Break My Bones

A PENALTY BOX PLAYERS NOVEL

GRACE MCGINTY

Also by Grace McGinty

To all my Thirsty Thursday, smut-loving angels.
Carpe Penes.

Break My Bones

Prologue

LUDO

"I'M GONNA KICK YOUR ASS."

I snorted at the girl in front of me, giving her a wink that made her cheeks flush with anger. "Girl, you couldn't kick my ass if I was lying dead on the ground."

She gritted her teeth at me as we waited for the drop. This was dumb. I had no idea why the coach was even letting her play. He'd said to treat her like one of the boys, and that's what I was going to do. Hell, she was so scrawny, she could probably *be* a boy.

Coach had caught me mouthing off to Johnny Lipkin about her, and now he'd stuck me down in defense. She was goalie, and that meant it was my job to protect her, instead of flying fast and scoring goals like I should be. I was pissed, and I was happy to take it out on her. I didn't care if it wasn't her fault.

"Me and you, on the lake behind my house, running drills. The first person to quit is the loser."

She skated hard at drills, I'd give her that. But a girl didn't belong on our team; it didn't matter if she was an okay goalie. Ruben had lost his spot on the team to her, and that meant I had to hate her on principle. When she'd moved here at the beginning of the season, we'd all laughed at her.

No one was laughing now.

"Just name the time," I muttered, but skated away before she could answer me, as the other team's offense moved toward our goal. I checked their winger hard against the boards. This was the first year we could check, and it felt good to be able to play properly. They'd raised the age to be able to check from U12 to U14 right when I'd gone up a grade, and I'd been *pissed*. We'd all been pissed. I wanted to bounce other players off the boards without being given a penalty, like a proper player.

We played for twenty minutes, without either team scoring. I wanted to pretend it was all my awesome defense, but the girl was a good goalie. Better than Ruben, but she still shouldn't be on the damn team. This was no place for a girl.

As if to prove my point, the front of the net was a fucking mess, with sticks and skates all over the place as the Littleton Hawks all converged to get the puck in the net. Their captain, Tony Meyer, was a dick. Definitely my archnemesis, since he'd first pushed me over in peewee.

He shoved me, and I shoved him back. "Back off," I

shouted at him, my voice doing that awkward breaking thing, ruining the dramatic effect I was going for.

"Make me, pussy," he yelled back. The fact that his voice had broken, he'd sprouted four inches, and could already grow a mustache irritated me more than it should.

I rammed my shoulder into his chest as Robbie got the puck away and fired it back to the other end of the ice. Tony flipped me the bird, then skated off at full speed.

I wanted to be down there, shooting pucks at the net. Instead, I was stuck up here in D.

"What a douche," the girl grumbled, but her eyes tracked the puck like a cat prowling around, waiting for its prey.

"He's a douche already being scouted by good schools," I snapped at her. "He's a douche who'll probably be in the NHL one day."

She was silent as the puck came back down toward us. She fended off another shot at goal, and I slid around the back of the net, passing the puck back up the ice to Kolbie.

"I don't think so," she said.

"What?"

"I don't think Tony will be in the NHL one day. He's just a loser. Some people have all this talent and just are too lazy to use it. It's a waste. I'd *kill* to be able to play in the NHL."

I dragged my eyes away from the other players,

looking over my shoulder at her. I couldn't see much of her face through the mask, but I saw that longing for a dream that wouldn't happen. Only one girl had ever played in an NHL game. But it had only been one game, one time, like thirty years ago.

As quick as a rabbit, the look was gone. She grinned at me. "You deserve it more than Tony the Asshole. You're just as good, probably better." It seemed to hurt her to admit that. "You're gonna have to get to the NHL for the both of us, Ludo."

I couldn't help the grin that spread across my own face at the picture she was painting. I wasn't so different from any teenager who played hockey—being drafted into the NHL really was the dream. "Sure thing," I shot back at her, but then the Hawks were flying back down the ice at us, and I skated up to intercept.

Their team was shit without Tony, since their whole strategy was just to pass the puck to that shithead. But what they lacked in skill, they made up for in chaos, and they were suddenly all back in front of the net again, trying to get a stick on the puck to take a shot.

Tony raced up, hooking his stick around the girl's skates and pushing her into the net. She went back hard, whacking the back of her helmet on the ice.

Fuck no. That jerk did not just do that.

You didn't touch the fucking goalie. Especially not *my* goalie. Without any conscious thought, I was shoving Tony across the ice. He was an idiot who liked to act tough, so he dropped his gloves and ripped off his helmet.

That asshole wanted to fight? I'd fight.

Throwing my own gloves and helmet off, I took a swing at the smug dickhead's face. My fist connected with his jaw, making his head snap to the side, but he didn't go down. He was bigger than me, which gave him some staying power, but I knew for a fact that would've hurt.

I was ready when Tony gripped my jersey, throwing a weak-ass punch at my face. I could take a punch just fine, and I followed it up with two of my own. Robbie was next to me, fighting off his own Hawk, though I couldn't see who it was. Johnny was there too, because he loved to brawl.

The ref was blowing the whistle, trying to jam a hand between me and Tony, but we all ignored it as we scuffled across the ice. I got Tony on the ground and sat on top of him, giving him another hard left to the face.

"Ludo, stop!"

I looked over to where the girl was tugging on my shirt, and when I stopped resisting, she tugged me right off Tony, overbalancing and landing on her ass again. I was heaving in oxygen, winded from the fight and the adrenaline coursing through my veins.

The ref sent me off—as well as Tony—which I'd expected, but I waited a little to help the girl to her feet.

"You didn't have to do that. He would have gotten the penalty."

I shook my head, reaching down to grab her wrist and tug her back up. "No one touches the goalie, Juniper. Especially not ours, and especially not you."

As I skated toward the box, I noticed my dad shaking his head at me. While his lips might've been pressed into a hard line, his eyes said something different. His eyes said he was proud of me for standing up for Juniper, our goalie. And that was all that mattered.

CHAPTER

One

LUDO

NINE YEARS LATER

"YOU LOOKED SO hot in that TimePeace commercial, Ludo." The woman beside me leaned in closer, her breasts pressing into my chest. "How about we go upstairs and do a recreation of the shoot?"

I wanted to tell her that we were missing an angry Russian photographer, three lighting dudes, and you know, the actual watch. But I knew what she meant—hell, a sea monkey with two brain cells would know what she meant.

I wasn't sure why I'd had to be naked on the ice with nothing but my stick and skates to sell a watch, but ever since I'd agreed, I'd been getting so much pussy that it was starting to wear thin. Which was worrying. I loved women, and all their soft body parts that I usually enjoyed sinking into.

But I wasn't feeling it tonight. I wasn't feeling the woman beside me, or this stupidly loud party, or the amount of cameras pointed in my direction. I wanted to go home and lick my wounds after being knocked out of the play-offs. I didn't want to be at a sponsor party with a bunch of models and social media influencers who were completely wasted from the free booze and getting more handsy by the hour.

Maybe I should get the team doc to check me out and see if I was suffering from brain damage after that hit last week, because normally, I loved all those things.

I peeled the woman's hand from my thigh, giving her the signature fuckboy grin that seemed to make them want to tame me instead of running the other way. "No thanks, babe." I looked past her head. "Hey, is that Joe Burrow?"

When the girl whipped around to search for Joe in the crowd, I ducked from her grasp and disappeared further into the swanky penthouse that was hosting this party. I grabbed two more shots of vodka from the scantily-clad waitress making the rounds, not hanging around for her to flirt with me too.

If I was honest, those things just weren't as fun as they'd once been. Since Rigby and River had settled down, I didn't have my wingmen anymore. It was lonelier than I wanted to admit. Especially tonight, with last night's loss so close to the surface. I wasn't a cocky rookie anymore, and the team's L reflected on me as a senior player.

I found a small alcove with a couch beneath the stairs. Luckily, no one was fucking in it just yet. You couldn't see it from the main area, which was probably why it was still empty. That, and the fact that no one else was wanting to hide. The whole point of these things was to be seen by all the right people, to network, to make nice. I didn't want to make nice tonight.

I threw back the first shot in my hand, appreciating the burn as it traveled to my gut.

"Hiding out in here, Ludo?"

I dragged my gaze up to Erik Luthersson, the goalie for the Detroit Infernos. They liked to pit my team, the Ann Arbor IceCaps, against his in the media. Fire and ice, and all that. Two Michigan teams, the endless rivalry. That meant this could go one of two ways— either Luthersson was here to gloat, or he was hiding from the bullshit out there too.

"It's a bit much tonight," I said honestly. If anyone was going to understand, it was another player. The Infernos had been knocked out in the first round of playoffs, so he knew my pain.

He gave me a sympathetic look. "It was a rough loss last night. You played well."

I breathed a sigh of relief that he wasn't going to be an asshole. I didn't have it in me to be a cocky dickhead tonight. I shifted over so he could sit. "They played better," I replied with a shrug, but Erik grunted his disagreement.

"They got better calls. You were evenly matched. It could have been the IceCaps going through." He folded down onto the couch. His feet stuck out from the alcove, so I didn't think our spot would be hidden for much longer.

He was a big fucker, like most goalies. Long arms and legs, wide shoulders—he was like a boulder in front of a cave when we played him. It was why they'd nicknamed him the Norse God. Playing the Infernos had been so much harder since he'd been recruited.

Opening his jacket, he pulled out a bottle of the vodka that was sponsoring the party. I raised an eyebrow as he cracked the top of it. "I am the face of this firewater, so I get free bottles." He took a slug, then screwed up his face. "Tastes like shit, though." He lifted the bottle, offering it to me.

I threw back the remaining shot in my hand, then held the glass out to him. He poured it with a steady hand.

"At least you got to keep your clothes on for the advertising."

Erik snorted. "Only because my dick was too long to hide behind the bottle," he said with a wink, making me laugh. "I've seen your ad. You look good." He smirked. "The models seem to agree, no?"

I rolled my eyes. "I never thought I would say this, Erik—and I'll tell everyone you're a liar if you ever repeat it—but I think I'm sick of meaningless sex with women who don't know that Ludo isn't my real first name."

Erik gave a mock gasp before chuckling, taking another swig of the vodka. "Meaningless, emotion-free sex begins to feel numb after a while. That's why they're called feelings. They help you feel things."

I squinted, because I wasn't sure if that actually made sense and I was too drunk to figure it out, or if he was drunk and it was just a load of jumbled horseshit. "*Please.* We both know everyone loves goalies. I bet you're getting laid more than a ten-inch dildo in a nunnery."

Erik crossed himself, letting out a deep, rumbling laugh. "You'd be surprised, Ludo." He rested the bottle of vodka between his thighs, stretching out on the couch. It was a two-seater, but not exactly built for two hockey players. "Are you staying with the IceCaps next year?"

"Yep, I renewed my contract." I loved my team. I loved the guys. I wanted to stay there forever. "How about you? Still gonna be my mortal enemy or are you getting poached by a team in the Eastern Conference? It'd make my job easier if you were," I said with fake gravitas.

Erik shook his head. "No, they've locked me into a two-year contract. After that, I'll see where I go."

I nodded, slumping back against the couch's overly hard backrest. Man, I hated modern furniture. "Going home for the offseason?"

He nodded. "My family misses me when I play in the US."

"What about your girlfriend? Taking her home too?" I had no idea why I asked that. The vodka was making the edges of my vision a little soft. *Good*. I was getting to the part of the evening where my thoughts got quieter and the world got a little more fun.

Erik sighed. "No girlfriend. I have no time for those kinds of attachments. No time to give any woman the love she needs. Not even enough time to give a dog the love it needs."

I nodded, because I got that. I was lucky. My best friend looked after my cat while I was traveling to away games. I always joked that we shared custody of the giant furball.

"Sounds lonely."

He grunted and drank some more. Conversation inevitably turned to hockey. We gossiped like little old ladies at the salon, talking about who was cheating on their wife on the road, who was going to get drafted at the end of season, who wouldn't be picked up again by any team. Never about our own teams, though. Loyalty went deep, no matter how much I came to like Luthersson as the night went on.

Women came over, but Luthersson shut them down and sent them on their way quickly. I guess he felt the same as I did—over the whole thing. It was actually kind of impressive to see. He managed to reject them in a way that still had them smiling as they left.

He had the kind of blue eyes that kept you trapped as he talked, and his Icelandic accent seemed to creep out, the more vodka he imbibed. It made me laugh hysterically, because his voice went nearly half an octave higher and lilted happily.

Eventually, our respective sponsors found us, and we were forced to take some extremely drunken promo photos until finally, we escaped. I was giggling like I was a fucking teenage girl as we crept out of the penthouse, taking the elevator down to the lobby.

I bumped him with my shoulder. "If you ever wanna stap—I mean stop—being a goalie, you could be a ninja." I wasn't wasted, but I was definitely on the happy side of being drunk. "Or a model. You're a handsome guy. Just not for vodka."

"Thank you, *Laglegur*."

I squinted at him. "Did you just call me lame in another language?"

He threw back his head and laughed. "No. It means friend in Icelandic."

I nudged him with my arm again, leaning into him because if I went too far over, I might end up on the floor. "Thanks, buddy. You smell nice."

The elevator doors opened, and I staggered into the lobby, Luthersson stumbling out after me with a laugh. We needed to hail a taxi ASAP before I passed out on the side of the road. Luthersson stood behind me on the pavement as I lifted my arm and hoped one of the passing cabs was empty. His body ran hot, chasing off the late spring chill. He was so big, he was basically a windblock.

A taxi appeared, and I climbed in, grabbing Luthersson's arm and dragging him in after me. I wasn't sure why, but sharing a taxi seemed like a good idea. I didn't want to go home to my empty apartment just yet. Actually… "We should go back to my place and finish your bottle of cheap-ass vodka while our taste buds are dead. We can play C.O.D."

"You got it, *Laglegur.*"

I grinned and gave the driver my address. We could stave off loneliness together for a little longer.

"On my left, on my left!" I shouted at Erik, but I was too slow and ended up dying. "Dammit." I laughed, falling back onto the couch. He also got the giggles and couldn't stop as he valiantly tried to hold our position, but soon enough, we were both dead.

The bottle of vodka was now gone, and everything was a bit spinny. I threw the remote down, slumping against the back of my overstuffed couch. I was close to Erik, our combined weights making us creep closer and closer to the middle. My whole body was pressed along his, though he was a couple of inches taller than me.

I kinda liked it.

When he threw his remote down next to mine and put his hand on my thigh, I kinda liked that too. Definitely the booze.

"I've had a really good time tonight, Ludo." He was harder to understand now, his accent thick. "It is nice to have someone for a night. I miss my friends."

I made a rude noise. "What about those fucks in the Infernos? Not you, of course. You're the one nice one. But don't you have friends on the team?"

He shrugged. "They're okay. They don't really approve of me."

I felt as if my eyebrows were about to fly off my head, I raised them so high. "You're the best goalie they've ever had."

He gave a sad chuckle, which made something in my chest feel hollow. "It's not my hockey skills they are disapproving of, *Laglegur*."

I frowned at him. "Then what?"

Instead of answering, he leaned forward.

Then he kissed me.

I sat still, my body turned to stone, as his soft lips ran over mine. One part of my brain acknowledged that he kissed differently to a woman. It was firmer. More aggressive.

The other part of my brain was still struggling with shock, but something low in my gut was stirring. Was I into this?

I tried kissing him back, his teeth scraping over my bottom lip, and a groan escaped me of its own accord. I deepened the kiss, my body feeling more languid than it had in a long time.

"We should stop. We are drunk. You don't know what you're doing," Erik whispered.

Maybe that was true. But both the hard line of my dick and the burn in my gut that I knew was desire were telling me that I wanted this. A small part of me wanted to know what it was like, and the drunken part of me decided the booze would be a good excuse to try.

So I grabbed his face and kissed him again. There was no more hesitation in Erik after that. There was just a clash of mouths, hands, bodies.

Tomorrow was soon enough for regrets.

Hours later, I snuck out of my own bed. Naked. The booze had left my system, and all that was left was panic and a fucking killer hangover. Heading to the bathroom, I pulled out a set of dirty clothes from my hamper. I shoved my feet into running shoes and walked to the table.

Grabbing a notepad, I wrote a message to Erik and tried to ignore the flashbacks of his hands on my body, his lips around my cock. Of sliding into—

I slammed a wall down on the thought.

Had to go out. Lock up when you leave.
  - Ludo

. . .

Then I got the fuck out of there. This had been a mistake. An epic, epic mistake. I'd just forget it ever happened. It was mostly a giant black spot anyway. More flashes of memory than actual recollections.

I snuck out of my own apartment and ran until I threw up over someone's front fence. Then I kept running, like I could outrun the feelings that seemed to have settled in my gut.

Not disgust.

Not anger.

Not even regret, though that was definitely there.

I tried to outrun the feeling that was worse than all of those combined. I tried to outrun the desire that was still coursing through my veins. The need to turn around and go back, to see if I enjoyed it as much sober as I had when I was drunk and carefree.

No, it was a mistake, and mistakes were best left in the past. That was all this could ever be.

CHAPTER

Two

LUDO

FOUR MONTHS AFTER *THAT NIGHT*

"MOVE YOUR ASS, LUDO!"

"It's hard to move it if you're riding it so hard, asshole," I grumbled beneath my breath. The captain, Muss, shot me a look, so maybe I hadn't said it as softly as I thought I had. I skated the drills again, pushing myself harder.

The offseason had felt way too long, stuck back in my hometown with my thoughts, but on the other hand, not nearly long enough. I wasn't ready to play again. To be back on the ice, to possibly be facing—

Shutting down the thought, I skated from one end of the ice to the other until my thighs burned with the effort. I hadn't worked out enough in the offseason, drinking too much beer, partying a little too hard with my friends from home. I was paying for it now as my lungs burned in my chest.

River skated up and nudged me with his giant body until I ricocheted into the boards. "Where've you been, shithead? Shack up with a girl over the summer?"

Lips on mine. Flesh between my teeth. Tongue sliding up my—

I slammed the mental wall back down. "Nah. I went home. Hung out with my high-school buddies."

River raised an eyebrow. "All summer?"

I nodded, lifting my shoulder into a shrug. "It was time. I hadn't gone back for more than a couple of days since I was drafted." That was the excuse I'd told myself over and over and over again during the break. It definitely wasn't that I was a coward, running away from Michigan as fast as my legs could carry me.

"Did Junie go with you?"

I smiled finally, because thoughts of my best friend always made me feel better. Juniper had been my teammate back when we were kids. When I was scouted, my parents had begged her to go with me. I wasn't sure why. Had they thought I was going to get into mischief or something? I was *perfectly* well behaved… if you didn't count getting busted boning that chick in the alley behind Smoke nightclub last season. Or the girl I'd gotten caught fucking in my Range Rover. Or that time I'd gotten drunk after we won the Cup last year and taken my clothes off on the bar.

Actually, Juniper did save me from that one. She'd

followed me when my parents asked, doing a marketing degree and eventually becoming the IceCaps social media manager. I'd told her that I had no sway in Management's decision to hire her, but if I was being honest, I'd definitely slipped it into my contract nego-tiations.

Juniper had hated my guts when we were kids, during those first few months in junior high, but now? Now, she was my anchor. The one person I could always count on.

I shook my head at River. "Nah, she went to the UK on holiday. Said she was disappointed she couldn't smuggle a cow and a hot Scotsman home in her bag."

River's lips curled into a rare smile. Everyone liked my Juniper. She didn't have a malicious bone in her body. Plus, she made us all look amazing as fuck on social media. Like hockey gods.

"Lucky for you, buddy."

I frowned at him, but he just shook his head and skated away. I was glad Juniper hadn't been here over the summer. I might've been able to fake it with my dad and my best friend, Robbie, but Junebug would have known instantly that something was wrong.

I sweated through another hour of training on the ice before hitting the showers. I'd have to book some ice time after training to get back to peak physical fitness. If I dragged ass like this during the season, I was gonna get sent back to free agency, or more likely, down to the minors.

The smell of cologne and ligament ointment, plus sweaty asscrack, was almost soothing to my soul. A locker room had been my happy place for so long—a place of solitude and focus before heading out onto the ice to play a sport I loved. A place to celebrate with my friends when I was high on the win, or to hide out in after a loss.

Throwing on a tee and some jeans, I headed upstairs to the team office to grab Juniper. We lived in the same apartment building. When I was first drafted, I'd wanted us to just share a place, but she'd put her foot down.

"There's no way in hell I'm sharing a wall with you, Ludo. You're a fucking manwhore. I don't want to listen to fake orgasms every day of the week." We'd compromised, and I'd gotten her an apartment in the same building as me, right across the hall. I also subsidized her rent, but she didn't need to know that.

She was in the open-plan office, her headphones on as she concentrated on the screen of her laptop. Friar Puck, my sweet boy, lay next to her on a massive, fluffy bed. He lifted his head and made a happy chirping meow at my entrance, then settled back to sleep.

The IceCaps office was pet friendly, for which I was thankful. Friar Puck had shown early on he didn't like to be alone, by chewing up every pair of shoes I had. Even my skates. The vet had said it was unusual behavior for a cat, but that Maine Coons were a special kind of crazy. It didn't help that he was the size of a beagle.

I knocked on top of Juniper's cubicle, and she jumped, clutching her chest in fright. "*Fuck,* Ludo. You scared the shit out of me," she hissed.

I just grinned. The fact she was so easy to jump-scare was one of the reasons she'd hated me as a teenager, and why I'd wanted to be her friend so bad. Her dark brown curls were sticking up from her head, and the apples of her cheeks were flushed pink with outrage. Sometimes she looked exactly the same as when I first met her. Then she'd stand up and she'd have all those very adult curves and I'd realize that neither of us were scrawny kids anymore.

"It's lunchtime, Bug, and I'm starving."

She rolled her eyes at me, but I could see her saving the document she was working on. "Well, why didn't you go to the cafeteria? Not like they don't have enough food for you guys down there."

"And miss out on eating with you guys? Never," I crooned, as Friar Puck stood and stretched, placing his big head beneath my hand for a pet. He was a smoke-colored Maine Coon, and honestly, he was the most handsome cat I'd ever seen. I wasn't even biased. He was basically the perfect blend between dog and cat.

Juniper stuffed her things in her oversized tote and stood. "Come on. Wouldn't want you to waste away." She hooked the harness on Friar Puck. I waved at the guys in the office, winking over at the other office girls, until Juniper punched me in the kidney. "Cut it out, asshole. Otherwise, I'll get them to ban you from this floor."

I snorted as we reached the elevator. "You can't ban me. I'm the team's star player."

"For now. The new drafts look good," she said, changing the subject.

Yeah, they did. We'd see how many made the cut after the preseason games, but I wasn't worried. Not at all.

"They're still green. We'll see how they go on the big stage before I start thinking about retirement."

She huffed a laugh as she strode out of the elevator in front of me, waving at Hank the security guard at the front desk. "Hey, Hank. How's Jude's knee?"

"Recovering from her second surgery. Doctors say she'll be up line dancing before you know it. Though last time she did that, she threw a hip, so maybe we'll skip the boot-scootin' for now."

Juniper squeezed his arm with a laugh, and he looked at her like the sun shone out of her ass. "Solid idea, Hank. Give her my love, okay?"

He grinned, then gave me a quick nod. That was the thing about Juniper. I was replaceable to the IceCaps team, but I wasn't sure she would so easily be replaced.

Hank gave Friar Puck a quick head pat before we moved through the parking garage to my Escalade. Back when I'd first gotten a Maine Coon, I'd upgraded from the truck I'd bought with my first paycheck. I wanted him to be safe, and also cool in summer. That was a lot of fur to have.

Juniper had rolled her eyes, making a crack about having a tiny dick, but in the dead of winter, she sure as shit wanted to ride to work with me and my heated seats, not in her shitty little Honda.

"Chicken and waffles?" I asked as I opened the rear door for Friar Puck, giving his ass a bit of a shove as he flailed around. He wasn't made for high jumps, that was for sure.

Juniper moaned as she climbed up into her seat. I liked to joke that she needed a stool to climb in, at just over five feet and two inches. "Hell yeah. Let's do it."

I drove her over to our favorite diner, parking right out front of the window. We left Friar Puck in the car. He'd hang out on the dashboard, glaring at people as they went by. It wasn't hot at all today, but still, I left the windows down a few inches. Actually, there was the bite of winter in the air, so I didn't have to worry about people calling the cops to bust him out.

Striding into the squat brick building, I kissed the waitress on the cheek. "Hey, Beth."

"Good to have you back, you two!" she gushed. Beth definitely wanted to get into my pants. It didn't even matter that she was fifty-two. "How was Scotland, Junie?"

Juniper also leaned forward to kiss her on the cheek. "Beautiful, Beth. You need to go. They're so nice, and that *accent!*" she gushed, fanning herself. "I met a guy in a pub, and he showed me what was under his—"

I slammed a hand over her mouth. "That's enough of that, thank you. It's too early in the day—hell, it's too early in the *year* to listen to you gloat about getting down and dirty with some Scottish laddie."

Juniper licked the palm of my hand. I pulled it away, screwing up my nose as I rubbed my hand on my jeans. Beth just laughed, used to our antics. This was our go-to place to eat. "We'll talk later, Junie; I need the details. Head on over to your regular table. Just the usual?"

"Please, Beth."

I could see Friar Puck out the window, and he looked back at me, letting out a silent meow. Some people would say it wasn't very tough to own a cat, even if he was a monster in size. But there was something extremely manly about being rejected by a feline repeatedly and continuing to come back for more. Almost masochistic in nature.

I sat in the booth right in front of him and waved, like he gave a shit I was here. "Maybe we should get him a girlfriend."

Juniper shuddered. "Hell no. He barely fits in your apartment, let alone mine." She wiped off the mouth of the syrup bottle, something she did every time we came for food. She had a bunch of little quirks. Next, she'd pour out the top layer of salt into a napkin. Then she'd fold it into quarters and wipe the whole table down.

Her mom had OCD and wouldn't ever leave the

house to eat, and while Juniper had never been that bad, she still had these tiny rituals. I didn't tease her about it anymore. It was just a part of who she was. Also, I loved Misha, her mom, who'd basically treated half the junior hockey team like her own children back when we were running wild in our teen years.

Ritual done, Juniper put the napkin to the side. "So, are you going to tell me what's wrong, or do I have to drag it out of you with torture?"

"What do you mean?" I choked out. I couldn't even blame it on swallowing my water wrong, because it hadn't appeared yet.

She rolled her eyes. "Really? We have to do this the hard way?" She sighed heavily, like I was the most annoying person she'd ever met. She did that a lot. "We've been friends for so long that I think I'd know when something is wrong." Linking her fingers beneath her chin, she cleared her throat. "Allow me to submit my evidence. Firstly, there's the fact you went home for your holiday. The entire offseason. You *hate* going home since your mom died. At the end of your first year, you legit hoped you'd busted your finger and would need rehab, just so you didn't have to go home."

I went to argue, but she raised a hand to stop me. "Exhibit two: Robbie messaged me and said you spent the whole break drinking beer and dodging Billie-Tayla, who you normally would've ridden off into the sunset like a long-in-the-tooth nag."

I gritted my teeth. "Billie-Tayla is okay, but I've been there before. No point going back again."

Juniper raised an eyebrow. "Since when have you been picky about who you stick your dick in, Andrei Ludokov?"

"I'm not a teenage boy anymore, Bug. I'm a grown-ass man."

She snorted again. "Sure thing. Basically a retiree." She reached over and gripped my hand. "But the most damning evidence is the dark circles under your eyes, and the shadows that seemed to be gathered in them. Rigby messaged and said you were missing shots on the ice that you could've made in your sleep last year. So what's the problem, Ludo? You're my best friend. I want to help."

I chewed my lip, looking down at where her small hand sat on top of mine. She was my best friend too. The one constant in my life. The person I'd leaned on every day since we turned eighteen and my mom died, and she stood by the grave with me, holding my hand as I cried.

I swallowed hard, looking Juniper dead in the eye. If she was going to be disgusted, I wanted to know straight off.

"I had sex with Erik Luthersson."

CHAPTER
Three

JUNIPER

OF ALL THE things I'd thought Ludo was going to say, that wasn't one of them. It was so far from what I'd thought he was going to say, my brain just blanked. Total whiteout.

"The goalie from the Detroit Infernos? That seems a little disloyal." He huffed and dragged his hand away, but I wasn't going to have that. I grabbed it back, pulling it to my side of the table. "Sorry, that was a shock. Fuck."

Man, what the hell did I say to that? No wonder he'd been off.

I lowered my voice. "By sex, you mean…?"

He frowned at me, his eyes fierce. "I mean, I put my dick in his ass, Bug. Sex-sex."

I tilted my head at him. "I always knew you'd be a top." I almost slammed my hand over my mouth to stop the words, but it was too late.

He growled wordlessly at me, still trying to drag his hand away, but I was holding onto his fingers for dear life. "What's that supposed to mean?" he hissed at me, his eyes darting around the restaurant.

What *was* that supposed to mean? Fuck, I was seriously screwing this up. I pulled an excuse out of my ass. "That I've heard you fuck enough girls at parties to know that you're dominant in the bedroom. Don't be so goddamn sensitive, you big baby." I leaned forward. "How did it happen?"

This was the information I really wanted. How did my manwhore, uber-masculine best friend fuck the goaltender of the opposing team? I mean, Erik Luthersson was smoking hot, but up until a minute ago, I would've bet my entire life savings that Ludo hadn't noticed that small fact.

"It was at that stupid promotion party after we lost to Calgary. I was drunk on shit vodka—"

I sucked in a sharp breath. "Did Luthersson take advantage of you when you were drunk? I'll kick his fucking Danish asshole right back to the Baltic sea if he got you drunk and forced you into anything."

I would *ruin* him. I would start with his career, then I'd start a social media campaign against him. I'd have to be careful, though, so that it didn't come back on Ludo. He was my priority. Maybe I'd start a rumor that Luthersson was a drug cheat first.

Ludo tugged on my hand. "Stop plotting his death. It was... consensual." His tongue peeked out and wet his lower lip. "We were both drunk. Like, really drunk. And he's Icelandic, not Danish."

Beth appeared with our food, but suddenly, my gut was churning way too much to eat. I gave her a strained smile, letting go of Ludo's hand. "Thanks. Looks delicious."

She smiled back brightly. "Let me know if there's anything else you need."

As soon as she left, I looked around, but the diner was quiet this time of the afternoon. "I don't want to get all Dr. Phil up in here, but how do you feel about it all?"

He sighed, pushing a fry around his small container of ketchup. "It's fucking with my head."

"Why?"

Spearing me with an angry look, he snapped, "Why do you *think?* I'm not gay, Juniper! I love women. Especially fucking them."

He slumped back, and I just wanted to hug him. Thankfully, the perks of our friendship meant that I could. So I stood up and walked around, sliding in close and wrapping my arm around his broad back, breathing him in. He smelled the way he always did, like sandalwood and Tiger Balm.

He held himself stiff for a moment, but then leaned into me, resting his head on my shoulder, seeking comfort. He was a tactile guy, which was probably why he played such a hands-on sport. It was a small fact I'd appreciated a lot over the years.

"Ludo, if there's any person in the world you don't

have to convince about your love of women, it's me. I was a room over at that Halloween party sophomore year when you lost your virginity to Myra Winters. I was also playing beer bong with Joey Linetti at that frat party when you had a six-way with half the pledging class of Delta Phi. I get that you love women. No one's doubting that for a moment.

"But it's not a cut-and-dried thing," I continued softly, my fingers scraping through his hair. "You can like both men and women. You can be completely straight, except for Erik Luthersson. You can desire just him, as a person and not as a man, per se. You can like none of them and become a crazy cat man. Pretty sure Friar Puck would love some more kitty siblings. Hell, get a dog too. Maybe a baby goat." He huffed a laugh at that. "What I'm trying to say is that this doesn't have to be a big deal. If you don't ever want it to happen again, just chalk it up to experimentation and forget about it. Go back to being Ludo, modern day Casanova. If you do want it to happen again, then you can experiment with that too."

I chewed my lip. "So… was it just Luthersson you were attracted to, or is it other men as well?" I'd dropped my voice even further, because this really wasn't a conversation we should be having in public. At least, not until Ludo figured out what he wanted.

"I've spent decades in locker rooms, Junebug, staring at hairy asses and dicks."

"And?"

"And I've never wanted to fuck any of them…"

Yeah, that didn't sound entirely convincing. There was definitely a *but* there. It was probably even hairy. "But?"

"I think there were times I definitely appreciated their bodies. I mean, I dare anyone to look at Rigby Engman naked and not think he was hot. You could be a dyed-in-the-wool homophobe and still think he was hot." He sighed, straightening slightly so he could eat his fries. "I wrote it off in my brain as just, like, an appreciation for his natural form or like, their gains in the gym and stuff."

"It could be just that. I definitely look at other women and think, 'Man, she has an amazing body. I wish mine looked like that.'"

He nudged me with his shoulder. "Your body is beautiful, because it's yours."

I rolled my eyes, despite the flush on my cheeks. Ludo hadn't let me put myself down since I was fourteen. He was big on self-love. Or maybe he was just protective of me. Who knew?

He'd been a prick to me for about three months until some switch flicked in his tiny pubescent brain. Then he'd decided I was his to protect from other assholes who would give me shit for being a girl on the hockey team, like he hadn't done the exact same thing.

"You're missing my point, but that doesn't matter. Let's assume you're"—I lowered my voice again—"bisexual. Is that something you want to explore?" The look of fear and uncertainty hurt my heart. I grabbed his hand and squeezed it. "You know this isn't going to matter to anyone who loves you, right? Me, River and Rigby, Muss. Robbie back home, Johnny—wherever the hell he is right now." I didn't mention his dad, because that old fuck would definitely have something to say about it. "We all love you, no matter what. If you want to forget it ever happened, I'll support you. If you want to explore this side of yourself, I'll be your wingwoman for life. If you want me to track down Luthersson and kick his nuts in, I'll put on the Doc Martins I keep especially for this kind of occasion. If you want me to reach out to him and test the waters, I can totally do that too."

He froze, turning to look down at me. "You could do that?"

My brain was already scrambling for ideas. How I could approach Erik Luthersson without letting him know that I knew? Fuck it, I'd figure it out. "I definitely can. I'll approach Stacey, their PR person, about maybe doing a series of crossover interviews or something. Leave it with me—if that's what you want?"

He was silent for a long time, and I could see the turmoil in his face. I wanted to soothe him, to tell him it would be okay, but honestly, he had to work this out on his own. All I could do was make it as easy as possible.

Finally, he nodded. "Just make enquiries. Don't tell him it's because of me, though?"

I smiled at him and kissed his cheek. "I promise it's

going to be okay, Ludo. When have I ever led you astray?"

Ludo scoffed, but shifted his plate closer. We couldn't let chicken and waffles go to waste. That would be sacrilege.

I went to slide out of the booth, but he gripped my arm. "Love you, Bug. You're my best friend, and I don't tell you enough how much I appreciate you."

I gave him a crooked smile. Once upon a time, back when I was a teen, those words would've set something aflutter in my chest. I'd had the hugest crush on him for the longest time. Even when he was dating other women, or I'd been with the one or two boyfriends who hadn't been threatened by me being best friends with a professional hockey player, a small part of me had loved him. That white-hot feeling of desire had eased as we'd settled into something more comfortable. Friends, but the ride-or-die kind.

I nudged him with my shoulder. "I know. You'd be lost without me." I slid out of the booth, moving back to the other side of the table to eat my own food. This was a heavy conversation for a Monday afternoon. I was putting on a stoic face, but fuck, I was still reeling from that bombshell. Time for a subject change.

"Did you see that new interview with Rigby, River, Nova and Devan? They seem really happy."

Disgustingly happy, actually. Which made me so thrilled for them all, but also, a little envious of Nova. I'd spent some time with her at IceCap social events, and she was so sweet and strong. I'd obviously seen the media posts about how she became sole guardian of her little brother, and all the bullshit that went down with her and the guys. I'd done my best to counteract that negativity, and the slut shaming, on our socials, but the PR team had quickly taken it out of my hands as they navigated the public backlash over the group's polyamorous lifestyle.

Ludo stuffed half a waffle into his mouth, chewing loudly before answering. If women could see him now, he'd never make the list of hottest athletes of all time. Disgusting. He was lucky I loved him.

"They're happy. God knows, Nova needed back-up dealing with those emotionally stunted fuckers." He shook his head. "With the things the media put them through, I wouldn't be giving interviews. I'd be telling them all to go fuck themselves."

I didn't tell him that if news of his sexuality—or his relationship with Luthersson—came out, there would be just as big a media storm. There'd only been one openly gay player in the NHL since the sport began. The key word there was *openly*. Statistically, there had to be dozens of players deep in the equipment closet. Even Luthersson wasn't out.

But I knew one thing with absolute certainty: I would protect Andrei Ludokov and his heart with everything I had.

We made small talk for the rest of lunch, Ludo filling me in about people from home, and me telling him all the draft gossip that came across the group chat I had with a bunch of other social media managers.

Ludo paid for lunch, leaving a big tip for Beth, and drove me back to IceCap Arena. I leaned over and kissed his cheek, then Friar Puck kissed me. Grimacing, I wiped the cat slobber on my denim jacket. Cats weren't even meant to do that, right? His tongue felt like sandpaper.

"I have a date after work at Shaggers, so I won't need a ride home."

Ludo waggled his eyebrows. "Anyone I know?"

I shook my head. As my grandfather would have said, I knew better than to shit where I ate, so I never dated players or any of the IceCaps staff. "Tinder date. Nice investment banker from the city."

Ludo screwed up his nose. "Sounds boring. Well, you know the drill. If you need me, send the emoji."

We'd come up with the emoji system back when we'd been in college. If I sent any green emoji, the date was on a one-way path to Bone Alley. An orange emoji meant that I wouldn't be going home with the guy, but it was going fine. Red meant that Ludo would track my phone, swoop in like an enraged lover or brother or something, and rescue me from my horrendous date. Black emojis meant he was coming in with a baseball bat swinging. I'd never used black, but the option was always there.

"I know, Ludo." I opened the door and slid out from

the giant motorized dildo he called a car. "Love you, you raging dickhead."

"Love you too, bitchface."

He drove away, and I finally let my face contort into the absolute mask of surprise I'd kept contained all of lunch. Ludo, *my* Ludo, was fucking bisexual. *Holy fucking fuck.*

I groaned, because the image of him kissing another dude was way, way too appealing. I had to lock that deep down in my brain and never let it out. I was just going to imagine Erik was really Erika, and that he— she—was just another Ludo conquest.

But as I pulled up Erik Luthersson's player profile on my phone and reached out to the Infernos media manager, the image kept creeping in. This handsome fucker, kissing my best friend.

This was going to be tough.

CHAPTER
Four

ERIK

"HIDE YOUR DICKS, boys. Here comes Luthersson."

I rolled my eyes at Rusket. I was used to his bullshit now, after two seasons of it. You'd think he'd get over it, but no. I kinda wished I'd never been upfront with the Infernos about being bisexual, but it wasn't a big issue back in Iceland. Plus, I'd figured that being open would prevent problems here later on, if it came out that I was equally as interested in men as women.

I'd been so fucking wrong. I couldn't go back in time and keep that shit to myself, and it was getting harder to ignore this asshole.

Laurens flipped him the bird. "Fuck off, Rusket. No one wants your shriveled cock, especially not Luthersson."

I grinned at Laurens, my closest friend on the team. He was a nice guy, a veteran player. I suspected that if it weren't for the love for his hometown team and the game, he would have asked for a trade and found a home that wasn't so fucking toxic. It was tempting for me too, but I knew that this shit would now follow me wherever I went. Players gossiped more than old ladies at church.

I changed out of my gear and back into my sweats, since I'd shower at home, but the coach pointed at me. "Luthersson, the PR team wants to talk to you before you run off."

I raised an eyebrow at him but nodded, throwing my shit in my bag and walking out of the locker room, smiling at Laurens but pointedly ignoring Rusket. I went across the parking lot to the Infernos offices. With a wave at Mo, the security guard, I took the elevator up to the second floor.

Stacey was there, talking to a sweet-faced woman, who was wearing a pair of tight jeans and a polo that had the Ann Arbor IceCaps logo on the pocket. She looked past Stacey at me, her eyes narrowed, like she was considering my worthiness, though I wasn't exactly sure what for.

"Erik!" Stacey crowed, her smile wide. She was thirty-eight, sick of sportsmen—hockey players in particular—and didn't take our crap. She had three kids under five, plus a carpenter husband who looked like he'd swing a hammer at anyone who thought about fucking with his wife. "This is Juniper Verne, the social media manager for the IceCaps. We're trying for Michigan unity this season, so we're going to do a series of side-by-side interviews between matching players on each team. We're starting with goalies. You're our test dummy."

I gave both women a tight smile. "Sounds great."

Stacey clapped her hands. "Great. I'll leave you two with it. Juniper, track me down when you're done, and we'll figure out where we go from here."

The woman stood and smiled. "Thanks, Stace." As the Infernos' social media manager left, Juniper turned those appraising brown eyes back on me. She thrust out a hand. "Thanks for agreeing to this."

I smiled, taking her much smaller hand in mine gently. "Well, she didn't phrase it like a request, and a happy PR department means a happy team."

Juniper snorted. "Isn't that the truth? Please, have a seat." She flicked through papers in front of her. "We decided to start with you and our goaltender Virtanen, because of the obvious parallels between you. You're both from Nordic countries. You're both goalies."

"Ah, but I don't have to train under Soukal, and I'm extremely thankful for that every day." The IceCaps goalie coach was a scary woman. She could make your balls shrivel up like raisins with just a look. "But she is excellent at what she does. Virtanen and Perrier are some of the best goalies in the league. You can't argue with the results."

Juniper smirked. "Very diplomatic of you, Mr. Luthersson."

"Please, call me Erik," I corrected.

"Erik." She said it like she was tasting the vowels on her tongue. "We thought we might do this kind of like a compliment box in kindergarten. You have to say something nice about the other team, and we work from there. It can be about our goalies, or the defense. Is there anyone you particularly like on the team?"

My mind went straight to that night, months ago, and the taste of Andrei Ludokov on my tongue, the feel of the hard muscles of his thighs as they flexed beneath my hands. "Virtanen is definitely an amazing goalie. His skill at covering the goal while remaining on his feet is definitely something I aspire to work into my own skill set."

I watched her scrawl notes across a notepad. "Your height would definitely give you an advantage, though, when it comes to goal coverage."

I nodded, speaking a bit about my own technique and comparing it with Virtanen's. She asked insightful questions, which told me she knew a lot about the game, and the goalie position in particular. I found myself enjoying the interview, which was probably a first.

She yawned widely, slapping a hand over her mouth. "I'm so sorry. I had a late night. I need about three more cups of coffee before I'm human again. I wasn't trying to be rude."

"Late night doing anything fun?" I internally winced at how inappropriate that sounded, but it was too late now.

She screwed up her nose, which honestly, was kind of adorable. "Not really. Just a date."

"Mmm, doesn't sound promising. No sparks?" Why did I even want to know?

She frowned. "No. He knew I worked for the IceCaps and really just wanted seats against the glass. Outside of hockey, we had nothing in common."

"His loss." I could say that without a shadow of a doubt. The woman in front of me was lovely. Soft curves, with big brown eyes that seemed to melt me on the inside. She was disarming in the best ways.

Her cheeks flushed pink. "Thank you. I'm not sure he feels the same way, but that's okay. My best friend said the same thing, and if both of you say it, then it must be true, right?" She tilted her head to the side, her eyes narrowing a fraction. "You might know my best friend, actually. Ludo? He's right wing for the IceCaps." She waved a hand at me. "Of course you know each other. You spend a lot of time together—on the ice, I mean."

Chills flashed along my skin, and I met her brown eyes with my own blue ones. "I know Ludo. He's an excellent player."

She chewed her lip. "He's an even better friend. He's loyal and funny, and he's so open and accepting that I worry someone will take advantage of him." She huffed. "God knows, every time he sleeps with a girl, there's a tell-all story in the tabloids the next day about the size of his cock."

I'd seen that cock, and I could vouch that it was pretty damn impressive. But I kept that to myself. We looked at each other silently for a moment, and I wondered if she knew what had happened.

"He is a renowned ladies' man. I can't imagine that's easy, as either his friend or as his social media manager."

"He's the easiest person on the planet to love, as long as you have a good pair of headphones and you don't get yourself emotionally caught up in his web." She gave me a hard look. "I love him, and I'd protect him against anyone, especially people who want to use his sexuality against him. One day, I hope he finds the right person who'll see past his bullshit and love him unconditionally."

I frowned. He'd mentioned his best friend Bug throughout the night, but he hadn't mentioned she was a woman. Or that she was so beautiful, and so very obviously in love with him. "Looks like he already has."

She shook her head immediately. "Oh, no. It isn't like that with me and Ludo."

Mmm, but I bet she'd wanted it to be at some point in her life. However, I was certain of one thing: Juniper knew what had happened between me and Ludo all those months ago. She was being just vague enough, but her comments were too pointed to be coincidental.

Folding my arms across my chest, I leaned back in the chair. "Then he's even luckier that he has someone so devoted coming to his defense." I sighed. "Look,

Juniper. Let's stop beating around the bush, yes? Ludo is safe from me ever mentioning what happened at that party. I'm not about to run to the papers and give them a tell-all. It'd sink my career as fast as his, and cause problems for us both."

She gave a relieved sigh, her shoulders slumping. "Thank *fuck*. I absolutely suck at that double-talk bull-shit. Saying what you mean by saying what you don't mean? It's confusing to even think about." She leaned across the small corner of the table that separated us. "He wanted me to come here and suss you out, to see how you were doing, I think. What happened between you two is just that—between you two. I just want to make sure that we both have his best interests at heart. Your interests, too. This isn't an industry that's known for being kind to people like you and Ludo. It stressed him out a lot over the summer break."

That made guilt burn in my chest. "I didn't realize he'd never... you know, until after. I would never have initiated anything if I'd known. A drunken hookup isn't what I'd wish for anyone's first time. If you see him, tell him I'm sorry for that."

Another appraising look. "Are you sorry?"

"For that? Yes. Not that it happened, though. Ludo's a special guy. I don't regret that night. I don't regret getting to know him."

She gave me another hard look, then sighed. "Then you should tell him all that yourself."

It was my turn to appraise her. What were her real

motivations? Because if I'd learned anything, it was that people were rarely as selfless as they made themselves out to be. "Would he want that?"

She shrugged. "It can't hurt to find out. Even if it's just to lay the whole thing to rest. Here, give me your phone."

I handed it over without question. She had a quiet kind of authority, and I wondered if it was because she worked with athletes every day. We could be an unruly bunch at times, especially with things that weren't the sport itself. Hockey was life, and everything else was a chore.

"I'm sending myself your number. I'll give it to Ludo, and if he wants to call, then he will." She looked up at me once more, her gaze searing me from beneath long, dark lashes. "If that's what you want too?" Her fingers paused on the screen of my phone.

Was it what I wanted? Should I leave that night in the past, just a nice—if blurry—memory? Or should I chase down this doomed connection?

"Put my number in there." If it was all for nothing, then so be it. But I didn't hadn't gotten this far by being a chickenshit, and I wasn't going to start now.

She gave me a soft smile, like I'd done the right thing. "I'll give it to him. Ludo has been searching for something for a long time; maybe this is it. No pressure," she said with a laugh, then groaned. "He's going to fucking kill me, though. I was supposed to be subtle and *not* let you know I was testing the waters on his behalf." She shrugged. "I was never good at subterfuge.

"Once, when we were seventeen, Christie Roberts became my friend to get closer to Ludo. She was the mayor's daughter. Anyway, she invited me and Ludo to hang by their pool, except when we got there, she disappeared upstairs with Ludo. And then her dad, the fucking mayor, came home and I panicked. He'd have murdered Ludo for debauching his daughter," she said, the expression on her face making her eyes sparkle with mischief. "Instead of saying I was there hanging out with Christie—which would have been fucking *logical* —I freaked out and told him I was robbing the place. He called the cops, and I got arrested as Ludo shimmied down the drainpipe at the back of the house and made a run for the woods, stark naked."

I laughed. "No shit. How'd you get out of that?"

"Ludo made Christie tell them I was there with her, and that I was just pranking her. In the end, I had no stolen goods and was there at the request of a member of the household. The police just reprimanded me and let me go." She laughed, and I chuckled along with her.

"Sounds like you've had his back for a long time. You obviously love him."

She shrugged, packing up her notebook. "He needed to escape that town, and I didn't trust Christie not to lie her way out of trouble and throw him under the bus." She met my eyes, and I found myself once again lost in their warmth. "He's my best friend. There isn't anything I wouldn't do for him."

Yeah, she loved him. It was there in the depths of her voice, the fire in her gaze. I'd bet my balls that it wasn't just the love you had for a friend, which made me wonder—did Ludo know his best friend was in love with him? Was he stringing her along for his own benefit? Or were they both in denial?

One option made him a monster, and the other made him a fool. Hopefully, I'd find out which soon enough.

CHAPTER
Five

LUDO

FRIAR PUCK RAN around my feet like a lunatic as I walked over to answer the door. "If you trip me over and bust my knee, I'll be too poor to buy you that gourmet food you like, you insane fur coat," I grumbled at him, and he looked up at me with an incredulous expression. Well, maybe not incredulous. He was probably just responding to me saying *food*.

I looked through the peephole to see Bug with an armful of grocery bags. Pushing Friar Puck out of the way, I opened the door and reached for the most precariously balanced bag. "What's all this?"

She stuffed one more bag at me, then bent down to herd Friar Puck back into the apartment. "Food. I'm cooking dinner."

Hmm. That was never good. The only time Junebug voluntarily cooked for me was when she wanted to carb-load me into a coma before having a "talk" with me. Or when she was giving me bad news.

Like the time some girl gave a tell-all story to the tabloids about my dick. Or the time Bug told me she was seeing someone, though why that counted as bad news was beyond me. The guy had been a dickhead, but that was more bad news for her than me.

Placing her bags on the counter, she turned to me. "Don't be weird about this, but I got Erik Luthersson's phone number."

My jaw unhinged. "You were going to *test the waters!* How is getting the number for the guy I fucked subtle?" Jealousy churned in my gut, though I wasn't entirely sure where that jealousy lay—over Erik or Juniper.

She rolled her eyes at me. "I got it for you, not me, you dumbass. Call him if you want to, or don't. I told him you didn't owe him anything, and he agreed."

"The hell, Bug? You guys just came right out and *talked* about it? You weren't supposed to let him know."

She threw her hands up in the air. "We both know I suck at subterfuge," she snarked back, like this was my fault. She started unpacking the food aggressively, as if she wasn't talking about tanking my whole damn reputation. "We are having steak. Also, Management just announced a charity match between the Infernos and IceCaps, in support of the Michigan Mission to help the Homeless. It's this weekend."

I'd thought her blurting out to Erik that she knew

about us was the bad news, but nope, there it was. My time hiding from the truth was officially over. I was going to come face-to-face with the man who haunted my dreams.

"Oh." I swallowed hard. "Isn't that a little short notice?"

"Apparently, the GMs met at the country club and arranged it over a few top-shelf whiskeys and cigars."

"Well, fuck."

Juniper pinned me with a hard stare. "This was bound to happen. It's better now than in front of thousands of people during a regular game with actual points on the line."

That was the thing about Juniper. She loved me, but she also loved hockey and the IceCaps. She wasn't going to let me fuck up the team's chances just because I was going through an emotional crisis.

She grabbed a card from her back pocket and handed it to me. On it were the initials EL and a phone number. Erik's phone number. "Call, or don't call, but either way, you better bring your A-game this weekend. You're going to get your ass benched before the season has even started if you continue to be too up in your head to fire a shot at your puck buddy." She chuckled at her own pun, then went to work on dinner, chopping onions.

I stumbled over to the couch, staring at the numbers on the card. Was this a crisis? It was kind of now or never, right? I had to either decide to go there again or forget it had even happened. I should do that last one.

Just skate out there and play, like I didn't care who was on the other team. Just some random goaltender. Treat him like every other person I played against.

Maybe I should go out and get laid. That's what I needed to do. I'd hardly been out with anyone in the last four months. I'd go out, find a pretty little puck bunny to bury myself in, and forget Erik Luthersson ever happened.

The smell of caramelizing onion dragged me from my thoughts. That's what I'd do, but not tonight. Tonight, I'd hang out with my best friend and my cat, and bask in this small window of calm before the season started.

I came back over to sit at the kitchen island, and Junie pushed a bag of salad at me to open. We chatted about everything and nothing, work and home. About Juniper's younger cousin, who was currently fucking his way through his freshman year of college in a way that she disapproved of.

"That went fine for me," I argued, and she pointed a big-ass kitchen knife in my direction.

"That's because you had me making sure you didn't knock up some sorority girl, or get blackout drunk, or whatever other bullshit teenage boys get up to in their spare time instead of focusing on their studies." I squinted my eyes at her until she frowned. "What the hell are you doing?"

I grinned. "Trying to work out at what point you turned into your mom."

She gave me the finger, making me laugh. If everything could be as easy as it was between me and Bug, life would be a breeze.

The conversation turned to her failed date with the finance guy from the city, and I got a sick sense of satisfaction knowing it had been shit. Bug would be wasted on a city boy whose idea of sports was the stock market. But I still felt outraged on her behalf that someone had tried using her to get closer to the team. The fact that no one could see how amazing she was, what she'd bring to any relationship, was baffling to me.

"His loss," I told her.

She smirked at me as she plated up the food like she was a Michelin star chef. She liked to say you ate with your eyes just as much as your mouth. I always joked that was why I liked watching a girl while I ate her out, then Bug would usually throw something at my head. It was a tale as old as time, a routine that was comforting as much as it was amusing.

She handed me the perfectly cooked steak. "You know, Erik said the same thing."

I turned away so she couldn't see my flushed face. "Obviously, because it's true." I grabbed her plate too, taking them both over to my dining table. This was also part of the routine we'd had since moving here in my rookie year. Dinner together at least once a week, more in the offseason. Now we moved around each other like people who'd been each other's support system for years.

"I haven't said this yet, but Ludo?" I looked up as she said my name softly. "I like him. He was sweet, respectful. And so fucking handsome. If you do decide to pursue this, you have my support. I'll be there for whatever you need."

I squeezed her hand. "You always are."

It couldn't hurt to message Erik and see if I was worrying myself over nothing.

Yeah. That's what I'd do.

By Saturday's charity match, I still hadn't messaged Erik, and worse still, I'd worked myself into a fucking state of anxiety over it. Bug was staying out of it, but I could feel her watching me with that thoughtful stare every time we were together.

I'd gone on a Tinder date, but couldn't make myself go home with the girl. Her kisses had turned me off, and I wasn't in the right headspace to fuck her. Knowing my luck, I wouldn't have been able to get it up, and then she'd sell the story of my impotence to the media. I'd have been Limpdick Ludo before the week was out.

So I was going into the game a sexually frustrated, anxious mess, and the guys were all giving me looks like they wanted to ask what was wrong.

Fuck, I really hoped they didn't.

Bug was floating around the locker room, getting content for ClockTok and the other socials. The guys knew to just let her flit around, and she knew not to bug them for anything before a big game. Afterwards, she'd probably pull us aside to get some soundbites, but she knew not to get in the way beforehand, when we were in the zone.

Though everyone seemed kinda chill about this game. It didn't mean anything. It was for the fans and the corporations that would donate to Michigan's Mission. It had no real consequences. The atmosphere before the game was jovial; we were all happy to finally be back on the ice.

Everyone except me.

Muss came over and slapped me on the back. I'd heard rumblings he was looking at retiring, but I'd believe that when he announced it with his own mouth. He loved this game as much, if not more, than any man on this team.

"You okay, Ludo? You're looking a little jumpy. You know this is a friendly game, right?"

I gave him my signature shit-eating grin, but it probably didn't reach my eyes. I hoped Muss didn't notice. "Anytime we get to hand the Infernos their asses is a good day."

"So you're all good?"

"Sure."

"Then why is Junie throwing you mother hen looks? You two okay?"

I just shrugged, like I had no clue that she was

watching me for a full meltdown. "Of course. Why wouldn't we be?"

Muss gave me a hard look. "I heard she went on a date the other day. Is she seeing someone?"

I raised an eyebrow at him. It was only because he was happily married that I wasn't giving him the stink eye. "Not that I know of. Why do you wanna know?"

"Just trying to work out why you're as jumpy as a virgin on her wedding night, and why Juniper's looking at us like she wants to rescue you from my clutches."

I searched for my best friend in the crowd of half-naked guys, finally spotting her. One of the rookies was flirting his ass off in her direction, though her eyes were on me and Muss, and she did look a little worried. My gaze flicked back to the rookie. Apparently, I needed to give the newbies the speech about keeping their hands off Bug.

"Probably mentally asking for help getting away from Rodney."

Muss rolled his eyes. "Roderick," he corrected, but he was frowning in their direction now too. "She'd be good for him. He reminds me a little of you when you started. Throws himself headfirst into the lifestyle of professional sports, but he has no one to keep him grounded."

I shook my head at Muss. "Nah, he's not right."

"Oh, and why's that, Ludo?"

I shrugged. "She deserves better."

Shaking his head, Muss slapped my back again. "Sure thing, kid." He huffed a laugh. "Now get your head in the game. This might be a friendly, but Coach will still be watching to see if we're up to scratch to start the regular season."

I went through the rest of my pregame rituals, finally feeling more settled. At least, I was until we were warming up on the ice and the Infernos came out to the cheers of the crowd. Normally, I'd ignore them, but I sought out their goalie. I couldn't help myself.

Only to find him looking right back at me.

I was so fucked.

CHAPTER

Six

JUNIPER

I FELT like a helicopter parent at this point, watching Ludo fly around the ice, but even I could tell he was holding himself back from attacking the net like he should. The first half had been rough. I was in the box with Mr. Monderra, the owner, and I didn't like the look on his face as he watched Ludo.

When the end of the first period rolled around, and we were down 1-0, I decided that I couldn't let him get on Coach's bad side—or worse, the owner's radar for a possible trade. Ludo loved this team, and his whole life was here. If he left, I couldn't follow him, and that made something in my chest ache like I was having a heart attack.

I made my way down the locker room and waited as the team came off the ice. When he appeared, looking like a kicked dog, I grabbed his helmet and pulled him away from the door. River Cooper gave me a look, but shoved the guy in front of him into the room, giving me and Ludo privacy.

"Juniper, now isn't—"

I tugged him down to my height by the chin strap of his helmet. "You listen to me, Andrei Ludokov. If you don't go back out there and play properly, I'm going to kick your fucking ass for a week." I dropped my voice. "If you don't play against Luthersson like you haven't seen his dick, I'm going to knee you both in the balls for fucking with your careers. You are a *goddamn professional hockey player.* You aren't some love-starved fucking teenage freshman pining after Billie-Tayla and playing like shit. So you're going to go back out there, show your team some fucking respect, and give Luthersson some professional courtesy by playing like the NHL star you are. Got it?"

He stared down at me, his eyes wide and maybe a little scared. "Got it, Bug." I let go of his helmet, and he straightened, giving me a grin. "Love you, dickcheese."

"You too, you giant wank sock. Now go win us this damn charity match."

He saluted and strode into the locker room, where I could hear the taunting from inside. They might tease Ludo about it, but they'd never tease me, mostly because the older members of the team treated me like a little sister. The others had quickly learned that if they didn't treat the female members of the team with respect, they'd get their asses handed to them over and over on the ice, where no one could bitch about it.

I walked back up to the owner's box, sitting down next to some of the other support staff to watch the next two periods. Apparently, something I said had sunk into Ludo's big, dumb head, because he stopped pussy-footing around and started firing at the net like the ruthless winger I knew he was.

He also seemed to linger down near the goal a little longer than necessary, but whatever Erik and Ludo were saying to each other, no one else could hear. However, I didn't miss Erik reaching out and bumping the back of Ludo's leg with his glove, or the grin on my best friend's face as he skated back to where he was meant to be.

Obviously, whatever they'd said appeased something in Ludo, though I wasn't sure why that made me feel all tangled up in my chest. I wanted Ludo to be happy. Maybe it was because this thing with Erik wasn't easy. Up until this point, all of Ludo's girlfriends had been easy. The swimsuit cover model. The Victoria's Secret model. The Instagram model. You get the drift. Beautiful women, but to Ludo, they'd always been a thing to tote around like a trophy. Something that said *look, I made it. I'm successful enough to have a model girlfriend.*

As much as I wanted them all to be assholes, a lot of them weren't. Most of them were nice women with bucketloads of beauty, on the inside and out. I mean, some of them were bitchy princesses, but they didn't tend to last long. Actually, none of them ever lasted long. I worked hard to step back when Ludo was in a relationship, because above everything, I wanted him to be happy.

I finally made it back to my seat, just as my pet-sitting app gave me an alert that Friar Puck was doing something that he wasn't supposed to. When I opened the camera, I saw he was chewing on my newest pair of Nikes. With a sigh, I sounded the whistle noise from the other room, hoping it would be enough to distract him.

Friar Puck didn't like being alone, and normally, he never was. Only on game days, or if I had to go away for work. But whenever he was, he managed to destroy as many things as possible to make up for it. Nothing was safe, especially given the fact he'd worked out how to open doors with his huge paws.

Saphie, who worked in Nutrition, looked over at me and laughed. "Is Friar Puck wearing Ludo's underwear?"

I squinted at my screen, and there was Friar Puck at his treat bowl, a pair of boxers hanging around his neck. I pressed the button to release his treats, and the under-wear slid off his neck as he ate his crunchy, fishy bite things.

"You know you're rewarding bad behavior, right?"

I shrugged. "He's not bad. He's just lonely. I can give him a little leeway."

Saphie snorted. "That explains so much."

I didn't get to ask what she meant, because the arena suddenly erupted. Looking up, I saw that Ludo had scored. There was a moment where he stared at Erik, and the goalie stared back. I could feel the tension from here in the box, and while most might consider it rivalry tension, I knew better.

There was something between the two of them, and it was tugging at them with more force than either of them realized. You couldn't fuck with fate, but apparently, you could fuck with the goalie of your archrivals.

One thing I knew with absolute certainty was if this thing between them ignited, I would be left behind. My head and my heart went to war over that one, because Ludo deserved happiness, and so did I. It wasn't his fault that those two goals were incompatible.

The Infernos won in overtime, and as the buzzer sounded, I headed out to do my job. My small hand-held camera recorded the guys as they came off the ice, smiling despite the loss. It burned to lose, but at least it wasn't going to fuck with their standings.

Rigby grinned down the camera, his perfect teeth flashing, and when he was just past me, he reached back and ruffled my hair. I didn't need to train Rigby Engman about the camera; he responded to it like he was born to be there. "'Sup, Junie!" he murmured as he went past, and Muss, the captain, winked in my direction. Ooh, the social media girls were gonna love that.

Muss definitely had that sportsman swagger, the one you got from being the top of the game for so damn long. A few of the rookies threw me shy smiles, and then River Cooper brooded right at me, tilting his head so I was compelled to follow them down into the locker room.

At this point, I'd seen more sausage than a Bavarian beer festival, but the guys always tried to keep their junk covered, which I appreciated. I'd missed Ludo coming off the ice, and I frowned back down the tunnel.

Following River, I covered my eyes as we reached the locker room. "Cover your junk—I'm bringing in a camera!" I shouted. "This isn't ClickHeart, and I don't get paid enough to see your dicks."

I heard shuffling noises as everyone turned away. As I peeled open one eye and then the other, I saw some serious ass cheekage, but no dicks. Well, that was a relief. I did appreciate a good ass, though, and no one had asses like hockey players.

I spun the camera over to Muss. "Muss, can you push the camera away from me, toward…" I spotted Rigby again. He was a social media darling, right up there with Ludo, who I still couldn't see. "Toward Rigby. Hey, Rigby," I yelled over at the man in question, who'd lost half his gear already. "Do you know any Taylor Swift songs?"

River snorted, but Rigby just grinned. "From her sweet, country-girl era, or from her kickass, take-no-prisoners Reputation era? Or like, her recent stuff? That new album is a bop."

River shook his head. "Who fucking says bop? What are you? Ten?"

I waved the huge-ass enforcer away. "Hush. He's making my life easier." Ten minutes later, I had a clip of a still sweaty Rigby lip-syncing to a pop song. It was brilliant.

I looked over at Coach Toons. "Have you seen Ludo?"

The coach lifted his chin back at the doors. "Shucked his equipment and said he had to go see someone. I assume it's the boss." Coach Toons ruffled my hair. They were all lucky I wasn't precious about my hair-style. "Don't know what you said to the kid, but thanks for getting his head back in the game. You'll be trying to steal my job before you know it."

I snorted a laugh. "Fuck no. If I wanted to direct a bunch of toddlers, I would have become a daycare teacher."

Toons laughed. "Girl, you aren't fucking wrong." He turned to one of the rookies who was trying to sneak past him, giving him a dressing-down about a high-stick penalty he'd gotten in the third period, and I smiled over at Coach Soukal. One day, I was gonna convince her to do a "women in sports" clip for International Women's Day, because she really was a badass.

I got a little more general footage before leaving the locker room, but the whole time, I was worried about Ludo. Maybe I shouldn't have been so hard on him.

I followed the sound of voices down the hall that led to the switchboard closet. My feet shuddered to a stop as I found Ludo, all right. Found him kissing Erik Luthersson, like the only thing keeping them from fucking was the padding between them.

"Jesus Christ," I whispered.

CHAPTER
Seven

ERIK

PLAYING against Ludo had been thrilling. Distracting as hell, but almost like foreplay. He was a great winger, and I could see why he was the team's top goal scorer alongside Rigby Engman. He'd rushed off the ice before our team had even finished celebrating, and I wondered if he was a sore loser.

I'd been the last through the gate, too busy watching the little social media beauty draw smiles from every one of those surly IceCap bastards. She was good at her job, that was for sure. I walked down the small catwalk and just caught the flash of a face coming from one of the small halls that led off the main tunnel.

Ludo.

Waiting until the last of my teammates had entered our locker room, I kept walking, following Ludo down the hall until we were away from the bright fluorescent lights and shrouded in shadows.

"Hello, Ludo," I murmured. This felt more awkward than it probably should. "How was your offseason?"

He shrugged. "It was okay. How was Iceland?"

I laughed softly. This really was awkward as hell. "It was fine. You played well tonight. That was a great shot in the third."

He chewed his full lower lip absently. "Thanks. Lucky shot, considering you blocked the rest."

Apparently, we were doing polite small talk today. That wasn't in my nature, so I sighed. "Look, Ludo. I don't expect anything. I didn't realize until afterwards that what happened... wasn't something you'd experienced before. I would've approached you differently, if I'd known. At least, pursued you when you were sober." I still felt like shit about that. "If you want this to go to your grave, I won't tell a soul—"

He cut me off by kissing me. For a moment, I just stood there, stunned, as his lips moved over mine. Then I kissed him back, and he melted into me, as much as he could with all my gear still on.

The kiss went on and on, the world falling away, and I moaned into his mouth, burying my fingers in his dark hair. This was dangerous; I knew it was, but I couldn't drag my lips from his.

"Jesus Christ," someone whispered.

Ludo yanked his face away, whipping around to look at the person who'd stepped into this hallway with us. I let out a huff of relief when I realized it was a stunned Juniper.

"I'm sorry. I didn't mean—shit, *fuck*. Should you be doing that here? I mean, not that there's anything wrong with it. It was hot. I mean, not that you kissing needs to be hot for me. Your kissing is definitely about you, and how I feel about it is completely redundant. Is it hot in here? I feel—" Her rambling was interrupted by more voices coming closer, and panic flared on Ludo's face.

I could see how this looked. I had to think fast. Luckily, I was known for my reflexes.

I flicked my eyes between Ludo and Juniper, then reached out to grab Juniper, dragging her close to my body. "Apologies, little one." I flicked a look at Ludo. "Look angry."

I gazed back down at Juniper, then spun her toward the wall, kissing her. I caught her small gasp in my mouth, and chased the sound with my tongue. I smiled against her lips. She tasted like berries. My hands spanned her back easily, and I knew I could pick her up and press her against the wall as I fucked her. Or against Ludo.

I shuddered in pleasure even as Ludo cussed. "The *fuck*, Juniper? The goalie for the Infernos? *Really?*"

"Oh shit... Sorry, Ludo, we didn't mean to interrupt," another voice called, and I heard the hurried footsteps of people leaving. I also heard the whispers of Juniper's name, which made me wince. This would probably cause problems for her within the team.

I reluctantly dragged my lips from hers, and she

blinked up at me with those big, round eyes. Man, I kind of wanted to kiss her again. Maybe keep on kissing her until she kissed me back, like she couldn't get enough.

Instead, I gave her a little space. "Apologies. I couldn't think of any other reason why I'd be down this hallway." I looked around. There was a *Staff Only* door with a danger sign. If I wasn't making out with a beautiful woman, the only other reasons to be in this abandoned hallway were slightly nefarious.

She nodded, her cheeks flaming pink, even in the darkness. "No, it's fine. Totally fine. Good, even. I, uh, I should go. I'm sorry I interrupted. And that I kissed you."

I grinned, because how could I not? "I believe I kissed you, *Einiber.*" I winked at her.

Ludo was looking between us, his forehead creased tightly in a frown. *Uh-oh.* Maybe it wasn't so much of a stretch for him to be angry. Maybe their relationship wasn't as platonic as they'd made it out to be?

"I'll see you around. Both of you." With that, I wandered off, with as much nonchalant swagger as I could in skates.

When I made it back to the locker room, a fully dressed Laurens raised an eyebrow at me. "Where have you been?"

I gave him a tight smile. I didn't think he actually wanted the truth, and besides, I wasn't sure I could trust him with it, even if he was the most open-minded guy on the team. "Sorry, got caught up with a fan. Some of them know how to talk," I said, making a face, and Laurens laughed.

"Well, at least you got out of doing a little bit of baby-holding and hand-shaking." He heaved a sigh. "Coach wants us all out the front, talking with corporate sponsors and doing photo ops for the PR department. The GM made it very clear that we need all the good publicity we can get, after last year."

Last year had been a shitshow. Most of our team had been off on suspension when playoffs came around, a combination of dirty hits and bad calls putting us significantly off our normal game. Honestly, the owner could whine all he wanted, but until he cleaned house —including Rusket and Assistant Coach Craig—he was going to have the same problems. Coach Craig had never left the eighties when it came to gameplay, and that included dirty enforcers masquerading as defense.

Laurens pushed his fingers through his hair, tousling the dirty blond waves. "I'll see you out there."

Nodding, I pulled off the rest of my gear. I smiled tightly at the rookies as I stepped into the showers, setting it to blast cold. I needed to get control of myself. I shivered beneath the icy water, but it did its job, calming the fire in my blood.

When I'd stepped onto the ice this morning, I hadn't expected this. I'd just expected to make moon eyes and be ignored by Ludo, who'd had my number for a week but hadn't called—if Juniper had done what she said and given it to him. Maybe she'd kept it out of spite, but then why would she even ask for it? That didn't seem like the woman I'd met. She seemed to genuinely want her friend to be happy.

Which meant it was Ludo dragging his feet. So the kiss had been a surprise. His response to me was as wild as it had been that night at the end of last season, if a little less uninhibited. But it meant more because he hadn't been drunk on terrible vodka. He'd been high on the game, and I'd take that.

How I felt when I kissed his little bestie? That was a different matter altogether.

Sighing heavily, I stepped out from beneath the water. After all that, I still didn't know where I stood with Ludo. More questions than answers, yet again.

I dressed in my game day dress pants and a white button-up shirt. It was colder outside now, so I slipped into my soft, gray wool jacket. I looked like the personable goaltender that the team needed at these events, but my mind wasn't in it. It was still in the hallway pressed tightly to Ludo and with the taste of a certain little berry on my tongue.

I made nice as I schmoozed philanthropists, in the hopes that their love for my team would make them pull out their checkbooks and give back to society. I also talked to little kids who were having free time on the ice, which I much preferred to kissing the asses of rich old dudes. Kids were easy. They didn't want anything from you but attention.

By the time we were done, I was exhausted. I'd lost sight of Ludo and Juniper early on, but that hadn't stopped me gazing into every crowd in the hopes they'd reappear.

I needed to go home, maybe drink a beer and watch some mindless TV. Then I'd climb into a hot shower and rub my aching dick to memories of the past and fantasies of the future.

CHAPTER

Eight

LUDO

I WAS A FUCKING MESS, but at least I was playing better on the ice. It had been three days since the kiss after the charity match, and I still hadn't messaged Erik. I was normally so confident, so sure about the man I was, especially when it came to women. But Erik was very much not my usual conquest, and I was flailing.

On top of that was the odd sensation in my gut whenever I thought about him kissing Juniper. The image was forever burned into my retinas. I wasn't sure what I was supposed to have felt, watching the man I'd had sex with kiss the woman who'd been my best friend for nearly a decade, but I didn't think it was supposed to be raw lust.

I didn't want to examine that feeling too hard, because what if what I found fucked everything up forever? But Bug was making it hard—both my emotional ostriching and my dick—because she currently looked like a dream.

She was dropping Friar Puck back at my place before a date in Detroit. "You look nice," I told her, keeping my voice pointedly neutral, despite the fact an ugly feeling was taking root in my chest.

"Thanks," she chirped, reaching down to thump a solid pat on Friar Puck's ribcage. "My date is taking me to La Luna in the city."

Even I'd heard of that restaurant. It was a fancy Spanish place, where you had to know someone who knew someone to get a reservation, or be really fucking rich.

"Fancy. Who's the guy?"

"A stockbroker from one of those big city firms. And get this—he knows nothing about hockey, so he isn't doing it for the free seats."

I raised an eyebrow. "I don't like him already."

She laughed, giving Friar Puck one more thump before standing and brushing the cat hair from the skirt of her pretty wrap dress. It flowed over her curves like a dream, and was a soft pale blue color that complimented her ivory skin perfectly. It kind of did this weird, criss-cross thing at the bodice, which left most of her back bare and showed the curve of her breasts, almost all the way down to her belly button.

She slipped on a fluffy caramel-colored jacket and grinned. "Don't wait up."

I huffed. "Remember the emojis." She saluted as she

left, and Friar Puck sat down to stare at the door. I stared at it too for a while.

Eventually, I shook my head and moved to the couch. Maybe I'd play that new game I'd bought. Some needless virtual violence might be just what I needed to take my mind off everything.

I played it for a couple of hours, and at a save point, I got up to grab a beer and my phone. I stared at it for a little while, my finger hovering over Erik's number.

Tapping the message icon, I sat there, staring at the blank text box for way too long. Growing some balls, I finally wrote something and hit Send.

> Me: Hey

That was it. I threw my phone over to the other side of the couch, giving myself a stern talking-to about being a pussy.

I picked up the controller again and played some more, but when my phone flashed, alerting me to a text, I hit pause so fast, it was a wonder I didn't break the button. Snatching up my phone, I saw a message from Erik on my lock screen.

> Erik: Hey. I didn't think you were going to message me, but I'm glad you did.

I chewed my lip before I replied.

> Me: Just needed to figure some stuff
> out. How is everything?

So fucking cringe. But Erik took the verbal olive branch and ran with it. He texted me back about sponsorship negotiations with an insurance company and getting to keep his clothes on for the advert. He told me about preseason training and how he was doing physio for his knee, because he'd wrenched it mountain climbing over the break.

After that, we talked about good hikes in the area, and our dream climbs. I found myself relaxing into the texted conversation, and it was more like talking with an old friend than a guy I was interested in. We obviously had a lot in common.

> Me: So, do you only sleep with men?

I was braver by text as well. I could ask the serious questions if I didn't have to look him in the eye to do it. He'd kissed Juniper just fine, but even I knew it was easy enough to fake it.

> Erik: No, I've had my share of lovers of
> all kinds. I definitely desire the person,
> not their gender, if you understand what
> I mean.

> Me: I think so.

> Erik: I know I was your first, but you've
> been in a male-dominated industry for
> years. I can't pretend I'm so special
> that I'm the first man you've ever been
> attracted to.

I thought about it for a moment. Like I'd said to Bug, I'd definitely appreciated the physical form of a lot of men over the years—both professionally, and if I was truly honest with myself, sexually. But I'd never wanted to kiss any of them. Not until Erik.

> Me: Nah, not the first. Only one I've
> fucked, though.

There, I'd said it. *I fucked Erik.* There was no shying away from the fact now.

My phone rang, Erik's name popping up on the screen. I was half-tempted to let it go to voicemail, because I was braver when I didn't have to hear his voice.

But I steeled my spine and answered. "Hello?"

"Just wanted you to hear my voice when I tell you I'm honored to be your first." Erik's voice was a purr, and my dick stirred. "I wouldn't mind being your second, third, and one-hundredth."

I swallowed hard and forced a laugh. "Hey, I don't know if you've read the tabloids, but that sounds a little too much like commitment. I'm deathly allergic."

He gave a chuckle. "I don't know about that. You're pretty committed to Juniper."

"She's my best friend." Her pretty face flashed into my mind. "But that's all we are. Friends. In fact, she's on a date tonight with some stockbroker from your neck of the woods." I quickly looked down at my phone, double-checking the green emoji she'd sent earlier. "Sounds like it's going well too."

A noncommittal noise emerged from Erik's throat. "I figured she'd have a boyfriend. A woman like that is too sweet to be single."

I didn't know how we'd gotten onto the topic of Bug, but hearing him talk about her brought back the image of them kissing, yet again, and my dick went from stirring to semi-hard. "They don't stick around for long. I don't think they like the fact she works for the IceCaps. Too much temptation or something, like Bug is anything but a hundred percent loyal." I paused. "Why? Are you interested?" I kept my voice light, like his answer meant nothing to me.

"Mmm, in any other situation, I might've been. She's sweet and fierce, and I like that. But right now, I'm more interested in her best friend."

I groaned softly. Damn, there was hardly any alcohol in my system, yet I suddenly knew why drunk me had climbed into bed with him.

"Oh? Maybe you should come over and show me just how interested you are?" I was aiming for seductive, and if this had been any other situation, I'd have been one hundred percent positive that I was pulling it off with ease. Instead, I felt a nervous energy racing through my veins. The thrill of anticipation.

"Are you inviting me over, Ludo?" he purred down the phone.

"Yes," I breathed, and he groaned.

"I'll be there in 40 minutes, *Laglegur*. Wait for me?"

I was about to reply when my phone chimed. Pulling it away from my ear, I frowned at the screen. It was another message from Juniper.

> Bug: Just leaving La Luna now. Having a great time. [Black heart emoji x3]

It wasn't the message that made my blood run cold. It was the three black hearts after it.

Black meant danger. It meant come and get me with your baseball bat swinging.

"Fuck!" I swore, hanging up on Erik and quickly opening the app that tracked her phone. She'd added me so I could see her location back when we were in college, and I'd added her back. Once, I'd gotten blackout drunk and fallen into a dumpster, and it was the only reason she'd found me. We had each other's back.

Erik was already calling me back, and I answered as I stuffed my feet into my shoes. "Ludo, are you okay?"

"No," I growled, finding my keys. I was fucking forty minutes away, thirty if I broke all the road rules. That was still too long. Too many things could happen in thirty minutes. Things that made me sick to my stomach when I thought about them happening to my Juniper.

"What's wrong?" Erik demanded, but I could hear him moving around.

"It's Juniper. She sent me the message."

"What message?"

"The one that says she's in trouble. It's the emojis. Green means it's going well, and she's going home with him. Orange means she's okay, but to expect her home. Black means she's in trouble. She's *never* used black. Not in all the time I've known her. Somethings wrong, Erik, and I'm too far away." My voice was choppy as I raced down the stairs of my building. I didn't have time to waste waiting for the slow-ass elevator.

I could hear the jingle of keys on the other end of the phone. "Give me an address, Ludo. I'll go and get your Juniper."

Part of me knew that if it got ugly, it could jeopardize his career. Bad press, injuries—we didn't know what we were walking into. What I did know was that Juniper wouldn't have sent that message for no reason.

And in the end, she meant more to me than my career. God help me, she meant more to me than Erik's career too. I looked at the phone once more and realized her location had stopped moving.

I gave Erik the address and prayed.

CHAPTER
Nine

JUNIPER

THE DATE HAD STARTED like any other. Dean was charming, slightly older, and his eyes had lit up when he saw me. He'd told me how beautiful I'd looked, and had been a doting, and by all accounts wonderful date for most of the night.

There were a few red flags, but I was pretending I was colorblind for the night. It didn't hurt that he was extremely handsome in his beautifully tailored suit. It was a deep blue and obviously expensive. His hair was in a fashionable cut, and his teeth were so white that they belonged in LA, not here in Detroit. He obviously worked out—though if I hadn't already noticed that, the in-depth breakdown of his exercise regime over entrées would have made it clear.

But toward the end, after dessert, the flags become too big to ignore. He'd told me that I would be way more attractive to men if I considered doing his workout routine to shed a little cushioning. He'd been rude to the waitstaff when they'd brought him a single glass of the wine he requested, rather than the whole bottle—which was just for me, I might add. He was drinking top-shelf scotch on the rocks.

His grin that had seemed charming for most of the date got suspiciously more shark-like, the more he drank. "Did you enjoy your dinner, Juniper?" he murmured as I drank the last of my wine. He signaled for the bill from the waiter, waiting impatiently as the man returned and handed him the little leather folder with the bill tucked neatly inside. Dean slipped his black Amex into it and waved the waiter away again. He didn't leave a tip.

Red flags everywhere.

I forced a polite smile. "It was lovely. The food was delicious. Thank you."

"We should take this back to my place and you could show your gratitude for this lovely meal properly," he suggested, his smarmy grin back on his face.

Alarm bells sounded in my head, and my skin went cold. But I kept a pleasant smile on my face. "I really can't. I have to head to work tomorrow."

I stood, and the waiter returned with my coat. The wine was swirling around my head, making me feel more than a little drunk. This was bad.

Dean took the coat from the waiter and shooed him away. Once he'd stuffed me into it, he hustled me toward the door. I just had to make it to my car, then I could drive down the block and call Ludo to come and get me.

Once we were at the front door, I smiled politely. "Thank you so much for dinner. I'll give you a call tomorrow?" I forced sunshine into my tone.

Dean looked at me with flat eyes. "Let me see you to your car, at least."

I was already shaking my head. "No, it's fine. The valet here is ready to grab your car, aren't you?"

The valet rightly read my signals, and his eyes slid from me to Dean. "Absolutely. It's the brand new Mercedes, correct? Beautiful car, sir."

Dean spared him a look, his eyes flicking up and down to take in the kid's uniform. "I want to tell you that if you work hard, one day you could have one too, but that's a lie. Sitting behind the wheel of mine is the closest you'll ever get."

Holy fuck. What a douche.

"That was rude," I snapped. "You had no reason to be so cruel. Don't call me, asshole." I stormed off, keeping my steps even but brisk. I made it down the street and around the corner to where I'd parked, before finally breathing easier.

Thank fuck. That was a close call. I quickly unlocked my car, my hand on the open door, when I felt someone behind me, along with the unmistakable feeling of the sharp tip of a knife at my spine.

"You're the one being rude, bitch. Women like you are all about the games, the manipulation. You see me and see a free meal. You see a nice guy who shows you attention—even though I can get women way hotter than you—and all you want to do is trample all over me to get what you want. Well, guess what? I'm going to get what I deserve." He grabbed the door handle and pushed me into the car. "Climb over. I'll drive. Don't do anything stupid. I can chase you down without breaking a sweat."

My skin was ice, my heart pounding. Thinking fast, I held up my phone. "My housemate will call the cops if I don't check in."

He sneered at me. "Fine, do it. But don't fuck around. Show me before you send it." He locked the doors, watching me closely as I pulled out my phone and messaged Ludo.

> Me: Just leaving La Luna now. Having a great time.

I typed *black* into the emoji bar and clicked on the first black emoji I could find. The black heart. I sent three. I had to trust that Ludo would know. He'd disregard the words and trust the emojis. I prayed that the system we hardly ever had to use would work.

"What's with the love hearts?"

I shrugged. "It's just how women talk to each other. They'd think something was wrong if I didn't put in an emoji or two."

Dean muttered something derogatory under his breath as he started my car. "What a fucking shitbox.

How you thought I wanted to take you out for anything other than a quick fuck is insane. I'm obviously out of your league."

I was terrified, but also, what a *prick*. "Obviously, you're also out of your fucking mind, so I'll happily pass. I'll get the hell out of your way and your space." I subtly kicked off my shoes, hoping he didn't notice. If I got the chance to run, I was going to take it—I didn't need a broken ankle screwing my ability to escape.

He was still clutching the knife, and when I tugged the door handle, he thrust it at me. I saw it was a switchblade with an ivory handle, the blade shining under the streetlight. "Dream on, Juniper." He smirked at me. "Honestly, I couldn't have hoped for this to go better. I love it when my dates put up a little bit of a fight."

If I wasn't certain before, I knew right then that I was in real fucking danger. It sobered me up quicker than anything. He shifted into gear—or he tried to, because my car really was a shitbox, desperately in need of a new transmission—making him grind them loudly. He swore some more as he forcefully jammed it into first.

My stomach was now churning, all the rich food burning the back of my throat. *Fuck it*. I turned to face Dean and vomited right into his lap. There was red wine and roasted sea bass right across his four-thousand-dollar suit.

"You fucking disgusting *bitch!*" he screeched like a

banshee, scrabbling away like he could get out of the splash zone. But there was nowhere for him to go inside the car. He looked down at himself, and I took my chance. Flicking the lock, I wrenched open the door and started to run.

My stockings provided no protection against the rough concrete sidewalk, but I ignored the stabbing pains and ran. I ran as fast as possible back toward the lights of the restaurant. *Though he'll probably come back here, right?* I bypassed it and kept running.

I ran until someone yelled my name, which made me run even faster. What if it was Dean? It was a trap. When two arms came around my waist, I screamed. It echoed off the walls of the old brick buildings and down the side streets.

"Juniper, it's me. It's Erik," the body behind me puffed out.

I spun, not trusting my ears. But there, holding me loosely now, was indeed the huge goalie. I looked up at him and burst into tears, my knees giving out.

But Erik had fast reflexes. He caught me easily, pulling me closer to his chest and holding me while I sobbed. "Shh, it's okay now. I've got you. You're okay." He whispered the words over and over as my whole body trembled. Then he scooped me up into his arms. "Let's go. Ludo's on his way, and I'll take you back to my apartment to wait for him."

I let out a hiccuping sound. "How di–did you find me?"

He carried me easily, like I wasn't slightly too chunky for these kinds of heroics. "I was on the phone to Ludo when he got your message. He gave me your location, and I only live about six blocks away. I got my cardio in tonight."

My heart was still racing, but the black dots that had danced at the edge of my vision were starting to recede. "You don't have to carry me six blocks," I said in a tiny voice. We were attracting looks, but Erik didn't seem to care.

"You aren't wearing shoes, *Einiber*." When we reached a park bench, he placed me down. Pulling his hoodie off, he tugged it over my head. "You're cold, and I'm worried you're going into shock." I sank into the warmth of his sweatshirt, pulling up the hood like I could hide from the world. "We should call Ludo. Do you have your phone?"

I shook my head. I'd left it in the car when I ran.

He stroked my cheek softly. "That's okay. I have mine." Wiggling his phone from his pocket, he quickly pulled up Ludo's contact. "Ludo? I've got her. She's safe." Whatever Ludo was saying at the other end had Erik's eyes darting to mine. "No, I found her running down the street—no saving needed. She's an athlete; it took me two blocks to catch up with her." He turned away and dropped his voice. "I don't know what happened. It's not my place to pry. She needs you. There's time for retribution later."

I didn't hear the rest of the conversation, but Erik

recited his address and hung up. "Ludo is almost here. Come on, little one. Only a couple of blocks to go." He went to lift me, but I shook my head.

"I can walk."

His eyes said he wanted to protest, but in the end, he wrapped an arm around my shoulders and kept me close as we walked the remaining distance to his apartment.

CHAPTER

Ten

ERIK

I SAT on my couch with Juniper tight against my chest. I'd tried to give her space, but she'd crawled onto my lap, like she was trying to soak in all the warmth and safety I could provide. It was heartbreaking, and the rage brewing in my veins had no outlet right at this moment. I'd talked Ludo out of tracking the guy down and permanently disabling him, but the calm voice of reason wasn't something I was feeling myself. Not deep down. I kept seeing her wild, fear-filled eyes as she spun to look at me, the echo of her scream reverberating around in my brain. I wanted to kill someone.

The front door slammed open, making Juniper startle in my arms. I'd left it unlocked so I wouldn't have to disturb Juniper. I rubbed my hands up and down her back as Ludo barreled into the room, his eyes as crazed as Juniper's had been and equally as filled with terror.

"Bug!" He launched himself at us, gathering Juniper off my lap and into his arms. He squeezed her so tight that I wondered if she could breathe. She buried her face in his chest and burst into a fresh round of tears. "I need his name, Juniper. I'm going to kill that fucker with my bare hands."

She just sniffled, shaking her head softly. They stood there for a moment, him shielding her from the world, and I wondered if they realized how in love they really were. The two of them were like two parts of a whole. The fear on his face and his grip on her body, like she was about to disappear, told me that the feelings were greater than either of them were willing to acknowledge just yet.

"You're safe now," he kept repeating into her hair, and something in my chest twisted. He looked up at me, his dark eyes shining, and mouthed *thank you.*

I waved away the thanks, because I didn't need it. I would have done it for anyone, for a complete stranger.

He pulled away from her a little, kissing her forehead. "I know you aren't going to want to hear this, but you need to call the cops."

Her face scrunched. "And say what? My Tinder date was a psychopath? You don't even know what happened, Ludo."

He was shaking his head. "I don't need to know the details, Juniper. You wouldn't have used the black emojis unless you genuinely feared for your life. I know you." He let out a huge breath, like he'd been holding it inside his lungs for too long. "Do you want to tell me what happened?"

She shook her head immediately, but I could see the moment she stiffened her shoulders, like she was summoning courage. I wanted to tell her there was no rush, to take her time, but honestly, I wanted to know who I had to pulverize as much as Ludo did.

"It was a good date, though he started giving me too much fancy-ass wine with the entrées, so that should have been a sign. He seemed interested in me, and what I wanted to do with my life. My dreams. He was charming, charismatic. I was having a great time. Then I finished dessert and the rest of the wine, and it was like a switch flicked. He started talking about what I owed him for dinner." She swallowed, her face growing paler. "When I left, he followed me to my car and pulled a knife. He made me get in, and I told him that if I didn't message my housemate, they'd worry. I hoped—" Her voice broke. "I hoped you'd see it. I hoped you'd understand."

Ludo rubbed her back, whispering something into her ear I couldn't hear. She nodded, then continued. "He couldn't get the car into gear, and he told me about liking it when his dates put up a fight. Then I vomited all over his suit." I laughed, though it wasn't a mirthful sound. Her lips curled up as she looked over at me. "He freaked out, and I ran, right up until Erik found me." She swallowed hard. "Thank you."

"There's no need to thank me, sweet." I wanted to

wrap her up in my arms again, but I didn't think Ludo would let go of her anytime soon. "But Ludo is right. You need to call the cops."

"And tell them what? I don't know his last name or the company he works for. I don't even know if he's really a stockbroker."

Ludo was shaking his head. "That's the job of the detectives, Bug. But if you don't, could you live knowing he could do it to someone else? Someone who didn't have me or Erik to ride to the rescue?"

She shuddered in his arms, and I resisted that urge to bundle her back into mine again. Finally, she nodded.

"So fucking brave," Ludo whispered against her temple.

I called the cops, who said they'd send someone out. Then I sat down beside Ludo, who had her on his lap, and stroked the back of her palm until her adrenaline crashed and she drifted off.

"Can you describe the weapon again?"

It had taken the detectives the entire night to turn up on my doorstep. They'd buzzed my apartment at six a.m., looking pissed to be there. I'd gone and woken Ludo and Juniper, who were both still asleep on my couch, Ludo spooned protectively around Juniper.

The detectives had looked her up and down, taking in her bare legs beneath my oversized hoodie, her smeared makeup and rat's nest hair, and I could see them forming an opinion right in front of my eyes. Then when Ludo stood behind her, they straightened. They might not have been able to recognize me straight off, but everyone knew Ludo. Juniper's chances dwindled even further. I could see them making judgments about the kind of girl who hung around a playboy like Ludo.

It hadn't gotten any better, as they asked her the same questions over and over, until even I became aggravated. Not Juniper, though—she repeated herself on command, her story never wavering, her tone always even.

"And you didn't catch his last name? Didn't ask for any ID?"

Ludo snorted. "How long since you've been on a date, Detective? It isn't like gaining entrance to a nightclub."

One of the detectives gave him a haughty look. "Maybe it should be. Would solve problems like last night." He sighed. "Look, Miss Verne, I'm going to be honest with you. We get hundreds of these kinds of calls a month. Women who go out with men they meet on dating apps and get into trouble. You were lucky; most are not. Even if we track down the guy, there's little we could do to lead to an actual conviction. Without any real evidence, it'll be your word against his. You don't have any bruises, no evidence of assault. We'll talk to the restaurant, see if we can't pull up his plates and get a name. We can put a complaint in our system so if anything like this happens again, we'll have a pattern of behavior."

"Anything like this happens *again?*" she squeaked out. "You mean if he actually stabs someone? Or worse?"

The guy's jaw tensed. "It's the law. I don't like it anymore than you do." He stood, handing her his card. "If he contacts you or you think of anything else, give me a call." With that, both detectives nodded and headed to the door.

We all watched them go, and when the door closed softly, I walked over and locked it. I looked back at Ludo and Juniper on the couch. She still looked rough.

I went and squatted down at her feet. "Would you like a shower? I'll lend you some clothes, then make you some breakfast." My shirts were going to be like a dress on her, but at least everything would be fresh and clean.

She gave me a tremulous smile that didn't quite reach her eyes. "Thank you, Erik," she said softly.

I led her down the small hall to the bathroom. It only had a shower, and when I was in there, the shower head was up to my chest. But it was good enough. I pointed to a small linen press in the corner. "Towels are in there. I'll leave you some clothes outside the door." I stepped back and shut the door, heading back down to the open-plan kitchen and dining area.

Ludo was pacing around, looking absolutely livid. He looked like he wanted to smash something, preferably the face of that detective. If Juniper's date was in front of him now, I doubted he would stop at smashing. He would pulverize the guy, until all that was left was a goo. To be honest, I'd probably help him.

I touched his back, trying not to take his flinch to heart. "I'll make you some coffee."

Ludo nodded, trying to force a smile. "Appreciate it." He sucked in a lungful of air and let it out slowly. "I can't believe I made her go through all that, and it was for nothing. The cops are gonna do nothing. The guy's going to get *zero* fucking consequences."

I shook my head. "That's not true. When she isn't so raw from last night, she'll sleep better knowing she did what she could. That's the kind of person Juniper is—if she hadn't reported it, the guilt would have eventually come for her."

Ludo cocked his head at me. "And how do you know what kind of person Bug is, hm? You've had, like, two whole conversations with her."

I shrugged as I put a coffee pod in the machine. He made a good point. Maybe it was time for some hard truths. "I can tell because she loves you, but she still tried to set me up with you because she thought that would make you happy."

He frowned. "I love her too. I want her to be happy as well."

Could he genuinely not know? "No, Ludo. I mean she *loves* you. The way a woman loves a man." I walked over and lifted my hand to his cheek, turning his face to mine. "And you clearly love her too, the way a man loves a woman. That panic you felt last night? It wasn't just a man concerned for the wellbeing of his best friend. It was a man who was threatened with the loss of the love of his life."

He stared up at me, panic in his eyes. "You're wrong. She means too much to risk what we have," he hissed back at me. "You've seen my track record. I'll fuck it up."

"Your track record with everyone but Juniper, *Laglegur*. What if you don't fuck it up? Or what if you never try, and she marries another man in a year, or two, or five, then leaves you behind? Only you can decide what you're willing to risk."

"What about this then?" He pointed between us. "Is it nothing?"

A sadness welled in my chest, because I knew I wouldn't stand between them. "It's a diversion from life. My team—hell, the NHL—isn't ready for two of its players to be in a relationship. The fans would revolt. It's just a dream, Ludo. Juniper is a reality."

Scowling, Ludo stepped away. "No. That's bullshit." He winced. "Well, probably not about the NHL having a hissy fit." Then he grinned. I was getting emotional whiplash. "What?"

"I've got an idea. One that will help keep Bug safe and let us explore... whatever this is." He still couldn't even admit that he was attracted to me. This was insane. "I hate her going on dates she finds on those stupid dating apps, which are filled with creeps and weirdos. Next time, you mightn't be there to save her. I mightn't be either."

Yeah, last night had traumatized Juniper, but it had also left its mark on Ludo. Maybe me as well. "What are you thinking?"

He looked me dead in the eye, and I felt myself snared in those deep brown orbs. "I think you should date Juniper."

"What?"

"*What?*" My response was perfectly timed with Juniper's. My eyes darted over his shoulder to the slack face of the woman in question.

Uh-oh.

CHAPTER

Eleven

LUDO

"HAVE YOU LOST YOUR EVER-LOVING *MIND?*" Junebug's voice was shrill as she gaped at me. She was sitting opposite me on Erik's couch. Honestly, maybe I had lost my mind. But if I had, I'd lost it on the freeway halfway between Ann Arbor and Detroit, knowing she was in danger and I couldn't help her.

I unconsciously chewed my lip before releasing it. I had to project confidence in the idea; otherwise, there was no way Juniper would go for it. I knew this for a fact—I had to pretend like I had no doubts, or she'd try and talk us both out of it.

I'd learned this the hard way in our senior year of high school, when I'd wanted to fill the principal's office with goats. She'd talked holes in the plan until we just ended up with Timothy O'Lear standing in his office in a clown suit. Timothy had given Principal Mullins a minor heart attack, so I wasn't sure it was better than the goats, but Juniper had been correct about the clean-up not being quite so gross.

I wasn't wrong about this plan, though. This was the perfect solution. "It wouldn't be real, Bug. It would just be for show, and it'll give you some time to breathe after this, while also helping me out." I was selling this like my life depended on it. "Me and Erik can't exist in this world. We both know it."

"Ludo," Erik snapped. "I won't have you emotionally blackmailing her into it."

I dragged my eyes to the giant man. He hadn't even agreed yet, but that had sounded almost like he wanted it too, right? "I'm sorry. It's of course your decision. Erik and I can sneak around until we're ready to make things more open."

Juniper looked at Erik, giving him a small smile. "Don't worry. He hasn't been able to talk me into anything since Christie in senior year." Her gaze flicked to me. "Spell it out for me, Ludo. How would this even work? Erik and I hang out, and I bring you along as my bestie for the media or anyone hanging around with a camera phone, and then what? Sit in the room next door, listening to you fuck? Because I've been there, done that. It's not my favorite pastime."

I shook my head. "We'll figure that part out later, but the foundation's already been set, hasn't it? They caught you kissing in the utilities hall at the arena. People will already be gossiping about it. We just have to give them a little extra ammunition."

She frowned. "People will think I'm a traitor."

"It's already out there. We're just fanning the flames."

She was silent, spinning the ring her mother had given her around and around her finger. It was a gesture she always did when she was overthinking. "This has the potential to go really badly. We can all acknowledge that, right?" She looked at Erik again. "And you? What do you think?"

I held my breath. I knew eventually Juniper would relent, because I knew her well enough to know last night had shaken her to her core. Maybe it was callous of me to push this now. But I was running on fear, and there was very little I wouldn't do—unscrupulous or not—to keep her safe.

Erik gave me a hard look, before reaching out and grabbing Juniper's hand. "It is no hardship to pretend that such a beautiful woman is mine, little one. And as outrageous as Ludo's idea is, I would be lying if I said I wouldn't always wonder what could have been. But that isn't on you at all. We're grown men. If we can't stand up for what we want, do we even want it enough?"

That was directed at me, and I took it. He was right. Though I also knew he wasn't just talking about us. He was talking about my supposed feelings for Bug.

I'd purposefully never looked too hard at what I felt for Juniper, beyond the gratitude that she was in my life. I'd never tried to narrow down the other emotions that swirled in my chest, because I knew myself. I knew that I would fuck it up. I loved her too much to lose her just because I was a fucking idiot who thought with his dick and not with the two braincells God had seen fit to grant me.

However, if I was being honest with myself, those random hookups really were getting less and less satisfying. Until Erik.

She was back to twirling her ring. "How exactly would we sell this to the public? I'm with you all the time, and no one ever speculates that we're together."

Well, that wasn't technically true, but it hadn't taken much to shut those rumors down. I'd gone on a few dates with Rozelle, a fashion model, and all talk about me dating Juniper had died right off.

"I guess you guys would have to be touchy-feely in public for a little bit, just enough for people to take a few photos." I looked between them. "Maybe a well-timed kiss or two."

Juniper's eyes dropped to Erik's mouth, and I resisted the urge to smirk. I knew her next words would be outraged, but she couldn't control the way she looked at his perfectly shaped lips. "Are you pimping me out right now, Andrei Ludokov?"

"I didn't say you had to fuck him in an alley, Bug." I pushed the image of Juniper wrapped around Erik from my mind before I got a really inconvenient boner. "All I'm saying is give him a couple of chaste kisses when you see cameras around."

Silence fell again, everyone lost in their own thoughts. Juniper had a comically open face, and I could almost trace the swing in her emotions as she turned the problem over and over in her brain. She knew I was right; she'd said as much herself when I'd first told her about me and Erik hooking up. Bug was a problem solver, so she'd be turning this problem around and around in her brain. I just *knew* she'd end up in the same place as me. A place where she'd be protected from men like the guy last night—who I would gladly murder, if I had the chance.

"I'll think about it, Ludo." I grinned, making her scowl. "I mean it. I'll *think* about it. I'm not committing to a single thing. This doesn't affect you the way it'll affect me and Erik." She stood, straightening the clothes she'd borrowed. "Can you take me back to my car?"

I worked hard to keep a smile from my face. I knew when she said she'd think about something, it normally meant yes.

"Come on. We'll check if my car's been towed. I didn't exactly pay a whole lot of attention to the parking signs outside."

Erik stood too, towering over Juniper in a way that was almost comical. They looked warily at each other, but then the big goalie opened his arms, and I saw my Junebug melt. She stepped into the shelter of his long reach, and he wrapped her tightly to his chest, holding her steady again.

"I owe you one," she murmured against his chest,

making something inside my own ribcage thump heavily. This was a gamble. They might decide they liked each other better than they liked me. They might decide that they were more alike than they cared to admit, and fall in love. Erik might decide I was a fucking player and dump my ass, leaving Juniper in a shitty place with everyone. There were so many variables, so many possible outcomes, and only a few of them were good. But there was one outcome that wouldn't happen if Bug went along with my plan—the one where she ended up a news feature on the nightly broadcast. A statistic found dead in the park. Or worse, a silent victim of a predator.

I'd take the gamble.

She stepped back out of Erik's arms, and I moved toward him, meeting his eyes, which snared me once again like a honey trap. When he leaned down to kiss me, I didn't pull away. Instead, I let my lips linger over his, remembering his taste. I sighed into his mouth, and his lips quirked.

"If you can convince her, I'm in. But you can't pressure her into it," he whispered softly. I shook my head, but he caught my chin, his pale blue eyes bright, like an iceberg in the sun. "Promise me, *Laglegur.*"

I was going to have to Google Translate that soon.

But also, this was an easy promise to make. I'd never *make* Bug do anything. "I promise." With that, I pulled away and moved back toward Bug. "Come on, sweetheart. Let's go grab your car and get you home. Friar

Puck must be going nuts." I could only imagine the destruction he'd wrought, with us both away from home all night.

I led her from the apartment and down the elevator in silence. My car was still where I'd left it in front of Erik's apartment complex, which made me breathe a sigh of relief. I had a fine on my windshield for parking in a no-parking zone, but whatever. At least it hadn't been towed.

Bug looked pensive as she directed me to the on-street parking down a small alley from the restaurant. Her car stood out like a beacon, and my heart sank as soon as I saw it. That fucker had left it wide open. Even from here, I could see it had been picked over by thieves. All four doors were open, and it had no tires.

Fucking fuck.

"Stay in the car, Juniper," I growled at her, double-parking beside her car and flipping the bird as someone behind us honked. I walked over to her car and swore again. The stereo system was gone, along with the seat covers and her custom stick shift. The glove compartment was open and empty, and there was no sign of her phone. Luckily, she'd kept her cross-body bag on when she'd run, otherwise that would have been gone too, cash and cards included.

I stepped back, and something crunched under my foot. I looked down to see the shattered remains of her phone, bent beyond recognition. Someone had clearly taken their anger out on the piece of technology, and there was nothing on it that would remotely be considered salvageable. No wonder the people who'd stripped the car had left it behind. Still, I picked it up. We could take it home and wipe it properly.

I manually locked the car doors, not finding her keys either. We'd change the locks on both of our places as soon as we got home. I didn't know if she'd told that fuckwad where she lived, though I doubted it. Despite getting trapped in a shitty situation last night, Juniper wasn't known for being careless. Still, it was better to be safe than sorry.

Climbing back into the driver's side of my car, I pushed down the rage threatening to bubble out of my veins. "I'll get someone out to tow it."

Her back was shaking, and I realized she was crying. Grabbing her arm, I gently pulled her across the seats until I could hold her in my arms awkwardly.

"Don't worry. I'll make sure it's okay. I've got you, Bug. Always."

CHAPTER

Twelve

JUNIPER

AFTER THE DATE FROM HELL, I'd locked myself away in my apartment for the rest of the weekend. Ludo texted me updates about my car on the phone he'd insisted on getting me on the way home from Detroit. I'd have to email my insurance company, but they were going to assume it was a write-off, which meant I could get a new car. That was good, I guess. A silver lining, maybe.

Ludo had also had the locks changed on both our front doors. However, I still jumped at every loud noise, or every time my phone notification sounded. I wanted to brush it off, because nothing had happened, but that fear had somehow permanently altered me. There was no going back to a time where I hadn't watched the man I was on a date with go from charming to sociopath over the course of dessert.

How could I trust my own judgment ever again?

On the heels of that thought was Ludo's proposition. He might think I was an idiot sometimes, but I wasn't the one who'd taken way too many sticks to the head over the years. I knew he didn't want me dating after this fiasco either, which was why he'd come up with this harebrained scheme. He wasn't so insensitive that he'd focus on his own problems while I was in the middle of a breakdown. Not unless he was trying to talk me into something that benefited me as well.

He did have a point, though. Now that my nerves had settled a little, and the shock of what had happened had worn off, I could see how his suggestion might make it easier for them to explore their attraction.

Though Ludo didn't know how I'd felt when I was pressed against Erik's chest. That feeling of warmth and security was a memory I couldn't shake.

The other problem that Ludo couldn't have possibly accounted for was how I felt about *him*. How I'd loved him since I was fourteen. How I wished it was him that would be kissing me in public, claiming me as his.

I let out a frustrated scream into my throw pillow. I could wish for it all I wanted, but I couldn't force a man who saw me as a friend to suddenly have feelings for me. However, I could help him find his own happiness.

Besides, as much as I'd never admit it to Ludo, I kind of wanted to do this for me too. A convenient excuse to not go on any more dates, to maybe not look too closely at the panic in my chest whenever I thought about that night.

So when I picked up my phone, I pushed all the doubts, fears, and that cool voice of reason away.

> Me: I'll do it, if Erik is in. Don't force him. It's his life, his career, on the line.

A strong knock at my door had the blood freezing in my veins. What if it was Dean? I hadn't told him where I lived, but he was smart. Maybe he'd been able to track me down.

Panic surged through me until Ludo's voice came through the door. "Junebug?" I let out a shuddering breath and stood, straightening my shoulders, like I hadn't just been cowering on the couch a moment earlier. Flinging open the door, I saw Ludo standing there, holding a paper bag that bore the logo of our favorite Italian restaurant.

His face softened when he saw me. "I brought dinner. Come over." Hearing his favorite D word, Friar Puck lifted his head from the huge cat bed that took up about as much room as a two-seater sofa.

Nodding at Ludo, I called for the Maine Coon, who lumbered to his feet sleepily, plodding toward the door and across the hall. It had been lucky that they'd had these two apartments available when Ludo had made it pro. It made sharing Friar Puck so much easier, and cut down the inevitable commute that would've happened if I'd had to drive to see him.

Ludo put the food on one hip as he jiggled the key into the door. "It's still a bit stiff," he murmured.

I gave him a crooked smile. "That's what she said."

He chuckled. "You know it." He winked at me, and although it was subdued, it felt more like our regular banter.

I grabbed plates from his cupboard, and he laid out the food, then made me a G&T from the wet bar. Finally, we sat at his dining table, Friar Puck on a chair beside us, like he'd been invited to dinner. I slipped him a breadstick, and he took it back to his bed to gnaw on, like it was a chew toy.

"I saw your message."

I ate my gnocchi, meeting his eyes with a neutral expression. "Yep."

"You're in?"

I raised an eyebrow. "That's what it said. Did that knock you took on Thursday make your vision double?"

"Har-har, Bug." He grinned and walked around the table, pulling me from my seat and spinning me around. "You are the fucking best—you know that, right? I don't deserve you."

I gripped his broad shoulders, trying not to think about how good his body felt against mine. This was definitely for the best. Maybe if he settled with Erik, I could get on with my life. Let this go, no matter how much it felt like destiny. "I *am* the best, and no, you don't deserve me." I wiggled out of his arms. "So how does this work? I've done my time listening to you fuck people in the other room."

He held my chair out, and I sat as he went back to his own. "I'll arrange with Erik for us to go out this weekend. We'll soft-launch your relationship. You won't have to worry about anything."

Then he shoved an entire bird's-nest-size twirl of pasta into his mouth, his eyes alight with happiness. Yeah, I'd sacrifice a lot for that expression.

Turned out they couldn't arrange anything until the following Wednesday, between the season opener and their game schedules. Thankfully, not against each other. I got on with my life, though I was pretty sure I wasn't imagining several people giving me the side-eye. They couldn't possibly know what we'd arranged, but apparently, me being wrapped up in Erik's embrace after the charity game might've been enough to start the rumors Ludo mentioned.

Or maybe I was just being sensitive. As I took some short videos of the IceCaps guys after their win, zooming in on a grin, on the strong curl of a back, on the equipment manager examining the blades on a set of skates, it seemed like business as usual.

Until Rigby Engman came up and slapped me on the back. "Hey, Junie. How are you doing? I heard you were locking lips with the big Viking from the Infernos."

I flushed bright red. That was Rigby for you. He didn't beat around the bush. "Who told you that, Engman?" He zipped his lips and pretended to throw away the key, and I raised an eyebrow at him. "Wouldn't that make me a traitor to the team? They are our archnemesis, after all," I quipped lightly.

Rigby snorted, posing for me as he removed his shirt. Thank god for Rigby, and Nova too. Some of the WAGs got a little mad if I ever posted their partners shirtless on social media. Fair enough for the players who didn't want the attention—I'd never post anything the guys might feel uncomfortable with—but a couple of the WAGs acted like I was bringing hookers straight to their doors. If they couldn't trust their partners with a pretty set of tits on a puck bunny, they had problems, and those had nothing to do with the team's social media profile.

Not Nova though; she'd just laughed and said that Rigby kept printing them out and leaving them on her nightstand. Soon, she'd have enough for a whole wall of pictures. She had absolute faith in her guys, and I envied her confidence.

Rigby waved a hand at my question. "Nah, Junie. Love transcends hockey, but don't tell the guys I said that. If you wanna chase the Norse God, I say go for it. If he treats you badly, I'm sure Ludo will beat the crap out of him, right?"

Oh, he was fishing. *Cheeky.*

"I'm sure he would. You know Ludo, overprotective

to the max." I knew there was a reason none of the guys on the team ever flirted with me. I didn't think it was because I was a swamp troll. Some of these guys flirted with Soukal, though, and she was more likely to chop off their nuts with a skate than flirt back. No, I'd come to the conclusion early on that Ludo had put me off-limits.

Rigby tilted his head. "Yeah, I do know Ludo." He patted my shoulder again. "I don't mind beating the goalie up in the parking lot either. River will help. He's fond of you, and Nova thinks you're great. She'd probably come out swinging a baseball bat."

I grinned, because how could I not? "Thanks, Rigby. But I didn't even say I was dating the guy. You know one kiss doesn't mean commitment, right?"

The twinkle in the big center's eye made me smile. I knew that expression. It was the one he always got when he was thinking about his girlfriend. "Sometimes, one kiss is all you need to commit."

My inner romantic went *awww*, but this was a locker room and there was no place for mushy emotions. So I punched him in his overly muscular arm. "Get out of here, you big sap," I laughed. "I've got work to do."

With enough raw footage to keep me going for a week, I left the locker room and headed back to my office to store away my equipment. I should be done by the time the guys were finished. The plan was that Erik would pick me up just as most of the press and players were leaving. He'd kiss me, shake hands with Ludo, and drive me home.

Was it weird to be nervous? It wasn't a real date. It wasn't anything, really—just a peck on the lips and a trip home.

Still, butterflies fluttered in my belly, and my palms were a little sweaty. Grabbing my tote, I took the elevator downstairs to the ground floor. Waiting outside the shiny chrome doors was Ludo, looking showered and handsome in his chinos and white button-up. He was even wearing leather loafers. It should have made him look like a pretentious douche, but instead, he looked like the GQ man of my dreams.

"You ready, Bug?"

I gave a tight nod. I was worried that if I opened my mouth and said anything, he'd hear the nerves in my voice.

He waved an arm for me to step ahead of him, his other hand spanning the small of my back. The light touch felt as if it burned a brand across my spine, like a nineties tramp stamp. He led me through the glass and concrete foyer of the building, out into the side parking lot, where everyone who wasn't a regular punter parked.

My eyes were drawn immediately to Erik, who was leaning against a pillar under the spotlights of the building. It made him look almost angelic, the yellow light warming his pale blond hair. He smiled when he saw us, and anyone watching would think that smile was for me.

When he strode toward us—his long legs eating up the distance far quicker than I ever could—his smile stayed just as wide as he looked down at me. "Hello, little one. Are you ready?"

To drive home? Yes. To kiss in front of hundreds of people? Um... maybe.

Instead of voicing my doubts, I just smiled back. "Yes."

He placed his hands lightly on my hips and drew me closer. Dipping down, his lips brushed mine. Just like the last time, it was electric, his mouth running expertly over mine. Like they had a mind of their own, my lips parted so he could deepen the kiss. He took the obvious invitation, pressing his tongue into my mouth.

My body curled in of its own accord, and a tiny part of my brain shouted that this was more than was necessary to sell the story. Sighing, I listened to that annoying little voice that was such an epic do-gooder and pulled away. I slid my eyes to Ludo, who was watching us with a weird expression on his face. Not jealousy, which was what I'd expected. More like he was perplexed.

Had he thought Erik wouldn't kiss me? This was his idea, after all.

Erik uncurled from his position, wrapping an arm around my shoulder and holding me tight. I breathed in his cool scent, something like pine and mint, and he looked down at me fondly as I cuddled into his side. If he hadn't been such a damn good goaltender, he would've had an awesome career as an actor.

That's all this was. An act. My brain warned my heart to behave itself. My heart flipped it the bird. This was going to be a huge mistake, but there was no going back now. I'd thrown my hand onto the table, and I just had to let the chips fall.

CHAPTER
Thirteen

ERIK

JUNIPER WAS all but vibrating with nerves beneath my lips, and it was endearing as hell. I hadn't been able to help myself when I pushed the kiss. I wanted to taste more of her; she was addictive. Kissing her was like a gateway drug, and now I wanted more.

She fit nicely at my side now, her curves tucked tightly against me. I reached out a hand for Ludo to shake, trying to keep my laughter inside at the stunned look on his face.

"Ludo. It's good to see you."

It took Ludo a beat to reach out and wrap his hand in mine. I stroked my finger along the inside of his wrist, feeling the staccato beat of his heart. His nostrils flared, and I knew his desire matched mine. We'd done all this, created this elaborate ruse, and I still hadn't gotten him back into bed yet. It seemed risky—what if we weren't even compatible without cheap vodka dampening our inhibitions?

I didn't think that was true, but not for the first time, I wondered if we'd jumped the gun on this whole thing. This was a lot of hard work for something that may be just a passing fancy.

I looked down at the beautiful girl at my side. Even if this was a waste of time, I wasn't going to be mad that I got to share these small moments with her. I was greedy. Ludo had her heart; that was obvious to everyone but the man himself. However, judging by the way she clung to my waist, we both needed these moments. This contact.

"Good to see you too, Erik," Ludo finally responded, smiling brightly. The kind of smile you did for magazine covers and reporters. Not the kind of smile he'd given me that night, or the ones that he bestowed on Juniper.

I could see the faint flashes as people lifted their phones to take photos, so this could be breaking news in some shitty gossip magazines. People needed a hobby if it mattered who I dated, man or woman.

My tensing fingers on Juniper's hip drew her worried gaze up to my face, and I forced a smile. "Are you ready to head home?"

She nodded again, and Ludo stepped forward to give her a chaste kiss on the cheek, nodding at me in the way that men do when they want to convey how alpha they are. I let a smirk curl my lips and raised a single eyebrow.

Leading her through the throng of people still pouring from the building, I gripped her hand tightly as we headed toward my car. Most days, I drove a Range Rover, not to be ostentatious, but because my height was a problem in a lot of modern cars. There were very few made for a man of my height and breadth.

I opened the door for Juniper, holding out an arm so she could use it as leverage to climb in. Her small hand wrapped around my forearm as she hoisted herself up. "What's with sportsmen and their giant cars? If I hadn't been in locker rooms all my life, I'd say you were compensating."

I laughed. "We aren't all as height deficient as some. I don't like having to origami myself into a car to drive across town."

We were silent for the first half of the drive to her apartment, and it felt almost awkward with the amount of unspoken things between us. Juniper broke first. "That seemed to go well." I could see her face flush, even in the darkness of the car.

"It was a good way to float the idea of us as a couple into the world," I agreed readily, overtaking a Vespa with a man so big on the back, it's a wonder his knees weren't dragging on the ground.

"I hope it wasn't too weird, kissing me," she said with an awkward laugh.

I wanted to wrap her in my arms and kiss her again,

without the cameras this time, just to chase away that self-consciousness for good. Instead, I dragged my eyes from the road. "It wasn't a hardship."

She swallowed hard, her profile outlined by the streetlights. "Are you and Ludo going out tonight?"

Ah, back to safe waters then. I shrugged. "I'm unsure what Ludo has planned. I'm not sure even Ludo knows what he has planned. He's still struggling, I think, with all this." I waved at myself.

She chuckled, the hesitation finally leaving her voice and the usual teasing lilt returning. "You do seem like a lot to handle."

I grinned over at her. "You have no idea, but that isn't what I meant."

I wondered, perhaps, if Ludo had grasped this plan so wholeheartedly for more reasons than he wanted to admit. Juniper was now a small barrier between us, a form of protection in case he wasn't ready to fully jump into something more. If he wasn't ready, that was okay. I was prepared to go as slow as he wanted.

We pulled into the underground parking lot beneath Ludo and Juniper's building, and she directed me to her car space. Her car was still gone, totalled by that fucking piece of shit. I hadn't expected to see Ludo already waiting for us, though.

Or maybe I had.

He walked to the passenger door and helped Juniper out. "That went great, don't you think? You guys really know how to sell a kiss."

Juniper rolled her eyes. "I'm not a nun, Ludo. I know how to kiss a man."

This time, there was no disguising the jealousy that flashed in his expression, though Juniper seemed to miss it.

"But do you know how to karaoke?" he asked in a haughty tone, and she groaned.

I raised my eyebrows at them both. "Karaoke?"

"Ludo's favorite guilty pleasure. Better get it out of the way now, because once you've heard him warble out 'Sweet Home Alabama', you might want to run for the hills," she teased. "You guys have fun. My eardrums are going to be thinking of you."

Ludo shook his head, looping his arm through hers. "Uh-uh. Erik can't go out without his new girlfriend, right?"

Juniper groaned. "I didn't sign up for this. You should've mentioned that I may be subjected to auditory torture in the fine print."

He kissed the top of her head. "Bug, you signed up for exactly this when we were fourteen and your mom got you that karaoke game for your Playstation. It kindled a fire in me that can't be dimmed by your negativity." He herded us both toward his car.

Juniper looked over her shoulder at me. "Save yourself, Erik!"

I laughed, watching them goof around with the love and respect of two people who'd grown together. It was beautiful. "Do you think they have any Björk?"

. . .

An hour later, I wondered if maybe I should have taken Juniper's advice to run. Ludo was many things: an amazing hockey player, handsome as hell, and an overall good human being. But he couldn't carry a tune to save himself.

My ears felt bruised as he sang along to "Sweet Home Alabama". "...*they lost the Governor, boohoohoo!*" he warbled, and Juniper winced as the microphone screeched.

"Good lord," I murmured to her, and she threw back her head and laughed.

"Get him a shot. Surprisingly, the drunker he is, the better he sounds. By the time he can't walk straight, he's basically a slurring Frank Sinatra."

I nodded resolutely, trying to work out how many tequilas we'd need to make him not sound like a dying cat. The bartender flirted hard, and I gave her a polite smile, tipping her a twenty. She definitely deserved it, purely for pain and suffering.

Taking the six shots back to our spot, I laid them out in the center of the table just as the final chords played out and everyone clapped loudly. I had a feeling that the applause was because the song was done, not for Ludo's efforts. He was grinning as he pushed through the crowd of singers, basically anonymous. Apparently, people who hung out at Korean karaoke bars weren't the kind of people who also attended hockey games.

"Shots!" he yelled, picking up one as he made it back to the table. "Cheers." We picked up our own tiny glasses and clinked them against his. Then we all knocked them back with a wince.

Argh. Not good.

"Next up, we have Juniper and the Berries singing 'Don't Go Breaking my Heart'." There was an audible groan as Ludo downed his second shot and followed Juniper up on stage. I watched them interact as they sang the Elton John classic, and clapped and whistled wildly as they finished. Juniper definitely carried the song, but Ludo made up for it with sheer enthusiasm.

Actually, Juniper had been right. He *did* sound a little better after shots, though I didn't know if that was because I was pleasantly buzzed or if he'd actually improved.

Juniper remained up on stage for her solo. The beginning chords of "Hopelessly Devoted to You" filtered from the speakers, and she swayed gently from side to side, a grin on her face. She began to sing, and my lips parted. She sang softly to start, the sweet tune falling gently from her lips. But when she hit the bridge, *holy hell*. I looked over at Ludo, who was just as trans-fixed by the woman singing on the stage as the rest of the room.

"She doesn't sing unless we come to karaoke. She thinks we come here for me, but I do it for her. She looks so happy up there on the stage," he whispered. "Her dad wanted a boy, and pushed her toward hockey instead of singing. Now she'll only sing in the shower or here."

As she belted out the final chorus, I was entranced. Her cheeks flushed, her chest heaving, she looked so damn beautiful. Coupled with the starstruck look in Ludo's eye, I made a promise to myself.

I'd have them both. We'd have each other. Fuck what everyone else thought.

I lifted my final shot and downed it. *Cheers to that.*

CHAPTER
Fourteen

LUDO

I WAS RIDING a high that was fuelled by good times and too much tequila. We were all in the back of a rideshare, and Erik was singing "Mamma Mia" with Bug, doing the head-snapping thing. They were laughing, and it settled something deep in my chest. The driver was throwing us looks, like he was trying to work out if we were going to vomit in the back of his car.

We were all definitely at our capacity for tequila, but honestly, I needed the liquid courage. The first time I'd had sex with Erik, I'd been drunk off my ass, and I was worried that I wouldn't be any good sober. Like he'd see my awkward, fumbling attempts and change his mind.

I wasn't sure when I'd become a pussy, but here we were. I was out of my element. Even now, we had Juniper tucked between us like a buffer.

We stumbled out of the car toward the locked front doors of our apartment building. It took me way longer than I wanted to find the swipe card in my pocket, and I felt Bug shiver beside me.

Grabbing her hand, I led the two of them toward the bank of elevators. Erik was grinning widely as he stepped in, and Bug looked comically small between us. She looked up with her hands on her hips and huffed. Her hair had come out at some point and was curling down her back in soft, dark waves. I was too drunk to resist stroking my fingers through it, catching on the knots, and she gave me a sour look. So I wrapped it in my fist and gave it a gentle tug.

Her lips parted, and her pupils blew out. *Holy shit.* My Bug was into a little hair-pulling.

I grinned at her. "Do you like that, Junebug? Are you a bad girl? It's always the quiet ones."

She gave me a haughty look that was quickly destroyed by the fact she hiccuped. "Wouldn't you like to know?" she sniffed, and I realized I kinda would like to know.

As if reading my mind, Erik leaned closer. "I think I would like to know too." His lips were so close to hers, and I wanted to watch them kiss again. Even the thought was giving me a semi behind my tight jeans. Watching them kiss earlier had sent a strange bolt of pleasure straight to my dick. Apparently, I was a closet voyeur as well as a closet... other things.

Erik lowered his head to kiss her, giving her ample

time to move away. "But there's no cameras," she breathed, her eyes sliding to me. There was desire drenching her expression. Female desire was something I could easily recognize. But behind that lust, her eyes were asking me for permission. She wanted to kiss Erik, but still, she thought of me and my happiness.

I really didn't fucking deserve her. I lifted my chin, granting them permission they really didn't need. A small smile lit up her face as she closed the distance between her lips and Erik's. He curled his hands around her wrists, pulling her closer as they kissed, and again, the view made my dick hard.

Their kiss was way too short, the elevator stopping at our floor a moment later. The doors opened and closed, but none of us got out.

They pulled away from each other, but Erik slipped his hand down to Juniper's, wrapping her tiny hand in his massive palm. He grabbed the back of my shirt, pulling me in for an equally dirty kiss. I could almost taste the sweet flavor of Juniper's gloss on his lips. I kissed him back, chasing the taste of them together.

When Erik leaned away, pulling Juniper closer, our faces were only inches apart. Her eyes were burning, and something rose up in my chest. A yearning I had buried for way too long. Letting go, I kissed her softly. A brief brush of our lips, but it was everything.

A sober part of me was screaming to *stop*, frantic that I would ruin everything. But I couldn't stop. I was addicted to the lust swirling around in this metal box.

Before I had time to second-guess everything, Erik had taken my lips again, as we stumbled from the elevator.

I was drunk. I should have been paying attention.

"Holy fuck." The gasped exclamation echoed around the empty hall.

I wrenched away from Erik and toward the voice I knew all too well. Spinning on my heel, I stumbled—because tequila—and almost faceplanted. I definitely would have, if Erik didn't have those goalie reflexes, even drunk as fuck. He grabbed the back of my shirt and righted me.

"Johnny?" Juniper asked, squinting at the man in front of our doors.

"Hey there, Junebug. This is... an interesting turn of events."

Juniper squealed loudly. Fuck, she was always a lightweight. Fear burned through the last of my alcohol high, but not Bug's. She shook her hand from Erik's and ran toward our longtime best friend, launching herself into his arms. He caught her easily, spinning her around, and she laughed with happiness. "When did you get back? Are you just on leave or...?"

Darkness flashed across Johnny's face. He lowered her to the ground. "Nah, Junebug. I'm out for good. No more Marines, just an average Joe."

She wrapped her arms around his waist, and jealousy finally reared up in my chest as he held her back, a look of affection punching light in the wall of darkness surrounding him. "I'm glad you're back. I worry about you every single day."

Erik cleared his throat, and all eyes turned to look at him. "Maybe I should go."

Fuck. Fucking fuck fuck. Juniper looked at me, and I saw what she was going to do, but I didn't have the words to stop it.

"Sorry, bad manners. Erik, this is one of our best friends from childhood, Johnny. We all grew up together in the same town. He's been in the Marines since he turned eighteen." There was still that note of betrayal in her voice. She hadn't wanted Johnny to join, but there was an anger in him that needed an outlet. I'd supported him when he wanted to enlist; it was the first serious fight Bug and I had ever had. "Johnny, this is, uh, my boyfriend, Erik."

I hadn't seen Johnny since I'd left for the NHL. A week later, Johnny had headed off to bootcamp, and it was the end of something special. Teenage friendships always struggled to survive the hardships of adulthood and distance.

Junebug had come with me to college a month later. Robbie, our other friend, had stayed back home to apprentice at his dad's construction business, and eventually married Marianne, who was his high school sweetheart. Marianne had always hated Juniper when we were teens, but now that we were all in our twenties and she had two kids and a lake house with Robbie, she seemed to be over it.

All that history washed over me like a tsunami, making me both happy my best friend was back and terrified that he'd caught me kissing Erik.

I clung to the hope that maybe Johnny hadn't seen anything, especially when he reached forward and shook Erik's hand. "Nice to meet you, man." He raised an eyebrow at me. "Don't want to make waves, having just got home and all, but Junebug, did you know your boyfriend was kissing Ludo?"

My face felt like it was going to sear right off my skull, and my heart pounded in my chest with such ferocity, I was worried it would seize up and stop altogether.

"I did see that, Johnny. Luckily, nothing happened to my eyesight while you were away," Bug quipped snarkily.

Johnny smiled. "All right then."

And that was it. Juniper gave me a smug look, her expression practically screaming *I told you so*. She'd said our friends wouldn't care, but I'd still worried. Johnny was always on his best behavior in front of Juniper. Always trying to impress her, like somehow her approval was what mattered most in the world. Even back when we were teenagers, when he got a B in math for the first time ever, the first person he'd told was Bug. Whenever he learned a new trickshot, he'd show her first.

We'd all loved her, but she'd given him something

extra. She'd anchored his lost-boy soul; she was Wendy to his Peter Pan.

Except without the romance. No one had touched Juniper like that. It was a pact between us all. Her friendship was worth more than dry-humping in the back of Johnny's beat-up truck. That backseat had seen many a hump through high school, as it became the unofficial place to take our girlfriends on dates. And there had been so many girlfriends—more than enough to keep a couple of teenage boys occupied. There'd been no reason to fuck around with Juniper, so keeping the pact had been easy.

Until now. You broke the pact. The memory of the brief touch of her lips to mine felt almost visceral.

"Ludo?"

Dragging myself from memory lane, I looked over at Juniper in the doorway of my apartment. Friar Puck had his huge head stuck out the open door, probably wondering what the hell I was doing and if he could come with.

"We're going inside to have coffee. Are you coming?" Bug's voice was gentle, coaxing, and I nodded. Her eyes told me she'd have my back. No matter how much she loved Johnny, I knew she'd kick his ass if he had anything to say about me kissing Erik.

"Okay, I'm coming." This was the first big test. If I couldn't cope with coming out to a guy who'd once held back my emo fringe as I hurled in my next-door neighbor's yard, then I wasn't ready for what I'd proposed to Juniper and Erik.

Straightening my shoulders, I walked through the door. Johnny met my gaze, all sorts of questions in his eyes, but his smile was genuine, and I couldn't help but grin back. "It's good you're home, Johnny. Juniper wasn't the only one who worried."

Darkness flashed across his face, like a stray cloud blocking the sun, but it was gone just as quickly. "It's good to be home." He sat down, and I knew that curl of his lips. It meant mischief was about to happen, and usually, that meant I'd be in the thick of it. "So, are we gonna talk about you playing tonsil hockey with Junebug's boyfriend, or do you want to pretend it never happened?"

All eyes turned to me. As much as I wanted to pretend for a little longer, it was now or never. I cast a quick look at Erik, and he gave me a reassuring smile, settling something in my chest.

"So, this is what happened…"

CHAPTER
Fifteen

JOHNNY

WHEN I WAS FOURTEEN, a girl joined my hockey team. She came to tryouts, dressed in brand-new equipment, with fierce eyes and a stubborn tilt to her chin that set everyone on edge straightaway.

When she was a damn good goalie, making Ruben —who had the coordination of a drunken llama anyway —lose his spot, Robbie had said being a team meant we had to be pissed at Juniper, in solidarity with Ruben. *Whatever.* I had enough anger in my body that I would happily direct it wherever they aimed it.

But at our second practice, I'd forgotten my gear out on the stands and had to run through the halls to grab it. I ran my skinny ass shirtless through the arena, and unfortunately, I'd run straight into Juniper as she was coming out of the other change room. I'd snarled at her like a feral animal, and she'd just given me an unimpressed look.

Until her eyes had traveled down to the bruises on my side and frowned. The boys in the locker room just knew I fought a lot, and assumed they came from that. They never asked questions. But little Juniper had looked at them, her young eyes analyzing something she shouldn't yet understand, and I knew that *she* knew.

She didn't say anything, though.

The following practice, she saw me dragging my feet, not wanting to go home, and again her young eyes appraised me. Saw things she shouldn't.

At our fifth ever practice, she barreled up to me, her brows drawn down and a determined look on her face. "My parents bought me a Playstation."

I'd thought she was screwing with me, rubbing her middle-class wealth in my face. "So fucking what?"

Completely impervious to my snarling, she'd pursed her lips. "You should come over for dinner tonight and show me how to use it. I can't make it work. My mom said you should stay for dinner too. Said she'd drop you back home later. You should call your parents and ask." She held out her phone, one of those brick types with no camera and no apps.

"My parents are dead."

I watched her wince, but she was determined. I'd say that continued to be Juniper's defining trait right up to this very day. "Then who do you live with?"

"My uncle and cousins."

Something knowing crossed her face again, and I wanted to run away from it. I'd never met a person who knew my secrets without me saying a word, and I wasn't sure I liked being so stripped bare. "Then you should call them and tell them."

My chest had felt too tight that day. The idea of not going home, of eating a meal cooked by a mom, was like a dream. "They won't care." Honestly, I doubted anyone would be home before the bar closed anyway.

She'd looked at me again, like she thought I was lying, but then nodded. "Okay." She'd walked off, like she hadn't just thrown me a life preserver. We went through practice, the guys gave her shit and she gave it back, then at the end of training, she stood beside the doors and waited for me.

When her mom pulled up in their minivan, I'd climbed in beside Juniper, ignoring the gaping mouths of our teammates. I'd eaten two bowls of pasta alfredo and taught her how to play *Final Fantasy X*. And then after the next training, I'd taught her how to beat the boss at the end of level one. It went on like that for months.

A year later, she told me that she'd known how to play when she invited me. She could just tell I didn't want to go home, and the fist-shaped bruises on my torso had told her why. So she'd talked to her mom, gotten permission, and made it her mission in life to ensure I always had somewhere to go where I was safe.

She'd said all this while playing the final boss in *Final Fantasy X*. As Yu Yevon was defeated on the screen of her bedroom TV, I'd realized I loved Juniper. It was a different kind of love than what a teenage boy should feel for a girl he has a crush on; it was an all-consuming love for someone who *saw* you. I also knew that if she ever realized, or the guys found out, I'd lose the only family I had.

So I'd continued with the status quo, right up until I left for the Marines. That girl, who'd become an integral part of our friendship group, even though we were a bunch of stubborn, shithead teenage boys who'd given her hell for months after she'd arrived…That girl? She'd saved me.

Her mom had basically adopted me, had sat in the stands and cheered when I got my diploma, and had hugged me extra hard when I'd gone off to bootcamp. Had written me letters too, though not quite as frequently as Juniper had.

My thigh throbbed as I lay quietly on Juniper's pull-out sofa, my trip down memory lane one I'd taken many times over the years. Juniper had actually saved me twice.

When a bullet had shredded my thigh, and I was bleeding out in the desert, I thought how disappointed Juniper would be that she'd saved me all those years ago just for me to die surrounded by the bodies of my fellow Marines, for a war that had no end. It had been the thought of Juniper's sadness that had me creating a tourniquet and dragging myself to the shade until I could radio for help. It had been Juniper who'd gotten me through the surgeries and the rehab, until I could walk good enough that she wouldn't notice I'd almost had my leg blown off.

She'd thought I'd been on a tour this whole time, but really, I'd been in a military hospital getting patched up and then honorably discharged.

I shifted, trying to ease the ache in my thigh, and it made the sofabed squeak. I wasn't surprised when Junebug's door opened and she cautiously stepped out.

"Johnny? Are you awake?"

"I'm awake."

She tiptoed out into the living room, and I watched her move through the darkness. "Do you want some hot cocoa? A whiskey?" She grinned. "Whiskey in your hot cocoa?"

I shook my head. "I'm good. Thanks, Junebug."

She moved to the other side of the pull-out couch, climbing beneath the covers. She turned on her side and looked at the profile of my face as I continued to stare at the ceiling. Many times during our teen years, we'd chilled in her room just like this, talking about the world and all the good and bad things in it.

I couldn't have comprehended the true amount of bad things at that age, but I knew now. But what I *had* known back then was that Juniper was one of the good things in the world. I still knew that with my whole soul. The fact she'd just crawled back in beside me, as if I hadn't been gone for over four years, made my chest ache.

"Can't sleep?"

I shook my head. "Don't need it. It's an old habit now."

We were silent for a little longer, although I could still feel her gaze on my face. "Johnny?"

"Mmm?"

"Are we going to talk about why you're limping?"

I let out a huff of laughter. "I couldn't ever get anything past you, Juniper May Verne." I sighed heavily. "I don't want to talk about how it happened, but I guess I didn't leave the Marines voluntarily. I was honorably discharged. I was shot."

She hissed and rocketed up in bed, full Exorcist-style. "John Percy Lipkin! You were fucking shot and you didn't *tell me?*" She moved toward me, throwing back the blankets, like I might still be bleeding from somewhere. "Show me?"

Her voice was a soft request, but I wasn't fool enough to believe she'd just let it go if I said no. She'd always been protective. She'd need to see I was okay before she'd be satisfied. As much as I wanted to hide it from her, a part of me warmed under her concern. Juniper might be the only person left in the world who'd care if I lived or died.

I tugged my sweats down my legs, giving my dick a

stern talking-to about behaving in my tight boxers. I watched her face as her eyes skimmed down my body, but I couldn't judge her expression in the dark. I knew the moment she saw the mess of my thigh, though, because she sucked in a breath.

"I was lucky, really. If the shot had come a little closer, or landed a little more to the right, it could have hit my femoral and I would have died out there."

"Fuck, Johnny," she breathed. That had probably been the wrong thing to say to her, because tears now fell over her eyelids.

Ah fuck. I could do many things without batting an eyelash. Face down enemy insurgents. Carry the body of my fallen buddy two miles to get help. Kill a spider bigger than my fucking face.

But Juniper's tears weren't something I'd ever been able to deal with. She wasn't a crier. She wouldn't have survived in our group if she had been. I'd only seen her cry three times before now. Once when Jimmy Myles had broken up with her in ninth grade, because he'd said she was a whale and a bunch of other mean-ass shit. Ludo, Robbie and I had beaten the absolute shit out of him for that. The second time was the day we'd buried Ludo's mom. She'd stood beside him, holding his hand, and cried right along with him.

The third and final time was the day I'd left for the Marines. I'd almost quit right then, changed my mind and gone home rather than cause her any pain.

So when a tear landed on my messed-up thigh, I

choked on the emotions in my chest. "I'm okay now, Junebug. I'm home and safe."

She reached out and ran her fingers over the ugly, puckered scars, and I clenched my teeth to keep myself in check at the soft touch on sensitive skin. My dick stirred, and I moved to pull up my sweats before she realized her gentle fingers were going to give me a boner. Better that she thought I was ashamed.

She continued to stare down at me. "So all these weeks, when I've been sending you letters, have you been stateside, recovering? How long?"

I winced. This was gonna be bad. "Four months."

"You've been here, in a military hospital, getting that all fixed for *four months*, and you didn't think to contact any of us? Ludo or Robbie? Mom?" She swallowed hard, and I knew her feelings were hurt. "Me?"

I shook my head. How could I explain to her that I felt like a fucking failure, the only survivor from my entire team? How the darkness had swamped me like an oil slick, and it had taken so damn long to stop feeling like I was drowning? How each painful moment of my recovery had felt like retribution, and that I hadn't deserved any of the softness she would have given me?

Luckily, the therapists had really helped. Darkness still chased me, especially through the nights, but I no longer had survivor guilt.

"I wasn't ready," was all I said to her right now, though. I'd explain the rest one day, but not today. Her eyes ran over my face, and she nodded. Lying back down, she pulled up the blankets over us both, then reached across the space between us to hold my hand.

"I'm here for you, Johnny. Always."

I swallowed back the feelings that surged up from my chest. "I know, Junebug." I squeezed her hand. "Can we talk about what you and Ludo are doing?"

Juniper had had a crush on Ludo for as long as I could remember. It was the main reason I'd never made a move on her—that and the stupid pact I'd made with Ludo and Robbie, that none of us would jeopardize our friendship by making moves on Juniper. It didn't matter, because Ludo had been the only one for so damn long. He'd been too blind to see it, though, and a jealous little part of me had always been happy he'd been oblivious. It would have been torture if my best friend and the girl I had a crush on had gotten together.

She sighed. "I want him to be happy."

There wasn't anything she wouldn't do for Ludo. Wasn't anything she wouldn't do for any of us. I knew that. It's why I hadn't called her when I'd been all fucked up. She would have moved Heaven and Earth to make me better.

She rolled onto her side, nudging me until I was on mine, then spooned herself against my back. "Go to sleep, Johnny. You can give me all the reasons why it's a terrible idea tomorrow. Tonight, I'll watch your back while you sleep."

With her soft, warm body pressed along my spine,

her hand still clutched in mine, I didn't think there was a chance I would sleep. But then her breathing evened out as she drifted off, and mine matched it. Soon enough, I was falling into a deep, dreamless sleep for the first time since I'd enlisted.

CHAPTER

Sixteen

JUNIPER

I WAS HUNGOVER AS SHIT. Though not hungover enough to forget that Ludo had kissed me, Johnny had seen Ludo kissing Erik, and the fact Johnny had been fucking shot. I pushed my fingers through my snarled hair as I sat up on the pull-out couch.

It squeaked, and Johnny's eyes flew open. He was up and out of bed before he'd even taken in his surroundings. "Woah there, soldier boy. Just me," I teased softly, hating the look of cold determination on his face.

I'd *hated* it when he went into the Marines. I'd spent months trying to talk him out of it. Ludo had said to let him go, that there was a part of Johnny that needed the strict structures of the military, or the only place he'd end up was in jail like his cousins. It had been the most adult conversation our group had ever had, but I'd still wanted to bundle Johnny up and lock him in the closet so he'd miss the bus to bootcamp.

I'd been worried that the Marines would finally burn out the sweet, sensitive boy who still existed under all that anger.

Given the way his chest was heaving, and the blank look in his eyes, I'd been right to worry. Standing there without his shirt on, I could see the rest of the scars I'd missed earlier. There were so many. Long, thin ones. Round, puckered ones. All on a body that had been honed into a marble statue of strength and pain. When my eyes traveled lower, I got caught on the slight tent in his sweats and quickly averted my gaze.

Rule number one of having a bunch of guys as friends growing up was that we never acknowledged their morning wood. Ever. It was like an *A Current Affair* special where they blurred out the whistleblower's face—we just pretended their bodies ended at their belly buttons.

Johnny cleared his throat, running a hand through his short brown hair. "Sorry. Instinct."

I waved a hand, like the fact he'd sprung out of bed ready to murder me meant nothing. "It's fine. Want some coffee?"

He grunted his agreement, and I went over to my fancy machine. Sliding his cup underneath, I pushed a couple of buttons. "I'll be back in a minute."

I walked into the small bathroom in my apartment and stared at my bloodshot eyes in the mirror. Despite being on the fold-out couch, I'd slept surprisingly well. Probably the tequila, and I'd always found something calming about Johnny, even if he was considered the "bad boy" among our group.

Not by Mom, of course. She'd loved Johnny from the day I brought him home. She'd always wanted more kids, and it was like Johnny—and to a lesser extent, the rest of the guys—had given her that. My dad had been away almost all the time, giving us a good, middle-class life, but I was pretty sure Mom had been bored and lonely, so having a baby bird to save gave her purpose.

I brushed my hair and my teeth, splashing water on my face in the vain hope it would make me feel half alive. Spoiler alert: it didn't.

Shuffling back out to the living room, I saw Johnny had put on a shirt. Shame, really. I mentally slapped myself, because thinking Johnny was hot was almost sacrilegious. I only had permission to lust after one childhood friend, and Ludo had held that mantle for a long time. But I was only human, and the Marines had chiseled away all the soft boyhood in Johnny, leaving only a dark, brooding man.

"Bathroom's all yours when you want it." I grabbed his coffee from the machine and put my cup under instead. "So, what's the plan now you're out? Do you need a place to stay?"

Johnny frowned into his coffee cup. "I haven't quite

figured it all out yet. I've got a hotel in Detroit at the moment—"

I snorted. "As if Ludo or I would let you spend money on a hotel when you could come and stay with one of us. Ludo has a spare room, or you could always stay on my couch if, you know, you don't want to listen to Erik and Ludo fuck."

He shrugged. "I've listened to Ludo have sex in the next room more times than I can count."

Yeah, Ludo was a bit of a manwhore. He'd always been too pretty and too charming not to have female attention all the time. Johnny got the attention too, but he was pickier.

I gave him a hard look. "It's different this time. I don't want you to be uncomfortable."

"Why? Because he's fucking a dude? That doesn't bother me, Junebug."

"I know. I didn't think it would. No, I meant because I don't think Erik is going to be just a casual booty call or a one-night stand. I think he's kind of enamored."

Johnny raised an eyebrow. "Enamored? Jesus, is this a Jane Austen novel?"

I threw a cinnamon roll at his head, and he caught it, tearing through half the carby goodness in a single bite. "You know what I mean. He wouldn't be doing all this if it didn't mean anything."

Johnny made a humming noise into his coffee. "And by all this, do you mean using you as a beard so he and his man love can fuck in the shadows instead of coming out to the world?"

I sighed, bringing the plate of cinnamon rolls to the table, as well as a punnet of strawberries. Johnny looked right at home at my dining table, and I was so fucking glad he was here.

I gave him a haughty look. "It works for us all at the moment." I tried really, really hard not to think about Ludo kissing me briefly in the elevator. It had definitely been the tequila. I was also trying not to think about Erik kissing me, like he wanted to strip me naked. This was supposed to be for show only.

Already, it was getting messy, and it had barely been a week since we came up with the plan.

"It works for you because you're scared," Johnny said softly. "If you could give me a name, I could make sure that fucker will never make you scared again."

That darkness was back, and instead of scaring me, it made me feel... something else. *Yep, gonna stuff that one right down.*

I shook my head. "It doesn't matter—"

He reached out and gripped my arm. "It *does* matter. No one touches you, Juniper, unless you want it. I'll break the fingers of any man who thinks otherwise. Understand me?"

I stared up into his stormy blue-gray eyes, my head nodding of its own volition. "Yeah, Johnny, I get it." I wrapped my arms around his waist and hugged him tightly. "You have my back, I know. But he isn't worth the trouble you could get into. I just want to forget it happened, and if that means spending a few months licking my wounds and pretending to be the girlfriend of a hot Nordic guy, then that's what I need to do."

He huffed a breath, and I felt it puff over my forehead. His arms held me tightly to him, like I was his own personal teddy bear. "Okay, Junebug."

There was a knock on the door, and I disentangled myself from Johnny's arms as Ludo strolled in. His eyes looked between us, a small frown knitting his brows. Just as quickly, the look disappeared.

Friar Puck appeared behind him, loping over to Johnny. The big cat had adopted Johnny last night. He reached down and scratched behind his tufted ears.

"You stealing my girl and my cat, Johnny?" Ludo joked, heading over to my coffee machine. I'd been telling him to get his own, but I had a sneaking suspicion he just liked to come over before training.

"Our girl, Ludokov. Our girl," Johnny teased back, and those two fell right back into the friendship they'd had all those years ago, like time—and sometimes oceans—hadn't separated us for the last few years.

Ludo grinned at Johnny, then his smile fell. "About Erik…"

Johnny waved a hand. "I don't care who you fuck, Ludo. I didn't care back when you screwed Tina, the school secretary in senior year, and I don't care if you make manly love with a giant now. Whatever makes you happy, man."

I gasped. "You did *what* with Tuna Fish Tina?" Unfortunate nickname, but teenagers were mean. Everyone had called her Tuna Fish Tina because she had a long, skinny face and really small lips right in the center, which she always painted red, making it even more obvious they were tiny. So she'd kinda looked like a tuna.

Thinking back on it now, I cringed. Kids were dumb.

Ludo flushed. "She offered to give me a blowjob, and I accepted. I didn't *fuck* her," he corrected, giving the stink eye to Johnny, who just shrugged with a grin. "I was going to take you to the rink, asshole, but now I might just leave you behind."

Johnny's face shut down, his hand going unconsciously down to his left thigh, rubbing it with the ball of his hand. I frowned again. "I'm going to shower and get ready for work. While I'm gone, maybe our best friend can tell you about the fact that he got shot while on active duty and *didn't tell us*."

Ludo gasped, and I turned away, heading back to the bedroom.

My phone vibrated on the nightstand, and I checked it, seeing thirty-five new messages. Some from my work buddies, some from people back home, and one from Erik.

Apparently, being seen together had worked, as a couple of hockey gossip sites had picked up photos of Erik collecting me from the arena. There were several messages from the girls at work that were all just emojis.

I opened Erik's message.

> Erik: Apparently, last night worked. We should go on another date. Tomorrow night?

I chewed my lip, trying to ignore the way butterflies took flight in my belly.

> Me: Sounds good. What should I wear?

> Erik: Whatever you like. Be comfortable.

Men. Being comfortable was almost universal for their wardrobes. Jeans and tee, and you're both fashionable for multiple locations and comfortable. However, being comfortable had a mountain of meanings to most women. Should I wear a sundress, or will we be doing a lot of bending over? Are we being active? Can I wear my yoga pants? Inside? Outside? Are we having dinner?

I was already stressed, but now I was also running late for work. Stressing would have to wait until tomorrow.

CHAPTER
Seventeen

ERIK

I'D EXPECTED THE RIBBING, and hell, maybe a little of the negative taunting from the team. Everyone but Laurens had given me the side-eye all through training, but I should have known that Rusket wouldn't let it go. After all, how could he poke at me for being gay if I was fucking a woman from our team's fiercest rivals?

"You know your girlfriend is going to go running back to that asshole Ludokov to tell him all our game play, right? She's definitely using you, and you're too fucking dumb to see it," he ranted, walking behind me as we headed to the ice. "She's definitely fucking Ludokov too. Though why he'd be fucking a little chubby girl like that when he's been out with Allegory Jones is beyond me. I'd much rather be fucking a Victoria's Secret model, personally." His mouth just kept running, and I was about ready to shut it permanently for him, sanctions be damned.

"Whatever," I grunted at him. "Just train. I don't need your commentary on my life."

I suffered through another hour of training, then hung around on the ice, in the vain hope that everyone would be in the showers by the time I made it back to the locker room. If I'd thought having a girlfriend would make it easier, apparently I was wrong.

Or maybe Ludo was right; my whole team were assholes.

A couple of the rookies came up to me and chatted, not having been turned against me by the rest of the team yet—or hell, maybe the next generation of players were just more tolerant and less hopped up on testosterone and their hillbilly daddy's prejudices.

I timed my shower just as Rusket was coming out, knowing if I spent enough time in there, I could probably avoid him altogether. When I emerged, the room was basically empty, except for a couple of rookies and the coach.

I had a lot of respect for Coach King. He was one of the best in the business and definitely one of the few reasons I hadn't begged to be traded. However, he believed in letting the captains deal with inter-team cohesiveness, which was a mistake.

"Luthersson, can we chat?"

"Sure, Coach. What's up?" I pulled on my sweats and a tee.

He cleared his throat awkwardly. "My wife tells me you're in a relationship with the social media girl over at the IceCaps."

Internally, I groaned. "Your wife is correct."

Coach nodded, chewing his lip as he looked past me and into the hall. "I don't have to worry that she's going to bamboozle you with her charms into giving up valuable team information, right?"

This time, I outwardly groaned. "Not you too, Coach. Come on. Juniper isn't like that. Plus, when we're together, we aren't spending a whole lot of time talking about hockey."

Coach made a huffing sound. "I don't want to know what you get up to behind closed doors, Luthersson. It's none of my business." He gave me a shrewd look that told me he'd heard the gossip from the other guys on the team about my sexuality. "As long as you play well and don't give away trade secrets, it's all good with me."

I resisted the urge to roll my eyes. "Got it."

Coach slapped me on the back and left, and I shook my head at the ridiculousness of the whole fucking thing. I could only imagine the kickback I'd get if they knew it wasn't just the pretty Juniper I was interested in, but the IceCaps wonderboy right wing.

I thought how close we'd gotten last night to something else, something I didn't think I could even hope for. The three of us in the elevator had been hot enough that we could have set off the fire alarm. I couldn't imagine what it would be like if I got them both into bed, under my hands and hopefully over this stupid barrier they had between them. You'd have be blind to miss the raw sexual tension between them, but apparently, they were far-sighted at the very least.

I hadn't planned for the hot soldier, though. His eyes had appraised me with a kind of cool calculation that made me wonder what he did in the Marines.

But the way he looked at Ludo and Juniper, all soft and protective, led me to believe he was only looking out for their best interests. I couldn't guess how his appearance would affect Ludo's master plan, but I found myself panicking at the idea Ludo would pull out of this arrangement. That he'd bury that part of himself he'd just begun to explore, because the scrutiny would be coming too hard and too soon. I needed to spend more time with him.

I pulled out my phone.

> Me: Do you want to hang out tonight?

I was about to shove my phone back in my pocket, but three little dots appeared immediately.

> L: Sounds good. Your place? Johnny is going to stay at mine for a while.

I chewed the edge of my thumbnail. That didn't bode well if he was hiding what we had from his friend already, even if Johnny had caught us kissing. I chastised myself. I was trying to push too fast, wanting everything all at once.

> Me: Sounds great. About 8? I'll order pasta, you bring the drinks? No vodka.

A laughing emoji, as well as a green-faced emoji, came up underneath my message.

> L: Beer it is. See you at 8.

Smiling to myself, I stuffed my phone back into my pocket and made my way out of the locker room.

Should I light a candle? Would that be fucking weird?

That was just the latest in a long list of stressed-out questions I'd asked myself. When Ludo buzzed from downstairs, I was relieved that I could finally stop being a pedantic bitch about everything, especially when he rolled through the door clutching beer and the pasta takeout.

"Met the kid at the door. I gave him a forty-buck tip, and he didn't even ask whether or not I was going to the right apartment," he laughed.

I tsked. "The ethics of delivery drivers isn't what it once was."

I took the pasta from him and leaned in for a kiss. Casual intimacy was the first step to something more meaningful—at least, that's what my sister's magazines had always said when I was growing up. Ludo relaxed quickly under my lips and kissed me back. I made a happy noise at the feel of his lips on mine.

"How was training?"

Ludo huffed. "Everyone kept asking if I was okay, but I wasn't the one on a skeezy gossip site."

I rolled my eyes, but I didn't want to beat him over the head with the fact that everyone knew about his feelings for Juniper except him. And Juniper.

Tonight, I wanted it to be about us. "It's nice that they care about you."

He frowned at my tone. "Do I need to head over to Inferno Central and kick some ass?"

I grinned and leaned forward to kiss him again. "Not today. I can fight my own battles. Come on, we'll serve up the pasta."

He put the beer on the counter, then reached out to grab the bag of food back from me, placing it beside the beer. "Erik?"

I sucked in a breath, the soft seduction in his tone going straight to my dick. "Yes?"

"I don't want to eat dinner just yet," he purred, stepping closer to me, his hands gripping the front of my shirt.

I grinned, my eyes drifting from his hooded gaze down the sculpted body that was barely hidden beneath his tight white shirt. "What do you want?" I murmured so low, it was almost a whisper.

He leaned forward until our lips were almost touching. "I want your lips wrapped around my cock."

A shudder of pleasure ran up my spine. My hands traced down his muscled lats to the tight rise of his ass. "Then I guess you better sit down then, because by the time I'm done, you won't be able to feel your legs," I promised, leading him to the couch.

I couldn't fucking wait.

CHAPTER

Eighteen

LUDO

I WAS TAKING the bull by the horns. Or the goalie by the cock. Either way, I was finally getting out of my head and back where I wanted to be: in Erik's bed. Well, on his couch.

He shoved me down, and it was odd being with someone who could move me so easily. If he were a woman—

I stopped myself from making comparisons. This wasn't one of my old, casual conquests. This was something new, and I couldn't be one hundred percent present if I kept thinking, "If Erik were a girl..."

Luckily, he made it easy by kissing me with such heat, every thought disappeared from my brain. He pushed me back onto the couch cushions, my knees spreading wide to make room for those shoulders. Grabbing the waistband of my sweats, he pulled them down to my knees, sucking in a breath at my already semi-hard cock.

"You're freeballing it? Man, I feel like a piece of meat right now," he teased, but then he ran his tongue over my balls, and all the oxygen got stuck in my throat. Could you choke on air? My dick got hard, and as his tongue ran up the vein on the underside of my cock, I couldn't look away. Especially not when he took the head between those lips, his blue eyes hazy with lust.

I wanted to watch every moment, but he had a mouth like a vacuum. It felt like he was sucking my damn soul out through the head of my dick. I buried my hand in his short hair, gripping the soft strands like he was an anchor so I didn't jack-knife off the couch with pleasure. I thrust my hips up slowly in time with his movements; he took my cock so well that I wasn't sure how I'd ever considered a blowjob good until this very moment.

"Fuck, Erik," I groaned. I was going to blow way too quickly. He'd think I was a two-pump chump, and my ego couldn't take that. Grabbing his head, I pulled him off my dick with a grunt. "I want to blow inside you."

Because that was the part I hadn't been able to forget. The tight feel of him clenched around me, all hard muscle. It had felt like I was conquering something, but also like I was giving something in return. That made no sense, but then again, it didn't have to.

"Straight to the main course? Is your Casanova reputation a lie?"

Gripping his face, I pulled him up for a sloppy kiss that tasted like my precum. I kicked my pants off, letting him drag my shirt over my head. He was wearing way too many clothes, and I tugged at them. I wanted to tear them from his body. Wanted to feel his hard edges against mine.

He moaned my name, his deep voice rumbling against my lips. It sounded fucking beautiful. His hands explored my body, his strong fingers tracing my collarbone, down to my pecs, and tweaking my nipples until I hissed. He smirked at me, making my blood heat. *Oh, it's on.*

I turned until he was under me, my mouth back on his as I tore at his clothes. Luckily, he was helping me this time, shucking his pants and shirt in record time. The hard bar of his cock ran along my stomach, and I was kinda glad he was a bottom, because *holy shit.* I spat in my hand and stroked his length, running my thumb over that spot that had made his knees shake last time.

"Fuck, Ludo," he gasped. He reached between the couch cushions, pulling out a bottle of lube. It was so fucking strange that a laugh escaped me.

Sitting back on my heels, I stared down at him and the magic couch cushions. "Well, aren't you prepared? Or do you just keep it there for special occasions?"

He gave me a cocky expression that made my dick jump, pouring some lube into his hand and wrapping it around my dick. I gasped at the coldness, but that was soon replaced by the hot sensation of him pulling my cock just perfectly.

"I had a suspicion we wouldn't make it to the bedroom," he growled, stroking me harder. I was going to last three fucking seconds if I ever got inside him. Gasping for air, I pushed his hand away and slid to the floor, pulling him down with me.

I bent him over the seat of the couch, going up on one knee, because fuck, he was tall. And *perfect*. His back was made by the gods and perfected by hockey. As he flexed his shoulders, it was like watching a muscular symphony. I could watch him bent over like this all day. I mean, if I wasn't dying to be inside him.

"Can I go bare?" I asked breathlessly. "I'm clean." I wanted to feel him around me with nothing between us, more than I wanted to breathe. We had to have regular STD and health checks, so I knew he'd likely be clean too.

"God yes. Just fuck me," Erik groaned as I poured lube between his cheeks, smearing it into his tight hole with my finger until he was moaning beneath me. Working in one finger and then two, I leaned forward, kissing the hard muscles of his lats, then biting his shoulder hard enough that it would probably leave a mark.

"I've dreamed about this every night for months. I didn't know if they were memories that I forgot, due to the alcohol that night, or if it was just something I wanted so fucking bad that it was an ache in my balls."

I scissored my fingers. "I've watched hours of porn to find out what to do to help you take my cock, and moan my name at the same time."

I mean, I'd read articles too—because porn couldn't always be trusted to be realistic—but saying I'd read how-to guides wasn't very sexy in the moment.

"I want you to crave me, crave this, as much as I do."

Erik let out a shuddering breath. "Fuck me, Ludo."

I lined my cock up with his ass, replacing my fingers with the head. That first slide was a fucking religious experience. Bottoming out inside him was like nothing I'd ever experienced.

"God, its so fucking *tight*." My balls pulled up, but I paused, breathing through my nose. I wasn't done yet. I couldn't be done yet.

Erik pulled back, until just the head of my dick was inside that tight ring of muscle, then impaled himself on my cock again. "Harder," he grunted. "Like you mean it."

Leaning over him, I snapped my hips against him, the slam of his tight-as-fuck glutes against my pelvis making a noise that I'd hear in all my dirty fantasies. "Stroke your dick. I want your cum painting your couch cushions," I ordered, my hips flexing so fast, I almost was losing it. But I couldn't stop now, the sounds of sex and the feel of him around my cock drawing me to madness, like a moth to a flame. I curled over his back, my hand reaching forward so I could rest my hand over his as he stroked himself in time with my thrusts.

My rhythm got wild, and suddenly, I was coming deep inside him, filling him full of me. Dark spots danced at the edges of my vision as he came all over my hand, his ass so tight around me that I was worried I was going to lose blood flow.

He collapsed forward, and I went with him, plastering myself to his back as we both breathed like we'd just run the Boston Marathon. Pulling out of him, I flopped back onto the couch, tugging him up onto it with me. It clearly wasn't made for two hockey players, but we'd make it work until I could feel my legs again.

"Holy fuck. I guess the first time wasn't a fluke then."

Erik chuckled, turning to face me. "You were worried it was? Bold move, literally changing three lives on the chance of a fluke."

I shrugged, running my fingers through the soft blond hair falling over his face. "I didn't *think* so, but we were pretty drunk. There isn't anything I wouldn't risk to keep Juniper safe, though."

He made a happy humming noise. "I understand. I'm taking her on a date tomorrow." He rolled onto his side. "Can I be honest with you, Ludo?" At my nod, he continued. "I really like Juniper. If I'd met her before you, I would have stolen her from you completely."

I laughed, the jealousy I thought I'd feel at his words nowhere to be found. "You could have tried."

"I can be persuasive," he teased, waggling his brows.

Yeah, no shit.

"There's something about her, though. She has this guileless kind of beauty that she doesn't even realize she has. And that sharp tongue. Her sweet loyalty. She's a catch that's wasted on you, *Laglegur,* if you can't appreciate it."

Now I frowned. "I appreciate all those things about her."

He nodded. "And one day, someone else is going to appreciate those things about her too."

Now the jealousy appeared, coursing through my veins. Juniper had been a steady presence in my life since... forever. The idea of her dating someone else, marrying someone else, having a life that didn't include me, made a tight ball of acid form in my stomach.

Erik gripped my hand tightly, looking into my eyes as he murmured, "Maybe that person could be me. I want... something more than this. Something more with her."

The betrayal in my chest burned. We'd only fucked twice, and he was already over me? I mean, we'd been texting every night and hung out a couple of times, but was I a dead lay or something?

I went to climb off the couch, but Erik's big arm banded across my chest. "No, Ludo, you misunderstand. I want you *both*. I want us to be something more. I want it to be the three of us."

Well, that was *not* where I'd thought that conversation was going.

"You want us to be a throuple? Aren't you getting ahead of yourself?"

"Didn't you feel what was happening in the elevator before we were interrupted? Couldn't you feel how *right* the three of us were together?"

I closed my eyes, remembering the sensation of Juniper's soft lips pressed against mine. The taste of her on Erik's tongue. "Erik…"

He lifted his hand. "Just think about it. I don't want to pursue her without your permission. I'm committed to what we have right now."

I nodded, relaxing back down onto the couch beside him. Soon enough, my eyes grew heavy, but the idea of the three of us spun around and around in my brain, eventually chasing me into my dreams.

CHAPTER

Nineteen

JOHNNY

I BENT down to secure my laces tightly, a routine I'd done so often that it was basically muscle memory. Even if I hadn't worn skates in over four years. When Junebug had found that out, she'd insisted we come straight down to the rink and do some free skating. My thigh ached a little, but this was probably good physiotherapy for it.

A part of me was excited to be back on the ice. We'd spent so much time training, racing up and down the ice, and generally goofing off in our teen years, that skating had been as easy for me as running.

But I'd been in the desert a long-ass time. I was scared that I wouldn't be able to do it anymore, that the Marines had stolen this from me too. Along with my ability to sleep, and my ticket to Heaven.

Juniper was already out on the ice, her curvy legs wrapped in thick tights with an old IceCaps hoodie hanging around her thighs and a soft, knitted cap tucked around her braids. It was like looking at teenage Junebug all over again, right down to the bright smile on her face. She loved the ice, as well as hockey.

Once, when she'd been twirling around on the ice, Robbie had asked her why she didn't go into figure skating. She'd simply said it was because you couldn't hit someone in figure skating. Our girl had been fiery, even back then.

"Hurry up, Johnny, before the ice melts."

Robbie used to say that, every time we took too long. He'd gone through a stage where he blamed everything on global warming, after we'd learned about meteorology in science class. It became a thing we said whenever anyone was being too slow.

The nostalgia hit me right in the chest once more, but I sucked in a deep breath and grew some balls. I might fall on my face, but I wasn't a pussy. I was going to try. Slipping the blade covers off, I walked to the ice and stepped out.

I skated a few steps without landing on my ass, so I took that as a win. I pushed out, sliding a little, and when my thigh didn't collapse straight away, I skated toward Junebug. I was almost there when my toe caught, and I flailed forward. Juniper was there to catch me, laughing, because that's just the kind of friend she was.

"Want me to go get you a support penguin? Help you keep balance while you get your legs back under you?" she teased, tilting her head toward the little walker things the kids used when they were learning to skate. They looked like the IceCaps penguin, complete with scarf.

"Fucking har-har," I grumbled, but my lips were already curving into a smile. "Give me five minutes to get everything working again, and I'll still kick your ass in a race."

Juniper snorted, skating confidently across the ice. "It's been too long since I've been on the ice myself. I forgot how much I loved it."

Finally, my brain and muscle memory synced, and I slid across the ice after her. "Why haven't you been out here for so long? When we were teens, I was worried you'd get frostbite, we spent so much time on the ice."

She shrugged, skating backwards easily. "Work. Life. It all gets in the way. Adulting is a trap."

Amen to that. Though I didn't think I'd ever been a carefree kid. At least, not since my parents died.

I pushed a little faster, overtaking her and forcing her to skate harder to keep up. We dodged around the figure-skating lessons, and the amateurs doing drills. Juniper tried to check me into the boards, and I bounced her back with my hip, her giggling so infectious that I found myself grinning too.

We goofed around until my thigh began to burn, at which point I headed back to the wall. Someone had brought out the peewee team for practice, and Junebug was talking to the tiny little goalie, giving him pointers.

"She's a natural with the kids."

I looked over my shoulder to Ludo, who was resting on his forearms on the wall. I hadn't even heard him come up. A few months out of the Marines, and I was already getting slow. Or maybe it was the Juniper effect. She was definitely distracting.

"She is. She was always so effortless with a stick in her hand." She had so much talent. If she'd been a boy, she would have been drafted right along with Ludo. Maybe she could have joined the women's league either here in the US or in Canada, but she'd broken her tibia in senior year, falling down a mineshaft at a party in the woods outside of Louviers, our hometown.

I could still remember the sound of that snap. Her scream of pain.

So her chances of selection had crashed and burned, and she went on with life in an extremely Juniper-like manner. Like the whole thing had never happened, like she'd never been so good that she'd almost made it big. She just rolled with the punches, a smile on her face.

But watching her now, moving from side to side, showing the tiny kid—whose equipment seemed way too big—how to move to cover the goal, I wondered how much of that pain was just buried.

"Are you enjoying being back on the ice?"

I nodded, looking over at my longtime friend. "Took a little bit, but it's like riding a bike."

Ludo tilted his head. "And being home?"

I shrugged. "Also a bit of an adjustment. Junebug

makes it easier—like I never left, you know?" He hummed his agreement, his eyes darting back to her in the goal. "Actually, I wanted to talk to you about this thing you have going on."

Ludo's shoulders tensed. "Yeah?"

"It's not really fair to her, is it? You're getting everything out of this arrangement, and she's getting what? A time-out? She deserves to live her life and be happy, Ludo, not just to be a pretty mask that you and Erik hide behind."

He frowned, his jaw flexing with tension. "That's easy for you to say. You didn't see her, Johnny. She was fucking *terrified*. She cried. She barely slept for a week afterwards. How am I meant to watch her leave on another date and wonder if she's okay?"

I shook my head. "Because it has nothing to do with you. It's her life—she isn't going to sit in the corner while you get your happy ending and she gets left behind."

He stood tall now, turning to look at me with a fierce expression on his normally jovial face. "No one is leaving her behind. She'll be just as important to me in a year, in ten years—hell, when we're old and retired—as she is now."

I sighed, because I felt like we'd had this argument before. "As what? Your best friend? Someone who sits around and pines after you, because you're too much of a dumbass to see what's right in front of you?"

He crossed his arms across his chest. "Where the

fuck is this coming from, man? You sound like a jealous stalker." He glared at me. "Is that it? Do you want Juniper for yourself?" he sneered.

"What would be so fucking wrong with that?"

He reared back. I guess he'd thought I was going to deny it. "What the fuck? Since when?"

Shit. Fuck. I couldn't take it back now. "Since we were fourteen, and she realized my uncle and cousins were beating the shit out of me."

He took a step back. "What?" he breathed. "How did I not know this?" Guilt clouded his features, tinged with pity. His dad had been an old bastard, but he'd basically just ignored Ludo unless he was playing hockey. After his mom died, the old man had fallen into a bottle and never dragged himself back out. Not for Ludo, and not for himself.

I'd avoided this conversation for so long. I knew my friends would feel bad that they'd missed the signs I was getting the shit beaten out of me. "I didn't want you to know, Ludo. I didn't want *anyone* to know. Junebug's just more empathetic than the rest of us fuckers combined."

All the fight went out of his body. "Man, I was so oblivious to everything, wasn't I?"

The mirthless laugh exited my lips like a hiss. "We were teenage boys. We thought about hockey, girls, and fucking a tube sock."

He looked over at Juniper again, and I could see the

conflict in his expression. "Does Bug know how you feel?"

I shook my head violently. "Hell no, and I'd like to keep it that way. She deserves better than me." I looked him dead in the eye. "She deserves better than you too."

He laughed—actually laughed. "Erik likes her as well. Actually, maybe he likes her more than me." He shook his head, like he couldn't believe someone else was more desirable than the great Andrei Ludokov. "He wants us to be a committed throuple."

Now it was my turn to be surprised. "And what do you want?"

Juniper started to skate back toward us, a smile on her face and her cheeks flushed pink. God, she was so fucking beautiful. Too beautiful for someone as ugly as me, that was for sure.

I didn't think Ludo was going to answer; he'd take the out that Junebug's imminent arrival would give him. Instead, he turned to me, his face more serious than I'd ever seen it. "I just want her to be happy."

It's what we all wanted. If that meant bowing out, that's what I'd do. But I wouldn't let her be cast aside by my best friend and his lover. I was going to have to take the measure of this Erik guy, more than our fifteen-minute chat over a coffee and a beer. He held the hearts of both my best friends in his hand, and I was going to make sure he was worthy of them.

CHAPTER

Twenty

JUNIPER

I WAS PUTTING the last touches on my makeup when Erik knocked on my door to pick me up for my date. Stepping back, I cast one more look over my outfit. Taking Erik at his word about being comfortable, I'd opted for classic blue jeans and a white tee, with a gray blazer that was tailored beautifully to my fairly steep curves. Combined with a cute pair of wedges, I felt ready for anything, except maybe scuba diving.

"Your date is here!" Ludo yelled from the living room, where he was watching game highlights from Montreal's last season with Johnny.

Running my fingers through my hair, I grabbed my purse from the back of my bedroom door and headed out. As I came into the living room, Erik was standing close to Ludo, saying something softly to him as their bodies leaned toward each other like they were magnets, destined to attract.

Whatever Ludo said made Erik smile, an expression filled with knowing. Something had happened between those two, because they were no longer dancing around the attraction they obviously felt for each other.

Still, a little pang struck beneath my breastbone. Jealousy, maybe. I pushed it away, because I'd agreed to this. Hell, Ludo exploring this thing with Erik had been my idea. I had no right to feel anything but happy for them.

I pasted a smile on my face, strolling into the room confidently. "Ludo, stop making that fuck-me face at my date. I spent two hours getting ready, and if you lure him over to your apartment, I'm going to be pissed."

I looked over at Johnny, who was watching the three of us with a frown. I rolled my eyes at him, like I couldn't believe Ludo's antics, but my smile felt a little too brittle.

Loping over to me in two long strides, Erik wrapped me up in a hug. "*Einiber*, you look beautiful." He kissed my cheek, and I flushed. "Let's go. Our reservation is in an hour, and we still have to make it to the city."

Ludo leaned against my kitchen counter. "Have her home by midnight, and no funny stuff. Wouldn't want to send her off to a nunnery this young," he teased.

Shaking my head, I walked over and kissed his cheek. "You're not my father."

He kissed my cheek back. "No, but I could be your

daddy," he purred jokingly, his eyes filled with laughter.

The response I had was pure, visceral lust. Hell, that wasn't even my kink—no hate to the people who were into that—but still my lady bits clenched, got down on their knees, and said *please sir, can I have some more?*

I laughed awkwardly. "I'll tell my dad you're trying to replace him."

A weird rumble echoed around the room, and I belatedly realized it was Johnny laughing. I wasn't sure I'd really heard him laugh since he'd arrived home. The sound made everyone turn toward him. Friar Puck even lifted his massive head from Johnny's lap, looking up at him with perplexed, golden eyes. It was the first flash of the old, less burdened Johnny I'd heard. A Johnny who wasn't so weighed down by darkness.

"I'd pay money to hear that conversation," he chuckled.

Ludo threw him a sour look and shooed us out the door, like this was his apartment instead of mine. I guess they'd been interchangeable for so long—why stop now? Even though Johnny was technically staying in Ludo's spare room, he had breakfast and hung out in my place just as often. I needed to get him a key, give him a little bit of permanence so he didn't feel like he was relegated to being an afterthought.

A warm hand spread across the base of my spine. "You're thinking very hard. Are you having second thoughts?"

I realized I'd followed Erik all the way down the hall silently, like a prisoner going off to the gallows. *Whoops*. Giving him a guilty smile, I shook my head. "No, sorry. I was thinking about Johnny."

He ushered me forward as the elevator arrived at our floor. "He seems nice. You can tell how close the three of you are. He seems to fit with you seamlessly."

A grin split my face, because Erik's words soothed a worry that had been plaguing me since Johnny's return, that perhaps we didn't fit so well anymore. That we'd developed rough edges and different layers that would eventually send us off in other directions. "We grew up together. You can't be as close as we were without some of your personality being a reflection of theirs, and there being little hints of you in them too."

Erik nodded. "My Ömmu always said that when you love someone, you share a little piece of your soul with them." He wrapped an arm around my shoulder. "She'd like you. You're both very wise." I flushed under the praise, or maybe it was because he was warm and smelled amazing.

The doors opened, and he led me out to his car, which was a vintage muscle car. Honestly, I couldn't have been more surprised.

"Holy shit... is this a 1970 Chevelle?"

Erik raised his eyebrows at me. "You know cars?"

"Under duress. Robbie wanted to be a mechanic when we were young, and he'd read those classic car magazines all the damn time. Ludo wanted a Ferrari, but Robbie was an American muscle car guy. I think I could tell you every decent car from, like, 1962 to 1975. It was all he talked about." I laughed, thinking about it now, but back when I was a teenager, it had felt like getting an icepick to the brain hearing about horse-power and RPMs and carburettors, or how fast each could go from zero to sixty. "Having a bunch of guys for friends wasn't always glamorous. Sometimes teenage boys are really damn *boring*. It was all boobs and cars, unless we were talking about hockey."

I slid into the car, and just enough of Robbie's passion had bled into me that I could appreciate the beautiful condition of the interior, and the growl when Erik started the engine. Grinning over at him, I reveled in the deep vibration. He pulled out into the traffic, and soon enough, we were heading down the highway to Detroit. The radio was on low, though I could see he had a pretty impressive sound system.

He cleared his throat, and I slid my eyes in his direc-tion, trying not to be so awkward. "So Robbie was the fourth member of your group?"

"Yep. He lives back home with his high school girl-friend—now wife—Marianne. She used to hate me. Once, she put laxatives in my drink bottle during practice."

We'd all gotten over those petty teenage rivalries a long time ago, but if I was honest, Marianne had always been a mean girl. She might have mellowed, but she was still a bit of a bitch. I'd never tell Robbie that, though. He loved Marianne almost as much as he loved his vintage Shelby that he'd restored from the ground up.

Almost.

Erik asked me pleasant, getting-to-know-you date questions the whole way to Detroit, and I reciprocated, and honestly, it was easy. So easy that I barely noticed the miles flying by. Pretty soon, we were pulling into a faux log cabin-style building.

I looked over at Erik. "Is this what I think it is?"

He chuckled. "Wait and see."

I was two martinis down and wielding an ax like a crazed person. The last three axes I'd thrown had bounced harmlessly off the target. "This is unfair, Erik. This ax-throwing bullshit is basically coded into your DNA. You know who weren't good with axes? The Italians."

"You're of Italian ancestry?"

"Like two percent, according to one of those DNA tracker things. The rest is Irish. I'm so white, I'm practically Miracle Whip."

He laughed, launching an ax in a perfect arch at the target, the blade burying itself with a solid *thunk*. "I'm fairly sure the ancient Gaels had axes. Not so different from the Vikings at all. Maybe you just need to unleash your primal instincts." He pulled me into our little cage lane and stood behind me, despite the safety warnings of the staff that there should only be one person in front of the line at a time—I guess so nobody got in the way of a vicious backswing.

He kicked my feet wider, and I could feel the hot press of his chest to my back. "Spread your feet." He wrapped his hand around mine and slid it down the wooden ax handle. "Hold your ax low. Look where you want it to go. Then give it a feral yell."

Man, was this meant to feel like foreplay? It was so hot in here. I didn't know if it was a faulty HVAC system, the booze, or the fact that Erik was so hot he threatened to singe my eyebrows.

He stepped away, and I tried to calm my wild heart. Doing as he said, I wound back, looked through the target, and shouted as I loosed the ax.

It hit just outside the target ring, and I squealed. "Oh my god! I did it!" Spinning in Erik's direction, I launched myself at him. He caught me with a soft *oof* but spun me around until the soles of my shoes brushed against the tall table that held our drinks.

"See! I told you that you had a little Viking in you."

"I wouldn't mind a big Viking in me either." I slapped my hand over my mouth. *Holy shit.* "Oh my god, I didn't mean that. I'm so sorry. The martinis were really strong." The bartender must have been slipping us doubles, because he'd definitely recognized Erik.

I opened my mouth to apologize again for being inappropriate, but he cut off my words by leaning forward and kissing me. His sweet lips were almost familiar now, moving over my mouth like he knew exactly how I wanted to be kissed. His large hands spanned my back, and I pressed my own hands to his chest to steady myself.

The kiss went on and on, dizzying in its intensity, making desire flood through my body like a torrent I couldn't hold back any longer. A little part of my brain screamed that this was all for show, that it couldn't go anywhere, but my body didn't care at this point. I just wanted to kiss him forever and ever. His lips. His skin. Other parts that were lower and rhymed with... uh, wenis?

Finally, that screaming little voice in my head managed to wade through the haze of lust that was currently swamping my brain, and I pulled away. "I... uh... should get another drink. Or maybe some food." I looked around, spotting someone with their phone pointed in our direction.

Oh, that made sense now—he'd seen someone filming him.

Disappointment curled in my gut, but I pushed it down. This was good. I had no reason to feel guilty now, because this was legitimately my job, no matter how conflicted and slightly shitty I felt.

Giving Erik a shaky smile, I walked back to the table and downed a whole glass of ice water. "We only have ten minutes left. I think it's your turn. I'll take some action photos for your Gram feed."

Nothing said relationship like posting the other

person on social media. He looked down at me, a slight crease between his brows, but eventually, he hefted the ax and walked to the line at the end of the lane. I took an action shot as he threw the heavy weapon perfectly, nailing the bullseye like a pro. I guess no one had better hand-eye coordination than a professional goalie.

I grinned as he turned around, triumphant. It was time to divert the conversation somewhere safe. "So, uh, you and Ludo looked a lot more comfortable this evening."

Erik's smile was that smug expression of someone who'd gotten dicked down real good. "We've definitely moved along in our friendship. He's really something special. We made the right decision, pursuing the thing between us. I guess we have you to thank for that."

Jealousy, thy name is Juniper.

Instead of letting the green-eyed monster free, I waved a hand in his direction. "Yeah, being taken on dates by a handsome hockey player is such a hardship."

I kind of wished it was. I wished I didn't enjoy Erik's company quite as much. I wished that my feelings for Ludo were only the type shared by two childhood friends. I wished that I could have everything I wanted without having to give up something equally as important to me.

But if wishes were fishes, that dream was Moby Dick.

CHAPTER

Twenty-One

LUDO

MONTREAL HAD KICKED OUR ASS, but the team had still gone out for drinks afterwards. Unlike when we won, there wasn't any partying or puck bunnies. I guess there might still have been puck bunnies, but I didn't have much interest these days.

I'd been on the road for almost a week, and I was chomping at the bit to get home. I wanted my own bed, my couch, the new video game that just had dropped, and an ice-cold beer. I wanted to see Juniper and Johnny.

I'd been rooming with Muss, and he snored like a freight train. How his wife, Julieta, hadn't smothered him in his sleep was a mystery to me.

If I was honest, I wanted to get back to Erik too. I was so fucking gone for him that it was a little pathetic. We'd texted the entire time I'd been away, and I hadn't seen him much before that either, our schedules not really lining up. That was one issue with dating another hockey player that I should have predicted. It was so rare that we weren't on the road at different times. We couldn't even Facetime, because while I may be able to pass him off in my phone as Erika, no one was going to mistake his low baritone voice as a Miss America contestant.

All we could do was text and call, like this was 2002.

I stood beside some of the rookies, with Rigby, River and Muss having gone back to the hotel rather than coming out with us. I couldn't go home, because I was maintaining the illusion of being the playboy I'd always been, not a guy who'd settled down with another guy.

One of the rookies, Cal, had a girl under each arm, and he was definitely trying to steal my mantle of IceCaps fuckboy. Let him—I was tired of that life.

A woman in a tight black dress that hugged just under her ass came up to me, batting lashes so long that either they were fake, or her daddy was a giraffe. "Hi, Andrei," she purred, and I gave her a smile that should be pleasant but felt almost painful on my cheeks.

"Only my parents called me Andrei. It's Ludo."

She grinned shyly. Definitely an act. "Oh, I thought maybe only your friends called you Ludo, and we weren't there yet." She stepped closer, running a finger down my chest. "I wouldn't mind being closer, though." She dropped her voice, beckoning me closer, but I ignored the come-hither gesture. "Don't tell anyone, but the IceCaps are my favorite team."

Someone took a photo, and I groaned internally. I wanted to reach out and grab the person's phone, slam it on the ground and stomp on it with my boot, but instead, I gave the girl my best pissed-off glare.

Erik would know better, and it wouldn't hurt to have a few pictures of me with other women on social media for a while. But I hated being a commodity. Hated people taking photos without permission and using me for clout and likes. It felt so fucking cheap.

I gave the girl in front of me a wink. "Your friend got the picture you wanted, so you can run along." My voice was still pleasant, but my whole face felt flat.

The girl laughed, like it was the funniest thing that she'd been caught out. "I'm sorry, but none of my girl-friends would believe I spent time talking to Andrei Ludokov without photographic evidence, you know." She leaned forward again. "If you think she's cute, we're sharing a hotel room. I'm sure we could both help you have a really, *really* good night."

I downed the rest of my beer, and her eyes lit up. Yeah, like me chugging a warm, flat beer meant I was going to stick my dick in her. "Thanks for the offer, but I'll pass. Have a good night, sweetheart."

I was going back to my hotel room. Hopefully, Muss would be sound asleep enough that he didn't sound like a chainsaw stuck in a kiddie pool of jello.

. . .

My head hurt from lack of sleep, and for the first time since going pro, I was homesick. I huffed a sigh, stuffing my crap back into my duffle so we could catch our flight home. It was almost time for check-out, and then we'd be back on a plane to Toronto. One more game tomorrow, then we could catch a bus home. I couldn't wait.

I met River and Rigby outside their room, which was directly opposite mine. They were both grinning widely, and I raised an eyebrow at them. "What are you so excited about? There's still two nights until we head home."

Rigby slapped my shoulder. "This is our longest away stretch. Almost done, and then we can head back home to Nova and Huey."

I narrowed my eyes at them, because even River was grinning, and that grumpy fuck *never* smiled. He was the polar opposite of Rigby. "What else is going on? Did you get a raise? Your contract renewed? Did Rigby suck your dick?"

Rigby snorted. "He wishes." He cast a quick look at River, who shrugged. If Rigby's smile grew any wider, it would crack his face. He dropped his voice low, leaning toward me. "You aren't allowed to tell anyone just yet; we're keeping it quiet for the moment. But Nova's pregnant."

"*Holy shit!*" I whisper-shouted at them. "Congratulations! I'm so happy for you guys." I didn't ask whose it was, because how could they possibly know? They were in that unconventional poly relationship, and I didn't think any of them abstained. Hell, I doubted it was even in their vocabulary. They'd all been stuffing their baby batter inside the cake tin as much as possible, if Rigby was to be believed. Looking at their smiling faces, I got the feeling it didn't even matter whose baby it was.

Maybe that's what it would be like if I agreed to Erik's plan for a throuple. I tried to imagine Juniper round with a baby, and not knowing if it was mine or Erik's. The idea of a pregnant Juniper made warmth spread through my chest. She'd be a great mom. She'd had a great example.

River patted my back. "Thanks, man."

We moved down the hall, toward the elevator that would take us to the foyer to meet the rest of the team. "When's she due?"

"Late May, I think."

I snorted a laugh. "Maybe we're gonna have to start throwing some games so we don't make it to the Cup playoffs. Don't want Nova giving birth in the family box." They laughed along with me, but their happiness filled the small space of the elevator, like a physical warmth that I just wanted to soak in. I wanted a little of their secondhand happiness, even for a moment. "Maybe you guys should have had a little more restraint during the offseason," I teased, doing the quick math in my brain.

Rigby snorted. "Yeah, right. Wait til you get yourself

a girl who's your whole world and you have to spend most of the year away from her. Honestly, it was a wonder she even remembered how to walk by the time preseason picked back up."

I screwed up my nose. "Too much info. I don't want to hear about your offseason orgies, man." I liked Nova. She was a sweetheart who didn't take any of the guys' shit. She was strong and independent, and she loved baby Huey with a fierceness so strong that you'd never know she wasn't his biological mother. She'd weathered that crap with stalkers and the press, then picked herself up and chased her own happiness.

"Speaking of offseason orgies, is that Inferno fucker still treating our Junie okay?" Rigby asked, his eyebrow raised. At least the team had stopped looking at me like I was about to explode. It had taken two weeks after the news of Erik and Junebug's relationship breaking for people to stop asking me if I was okay. However, fielding questions like this one made me regret that I hadn't acted more volatilely before. At least everyone would have avoided the topic if I'd acted like a jealous fool.

I shrugged. "You should ask Juniper. He seems nice enough, treats her well."

None of that was a lie. Whenever we were with Juniper, he treated her with the utmost respect. He included her in all our conversations and activities, like she was an extension of our relationship. I knew he was trying to show me how easy it could be. How well we'd fit together. I just wasn't willing to gamble Juniper on the chance that everything could be peachy keen.

River nodded. "Good."

I wondered what these guys would think if they knew it was me fucking the goalie of the Infernos, not Juniper. Would they turn against me? They might have an unconventional relationship, but as far as I knew, none of them crossed swords with each other. Nova was their center, and they floated around her like moons around a planet. Life had taught me that even the most open-minded of people could be weird about two guys fucking each other.

The coaches rounded us all up and loaded us into the bus that would take us to the airport. As we moved through the streets of Montreal, I sent a text to Erik wishing him luck for tonight's game. He was still on the road for another day before we were back in the same state.

Walking through the airport, we took photos with fans and signed random objects. When I finally buckled into my seat in the team's private plane, I closed my eyes immediately. Like a kid on Christmas Eve, I knew the sooner I fell asleep, the sooner I could wake up closer to all the things I'd ever wished for.

CHAPTER

Twenty-Two

JOHNNY

A LONG RUN of away games meant that Junebug got every night off. She'd told me if they were only doing one or two games, she'd sometimes travel with the team. But for such a long stretch, the team left her behind, and she used the backlog of promo clips and snippets of game play videos sent to her by the videographers to create content. It also meant someone was home to look after Friar Puck—though now I was here, there was an extra person to take care of the giant cat.

I was kind of fond of the fluffball, which had nothing to do with the fact that he had me wrapped around his paw and therefore never left my side. He'd just give me those big, soulful, golden eyes, and I'd give him a treat. He clearly knew a sucker when he saw one.

I was on the couch beside Juniper now, beers and pizza in front of us, as we watched Ludo play against

Toronto on the sports network. He'd always played like poetry in motion. I remembered watching him skate when I was seven and just *knowing* he was going to be a famous hockey player when we were older. He just had that kind of natural talent. He moved like a languid god across the ice. Fast and effortless.

"He's so fucking good." I'd barely gotten to see any games while I was a Marine.

She nodded, her eyes glued to the screen. "This team has really improved his game. He has a chance to be one of the greats." She cursed when one of the Toronto players high-sticked an IceCaps player at the back of the pack, but it was missed by the refs. She grinned over at me. "Not that I'd ever tell him that. He doesn't need a bigger head."

She stood and got more beers, coming back to sit down a little closer to me. She snuggled into my side the way she had through our entire friendship. Her love language was definitely touch; she was a hugger. Always had been, which was probably why Marianne had hated her so much. She'd hugged Robbie as much as she had me, and if Marianne had been open to it, she probably would have hugged the heck out of her too.

Robbie had just treated Juniper like a sister, and god knows, I'd tried to emulate that feeling. I would hold her respectfully, then go home and jerk off to the feel of her curves against my body. The only person she hadn't been quite as affectionate with was Ludo, and that's how I'd known she felt something for him. Whenever she'd hug him, it was always quick, and she'd pull away all flushed afterwards.

Man, what I would have given to make her cheeks that pink back then. Hell, what I would give to see her face flushed with pleasure now, her plump pink lips open as she came beneath my hands.

Ugh. Fuck. Stop thinking about her O face.

I ran through my sophomore-year hockey playbook in my head instead, moving from formations to trick plays, until my dick was back under control again.

She turned to me as the teams skated off the ice and back down to the locker rooms. "Have you made your mind up about what you're going to do?"

I was in this limbo, a kind of stasis. I had no plans now that I was out of the Marines. I had no real skills except killing people and surviving in terrible conditions. I'd applied for a couple of security jobs, but no one wanted security with a limp from a fucked-up thigh.

"I don't know, Junebug. I feel like I'm good for nothing but killing now," I murmured, not looking in her direction, pretending I was focused solely on the game in front of us.

Juniper grabbed my chin, turning my face toward her so hard it was a wonder I didn't get whiplash. "That's *bullshit* and you know it, Johnny. You're so much more than your fists and a gun. You always have been, and the only person who can't see that is you."

I closed my eyes slowly, and when I opened them

again, I'd made a decision. It was probably a stupid decision, but sometimes, they had the best results.

I leaned forward and kissed Juniper.

Her fingers on my chin went slack, and her lips stayed stiff beneath mine. I cursed myself. I was a fucking idiot, jeopardizing the only good thing left in my life. But as I went to pull away, her grip on my face tightened, and she deepened the kiss.

Holy shit. I was kissing Juniper Verne.

I lifted my hand to cup the back of her head, slipping my fingers through her silky hair. I'd fantasized about wrapping these dark locks around my hand for nearly a decade. She leaned closer, her breasts pressing against my chest, and I groaned. I wanted to whisper her name. I wanted to tell her that this would mean something, but I didn't want to break the spell.

We continued to kiss until I knew the shape of her lips on mine. Until the tender flesh was puffy and swollen from the force of my kisses, and she'd somehow made it onto my lap, my dick straining inside my sweats. Her eyes were hooded, and I dragged my face away.

"Juniper..." I breathed, though I didn't know if it was an ode or a warning. "God, you don't know how long I've wanted to feel you sliding that hot little pussy on my lap." She moaned into my mouth as she slid against me again, but I pulled away once more. "This will mean something." I hoped that the words would penetrate the lust around us, because I wasn't sure I had the willpower to warn her again.

I kissed down her neck and across her collarbone. "Johnny," she whimpered in a soft little voice, and I was done for.

I knew this might be the worst decision of my life, but I was making it with my eyes wide open. I slipped my hands under the edges of her oversized IceCaps t-shirt, slowly sliding it up her body, giving her plenty of opportunity to object. Instead, she wrenched it over her head, flinging it across the room. And there she was, looking like my teenage dream on my lap, her breasts at mouth height.

"*Fuck.*" The amount of times I'd dreamed of this exact moment... "You're so fucking beautiful." I leaned forward and took her nipple in my mouth, and she groaned, arching her back to press her breast against my face, her fingers scraping along my scalp, making me groan.

I gripped her perfect, heart-shaped ass in my hands and thrust upwards, trying to get some relief for my rock-hard dick. She rolled her hips as her hands tugged at my shirt, and somehow she managed to yank it off without removing her lips from mine for more than a fraction of a second. Her soft hands ran up my sides, over my abs, which made her make a small, satisfied hum in my mouth.

I didn't want to fuck her for the first time on the

couch. I wanted her in a bed, where I had plenty of room to work. I wanted to taste every inch of her, and I couldn't do that crammed onto her two-seater. Grabbing her arms and wrapping them around my neck, I looped my arms under her ass and prayed to the gods that my thigh would hold as I rolled to my feet.

"Ooh," she gasped into my mouth, wrapping her legs around my hips and hooking them tightly to me. Man, I wanted to fuck her against the wall like this, but I didn't want to test my thigh right now. Because if I fell over and landed on my ass, this would stop. Whatever spell was between us would be broken.

Moving to her room, I laid her gently down on the bed. I wanted to worship her while I had the chance. Tugging at her shorts, I dragged them down her thighs. Dropping them at my feet, I just stared. She covered the slight roundness of her stomach with her hands, and I nudged them away.

"I've dreamed of seeing you like this," I whispered. God, I hoped she didn't hear me being pathetic. "You're so fucking perfect."

She laughed, her cheeks flushed. "Oh yeah, straight out of a fashion magazine."

I climbed up her body, brushing my lips from her pubic bone, up over the swell of her stomach, between those heavenly tits, until my lips met hers. "Perfect to me."

The only thing that stood between us now were my

sweats, which she was using her feet to drag down. It was actually dextrous as hell.

"Off," she moaned between kisses, and I rolled back to my feet. I pushed my sweats down to my ankles, kicking them off, but hesitated over my boxers. She was going to look at that ugly wreckage of my thigh and all the desire swirling around us would dissipate into a lead balloon of pity.

Some of my thoughts must have shown on my face, because she was kneeling in front of me before I'd even managed to hook my fingers in the waistband. She looked up at me, her eyes burning with emotion I was scared to name. "You're perfect to me too."

Fuck, this woman. I kicked out of my boxers, and she sucked in a breath. But she wasn't looking at my thigh. She was looking at my cock, and her expression was *hungry.*

She gripped my ass and dragged me back onto the bed, where I settled between the soft warmth of her thighs. I slid my hand between our bodies and slipped them along her wet slit. Finding her clit, I brushed my finger across it. I watched her face, not wanting to miss a moment of her reaction.

She curled, but when I twisted my fingers, she gasped as well, her breathing picking up. Keeping a steady pace, I fucked her with my fingers, playing with her clit.

"Johnny," she whimpered. There was no other word

for it. Part gasp, part moan, part plea. I loved it. I added another finger, stretching her around three of mine, curling them up to where I was pretty sure her G-spot was. Man, it had been a while since I'd been laid.

"Oh god, oh god, *oh god*, right there," she chanted, and I stayed on course. She was fluttering around me, and I knew she was close. I wanted to taste her as she came around my fingers, but didn't want to stop. "Yes!" she screamed, coming hard until her whole body was like electrocuted spaghetti.

I continued to stroke her through her orgasm, committing her face as she came to my memory forever. She grabbed my hand, pulling me further up her body. "I need you inside me. Please."

I wanted to make her beg. I really did. But I couldn't wait.

I rolled us so she was straddling my hips. "I want you to ride me."

She grinned down at me, her face flushed and her eyes hooded. "I think you are overestimating the endurance of my thighs." She reached over to the night-stand, grabbing a condom. She tore it open with her teeth, and I laughed softly. Damn, she was perfect.

Then she was sliding down my cock, and I fucking saw Jesus. He mightn't entirely approve of the premar-ital sex, but I think he'd probably give me a high five if he knew how good she felt.

Plus, I loved her. I loved her so fucking much.

"Junebug," I groaned as I slipped balls deep inside

her. "Fuck." I was going to blow my load. "Don't move. God, you feel so damn good." I'd jacked off so many times in her shower over the last three days, it was a wonder I could come at all.

Grabbing her hips, I moved her back up my dick, then slammed her back down, her tits bouncing gloriously. *Yep. Definitely a high-five.*

She began to ride me in a soft, slow roll, for which I was insanely grateful. We were a panting, sweaty mess as I finally reached the end of my tether, my balls beginning to ache with the need to come.

She shoved her sticky hair from her face, giving a pleasure-drenched whine. "Please, Johnny."

Fuck, I didn't know what she was asking for, but I rolled us until I was wrapped in her thighs and thrust hard.

"Move, *please*. Fuck me, Johnny."

I was done. I slammed into her, trying to brand myself inside her. Slamming home, I bent her in half, both of her legs over my shoulders, clearly hitting somewhere good because she was clutching my shoulders as if she was holding on for sanity's sake.

"Come for me, Junebug. Be a good girl for me and come around my cock. Now, baby," I groaned, because I was coming. Junebug really would do anything for me, because she was milking me like she could bind my soul to hers with her sweet pussy. I emptied myself inside her, jerking hard until my muscles died, starting with my thigh and closely followed by my arms.

She wrapped her arms around me as I buried my face in her neck. "Perfect," she panted in my ear. "Just perfect."

I withdrew from her body, leaning up and grinning down. "I'm not done yet, Junebug. Hold on." Then I moved down her body to eat her like a meal.

I spooned around Junebug, neither of us speaking. Fuck, what would we even say? Luckily, I got a reprieve, because apparently, I'd tired her out. She'd snuggled into me and murmured, "So good," which was the last thing she said before the soft, even puffs of her breath told me she was asleep.

Sleep was always harder for me. I could hear what sounded like a party out the window, laughter and shouting telling me that it was really ramping up.

I'd started to drift off to sleep, when someone screamed. There was the sound of gunshot. Something exploding.

Blood everywhere.

Fuck, where was Lopez? I couldn't find him in the smoke. Bullets were pinging off rocks around me, shards flicking up and stinging my cheeks.

It was a fucking ambush.

"Get down. Get down."

"Johnny!"

Where the fuck was Lopez? A bullet grazed my shoulder, and I knew we were pinned down.

"Fall back. Fall back."

"Johnny! I'm here!"

Pain tore through my leg, as it was blown to pieces. Fuck, Lopez… His body flew through the air, landing on me. I tried to push him off, but he was crushing me. Where was the rest of my unit? I scrambled back until my back was against cover.

I couldn't die like this. Not now. I wasn't ready.

I could see the blank eyes of Oliphant staring at me, death leeching their color away. I had to call in. Had to stop the bleeding before I was as lifeless as Oliphant. Where were the rest of the guys?

"*JOHNNY!* Wake up! It's Juniper. Come back to me."

Her voice pulled me from the nightmare. No, not a nightmare, a flashback.

As my gaze snapped over to her, I saw her head was bleeding, and the sick feeling in my stomach made me want to vomit in horror.

I'd hurt her.

She was hovering over me, a shirt pulled over her naked body. "Are you back with me?" She reached out a hand, and I scrambled back.

"No, stay there. Fuck!" I stood, looking for my clothes, dragging them on. Finding my shirt, I pulled it over my head roughly. "I have to go," I mumbled, searching for my shoes and wallet. "I can't stay. I gotta go."

Her eyes were big and shiny, hurt pinching their

corners, but I just had to look at the huge gash on her head for my resolve to strengthen.

"I'm sorry," I whispered, as I ran out of there like the enemy was still on my tail.

I didn't deserve perfection. I didn't deserve her. This was all the proof I needed.

CHAPTER
Twenty-Three

ERIK

> Ludo: I can't get hold of Juniper. She
> hasn't answered any of my messages
> in the last twelve hours. Can you go
> and check she's okay? I'm on my way
> home, but I'm worried.

I FROWNED DOWN at the message once more as I buzzed Juniper's apartment. No one answered. I tried Ludo's too, in case Johnny was there, but no one answered that one either. I waited for one of the residents to leave, then ducked in through the open front door.

There was something wrong. My instincts were screaming it.

I took the stairs to Juniper's floor three at a time, skipping the elevator. Her door was locked, and I swore beneath my breath. I knocked loudly. "Juniper? It's Erik.

Are you in there?" I could hear Friar Puck letting out an irritated meow on the other side of the door, which was slightly reassuring. I knocked again. "Juniper! Let me in."

Finally, I could hear footsteps moving toward the door, and I let out a relieved breath. I'd been a little worried that she'd been dead in there. The door swung open a fraction, just enough that I could push it open further and step into the room, even as the footsteps hurried away. Her whole place was dark, the curtains drawn tight against the midday sun. There were beer bottles on the coffee table, but the TV was off.

I looked for an intruder, signs of a struggle, anything. It took me a while for my eyes to adjust enough that I could find Juniper curled up in a ball on the sofa, her chin resting on her knees. Her eyes were puffy, her hair was a mess, and she was only in a t-shirt, by the look of it.

Walking toward her slowly, I frowned as I tried to work out what had happened. Friar Puck chirped, pushing his cheek against Juniper's thigh. "Are you okay, little one?"

She turned those huge eyes to me and shook her head. My heart broke for her, anger simmering in my gut. Who'd put that look of defeat on her face? I would break theirs.

I sat down beside her, not touching her but leaving my arms open in case she wanted to come to me. "Do you want to tell me what happened?"

When she turned her face to me fully, the rage that was simmering in my chest turned into an inferno. A cut was raw on her face, held together with a couple of butterfly bandages.

"Who the fuck *hurt* you?" I gripped her chin, turning her head so I could examine it properly. The bruise around it was dark and purple, the cut a solid inch long. "*Einiber*, I asked you a question. Who did this?" I looked around the room, icy dread filling my veins. "Where is Johnny?"

Fresh tears spilled down her face, and I grabbed her up and sat her on my lap, holding her tightly in my arms. I was going to kill that fuck. Even if he could probably murder me a million different ways with just his hands, I didn't care. I didn't care if he was Juniper's best friend, or Ludo's. No one hurt her. No one.

I let her cry into my chest, trying to not let her feel the anger that was pounding through my veins. I stroked her back, wrapping myself around her tightly, like I could protect her from the world and anything that could ever hurt her again.

When her sobs started to subside, I kissed the top of her head. "Did Johnny hurt you?"

"Yes." Her voice was a shaky whisper. "But he didn't mean it."

I growled in my chest at her words. "He had no right to hurt you, whether he meant it or not."

She was shaking her head. I wouldn't have thought Juniper would be the kind of person who would make excuses for a man. She was tough. She took no shit. She wasn't this broken doll in my arms.

"No, I mean, he didn't realize he was doing it." She paused, as if she was weighing up how much to tell me, before she sighed and buried her face back in my chest. "We had sex. Johnny and me."

Burning rage was replaced with a fear so big, it froze my body. "Was it... consensual?" Had I completely misjudged Johnny? I liked him enough; I liked how supportive he was of Ludo and me. Had I been wrong?

Juniper shook her head violently. "No, Erik, no. It wasn't—he didn't..." She sucked in a breath. "It was completely consensual. The sex was fine. Great. Amazing, even. And afterwards was too. It was..." Another shaky exhale. "It was perfect. Then he fell asleep."

The rest of the story poured out of her, and I found my heart breaking for both of them, despite the jealousy that reared its head at the fact Johnny had touched my Juniper berry. My *Einiber*.

I locked that feeling down. She didn't need me to be territorial right now.

As she told me about waking up being shoved off the bed, her head clipping the corner of the nightstand, cutting her head, I fought to remain calm. She was right. He hadn't meant it, but that didn't mean he wasn't a danger to her.

And when she told me about him leaping off the bed, crab-walking to the wall, calling for someone called Lopez and screaming to fall back, my heart broke for the strong, silent man. He'd run out of there like it was goodbye, and as Juniper explained the pain and self-loathing on his face, I couldn't blame him. If it had been me, and I'd seen her bleeding because of something I'd done? I would have run the fuck out of there too.

What a freaking mess. "It will be okay, *Einiber*. He'll come back."

She shook her head again. "He won't, Erik. You didn't see his face. It was goodbye." More tears, and I had no idea how to fix this. Whether it was his fault or not, Juniper had been hurt, both physically and emotionally.

The protective beast inside me argued it was better this way. She wouldn't be in harm's way if he left and never came back. The rational part of me knew that both Juniper and Ludo wouldn't recover from the loss of their friend forever. No, this was a problem that had to be fixed, but I had no fucking idea where to start.

Juniper pulled away. "Are you mad at me?"

Shock had me rearing back so I could look at her face properly. "Me? Why would I be mad at you?"

She shrugged, burying her face in my neck again. "You're technically my boyfriend. I made a commitment to you and Ludo, and then I went and slept with the first guy who sat too close to me on the couch."

I stroked her hair, though it was wild and knotted.

"He wasn't just a random guy, little one. He was a man who you've loved for a decade, even if not in quite this way." I stood, picking her up. She wrapped her legs around my waist instinctually to stop from falling. "Come on. We better go clean you up, because if Ludo comes home and sees you like this, he's going to rage first and ask questions later, and I don't think anyone wants that."

She groaned, but didn't protest as I walked her to the bathroom. "You're always rescuing me, Erik." Her cheek was pressed to mine as she hung on like a baby koala. "I'm not usually this much trouble."

My hands were under her ass, holding her up, and I resisted the urge to squeeze those delightful globes. Now wasn't the time.

"I think we're saving each other, *Einiber*." I set her in front of her bathroom door. "Go and have a long, hot shower, then I'll redress your head. Ludo's on his way, but hopefully, I can help you get everything set to rights before he turns up."

She gave me a soft smile that made butterflies take flight in my gut. "I owe you one. More than one."

I kissed her forehead. "No one's counting."

She closed the door, and I walked back to the living room. Pulling out my phone, I saw fifteen messages from Ludo. The last four were in varying levels of panic.

Ludo: Are you there yet? Message me when you get there?

Ludo: Is she all right? Why aren't you answering your phone?

Ludo: Fuck, I'm freaking out. Is Juniper okay?

Ludo: Answer the fucking phone!

I hit Call on my phone. He answered in one ring. "Thank fuck. Where the hell have you been? Is she okay?"

I hesitated before I answered. "She's okay. How far away are you?"

"Why did you pause?" he snapped, and I rolled my eyes.

Sighing heavily, I walked into her kitchen. "There's a long story, and I think it's best if it comes from her."

"But she's okay?"

"Yeah, Ludo. She's gonna be fine."

He growled. I understood his frustration at my vagueness, but I didn't know how to tell the man who obviously loved his best friend, that his other best friend had fucked his dream girl and then freaked out. That definitely wasn't my business, despite the fact I was kind of in a relationship with one of the parties involved, and in a fake relationship with the other.

I could hear Ludo heaving in calming breaths. "Thank you for rushing over there. I'm sorry I snapped at you."

Smiling despite the circumstances, I dropped my voice. "You don't have to thank me for taking care of the people you love, *Laglegur.* It's what lovers do for each other."

CHAPTER
Twenty-Four

JUNIPER

I'D SERIOUSLY CONSIDERED STAYING in the shower until I just dissolved and slid down the drain. Couldn't take that long, right? Instead, I'd steeled my spine and walked out into the living room like I'd done nothing wrong. Which I hadn't, not really.

That had been the plan, but right now, I was regretting not going with the whole dissolving idea. Ludo had been waiting for me when I emerged from my bedroom, his eyes on my face like a laser beam as I unloaded the whole story in one extremely long, run-on sentence.

He hadn't said anything. Not in ten minutes. His face was twisted into this kind of blank expression that I couldn't read, and that was freaking *me* out. I'd always been able to read Ludo like a book, ever since we were kids.

Erik cleaned up the cut on my head, putting salve

and a fresh set of butterfly bandages on it. He kept stroking my back, like he knew I needed the support.

Finally, Ludo sucked in a shaky breath. "All right. Okay. You slept with Johnny. You're both adults. That's fine. No big deal."

I winced. I wasn't sure who he was trying to convince right now, but it definitely wasn't me.

Erik frowned at him. "Of course it's okay. Anything Juniper decides to do with her body is okay, because you certainly have no say over it, Andrei Ludokov," he chastised. "I think the real issue, as his friend, is where the hell Johnny is right now. If Juniper got a good read on his emotions, he's probably spiraling bad, and I know neither of you want that."

That seemed to shake Ludo from his shellshock. He grabbed his phone and jabbed the number for Johnny. It rang out. So he did it again. Still nothing.

I'd been trying to call him for half a day, and he hadn't answered. I'd held out hope that he'd be a noble asshole and at least answer Ludo's calls so he could confess to debauching me and breaking whatever pinky promise they'd made as kids that I was off limits.

Yeah, they thought I didn't know about that. Assholes.

I had this overwhelming fear that Johnny was going to do something terrible. Something he couldn't take back. I grabbed my phone.

> Me: I swear to god, Johnny Lipkin, if you do anything stupid because of this accident, I will find you and drag you back home. Even if I have to march into Hell to get you. Answer Ludo's calls. If you never want to speak to me again, fine. But don't make it worse by making me worry.

I sent the message and put my phone back on the table. Friar Puck still had his head on my lap, and I stroked his fluffy tail. "You're the goodest boy," I whispered. He hadn't left my side during my breakdown, and honestly, he normally spent most of his time sleeping on the windowsill, so the fact he was glued to my side was unusual.

When Ludo hit redial, someone answered. "Johnny, are you all right?" I couldn't hear what Johnny said on the other end of the line, but Ludo's eyes flicked to me. "She's fine, man. She's right here in front of me. The only thing wrong with her is that she's worried about you." He stood, moving away from us into the kitchen. Whatever Johnny was saying on the other end of the line had Ludo frowning. His jaw tensed. "She told me. That's between the two of you." Then he dropped his voice, which meant I couldn't hear the rest of the conversation.

A sigh left my body, and I realized I was emotionally exhausted. I felt like the last month and a half had been an emotional rollercoaster. I was so damn *tired*.

Erik wrapped an arm around my shoulder, and I

melted into his warmth. I was beginning to think touch was Erik's love language too, because he just seemed to know when I needed someone to hug me.

"At least you know he's okay now," he murmured against my hair.

He was right. It was a relief that Johnny hadn't done anything drastic. The sheer panic in his eyes when he'd seen the blood on my face haunted me. The fact he hadn't answered my calls just made the panic even worse.

"I'm relieved that my fuckup has only destroyed my relationship with him, not ended in his death." My self-pity was dressing itself up as sarcasm now. "Why didn't I keep my hands to myself? I'm so fucking desperate for someone to want me that I've ruined things."

Erik huffed an irritated noise. "Nope. That's enough of that. I've waited long enough for Ludo to get his act together, and this is the final nail in the coffin. I won't have you speaking this way." He put a hand on either side of my face. "Juniper, both of those men love you. Maybe they can't admit it to themselves yet, or maybe they're too scared. But as an outsider, there is no doubt in my mind that when Johnny looked at you, it was full of love and desire. More than a friend feels for his child-hood bestie, or a man feels for an attractive woman. The way he looked at you was like the sun rose at your whim."

He squished my cheeks a little more. "So hear me when I say that whatever happened between you two was probably a dream come true for Johnny. He has his own demons, and none of them are your fault."

I blinked at him slowly, my head shaking in his hands like I could deny his words. I opened my mouth to dispute them, but he placed a finger over my lips.

"Not done. Johnny isn't the only one who thinks you're special, Juniper. I told Ludo, way back at the beginning, that if I had met you before him, I would have chased you to the ends of the Earth to talk to you once more after that first interview. If you'd have let me, I would have made love to you every morning, just so you could wake up with a flush in your cheeks and a smile on your face." He leaned in close, pressing his forehead to mine. "If I had met you first, you would know that you are so damn special, all three of us would fall to our knees to have you for a lifetime."

My brain was reeling. "But you met Ludo first." That was all that squeaked out of my bamboozled brain.

Pulling back, Erik grinned at me. "I'm beginning to think that it doesn't matter, that everything is working out exactly how it should." He leaned forward, brushing his lips across mine. "I'm beginning to think that if you let me, perhaps I can have you both and be the happiest man alive." He kissed me once more. "I have a game tonight, so I have to go, but think about it, okay? Sometimes, we don't have to choose."

With that, he walked into the kitchen, tapped his watch, and kissed Ludo on the cheek. Then he strolled out the door, like he hadn't just dangled the biggest temptation of my life, right in front of my face.

Ludo was on the phone with Johnny for over an hour. Exhaustion swamped me after Erik left, and I curled up on the couch, Friar Puck half on top of me, pinning me down like a giant, fluffy weighted blanket. The steady thrum of his purr was the only indication I had that Ludo was now standing over me, concern written all over his face.

"Is Johnny okay?"

Ludo nodded. "Yeah. I think you being injured fucked him up a little bit. I talked him through it, but he won't come back. He's gone home to Louviers. I called Robbie, and he'll meet him at the airport."

I nodded, trying not to feel heartbroken. At least Johnny was safe. Robbie would take care of him; he loved Johnny as much as we did. "That's good. Did you tell Robbie…" I choked on the words. Had he told him that me and Johnny had sex?

Ludo sat down at the end of the couch, shaking his head. "Didn't think it was my place. I just told him that something happened between you two that set off Johnny's PTSD, and that he was all fucked up about it. Robbie hadn't known Johnny was stateside either. He kept that shit close to his chest." Apparently, that wasn't all that he was keeping close to his chest. "Robbie said

Johnny could work with him at the construction company. Keep his hands and mind busy."

I nodded again. It was a good idea. I should have suggested it earlier, but I'd selfishly wanted to keep him with me.

The silence stretched between us, Erik's words pounding around and around in my head. Shaking the wishful dream away, I stared at the black screen of the television in front of me. "I'm sorry, Ludo."

"What are you sorry for, Bug?"

Gah, so many things. "I shouldn't have... done that with Johnny. I've put you, and our friendship, in a shitty position."

He heaved a sigh. "Come here." He lifted his arm, and I slid under. "Short of murdering someone, you probably never need to apologize to me for anything. You're my Juniper. You've been my Juniper since we were fourteen. In my eyes, you can do no wrong. So you don't ever have to apologize to me."

I shook my head, my head turned into his shoulder. "We only just got him back."

Ludo leaned his cheek on the top of my head, the way he had a million times before. "Do you want to keep him, Bug? Do you want something more?" The strain in his voice was barely evident, and if I hadn't spoken to Erik earlier, maybe I would have missed it.

Could he be right? Did Ludo feel something for me too? Or was it wishful thinking on both of our parts?

And if he did feel like that about me, would I choose them over Johnny?

Life was so fucking confusing.

I sighed, shaking my head. "I don't know what I want."

No, that was a lie. I knew what I wanted. I wanted *everything*. I wanted them all. But the only thing that lay down that path was heartbreak and pain, no matter what the sweet Viking promised me.

I would learn my lesson and wait, because there was no way I was jeopardizing another friendship for something that wasn't mine to have.

CHAPTER

Twenty-Five

LUDO

I WAS PLAYING like trash again, but at least it was just in training. Coach Toons was chewing me out every five minutes, and Muss was casting me those worried looks again, but I had a lot on my mind.

However, everyone seemed to jump to the wrong conclusion when Juniper came into the dressing room to do her regular social media bit. The team had taken one look at the gash on her head and the big bruise creeping down the side of her face, and freaked the fuck out.

River was in front of her in an instant. "What happened to your face?" he growled. Granted, a growl wasn't that far from his usual style of speaking.

"Fell out of bed and cracked my head on the nightstand," she replied, raising an eyebrow, but ruining it by wincing in pain. Wrong eyebrow.

Even to my ears, that sounded like the type of bullshit excuse that women made up to hide domestic abuse.

Muss came over, frowning. "Are you sure, Junie? If you need it, we can help," he said softly. Given the thunderous look on River's face, he'd probably help Erik right into an early grave. River had had a fucked-up childhood. He took violence against women really hard, as did his best friend, Devon.

Bug just rolled her eyes. "I promise you guys. If a man hit me, I'd be the first one to feed him his balls, and you know it."

Rigby patted her on the back. "We know you're tough, Junie. But maybe we should pay Luthersson a little visit anyway?"

She let out an exasperated sigh. "Not you too, Rigby. I thought you were a lover, not a fighter?"

"Junie, baby, we're hockey players. We came out of the womb fighting."

She smiled, shaking her head. "Erik wasn't even in town when I hurt myself, so you guys can push all that protective machismo back into the little box that you keep it in. I'm fine. It really was just an accident. Now, River Cooper, you can stand still so I can take a photo for the Gram." She snapped a photo while River scowled at the camera. Grinning, she squeezed his arm. "Thanks for having my back, though. You guys are the best."

They really were the best. I had the greatest teammates in the league. Though they all disappeared before Bug made them stand around for more photos.

She sighed as she rubbed a hand across her face. "I guess that explains all the weird looks I've been getting today."

I shrugged. "The team loves you. Can't fault them for that."

"No, I can't. Guess I better message Erik and give him a heads up. Or maybe he can give his PR team a heads up. I'll try and put something on the Gram to head off any rumors too, just in case other people jump to a similar conclusion."

I watched as she strode away, already on her phone, emailing or texting, or however all the social media managers conversed with each other. I was pretty sure it was like a secret society that was designed to make us look equally like hockey gods and thirst traps. It was a fine line that took skill.

As soon as she left, Muss was back in front of me. "Do you believe her? Luthersson isn't hurting her?"

I nodded. "I believe her, one hundred percent. If I thought Erik even laid a finger on her, I'd break those insanely insured hands so he could never use them again." And I fucking would, even if I was in a relationship with him, because no one hurt Juniper. "But I was there when she cleaned it up, and saw the offending nightstand myself, so I promise she's fine."

Muss nodded, satisfied with my answer, but I didn't doubt he'd be keeping an extra eye on Bug. "Good.

Then what excuse do you have for playing like River's left testicle on a bad day? You're slow as shit out there, missing shots all over the place. You even fell on your ass."

I flushed with embarrassment. I had no excuses—well, none that I could give Muss anyway. Somehow, I didn't think he'd want to hear that I was in a relationship with Juniper's boyfriend, but she'd fucked our best friend, sending him into a PTSD episode, and then he ran back to our hometown. Oh, and Erik wanted to be a throuple with my best friend, who I might actually love, if I let myself identify the feelings in my chest rather than shying away from them, like a dirty little grub under a big-ass rock.

So instead, I replied, "Just an off day today. Think I had bad Chinese food last night. I'll be better for tomorrow night's game."

His eyes ran over my face in that disconcerting manner he had, before he nodded. "Get your head straight, kid. We need you out there at one hundred percent."

"I understand. I swear, I'm fine."

What a fucking lie.

My personal life was a mess, but hockey was that one thing I could rely on. I'd kept my promise to Muss, getting my head back into hockey in time for our home game against the Chicago Matadors. They weren't the best team in the league, definitely toward the bottom of the standings, but even the bottom team could come up and surprise you if you got too cocky.

It helped that Bug and Erik were in the stands, watching me play. I might have skated a little faster, hit a little harder, took shots I normally wouldn't, because I wanted to impress them. Sure, they'd both seen me skate before, especially Juniper, who'd attended all my home games since I was given a scholarship to college out East.

I scored again, finding a hole and firing it in like a sniper. The crowd went wild, and there were hundreds of hats thrown onto the ice. I grinned and skated around the wall, my stick raised in the air as my teammates came up and slapped my back.

Music pumped through the speakers, and I looked up into the crowd as the jumbotron flashed *HAT TRICK* below my name and number. I found Erik and Bug behind the glass and I pointed at them through the barrier. Of course, Junebug had her camera out, taking footage for the social media pages, but she was grinning so wide that I knew she was proud.

Finally, all the hats were scooped up and taken off the ice. They'd be waiting for me in the locker room, and I'd take every single one of them home.

Muss slapped my back again, his grin wide. "You definitely brought that hundred percent, kid." The rest of my team gave me congratulations, and I was flying high for the rest of the game. I assisted one more shot where Rigby scored, then the game was over.

The goalie for the Matadors, Rochelle, shook my hand hard, a smile on his face. "Good game, Ludo. I would have liked to keep a few more out, but you were on fire."

"I felt good tonight, man. You guys coming down to Shaggers after the game?"

"Yeah, me and a few of the guys will be there. No one parties like you Ann Arbor boys, and the women in this town are fine."

Laughing, I slapped his back. "You know it. See you there, brother."

An hour later, I'd done all the press conferences, and I was chomping at the bit to head out and celebrate. I met Erik and Juniper at the car, although it took me a lot longer to get there than I'd hoped—I had to stop and take photos with at least thirty-five people just in the parking lot.

Juniper ran at me, and I dropped the bag of hats so I could grab her up in my arms, spinning her around. "You played so freaking good!" she squealed, and when I put her down, she punched me in the arm for emphasis.

I flinched away and faux pouted, but soon enough, the grin was back. I hauled up my hats in the air like the trophy they were. It wasn't just that I'd played well, it was that so many fans had appreciated me enough to toss their hats onto the ice. That was the real accolade.

Erik leaned forward and gave me a bro hug. Maybe he squeezed me a little too long and hard, but I loved it.

"I told the guys we'd go to Shaggers for drinks," I told them both as we climbed into Erik's Chevelle. The first time I'd seen this thing, I'd almost jizzed myself. Robbie would literally jack off to thoughts of this car every night if he could drive it.

It was a short commute to the bar, and the parking lot was already packed. I waved at Rigby and River, as well as Nova and Devan. They didn't normally come out after a game, so I knew the mood was going to be great.

The bar was hopping when we walked in, fans and players alike high on the win. Half the team were already here. Hell, half of the Matadors were here too. The music was pounding from the speakers, the mood already wild. Puck bunnies in the smallest dresses possible stuck out like dildos in a church, but with the way some of the players were eyeing them, I knew they'd get what they wanted tonight.

One sashayed up to me, her gaze flicking up and down with exaggerated slowness, a small smirk on her face. "Great hat trick tonight, Ludo," she purred, stepping into my space. She was hot, and once upon a time, I would've spent fifteen minutes getting to know her, another fifteen minutes getting my dick sucked in the restroom, then I would have forgotten her name within the hour.

I'd definitely once been the manwhore Juniper had

always accused me of being, and Shaggers had been my brothel, with women here for the taking. But not tonight.

I grabbed the woman's wrist softly before she could touch me. "Thank you," I said politely, then moved her to the side, stepping around her so I could follow Erik and Bug into the hazy darkness.

I made it over to a clump of the team, waving to Rochelle of the Matadors. He was grinning down at a pretty little thing, who was all but rubbing his dick in public. Bug moved toward the team, congratulating the guys who'd played well, air-kissing the wives and girl-friends she knew.

I'd realized early on that Bug held a weird position in the IceCaps world. I'd always considered her an extension of myself—my right hand, my best friend. But I'd quickly seen that people loved her in ways completely unrelated to me. Tonight, the guys were busy ribbing her like she was one of them, and the women eyed Erik up and down before giving her the *hooboy, you did good!* look.

Juniper just *fit*. She'd always fit wherever she landed. Even in high school, she could hang with the hockey jocks, the student reps, or the theater kids. She floated through life with empathy and openness, though for a short time, I'd delusionally thought it had been me that gave her clout.

She pulled Erik forward, and I watched the guys all give him the side-eye as they shook hands with him.

Some of them still weren't convinced he wasn't responsible for her injury.

We all knew each other professionally, but despite our close proximity, we didn't spend much time with the Infernos—basically because their culture was fucked and most of them were assholes. Not Erik, and his only friend on the team, Laurens. But the rest? Absolutely cock-cheese human beings.

He'd have to win the IceCaps all over himself, but I had no doubt he would. He was a lot like Juniper in that way. Open and honest. It was easy to be disarmed by him.

Devan and Nova came over, and Nova was grinning at me. "How's it doing, Ludo? Great game."

I gave her my goofy, flirtatious smile. I always flirted with Nova, because it riled her guys. She wasn't really my type. She screamed commitment, and normally, that was something that I ran from faster than Usain Bolt.

"Thanks, Nova baby!" I pulled her in for a hug. "Someone has to make your boys look good. It's hard, thankless work, but I'll take one for the team."

River was chatting with Muss, but he still shot me a flat look over his shoulder. Even if he was holding a conversation, he always had one eye on Nova. He loved her so fucking much; it had actually been kind of disgustingly sweet when they were first figuring out their relationship.

"Junie looks happy," Nova commented, her tone forcefully light.

I nodded, but it was a lie. Bug was happy tonight, but the shit that had happened with Johnny had knocked her for six. She wasn't happy, but she was getting on with it. "She seems to like him."

Nova tilted her head at me. "And what about you? Do you like Erik?"

I froze, my eyes getting wide. Fuck, had she guessed? It took me a split second to realize she meant whether I liked him *for Juniper*. Not whether I like-liked him.

"I want whatever makes Junebug happy," I said in a strangled voice, and Nova narrowed her eyes at me. Clearly, I'd screwed up and if she wasn't suspicious before, she would be now.

Abort. Abort.

"I better get a drink," I told her quickly.

But Nova grabbed my arm. "Don't let your pride get in the way of your happiness, Ludo. You can love who you want. She can love who she wants. That doesn't mean there isn't enough love to go around; it's not a finite amount. You can have it all, and so can she."

I wanted to make a joke to throw her off, but nothing could make it past the lump in my throat. So I just nodded, heading to the bar like a coward who'd been stripped bare with just a few words.

CHAPTER
Twenty-Six

ERIK

IT TOOK me an entire hour to convince all the IceCaps that I would never hurt Juniper. That I would rather chop off my hands than lay them on her in anger. But once they were convinced, they folded me into their group like I belonged. This was what a real team should be like—this bond that was almost like family.

The drinks flowed as much as the laughs, and the revelry in the room was something that had been missing from my life. It didn't hurt that Juniper stood tucked into my side, Ludo bracketing her in on her left. Sometimes our fingers would brush where they met on Juniper's back.

I watched River Cooper and Rigby Engman—who were in a polyamorous relationship with one woman— interact with the other players. The team seemed to accept it easily, and Nova laughed and smiled with the men and their significant others. Everyone had embraced their little polycule like it was the most natural thing in the world.

Would it be the same if Ludo came out to them? That it was me and him in a relationship, and not me and Juniper? Or would Juniper being our center make it more palatable? I didn't want to think of Juniper like that, as a means to an end. If she entered a genuine relationship with us, it would be because we both wanted her passionately, not because she would help us hide this side of ourselves from the public.

I shook off the dark thoughts, smiling down at Juniper. I'd had just enough drinks to make my limbs feel loose and my grin feel goofy. Enough for me to lean down and kiss her, because I wanted to, not because I thought it would make a good photo opportunity. She looked up at me with that dazzled expression, and I knew I was just as gone for her as I was for Ludo.

My gaze traveled over her head, and I could see my lover watching our kiss with need in his eyes. I met his gaze, then dipped back down to kiss Juniper once more. "I'm just going to the bathroom," I told her softly.

She nodded, but was dragged immediately into a conversation with one of the players' girlfriends. Cindy? Candy? I couldn't remember.

I didn't need to look behind me to know Ludo was following me. I could feel his eyes on my back like a physical caress. People kept stopping him to congratulate him, and I smirked. He deserved the accolades. He was a damn good player.

I'd be lying if I said I didn't get a small thrill out of watching him shut down every beautiful woman who came up to him, trying to cajole him into letting them take a ride on his dick. It mustn't be his normal style, because even his teammates had commented on the fact he wasn't making the most of the women who came to him so easily. They'd been ribbing him about going home with more than a collection of hats tonight if he wanted.

But Ludo had shaken off their good-natured ribbing, saying he was too exhausted tonight to shake off any Stage Five clingers and he just wanted to celebrate with his boys. I briefly wondered how Juniper had dealt with watching his playboy ways all those years. Loving someone so fucking oblivious, then having to watch him go home with a bunch of faceless women every time you went out sounded like torture.

Watching the team with Juniper was another eye-opener. They were so protective of her, like they'd adopted her into the team and would stand guard over her heart, especially from an Inferno like me. I'd gotten the impression that the IceCap players had a pretty poor opinion of my team, though I couldn't say I blamed them.

I went into the bathroom, which was as busy as you'd think it would be, with half an arena in a bar of this size. I walked over to the urinal to take a piss.

The guy next to me broke the cardinal rule and looked down at my cock. "Holy shit. What a monster," he laughed drunkenly. "Hey, aren't you the goalie for the Infernos? Man, no wonder you save so many goals. Have a third leg to block with! Get it some padding, and you'll be unstoppable." He cackled at his own joke, and I looked at him incredulously.

The guy on his other side elbowed him. "Stop looking at the poor dude's dick, Bob. Fuck, I can't *wait* to remind you when you're sober that you told Erik Luthersson he had a big dick. Shirley is going to die with laughter."

Bob flushed, and I put my cock away and nodded at him. "Thanks for the compliment, Bob. But my eyes are up here."

His friend laughed so hard that I briefly worried he might fall into the urinal, but I washed my hands and pushed out of the men's bathroom. Ludo was leaning against the wall opposite the door. He tilted his head to the left, down the darkened hall. I worked hard to keep my face neutral, just raising an eyebrow.

However, when he moved through the *Employees Only* door, I followed—like I could resist. He moved into a storage room, pushing the door open quietly and slipping inside. I looked left and right, then followed behind him.

Hands grabbed me in the darkness, and suddenly, I was slamming against a hard body. Fingers buried in my hair, then Ludo dragged my lips to his. "Fuck, I've wanted to do this all night. Watching you kiss Bug, knowing how those lips felt, knowing how you taste…"

He groaned as he trailed off, kissing me hard. I backed him against a set of shelving, pressing my hips into his. I could feel the hardening of his cock against mine.

His hand slid down to massage my cock through my jeans, making me moan. "You almost missed out. Bob in the men's room told me I had a monster cock. I almost invited him home," I teased, and he squeezed my cock, making my thighs feel shaky.

"Oh yeah?" Ludo unbuttoned my jeans, pushing them down until he could wrap his hand around my dick. "I don't think Bob could take this. Fuck, I don't think I could take this," he murmured with a laugh. Yeah, I definitely bottomed in our relationship, and I was fucking A-OK with that. Then he dropped to his knees. "But I think I could swallow it down just fine."

I prayed to any deity I could that I didn't just blow all over his pretty face right then and there.

He grabbed my dick, licking a long stripe from root to tip, and my eyes rolled back as I buried my fingers in the soft waves of his hair. When he wrapped his lips around the head of my cock, I wondered if I was going to embarrass myself straight up.

He sucked me deeper and deeper into his mouth until I could swear I was brushing the back of his throat. "Jesus, *Laglegur*. That mouth." My words sounded strangled, and as he slid his mouth up and down my cock, his tongue stroking me, I could feel the pleasure through my whole damn body.

The hum of the crowd outside added to the forbiddenness of the moment, and it was amplifying my pleasure already. I didn't want this to end, but my balls were already pulling up tight.

"Fuck, Ludo. You feel so fucking good. Everyone in this room wants you, but you're mine. On your knees for me. I can't wait to get you home so you can fuck me just right." I was thrusting into his mouth now, my fingers in his hair holding his head still. I was so close to coming. "I'm almost fucking there, *Laglegur.* So close. Fuck, that's it. So good for me."

He moaned around my cock, and I'd swear I saw Odin. *So close. So close.*

Just then, the door swung open, and the light flicked on. "I found this room last time I was here and I—" The high-pitched voice of a puck bunny trailed off as her eyes flicked between me with my cock out, Ludo on his knees, and the fucking Matador goalie behind her, his mouth wide open with shock. "Holy shit! Oh my god. *Oh my god!*" she screeched, stepping around Rochelle and back out into the hall.

We all stood there, frozen, and I quickly stuffed my cock back in my pants. Ludo scrambled back onto his ass, like if he put distance between us, Rochelle might forget what he'd just seen. Finally, Rochelle shook himself from his stupor and stepped back into the hall, quietly closing the door.

"FUCK!" Ludo yelled. "Fuck, fuck, *fuck!*" He punched the shelf, sending a wave of paper towels down around our heads.

Frozen shock slid through my veins. We'd fucked up. This was bad. This could be the end of my damn career.

A little voice in my head told me this had to happen eventually. It told me that I couldn't live in the dark forever. But Ludo, he'd only just stepped into the sun, and now he was going to be thrust under the harsh burn of the limelight.

I needed to be confident for him. "Ludo, stop." I grabbed his fist, stopping him from taking a swing at the wall and potentially fucking up his hand. "Don't panic. Maybe they won't say anything."

Even as I said the words, I knew that was naive. That girl had seemed way too excited to not be out there telling every person she could find.

Ludo whirled around to me. "Don't panic? Don't fucking *panic?* Some bitch just caught me on my knees for you here in a bar filled with my team, and half the fucking fanbase, and you're telling not to panic?"

Okay, so he was freaking out. That was to be expected. "This isn't ideal, but it had to happen eventually. We need to get Juniper and get out of here."

Ludo groaned, running his hand down his face. "Fuck. Juniper."

We needed to get back out there, but first, Ludo needed to *not* be three seconds from a complete panic attack. "Take a deep breath. Don't go borrowing trouble just yet."

He sucked in air, and when he looked like he was

holding it together, I straightened my spine. We weren't doing anything wrong. We were fucking grown-ass adults making informed, consensual decisions.

I'd finally convinced myself everything was okay—that I could take whatever was dished out and protect Ludo and Juniper from the worst of it, even if it killed me—when there was a knock at the door. I was too scared to open it.

CHAPTER
Twenty~Seven

JUNIPER

I WAS LAUGHING WITH PERRIER, one of the IceCaps goalies, when a girl rushed out from the bathrooms and all but yelled at her friends, "I just saw Andrei Ludokov sucking the dick of the Infernos goalie!"

The sounds in the bar didn't stop immediately, but the banging of laughter and merriment turned to hushed whispers of disbelief.

Oh no. No, no…

I looked around as if I could see the guys, like this was all some big mistake. They were both nowhere to be seen, and I knew immediately that this was not some drunk girl's fantasy. I turned to look back at the guys, Ludo's team, and I knew they'd all heard it too.

Rigby stepped in front of me. "Are you okay?"

Oh. Of course. They probably thought I'd just found out about my boyfriend and my best friend fucking.

That would mess a girl up. "I'm fine." I winced. "It's a long story, but I have to find the guys."

Rigby stared at me, his eyes comically wide. "Wait, you *knew?* Ludo is, uh… you know?" He was shaking his head, like he couldn't find the right words.

I planted my hands on my hips and gave him my fiercest glare. "I did. Does it matter to you if he is?" I growled out the words, ready to go to war with this man I considered a friend. I looked around at the rest of the team. "Does it matter to any of you?"

Rigby was shaking his head so vigorously, I was worried he was going to dislocate something. "Fuck no, it doesn't matter to me. Us. I'm just surprised. Ludo is such a…"

"Manwhore?" River supplied, a dumbstruck look on his face too.

Nova, bless her fucking heart, came to their big, stupid rescue. "You can be a manwhore with women *and* like guys too, you Neanderthals. The problem right now is that your friend needs you. So snap out of it. Go find them and move them out the back door. They can't walk through here," she hissed. She turned to Devan. "Go get the car and pull around back."

Devan gave her a salute and disappeared through the crowd. I followed River through the bar, people naturally moving out of his way until we made it to the back hall, just past the bathrooms. Rigby and Muss took up sentry duty at the entrance to stop anyone following us down.

"Should I be worried that you all know where this infamous supply closet is?" I asked River, and he just gave me a wry expression.

"I wouldn't go in there with a blacklight if I were you." He knocked on a door that said *Employees Only*.

There was nothing but silence on the other side, and once again, I hoped the guys hadn't been outed in the most public of ways. I wanted to shake them both for fucking in a goddamn public location like idiots, but that could wait until later.

After a moment, the door crept open, and Erik was there, staring at River like he was the boogeyman. I stepped around him, into the room with him and Ludo.

Ludo was a mess. He was pale and sweating, his knuckles red, probably from punching something like an idiot. "Juniper..." he started, and I raised a hand.

Taking a calming breath, I gave him a reassuring smile. "It's gonna be okay, Ludo. I promise. But first, we have to get out of this bar. We'll talk about everything at home. Let's go."

River stepped back, doing his best impression of a six-and-a-half foot privacy screen. I shoved Erik out of the room gently, grabbing Ludo's hand and dragging him out after me.

"Wait," River grunted. And then he surprised the shit out of me by hugging Ludo. "Wanted you to know this changes nothing. We still love you, and we've got your back, no matter what."

Gah. Big dumb jocks who are in touch with their emotions. Makes me want to cry girly tears.

Ludo swallowed hard. "Thanks, man."

Then I was dragging him down the hall, through to the back exit, where Devan was idling with his fancy SUV. Erik opened the rear door for me—a gentleman even in a damn crisis—and I scooched over, bypassing the baby seat.

Ludo climbed in beside me and shut the door. He was mouthing the word *fuck* on repeat, and I got the sentiment. Still, I wrapped his fingers in mine and held him tight, while Erik looked back at us worriedly from the passenger seat.

Devan drove back out onto the main road, only casting small glances at the guys. Of all Nova's part-ners, I knew Devan the least, but he seemed like a nice guy. He didn't say anything, or ask any questions, other than where we wanted to go. He just let us deal.

"I'm sorry, Bug," Ludo whispered, and I squeezed his hand tightly.

I wanted to hug him, but we didn't need to add being pulled over by the cops for not wearing seatbelts to the list of tonight's drama. "You have nothing to be sorry to me for, Ludo. It was going to come out, one way or another. I'd rather it hadn't been in quite such a spectacular fashion, though. We'll discuss your inability to keep it in your pants later."

He cleared his throat. "Technically, it was Erik who didn't have it in his pants."

I pinched the bridge of my nose. "For fuck's sake, Ludo."

Devan snorted a laugh, the first indication he was listening. "Sorry. For the record, your sexuality—or whatever the hell you guys have going on here—makes no difference to us. We're here for you, no matter what. You were there for the guys when we were figuring out our own relationship. It's our turn to do the same." He met Ludo's eyes in the mirror, and I tried to swallow down the emotions clogging my throat again.

Ludo cleared his throat. "River said as much. I appreciate it."

The rest of the ride was silent, except for the steady buzz in my pocket as the team's social media accounts were tagged over and over in whatever stories were being posted about Ludo. I was going to have to talk to Caitlyn in PR in the morning about getting ahead of this, as well as Stacey from the Infernos, who I assumed would be finding out about this really soon, if not right now.

It could all wait. At this moment, I wanted to deal with these two men who meant more to me than any job or reputation. I wanted to make sure they were okay. I wanted them to know what to expect, and how we were going to navigate any problems we might have.

Devan dropped us off at the apartment block, and I thanked him again. I was going to send Nova the biggest box of chocolates I could find. I would've sent her the largest bottle of vodka I could find, but Ludo had confided that she was pregnant, so I doubted she'd appreciate that just yet.

We swept into the building, like paparazzi were going to jump from the bushes at any moment. I foolishly hoped that perhaps they wouldn't pick up on this. Maybe they'd leave it alone. But the combination of Ludo getting a hat trick and then getting caught on his knees, all in one night, was going to be too good for the papers to pass up.

Holding both their hands, I led the guys up to Ludo's apartment. Friar Puck met us at the door, weaving through our legs, a piece of broccoli hanging from his mouth. *Where the fuck did he get broccoli from?* Giving me a soft meow, he trotted away happily, back to his still-full food bowl.

We all sank down on the couch, sitting there in silence.

Finally, I swallowed hard. "Well, I guess that's one way to announce your relationship?" I squeaked out into the silence, and Erik gave me a shaky laugh. Ludo just looked at me incredulously. Shrugging, I climbed onto his lap, hugging him close to me. He wrapped his arms around my waist and buried his face in my neck.

"Honestly, Ludo. I'm not going to sugarcoat it—it's probably going to be rough for a little while. But once it all dies down, you know what you'll be?" He shook his head where he was buried against me. "You're going to be an inspiration for boys who like boys, but still want to play hockey. You'll be an idol for kids who think they have to choose between being who they really are, and playing the sport they love.

"They'll be able to look at your story and say, 'Sure, I'm gay—or bi, or whatever else—but so was Andrei Ludokov, and he was one of the greatest NHL players of all time.' When they pinpoint the moment that the NHL dragged itself out of the Dark Ages, you'll be there as one of the first openly bisexual players in the history of hockey." I looked over his head at Erik. "You both will. And while this seems like a fucking disaster right now, one day, it will be one of the greatest legacies you'll have. After the hat tricks and the career saves have faded from memory, there'll be this."

Ludo pulled back to look into my face. He rested his forehead against mine, a sigh deflating his body. "You are the greatest thing that ever happened to me, Juniper Verne. The single greatest thing."

He kissed me then, soft and filled with feeling. He poured everything that had happened today into that kiss, and a part of me wondered if I should pull away. He was not in a good place right now. Maybe he didn't know what he was doing. I didn't want this to be one more thing that happened tonight that he'd want to forget about tomorrow.

So I cupped his cheek, pulling away. "Ludo…"

He was shaking his head. "Did I read this all wrong?" He flicked his eyes to Erik. "Did we read this all wrong?"

I actually laughed. "No, Andrei Ludokov. You didn't read this wrong. The way I feel about you—" I cut myself off before tonight became even messier. "But right at this moment? It's not the time for anything to happen. You're feeling emotionally vulnerable, and I don't want you to do anything you'll regret later. When everything is right in the world, we'll pick this up right here, if that's what you want."

Ludo nodded, his eyes sliding from me to Erik and back again, a look in his eyes that I couldn't decipher. Erik stood, reaching out a hand to me. "Come on. Let's go to bed. We'll need to be well rested for whatever shit tomorrow brings. Tonight, I just want to lie beside the two people who make me happy."

I placed my hand in his, and he led me to Ludo's bed. I took off my bra, shimmied out of my jeans, and climbed between Ludo's silk sheets in just my IceCaps jersey, Ludo's number on the back.

Ludo climbed in on one side of me, Erik on the other, and I fell asleep, cocooned in their warmth. If this was the only moment I'd have with the two of them, then I'd cherish it.

Because no one knew what tomorrow would bring.

CHAPTER

Twenty-Eight

JOHNNY

RUNNING home with my tail between my legs was not my proudest moment. I was man enough to admit that I was a fucking mess, though.

The look on Juniper's face when I'd run out of that room was going to haunt me for life, right along with the bleeding cut over her eye and the big-ass lump that I knew would have bruised. Every time I went to bed and closed my eyes, it was the same series of moments.

Watching her orgasm beneath me, her face flushed.

Waking up from a flashback with her hovering in front of me, bleeding.

The look of devastation on her face as I ran out the door like a coward.

Swinging my hammer harder, I framed up the tiny house I was constructing in the woods for Robbie's company. It was some holiday home for a rich Denver couple who wanted to see what it was like to live in a twelve-by-twelve box like the other half—every other weekend, that is.

Robbie had stuck me out here to put this shit together, because I could do it in my sleep. We'd all had summer jobs with Robbie's dad through most of our childhood—except Junebug, which had irritated her to no end—so we all knew our way around a hammer. We could build most things.

When I'd been too irritable with the rest of the crew, Robbie had done me a solid and given me this job, with strict instructions not to accidentally saw off anything while alone in the woods. He knew I needed time to get my shit together. He wasn't going to hover over me like a mama bear about it either.

I was staying in his and Marianne's spare room. They'd both been good about it, but they had a couple of kids, and I was fairly sure Marianne was waiting for me to move out. There was no way I was going back to my uncle's house, though, and renting a place here seemed too permanent.

Maybe I'd check out the B&B on the other side of town. I had a bit saved in the bank for emergencies.

Doing as much as I could before the sun went down, I loaded my tools into the tray of my borrowed truck and drove back to town. I didn't want to be out in the woods after dark by myself if I didn't have to.

I pulled up in front of The Bar, which seemed busy for a Sunday night. Only two places people of Louviers went on a Sunday: church and then The Bar.

Finding a parking spot, I rested my head against the steering wheel. I should just go back to Robbie's house, hide in their spare room and pretend to sleep for the tenth consecutive night. I just couldn't bring myself to field Marianne's passive-aggressive questions yet. Decision made, I sucked in a deep breath and let it out slowly, then climbed from the car.

I knew something was up when everyone's conversations dimmed as I stepped into the room. My phone began to ring in my pocket almost immediately, and I pulled it out. Robbie's name flashed across the screen.

Shaking off the weird feeling that everyone was looking at me, I answered the call as I walked across the room. "Robbie?"

"Hey, where are you?"

"The Bar. What's up?"

"Stay there. I'll be three minutes." Then the fucker hung up.

I sat in my spot and eyed Ruben, my former peewee teammate and friend. Not as close as me, Ludo, Robbie and Juniper were, Ruben had still been a fixture in my life for just as long. He was down the other end behind the bar and kept casting me weird expressions.

I lifted my chin. "What the fuck is going on?"

Ruben shook his head. "Robbie said to wait until he got here."

"Did someone die or something?" I asked, my heart beating harder in my chest. Had something happened to Juniper? I tried to think how Robbie sounded on the phone. He hadn't sounded messed up, which I knew was exactly how he'd be if something happened to Ludo or Juniper.

Ruben was shaking his head. "Nah, it's not that. Uh, I have to go top up Old Russell's beer. I'll be right back." Then he ran off, like I was chasing him, not even giving me a beer first.

The room quietened down again, and I turned to see Robbie stride in. Okay, something was definitely up. He came over, sitting down close to me.

"What the hell, man? Did my uncle finally kick the bucket? Because if so, I want to crack the champagne."

Robbie shook his head, taking out his phone and passing it over to me.

The headline was huge.

IceCaps star caught in compromising position with Detroit Infernos goalie

"Ah, shit." Fucking Ludo. Once an exhibitionist manwhore, always an exhibitionist manwhore.

I quickly read through the rest of the article. Apparently, after Ludo's amazing hat trick against the Chicago Matadors, he'd tried to extend the celebration and was caught giving head to Erik in the storeroom of a fucking bar by some wasted "source on the scene."

Robbie nudged me with his shoulder. "That's all you have to say? Ah, shit?" He frowned at me. "Did you know?"

I looked my oldest friend dead in the eye. "Know what?"

Robbie shook his head. "Don't fuck around with me, Johnny," he hissed. "Did you know Ludo was gay?"

I snorted. "Ludo isn't gay, Robbie. Ludo fucked three of the cheerleaders in your billiards room at the senior year grad party. Ludo fucked Billie-Tayla behind the bar of this very establishment. Several times."

Robbie's jaw clenched. "Ludo also just got busted blowing the goalie of another team."

I narrowed my eyes at him. "Would it be less offensive if it was his own goalie?"

He narrowed his eyes back at me. "It's not offensive at all. I'm just mad he didn't tell us." He tilted his head at me, his brain finally catching up to my non-answers. "Wait a fucking second. *You knew!*" he whisper-yelled. "You knew, and you didn't *tell* me? I had to find out from Marianne, who found out from Linda at the high school, who found out from her daughter Valery, who found out from the damn internet. That's a lot of hearsay when my best friends were keeping the truth from me."

I'd forgotten Robbie was such a fucking softie. "It wasn't my truth to tell, Robbie. If it makes you feel better, I kinda found out by accident too. Only person he really told was Junebug."

Robbie digested that, nodding softly. He didn't seem quite so indignant that Ludo had confided in Juniper. We'd all confided in Juniper the secrets that we held deep down, because we knew she'd take them to her grave.

"That's just it, though. The guy Ludo was blowing was Juniper's boyfriend. Though I guess it mustn't be too serious, considering you and her... you know."

I winced. Yeah, that probably looked bad. I weighed up how much to tell our friend—not because I thought he'd care, but because he'd tell Marianne, who would tell the entire town and then the rest of the world. By extension, that meant Robbie always got the censored version of events.

I'd told him that me and Juniper had hooked up, though. He'd wanted to know why I was being shipped to him and not her, who was definitely the more nurturing of our group. Plus, he was still my friend. I'd needed to confide in someone, and this wasn't something I could talk to Ludo about.

All I could do was shrug. "I don't know what's going on with them. But just know, if anyone in this town has something to say about Ludo's choice in partners, they're welcome to come and talk to me about it. I'm more than happy to set them straight." I said that last part loudly, looking around at all the close-minded bigots in the room.

Robbie nodded. "Or me. I'm more than happy to discuss how your opinion is wrong."

Ruben cleared his throat. "Anyone who has a problem with Ludo can drink somewhere else too." He slid a beer in front of me, and I nodded at his solidarity. We'd learned back when we were kids that a team stuck together. We hadn't been on the ice together in a decade, but that didn't mean we didn't still have each other's backs.

"Thanks, man."

I Googled Ludo's name, seeing a hundred different articles and posts immediately pop up. Shit, this was going to get real bad before it got better. I wanted to be there for my friend who was having his whole life flipped, for Juniper who was just as plastered throughout these articles as Ludo and Erik, the Plain Jane jilted lover, but I was still hiding away here like a kicked puppy.

There were grainy pictures of the bar, and pictures of Ludo and Juniper trying to get into the arena today, as well as quotes from an "unnamed teammate" saying that he felt uncomfortable in the locker room with Erik now. It was a fucking mess.

Robbie's phone buzzed, and he frowned down at it. "It's Juniper." I raised my eyebrows, ignoring the little stab to my heart that she'd messaged Robbie and not me. "They've both been put on leave until this shit dies down. They're coming home for the week."

Well, fuck. I guess there was no hiding anymore.

Twenty-Nine

ERIK

I WAS IN HELL. Players on my team who'd ignored the fact I was bisexual since I started with the Infernos now actively moved away from me. There were snide comments, with Rusket calling me a fucking fag every chance he got. He was riling the team against me, like sleeping with another player on a different team not only made me a traitor, but somehow put their own virtue on the line.

Laurens had gotten into a fight with one of the older players, breaking his nose, which resulted in a warning from the coach. I'd told him not to jeopardize his place on the team for me.

"I don't want to be on a fucking team that treats its players like this, Erik. This team is fucking toxic—I don't want any part of it." He'd stormed out after that, and I hadn't seen him since.

Dressed in just sweats, I sat in my locker, my fingers

tugging my hair like the pain would center me. I could withstand this. It would die down eventually. I just had to hold strong.

I sensed someone sitting down beside me, and I scowled. I wasn't sure I could take anymore of their bullshit right now.

"Luthersson?"

I looked up to see one of the new season rookies, Jason Melville. "Yeah?"

Melville bit his lip. God, if Rusket had put him up to saying something as a kind of fucking hazing ritual, I was going to murder the bastard, my position be damned.

The kid's eyes darted around the room, making sure no one else was around. "I just wanted you to know that, uh, us rookies, we don't give a fuck who you want to have sex with, or you know... love." His voice dropped, like love was some kind of dirty word. I guess when you were an eighteen-year-old rookie, love and commitment would seem horrible.

He cleared his throat. "I'm, uh, gay, but I don't want it out yet. I'm not that brave, you know? I don't have to tell you what the league will think, and I'm just a rookie. Not one of the best goalies in the NHL. I just want you to know that I really respect you. You were out to the team, despite the shit they give you. And now you're seeing Ludokov, and it's just... It'll mean something one day, you know? Maybe one day, I can do the same, and another rookie will be sitting beside me, confessing he's scared but that I make him feel like there's hope. Then maybe one day, when he has a rookie beside him, it won't matter at all by then."

Fuck. I was going to ruin my tough guy image by crying at the kid.

"I guess I just wanted to say that while it's hard, me and the other rookies have your back. We don't have a lot of sway yet, but we won't put up with Rusket's bullshit."

I sucked in a shaky breath. "Thanks, kid. Tell the other rookies the same. I appreciate your support."

Coach walked into the locker room, and the look on his face made my gut fall out of my asshole. "Luthersson. We're needed upstairs."

Melville stood in front of me. "Coach, I just wanna say that I don't think Luthersson should be punished for his sexuality or whatever. That shit is backwards as fuck."

I huffed a laugh. If you'd told me I'd be able to laugh today, I would have called you crazy.

Coach just raised a cool eyebrow at him. "Duly noted, Melville. Now hit the weights, like you're supposed to be doing."

Melville nodded like an eager puppy, and I slapped his shoulder in thanks as I walked toward the gallows. At least I wasn't facing the firing squad on all sides. I followed Coach out of the locker room silently, and he didn't speak to me in the elevator up to the offices above the arena. He led me to the conference room, where there were at least fifteen people all sitting around the table, looking like someone had died, instead of me just getting a blowjob.

The team's GM pointed to an empty chair at the end of the table. "Take a seat, Mr. Luthersson."

Sitting, I tried not to look like I'd done something wrong. I held my head high, meeting the eye of every single person in the room. If they were going to cast judgment on me, they were going to meet my eyes as they did it.

"We seem to find ourselves in a bit of a PR nightmare," the GM boomed.

Someone pushed a sheet of numbers into the center of the table. "Our approval is down five percent."

I raised my eyebrows. "How is that my fault? The news of my relationship with Ludo is less than twenty-four hours old."

The guy from PR sneered at me. "That's all it takes to crash our membership numbers." He looked at the GM. "This is a disaster. As you know, our membership is a certain demographic—"

"Homophobic isn't a demographic, Paul." Stacey, the social media manager, interrupted, and I threw her a grateful look. "And if it is, that isn't one we want to cultivate anyway."

Paul glared at her. "Our demographic is anyone who wants to spend their money to follow our team. Our job is to retain the members we already have, which means our star players can't be found face-fucking the opposition."

Someone made a protesting noise at his vulgarity, and the GM gave him a stern look. "Keep it professional, Paul." He looked around the table. "What are our solutions?"

The recruitment manager looked down at his folder. "We can put out a statement that says while we support the LGBTQI+ community, we hold our players to a high standard of public conduct, and therefore Luthersson has been suspended. Masters can step into his shoes. We can then decide what to do once it isn't everywhere in the media. Trade, maybe?"

They were going to fucking *fire me?* Shock stole the words from my lips. I felt like I was outside my body, listening to them decide my fate.

"Or we can *not* be stuck in the Dark Ages and actually come out in full support of one of our players? Jesus, how is this even a question?" Stacey argued, outrage written all over her face.

"It isn't just that he was found with another man, Stacey. Ludokov is an IceCaps player. You know the rivalry between the fanbases is rabid. They'll see Luthersson as a traitor."

"Then they need to get a fucking grip," someone else argued. "This isn't the English Premier League. We don't have damn blood feuds between teams."

The GM's eyes slid past me to Coach King. "What do you think?"

Coach looked back at the boss. "Sir, no one's going to pay to be our member if we're losing every game after getting rid of the best goalie we've had in a decade. The fans will overlook a lot if we're winning games."

Assistant Coach Craig glared at me. That old fuck had hated me since I first arrived. "The morale of the team is low, and it's because of Luthersson. Even if we keep him, he's a divisive presence. We won't win games if there's too much internal conflict."

"One gay player shouldn't be able to sink morale that quick, Craig," the GM quipped, but Coach Craig wasn't done.

"They don't feel comfortable with him in the locker rooms."

Coach King shook his head. "That's just Rusket stirring up shit. I told you to deal with him."

Coach Craig frowned. "He's entitled to his opinion."

"He's a fucking troublemaker, and I've told you to get him in hand."

They argued among themselves, until finally, I'd had enough. "How about I make this really simple for you —I quit. Trade me or I'm going back to Iceland to sit on my ass until you're *forced* to trade me. Put that in your fucking press release."

Coach King looked up at me, startled. "Erik, wait."

I shook my head at him. "No, Coach Craig is right. I can't play on a team with a bigoted, sadistic, B-grade bully like Rusket. Or a team who thinks that who I choose to love should be the subject of a fifteen-person meeting. If you can't support me as a player, then I don't want to play for your team."

I ignored their yelling as they all spoke over each other. Grabbing my duffel bag, I stomped from the room, not looking at any of the administration staff. I strode into the elevator and jammed the button to the parking garage.

Fuck this team. Fuck Coach Craig. Fuck them all.

Pulling out my phone, I opened a group text with Juniper and Ludo.

> Me: I quit. They were talking about suspending me anyway. Fuck this team.

> Ludo: Those fucking cunts. I'm going to come down there and beat the shit out of every single one of them. They'll soon realize that they need you more than you need that shitty-ass team.

> Juniper: I got put on mandatory leave today as well. Come over, Erik. We're going home.

CHAPTER

Thirty

LUDO

IT HADN'T BEEN that long since I'd been back to Louviers. I'd normally stay with Robbie, but Johnny was already taking up space in his house, and I was pretty sure Marianne would have an actual bitch fit if I rocked up with Erik and Juniper in tow.

My house was out of the question. I hated staying with my dad normally, but after a media storm about me being gay with the goalie of another team, I couldn't even imagine the shit he'd throw my way.

My dad had been the perfect father up until the day my mom died. Then he'd hit the bottle, and sometimes me, like he'd just wanted to burn the rest of his life down around him. To say we no longer got along was an understatement.

So we were going to stay at Bug's house. Apparently, her mom was so excited, she'd already started baking. Juniper's mom had been this warm figure throughout our childhood, even if she did have some OCD quirks, like the ones she'd passed on to Bug. She'd taken in Johnny, like he was her own flesh and blood. She'd been at every single one of Juniper's games, even some of my college ones when we lived closer. She'd cried when Johnny had left for the Marines, and also at Robbie's wedding. If she thought it was weird her daughter had three guy best friends, she'd never said so.

Juniper's dad... was more complicated. He'd almost never been home, and Robbie had once said he heard him having phone sex with someone who wasn't Bug's mom. We'd never told anyone that, especially not Bug. I mean, we were fifteen at the time, and that was grown-up stuff.

In the end, it didn't matter. They'd gotten a divorce when Bug left for college, though it was amicable enough, apparently. Juniper loved both her parents. Now her mom lived in their house alone, but Robbie said that she was dating the guy who owned the hard-ware store down in Sedalia, at least casually.

As we drove the rental car into Louviers, I sighed. One thing you could count on with Louviers was that it never changed. It had looked exactly the same way my whole life. Erik had his nose pressed to the window, making comments about how it was exactly how he thought a small American town would look. It had been built as a model town for a dynamite factory, so it did have that cookie-cutter, Christmas cottage vibe, especially being blanketed by a small layer of snow.

I was nervous as fuck. Maybe coming back here was a bad idea.

"Maybe we should have just headed somewhere random for a week instead," I muttered to Juniper. "You know that everyone here is going to *know*, and if the grapevine hasn't already run riot, I'll be surprised."

Bug shook her head. "We aren't running scared, Ludo. Fuck them. We can't avoid coming home forever, and it's going to be a gossipfest whether we're here or not. At least this way, they have to say their shit to our faces."

She was furious—at the Infernos for screwing Erik over, at the puck bunny who couldn't keep her mouth shut, at the social media trolls who'd had a field day with everything. But mostly, she was mad with the IceCaps. The team we'd both committed our lives to had—very gently—taken her social media responsibilities off her until this whole thing died down. I guess they wanted to control the narrative, and you couldn't do that if your social media manager was balls deep in the controversy.

People turned to look at the car as we drove through the town, because while we were close to Denver, there wasn't really anything here to draw tourists off the highway, so it was unusual to see unknown cars driving through.

I drove through the streets which I knew so well, I

still dreamed about them. I'd ridden them on my bike, crashed the aforementioned bike on that corner, kissed my first girl behind that tree. So many memories, both good and bad, but mostly amazing. I'd lived a charmed life for a lot of my childhood, and I knew it.

Juniper's mom's house was a cute little white-washed, two-story place. It had a huge backyard that backed onto a wide-open expanse of land.The mountains in the distance were like a silent wall between us and everything that had happened.

There was a small pond out the back which froze over in winter, and we'd all spent so many hours out there, shooting at a goal. Juniper was the reason my sniper shots were so good. Drill after drill after drill we ran, right up until I was drafted. We'd grown together, so our skills matched.

"Do you think the pond is frozen?" I asked Bug, and she grinned, her eyes wistful.

"Mom said it was. Want to try your luck against the Dynamite's secret weapon?"

Erik snorted. "Seriously?"

"Yep, they used to call her that in juniors. She was pretty good," I told him, proud of her even if she'd never pursued it going pro. When she'd broken her leg in senior year, ruining her chances to be scouted, deep down inside I was selfishly happy about it. It meant she could come with me wherever I went. I'd always needed Bug more than she needed me. I still did.

Because I loved her.

Fuck.

Because I *loved* her.

I was so fucking stupid. So blind and stupid. All the one-night stands. All the sorority girls and models and shit—none of them compared to the one woman I wouldn't let myself have.

"Ludo?" Her soft voice drew me from my thoughts.

I realized I'd been driving in a daze. I'd even parked out the front of her mom's house, then just sat there like a weirdo. "Sorry. Lost in memories."

She smiled, climbing out of the car. Erik was already out, holding her door open for her like a gentleman. He'd been right all along. I mean, I knew he was, but I didn't realize how long I'd been in love with my best friend. Maybe forever?

Juniper's mom appeared in the doorway, her hands rubbing together. "Juniper!"

"Mom!"

Bug ran up the path that had been freshly shoveled, and I wondered if the hardware guy did that for her. Last time I was here, the hardware store in Sedalia had been owned by Terry St. Clair, and he'd been seventy-eight back then. I doubted Bug's mom—who was only in her late forties—was dating Mr. St. Clair.

She wrapped her only child in her arms and squeezed her tightly. She kissed the side of her head, then let her go, holding her arms out for me. I stepped into the embrace of the woman who'd been my second mother.

"Andrei!"

Bug laughed as I screwed up my nose. This was the only person I permitted to call me Andrei. "Hi, Misha."

"My boy! You're doing so well. I saw your game against the Matadors. That hat trick was spectacular."

I flushed at her praise. "Thanks." Unfortunately, what had happened after had probably forever tainted the memory of my first hat trick.

Misha stepped back and looked past me. "You must be Erik," she said warmly, waving him closer and hugging him too. "Welcome to Louviers."

"Thank you for having me in your home, Ms. Verne."

Misha waved her hand. "Please, call me Misha. Come in out of the cold. Winter decided to hit a little early this year. The pond's been frozen over for three weeks already."

Bug whooped, leading us all into the house. It was exactly how it had always looked, except maybe the wall color had changed a little. It was still littered with photos of Bug, and by extension, me, Johnny and Robbie. There was even a photo of Johnny in his military uniform.

"Have you seen Johnny?" I asked, keeping my face politely neutral, not looking at Juniper.

Misha bustled around until we were all sitting on the couch, a plate of cookies magically appearing in front of us. "He comes around for dinner once a week, though you'd think I was trying to torture him when he agreed."

I snorted. I bet it was torture. He had to look into the face of the only mother figure he knew, knowing he'd fucked her daughter. Sounded like hell to me.

"How is he?" Juniper asked softly, and Misha narrowed her eyes at her daughter.

Whoops. Mom instincts activated.

"He's fine. Are you guys not speaking at the moment?"

Juniper flushed. "No. We just had a difference of opinion."

Misha tutted, but dropped it. We were all adults now, despite the fact she probably still saw us as errant teens. "Well, you better get over it, because he's coming over for dinner tonight." She kissed the top of Juniper's head again. "I'll get some coffee to have with your cookies."

Erik looked at the retreating back of Misha, a small smile on his face. "Good to know where you get your sass from, *Einiber*." He reached over and held her hand. "She didn't say anything about Ludo and I. Does she know?"

Bug nodded. "Yeah, she knows. You should assume everyone in Louviers knows. Mom just doesn't care. I sort of explained the situation with me and you and Ludo, and she gets it. She won't push you guys about it."

He nodded, twining his fingers in hers where he sat

beside her on the couch. "And the idea of us? As a whole?"

Juniper winced, her eyes darting to me and then away again rapidly. "There is no us, Erik."

He grinned at her, his eyes filled with promise. "Not yet, *Einiber,* but soon." He looked over at me, that knowing glint making me squirm in my seat. "Some things are written in the stars, sweet one. Sometimes we have to wait until the right time to have everything we want. I think your time is now, if you just give yourself permission to grasp it. *Carpe Penes.*"

I frowned at him. "Did you just tell her to seize the cocks in Latin?"

Juniper snorted, then giggled, until she was full-out belly-laughing. "I need to stitch that on a throw pillow."

Laughter bubbled up in my chest, and soon I was chuckling along with her. Erik smirked, and I realized perhaps he was telling me something too. I had a week before I had to return to the team. I had a week to decide if this alternative lifestyle Erik was proposing was the right one for me, if I had the balls to hold fast through the scrutiny that would come from it.

At this moment, watching Erik and Bug cuddled up on the couch happily, I knew that if I didn't try, I would regret it forever.

CHAPTER
Thirty-One

JUNIPER

MOM CHASED us out of the house after she'd fed us adequately. And by adequately, I mean until my stomach strained almost painfully against my jeans button. All rugged up, we stepped out into the back-yard. The pond was right down the back of the yard, but between that and us was the greenhouse Mom loved so much. She had a green thumb, and I knew for a fact that if I walked into that small glass building, it would be like walking into the tropics.

I noted that someone had built her a little wooden shed off the side, and I wondered if it was her new beau. She hadn't told me much about him, except that his name was Henry and he'd bought the hardware store in Sedalia from Mr. St. Clair when he retired a few years ago. Apparently, Henry knew his way around a hammer too, given the craftsmanship of that tiny wooden shed.

Strolling over there, I hoped it was a garden shed and not an outdoor sex den. I couldn't deal with knowing my mom still had sex, even though as an adult, I logically knew that she was still in her prime. The idea just made me want to puke a little, that's all.

Luckily, it just held my mom's larger garden tools, but also my old hockey goals. I looked over my shoulder at the guys, who were playing on the old tree swing like children. They were so fucking handsome, like a Hallmark movie poster. The blond ends of Erik's hair curled out the bottom of his knit cap. His jacket was black wool, and his jeans hugged his ass like a dream.

Ludo was like his dark-haired equivalent, his black puffer well loved, and his boots laced up over the top of his jeans. When he looked over at me and grinned, he looked so much like the boy I'd fallen in love with that butterflies fluttered in my stomach.

I'd loved and hated Andrei Ludokov over the years. I loved the man he was, funny and kind, handsome and mischievous. I hated that he was the standard I held everyone else to. No one ever made my stomach swirl with giddiness the way Ludo did when he looked at me like that. It was part juvenile crush and part very adult desire.

My gaze switched to Erik, who was forming a snow-ball in his glove-covered hands. His grin was wide and bright as he lined up the back of Ludo's head and let it fly. It exploded in a shower of white.

Ludo gave him an aggrieved gasp. "You asshole!" He tackled him into the snow, rolling around like they were fighting, but I had a sneaking suspicion that if I could see their faces, it would be more like foreplay.

"Junebug?"

I spun on my heel, slipping on the icy sidewalk. Johnny reached out and grabbed me, holding me up until I could get my feet under me again.

"Johnny," I breathed, and the visceral desire that hit me was like a freight train.

His eyes drifted straight to my forehead, which was covered by my fleece beanie. There was barely a mark anymore, but I didn't show him, in case even that faint pink line triggered him.

I wanted to throw my arms around him. I wanted to hug him close to me so he could never leave again. But I didn't know if that would be inappropriate, now he'd made his choice to leave.

You know what? Fuck it.

Stepping into him, I locked my arms around his waist and pressed my cheek into his chest. "Thank god you're okay. I was so fucking worried."

His hands came up to lightly rest on my back, and I hated it. Hated that he could no longer hug me the way he always had. Hated that we'd lost something that night.

"Robbie didn't tell you I was fine? Ludo?"

I waved a hand. "Of course they told me you were fine, but they're *guys*, Johnny. Their idea of emotional intelligence is thumping you on the back and telling you it'll be all good."

He chuckled. "Robbie did that exact thing."

I rolled my eyes, because of course he had. I knew my friends. "Johnny, about that night—"

But he was shaking his head. "It was a mistake. I shouldn't have... We shouldn't have..." He choked off the words. "Look, I know you're in love with Ludo. We all know you're in love and have been in love with Ludo since you were, like, fourteen. The only person who has no idea is the man himself. Maybe." He let out a long sigh, looking past me at the mountains in the distance. "So it's okay. I don't regret it, but I don't want anything more from you either."

Ouch. Well, that hurt.

I swallowed hard, looking out over the pond. "Oh. Okay, no, that's fine. We'll just chalk it up to a failed experiment and pretend it didn't happen." I would try to forget how he'd made me moan his name until my whole body shook with orgasms. How he'd told me to come like a good girl. That shouldn't be hard, right? I let out a humorless laugh. "My love life is a mess anyway, so what's one more layer of sand to bury my head in?"

Johnny cleared his throat, his eyes drifting to where Erik and Ludo were kissing in the snow, completely oblivious to us. Erik hovered over my best friend, staring down at him like he wanted to swallow him whole. "Oh, did you meet someone?" he asked, his voice purposefully neutral.

I laughed, the sound lined with hysteria. "No, Johnny. I didn't meet anyone." I shook my head. "Fuck me, when would I have time? The paparazzi have been at my front door for a week. Erik wants us to be in a throuple situation, and I'm tempted, even though it kind of feels like I'm poaching him from my best friend. Like I'm somehow taking a shortcut into something more with Ludo after standing on the sidelines for *so fucking long*, and now I'm forcing myself into their relationship."

I looked up at him. "On top of that, I had amazing sex with my other best friend, which was messy in itself, but then he ran away like my vagina was an IED. I've had to come to terms with the fact that every time I look at you, I'll picture the face you made while you hovered over me, fucking me like you needed it more than your next breath. I've had to come to terms with the fact that I've ruined something between us too, and yet I can't regret it either. So now I have *no fucking idea* where I stand with anything or anyone." I let out a shaky laugh. "Oh, and my career might be over."

During that tirade, the guys had stopped kissing and were now staring at me. Actually, Johnny was staring at me too. *Fuck.* I turned and fled into the house, leaving the three of them out there, staring after me.

My life was already in flames. What was one more match?

. . .

I hid in my bedroom for a couple of hours and then grew some lady balls. My mom would kill me if I stayed up here, so I was forced to leave the room in time for dinner. I made an exaggerated show of yawning as I walked into the living room, like I'd been napping, instead of just hiding under the blankets on my childhood bed, mortified.

Mom was just pulling the pot roast out of the oven, and the table was already set. The guys were sitting around watching hockey on the TV, which reminded me that soon Ludo would have to go back to Ann Arbor to play. I'd gotten an unexpected "holiday", but he only got a couple of days off.

As pissed as I was at the IceCaps, they hadn't blinked at the fact that Ludo was blowing the goalie of the Infernos. No, they'd just been annoyed that he got caught in a compromising position again. To them, it was no different to the time he got caught plowing the trust fund princess in the alleyway behind a nightclub in Florida. Or the time he got caught balls deep in a puck bunny in Ann Arbor by the press. The fact it was a guy this time was neither here nor there for the IceCaps.

I had to respect that, at least. They'd given him two games without pay every time he fucked up and embarrassed the club, so at least they were consistent.

Ludo looked over at me, his brows pulled together with worry. *Ugh.* Hightailing it into the kitchen, I saw Mom was almost done. "Is there anything you need me to do?"

She pointed her oven mitt at the stovetop. "Save the gravy."

We worked together in the kitchen, and I realized how much I'd missed my mom. I loved Ann Arbour, but there was nothing like being in the kitchen of your childhood home with your mom to give you the warm fuzzies. I stirred the gravy with a spoon, resisting the urge to taste it.

Mom plated up the pot roast on a large platter. "So, did Johnny finally come clean about his feelings, and that's why things are weird between you?"

I dropped the spoon into the gravy, hissing as I burnt my fingers fishing it out. "What?"

She shook her head. "Oh, Juniper. That boy has loved you forever. I was kind of hoping he'd finally told you. Ever since the second time you brought him around, I've known he worshiped the ground you walked on."

"Mom…"

She waved away my protests. "Forget I said anything. But I know you, and I know Johnny, and I think you'd make an amazing couple. I've been shipping you two since you were teens. Hashtag team Johniper."

I blinked. My mom had clearly been bodysnatched. "Shipping? Seriously, Mom? What have you been reading?"

She snorted at me. "I'm not a hundred, Juniper May. I can work social media just as well as the next person."

She grinned. "Henry is Team Judo, but I think he just likes the ship name better. I didn't think Ludo would ever settle down enough to realize how much he loved you, but maybe I was wrong all along. He seems very smitten with Erik. I don't blame him, because holy smokes, what a hottie!"

Having a young mom was sometimes horrifying. It had felt cool when I was a teen and she was in her thirties, so she could go mountain biking and ice skating and shit with me. But right now, I was horrified.

"Stop, Mom. He's young enough to be your son."

She waggled her eyebrows. "Or my toyboy." I threw the tea towel at her face, and she laughed, wrapping an arm around my shoulders. "About Johnny. Give it a chance. He's been devoted to you since before you had boobs. That's true love right there."

I pointed a finger at her face. "If this hadn't been the reason we were fighting, you would have put your foot in it."

She rolled her eyes at me, thrusting the platter into my hands. "I know my kid. I know Johnny too, even if he isn't biologically mine. I know how to read between the lines, and when he can't even look me in the eyes without blushing, it's pretty obvious that something happened between you two."

Sticking my tongue out at her, I headed toward the table. Somehow, I knew then that Mom would support whatever I decided to do. I was really lucky there; she loved me enough that there was nothing I couldn't tell her. Even if it was banging my childhood friend, or entering some polyamorous lifestyle with two professional hockey players.

"I love you, Mom."

She hugged me one-armed, placing a bowl of mashed potatoes on the table. "Love you too, Junie. No matter what."

Thirty-Two

JOHNNY

WHEN JUNIPER HAD RUN off to her room, I'd felt like the biggest asshole on the fucking planet. Again. Why did I keep hurting her like that? I'd tried to make things better, and instead, I'd ruined them more.

Sucking in a deep breath, I faced the guys. Ludo was on his feet, like he wanted to run after her, but Erik had his hand around his wrist. Erik was right; Juniper hated it when we saw her vulnerable.

Ludo walked over to me, and for a second, I thought he'd take a swing at my face. Instead, he just pulled me into his arms. "You look good, Johnny."

I hugged him back, because I needed it right now. "Thanks, man. Congrats on the hat trick. Also, congrats on flying out of the wardrobe like Aslan the lion."

"Technically, I came out of the storage closet."

Such a Ludo thing to say. I slapped him on the back,

lifting my chin at Erik in greeting. "So, they didn't take it well then?"

Ludo sighed, and we walked back toward Juniper's back porch. "You could say that. The IceCaps put Juniper on hiatus, even though none of this was her fault, and those fucks over at the Infernos tried to suspend Erik."

The big Viking bared his teeth. "I quit instead. Fuck them."

Picking up the twelve-pack of beer I'd left on the porch, I handed one to each of them. I clinked my beer bottle to Erik's. "Fuck them."

The guys sat on the porch swing, while I sat in the wicker chair by the back door. The cold was making my nose numb, but there was nothing quite like the silence of Louviers.

"Are we going to talk about the fact you had sex with Bug?" Ludo asked suddenly, and I gave him a panicked look. Misha was just inside the house.

"*Shh!*"

Ludo gave me that shit-eating grin he was so well known for. "What? Don't want Mama Verne to know you debauched her sweet daughter?" he teased.

I was gonna punch him in his smug mouth. "Like you can talk, asswipe. You want to fuck her so bad, you're basically repressed right now. At least I *know* I'm bad for her!"

We fell back into silence. This was so stupid. I

should have just stayed home, told Misha I couldn't make it to dinner. Told her I'd come next week, once I knew they were safely back in Ann Arbor. But I had to see that they were okay. They were my best friends, even if I had fucked it all up.

"Why?"

Frowning, I stared at Erik. "What?"

"Why are you bad for her?" he asked, his deep voice accented enough to add to his appeal.

Was he stupid? "Didn't you see the cut on her head? I did that. My demons did that. I hurt her." Dragging my eyes away from them, I looked down at the warped floorboards of the porch. I'd have to fix those. Maybe I'd see if Henry wanted to do it next weekend. Finally calm, I looked back at Erik. "I'm broken, and Junebug would spend every day of the rest of her life trying to put me back together. She deserves more than that. She deserves someone who can love her and give her the best life. The life she *deserves*, where she's the most important thing in the world."

Ludo was shaking his head. "You aren't broken, man. You need some serious therapy, but you aren't fucking broken. You're a hero."

I made a rude noise in the back of my throat. "Hero. I don't feel like a hero." I felt like the villain, bathed in blood. But Juniper's blood was the worst. "What if I snap, and don't know I'm here and safe? What if I think she's the enemy and really hurt her?"

Erik tilted his head at me, his head almost resting on top of Ludo's. He really was huge. "Have you had those kinds of lucid flashbacks? Triggered while awake?"

I shook my head. Mostly, I just had nightmares. They were bad enough, but I thanked god everyday that I didn't have it worse. The men and women who did were shells of themselves; I hated that for them, but praised every deity who'd listen that I wasn't one of them.

Erik looked between me and Ludo. "What if you could be with her, but have others to lean on too?"

Ludo's head snapped toward him, and mine did too. "What are you suggesting?"

Erik shrugged. "Ludo loves you." Ludo opened his mouth to protest, and Erik raised a hand. "Not like that, obviously. But you care about him. And we all care about *Einiber*."

"Einiber?"

Erik smiled, and it was filled with warmth. "It means Juniper berry in Icelandic. My berry."

I resisted the urge to go *awww*, because I wanted him to get to the point. Ludo must have agreed, because he nudged him with his elbow. "You were saying?"

Erik wrapped an arm around Ludo's shoulder, and it was surreal watching someone else pull moves on my Casanova friend. Ludo was so big, so dominant, and to see him relax into the arms of another dude was trippy as fuck.

Erik cleared his throat. "So we all care about her, and she very obviously cares about you two. And I'm definitely winning her over," he teased with a wink. "I say we just add Johnny to our happy little throuple. Make it foursome."

"I don't... Not that there's anything wrong with two guys, I just don't swing that way."

Ludo laughed. "I've seen your microdick, Johnny. I'm not interested either."

My face burned. "I don't have a microdick, you fucker," I shouted, then dropped my voice, looking over my shoulder for Misha. "You wish your dick was as big as mine, asswipe."

Ludo just winked at me as Erik rolled his eyes. "Kids, can we focus on the conversation at hand? I'm also not interested like that. But I am interested in Juniper. As is Ludo, even though he's being stubborn. I see no harm in bringing you into the fold." His eyes grew soft. "You need the support, and you're all basically family already. This would just make us all closer. Give you more hands to help you through the darkness, until you can stand in the light on your own two feet."

Ludo snorted. "You've been spending too much time reading about the weird set-up River and Rigby have going on."

Erik shrugged. "I met them, and they seem happy. In love. They treat Nova like a queen."

I was shaking my head now. This was a utopian ideal. It wasn't a catch-all solution for people so fucked up, they couldn't exist in a relationship by themselves. What the guys on Ludo's team had was an anomaly, not the norm. I might have been able to share with Ludo, because I'd kind of known since we were teens that if I wanted Juniper, I'd have to share her affections with him. I would always come second to him.

Could I live in a relationship where I came third to everyone?

But I was looking down the barrel of a life of fucked-up loneliness right now. "I'll think about it. I honestly don't think Junebug would go for it."

Erik gave us both a lopsided smile. "Juniper wants it all. She just doesn't believe she can have it, or that she deserves it. But don't worry, I'll make it my mission to teach her that she's a goddess to be worshiped, and I'm ready to do so at the altar between her thighs. Then I'll convince her to let us keep her heart safe."

I closed my eyes as the memories of Juniper's soft thighs around my ears as I licked her pretty pussy bombarded me. Fuck, I hated that I jerked off to the sounds of her moans in my head, the memory of her taste on my tongue. I hated that I'd ruined it before it had even begun.

If Erik could give the chance back to me, could I take it? *Should* I even take it?

We sat in silence for a while, until Ludo stretched his arms above his head and yawned. "Come on, let's go inside and watch the Infernos get their ass kicked without their star goaltender. Revenge isn't a dish best served cold—it's best served boiling hot so there's no fucking doubt about what led to their downfall."

I grabbed the beers, and we headed into the house. Misha was busy cooking, humming softly to herself. I hoped she invited Henry over tonight too. He was a nice guy, but I knew Misha was nervous about introducing him to her grown daughter. She respected Juniper's opinion, so if Juniper hated him, I knew that would be the end of it.

But Juniper wouldn't hate him. I doubted Juniper had ever hated anyone in her whole life, except that kid from the Littleton who was an arrogant bully. Tony Meyer. Man, we'd all hated him.

I walked over to the sideboard where Misha had kept her cutlery since I was a boy. "Am I laying out five places or six?" I asked her softly, and I could see the hesitation on her face. "She'll love Henry. You can't keep the guy on the hook forever—we both know he's head over heels for you. They'll get along great."

Misha looked conflicted, but finally nodded. "I'll message him now. Set six places, Johnny. I can always remove the place setting if he can't make it."

I grinned and gave her a tight squeeze. She deserved to be happy. I remembered how miserable Juniper's dad had made her. I wasn't sure Junebug ever noticed—she saw the good in everyone, and after all, he was her dad—but I could see loneliness in others, because I'd been there. People who had been gripped by hopelessness could always sense it in others, even if I was just a dumb kid with a bad attitude back then.

I moved to leave the kitchen, but Misha grabbed my arm on the way past. "You're a good man, Johnny Lipkin. You deserve to be happy too."

Thirty-Three

ERIK

IT WAS hard to watch the rookie Infernos goalie get hammered by Montreal, but only because I felt bad for the kid. He was going to get the blame for the loss, when it wasn't his fault at all. Watching Laurens swear at Rusket, watching the team fall apart—it should have made me feel vindicated, but really, it just made me feel like shit.

For kids like Melville, the Infernos were the beginning of their future. They didn't need this kind of thing haunting their careers, especially when it was completely out of their control. The younger players really stepped up, and Coach should be proud of the talent he'd recruited.

They still lost 8-2.

At some point, an older man appeared in the doorway of Juniper's house, looking nervous. Johnny stood and shook his hand, before introducing him to me and Ludo. The guy, Henry, smiled as he shook both our hands. "Lovely to meet you both. Ludo, I've heard so much about you from Misha."

Ludo grinned. "All wonderful things, I'm sure. I never did anything to give Misha gray hairs."

The woman in question walked into the living room, Juniper behind her. I appraised Juniper quickly, and she seemed okay, though she wouldn't meet any of our eyes.

"Andrei Ludokov, I have at least three gray hairs on this head that have your name on them. The four of you together would send any mother prematurely gray."

Johnny laughed. "Do you remember when Juniper wanted to be Katniss Everdeen, and we went out and practiced archery every day for a month? And then one day, she shot Robbie in the ass?" I chuckled at Juniper's horrified face.

Ludo got the giggles too, looking over at Henry. "We had to call Misha, because Robbie couldn't get hold of his parents. By the time we got back there, Juniper had tried to pull out the arrow and then passed out from the sight of the blood."

Juniper stuck her fists on her curvy hips. "It wasn't the blood. We were hockey players; we saw plenty of blood. It was the sensation of the arrow moving through muscle—" She gagged at the memory. "That's what made me feel a little woozy."

"A little woozy? Ludo had to carry you out of the

woods, and I basically dragged Robbie out. He still has the scar on his ass," Johnny teased.

Juniper stepped around her mother. "Don't listen to them. They were the mischievous ones." She thrust a hand out at Henry. "I'm Juniper. It's nice to meet you."

Henry shook her hand enthusiastically. "It's lovely to finally meet you. You're the light of Misha's life. She talks about you all the time, about how proud she is of everything you've accomplished." He looked at Johnny and Ludo. "How proud she is of all of you."

I saw the happy flush on both Ludo and Johnny's cheeks, and I knew that Misha was someone I really needed to like me. Not just for Juniper, but if I wanted this relationship to work, I'd need her support. Luckily, every interaction I'd had with the woman in question had been positive so far. She reminded me a lot of Juniper.

Misha clapped her hands together, directing everyone to the dining room. It was set out like a Rockwell painting, and I was beginning to think this town was about as picture-perfect Americana as you could get.

Henry did his best to engage Juniper, and she grasped the lifeline, still not really looking at us. I hated that she wouldn't look at me. I didn't want her to feel embarrassed about anything she felt.

Misha was seated beside me and handed me the mashed potatoes. "So, Erik. You're from Iceland?" she asked lightly, and I nodded.

"Laugarvatn. The home of the world's most beautiful waterfalls. And elves, but not the kind Santa uses. I can't get you off the naughty list."

"The only person here who's on the naughty list is Andrei," she teased, and Ludo looked indignant once more.

I chuckled low. "I think I quite like him on the naughty list."

Passing me the bean casserole, she laughed. "I just bet. He is a sweet boy. Behind all that bravado, though, he's been through a lot. With his mom dying so young, and then his dad…" She shook her head, sadness washing over her face. "You'll know this soon enough, of course, but that bravado hides quite a vulnerable heart."

She looked me directly in my eyes, her stare unflinching. Those intense brown eyes were so similar to her daughter's, reminding me of the interview where Juniper had given me pretty much the same speech. "I know you'll help him protect it, and won't go into it thinking you're just fucking around with a playboy. I can already tell you mean more than that to him."

I wanted to tell her that I wanted to mean more than that to her daughter too, but that was something Juniper needed to address with her mother, not me. "I promise."

Misha nodded, her hand patting mine. "Good. Now, tell me more about you. I want to know everything there is to know about the man who managed to lock down my favorite rebel."

Before I knew it, I'd told her all about my own family, and how hard it had been coming to the US and leaving everyone behind. The way I wished I had a Juniper of my own to lean on.

In return, she told me countless stories of "her kids" growing up, and I got a better understanding of how close they really were, and why Ludo had been so hesitant to make a move. That was a lot of history to jeopardize.

Deep down, I knew this was the right thing, though, for all of them. I just had to convince them to take the leap into the unknown, the unconventional. Then I had to convince them to let me into their world, because I desperately wanted to be part of their story.

Johnny and I shooed Misha from the kitchen to clean up and do the dishes. I stood beside Johnny, who was elbows-deep in the sudsy water, while I dried. We were silent, but it wasn't awkward. I got the impression that Johnny just wasn't a big talker, and that was okay.

"You're good for her, you know? For him, too," Johnny said quietly, looking out the window into the darkness of the backyard. "You make Juniper braver than she ever would've been without you. She loves Ludo. She never would have made a move before you." He chuckled low, and it was a sad, resigned sound.

"Junebug was a late bloomer. Didn't get boobs until she was almost sixteen. So we'd spent years treating her like one of the boys, you know? Mountain biking down the foothills, climbing trees, playing hockey. She was just Bug.

"Didn't help that we'd all decided early on to treat her that way. She was off limits to us all. Robbie had made us swear to that, and he held us to it—even though he got with Marianne when he was fifteen, so it didn't even matter to him. But sometimes, I think he saw more than we did. He saw that I loved her. Saw that she loved Ludo. I think he knew, back then, that if we succumbed to our teenage hormones, the whole friend group would have imploded."

He handed me another plate. "Anyway, at sixteen, she grew boobs. That year, at Christie's first pool party for the summer, I remember she wore this tiny pink bikini with ruffles. She had all these new, soft curves, and I spent a good portion of that party in the deep end of the pool with a hard-on. But the other girls finally saw Juniper as a girl, and a potential threat to their pursuit of the jocks, you know? The other guys on the team and boys in our class, they finally noticed what I'd known all along—Juniper was fucking beautiful."

"She is," I agreed softly. "On the inside too."

Johnny nodded. "Anyway, one of the guys from our senior class made a crude comment about her, and Ludo lost it on him. We had to drag him off, and he told everyone who was there that Juniper was off limits, or he'd make their life miserable. He probably could have done it too; he was a god in high school.

"What I didn't know until way later, was that the girls had spent the whole party telling Juniper that you shouldn't wear a bikini if you were over 110 pounds. That she looked fat and bulgy and all sorts of other mean-girl shit that fucks with your self-confidence as a teen. That she was lucky Ludo was her friend, because there was no way guys like Ludo or me would give her the time of day if it wasn't for hockey."

He shook his head. "She was a different Juniper from that moment. Not so carefree. More self-conscious. More shy. Coupled with the fact that because of Ludo's decree, guys kept turning her down when she asked them out, she believed the things those girls said. It fucked her up a little. She never would've made a move on Ludo, because she still believes she's unworthy of him, when it's actually the other way around." He let out a heavy sigh. "You need to remind her that she's so fucking perfect, it hurts."

I slapped him on the back. "We'll remind her, my friend. Together, she'll never doubt how fucking beautiful she is ever again."

He shook his head again, but I could see him wavering. Apparently, long-term pining had the same effect on Johnny that it had on Juniper—a false sense of unworthiness. I wanted to hug him, but I didn't think he'd take the embrace from me in the same way he'd take it from Juniper. I'd cure him of that. He needed the anchoring, the foundation. We could be that for him.

We were silent for a long time, the only sounds the steady clank of china on china. Finally, he nodded, handing me the platter. "I want what you're proposing. But I want her to be one hundred percent on board with this. Not just so she can have Ludo in some roundabout way, but because she wants us all. I don't want *any* doubt in her mind, because if she decides later on that this isn't what she wanted at all..." He stared out into the darkness. "I'm not sure I could recover from it."

I nodded solemnly. "I know that you're gambling something precious, Johnny. We won't take unnecessary risks with your heart or hers."

We fell back into silence, but I began to plan. The plan rose and fell on someone other than Johnny and me, however. The one person who could convince Juniper that this idea wasn't insane was the one person she didn't believe she deserved.

Yet.

CHAPTER
Thirty-Four
LUDO

JUNIPER WAS AVOIDING US, which was kind of impressive in a house as small as hers, in a town the size of Louviers. But she managed it, and I was getting frustrated. I messaged Robbie, knowing I needed to get this part out of the way.

I had to tell my best friend that I liked guys. I'd never had to have this conversation, not really. With Juniper, it was different. I could tell Juniper I liked to stick my dick in a meat grinder, and she'd just figure out a way to make sure I didn't permanently injure myself in the process while encouraging me to be true to myself.

Johnny had stumbled on the truth himself and taken it in his stride, with very little conversation about it.

But Robbie? I was going to have to sit down and have the whole awkward conversation, because Robbie would have questions. He wasn't a live-and-let-live type of guy like Johnny. I'd showered in locker rooms with these guys for decades, and I was kinda scared that they'd think I'd been... I don't know, checking them out the whole time. Which I hadn't. Well, not in a sleazy way. I'd always just kind of taken in their muscles, the long leanness of their bodies, and thought it was clinical, in a way. If it stirred anything like desire in my gut, I'd never acknowledged it.

I mean, I'd been way more attracted to Juniper, but had managed to keep that under control for all my horny teen years. No, it had been Erik who changed it all. Erik and the vodka that gave me permission to explore that low burn in my gut. I would tell them that. They'd understand.

I needed Juniper, though. I needed her to be the buffer between Robbie and reality.

"Juniper!" I hollered up the stairs, because she still hadn't come out of her room, and I was tired of her hiding. "Juniper May! I will climb up the tree outside your window, and then when I fall and break my arm, you can tell Coach Toons it was because you were ignoring me."

I heard her door slam open. "I'll tell him it was because you're a fucking child, Andrei Ludokov. He won't even argue with me!"

I grinned at where she stood at the top of the stairs, glaring down at me. Man, I loved it when she gave me that look, like she didn't know whether to kiss me or punch me in the face. That simmering lust had been between us for so long that we'd gone on with our lives despite it. It was like long-term pain; you just pushed it to the back of your mind and ignored it when you could.

Now I recognized what a fucking asshole that made me.

Shaking my head, I gave her a lopsided grin. "I need you, Bug. I have to go see Robbie, and I need you to protect me."

Her face softened briefly, but then she narrowed her eyes at me. "Robbie isn't going to give a fuck, Ludo, and we both know it."

I shrugged. She was probably right. But his dad was a bit of a homophobe, so maybe it was something that developed later in life? I needed her. She was my biggest supporter. My safety blanket.

"Please, Bug?"

She huffed, but made her way down the stairs. She was dressed in her jeans and snow boots already, her long-sleeved thermal undershirt peeking out under a purple flannel shirt. I loved her in that color. It made her eyes pop.

"Where's Erik?"

"Talking to his agent, trying to negotiate this bullshit with the Infernos. I can't take him for this part anyway. We'll go have drinks with Robbie and Marianne tomorrow, if this goes okay."

Bug waved her hand, like I was being ridiculous. "It's going to be just fine, but okay, if you need me to hold your hand while you tell the man who literally spent an entire *summer* talking about Vin Diesel and how amazing he is, then let's go."

"You think Robbie is bi too?"

She snorted. "God no. But if anyone can appreciate having a man crush, it's him." Walking over to the closet, she grabbed our coats. "Mom! Just going to see Robbie!"

"All right. Don't get arrested."

I smiled to myself. Her mom had said the exact same thing every time we'd left the house for as long as I'd known her.

We climbed into the rental car and pulled onto the road that would take us over to The Bar. It was just The Bar, since it was the only one in Louviers. It was also the only place to eat or get coffee. Ruben had started managing it for his aunt and uncle after they'd retired to Florida. At this time of the day, after the breakfast crowd and before the lunch rush, we'd have the place pretty much to ourselves.

While we drove, I had her trapped, and as much as I didn't want to make shit awkward between us again, I knew we had to talk about what had happened yesterday. "Juniper…"

She raised her hand. "Nope. I'm going to stop you right there. We are going to pretend it didn't happen."

I frowned at her. "You don't even know I was

going to say something about that. I could have wanted to tell you I was... quitting hockey or something."

Snorting, she rolled her eyes. "Sure. Maybe if you were dead." She gave me a serious look. "Please just pretend I didn't say anything."

At least we were driving, so it was too late for her to escape this conversation. "Nope. I can't do that. Because you basically told us all that you had feelings for me, and I don't think I can just unhear that."

She gave me a burning look, and it made my skin feel uncomfortably tight. "I know you don't think of me like that, Ludo. We've got that unwritten rule. A line we don't cross for the sake of friendship." She gave a mirthless laugh. "Honestly, what happened with Johnny should be enough warning to us both." She turned, looking out the window. "I know what Erik wants, but he can't have his cake and eat it too. I'll tell him as much. He'll respect my choice. Your friendship means more to me than some kind of half-relationship we'd have to be in to make Erik happy. Sometimes nothing is better than the alternative."

I pulled the car over to the side of the road and turned to her, grabbing her chin so she was forced to look at me. "Who said I don't think of you like that, Bug? Pretty sure it was never me. You're right; we had that unspoken rule, but it was never because I didn't *want* you. Fuck, I think I've jerked off in the shower to you more times than I care to count since you got those." I pointed to her boobs, and she looked down at them too.

"But you were my Juniper. My Bug. I've never had a relationship that I haven't fucked up in three months or less, and I couldn't take that risk with you. Losing you would be…" I let out a shaky breath. "It would be like losing a part of myself, and I always believed that to protect our friendship, to keep you in my life, I had to put you on a pedestal I couldn't reach." Her pretty pink lips parted, and I leaned closer. "I'm starting to learn that perhaps I hurt us both by doing that. But not anymore, Bug." I brushed my lips against hers. "I want to get you off that pedestal so I can play with you how I like. You've always been mine, Juniper Verne—we just didn't know it."

I kissed her hard, branding myself onto her lips, my hand cupping her jaw until she was stretched toward me, her mouth mine to conquer. She moaned as I kissed her in the way I'd always dreamed. The way I'd emptied my balls imagining over and over, every time I touched my cock. As my tongue thrust between her teeth, she released a little moan into my mouth, and I grew hard. I wanted her to make that noise around my dick.

Finally, I pulled back, and she looked up at me with that dazed, blissed-out expression that I wanted to see every day, for as long as she'd have me.

"Who do you belong to, Juniper?" I asked her softly.

She blinked at me, her lips pursed, though her eyes

were filled with warm mirth. "I belong to myself, Andrei Ludokov, and don't you forget it."

I threw back my head and laughed. "Fuck yeah, you do, Bug. And I belong to you too." I kissed her cheek. "Take whatever you want, whoever you want— as long as you choose me too." Sitting back in the driver's seat, I put the car in drive and pulled back onto the road.

Well, I tried to. Instead, the wheels spun on the snowy shoulder of the road.

Ah fuck.

Bug started to giggle, which turned into an all-out laugh. "You're gonna have to call Robbie and tell him you got us stuck in the snow." She hissed out the words through her laughter. "He's going to give you so much shit about this. You won't even have to worry about him giving you shit about Erik."

I glared at her and climbed out. "Just drive the car. I'll push." Even though I could see the back tires were well and truly stuck, I didn't want to subject myself to the absolute ribbing I'd get from Robbie, unless I really, really had to.

Three attempts and being splattered in slush later, I called it quits. Pulling out my phone, I called Robbie and listened to his howls of laughter as he told me he'd be right there.

I tugged the still-giggling Juniper out of the driver's seat and pushed her against the side of the car, kissing her like I could breathe in the very essence of her happiness. She curled her body into mine, and I squeezed her hips as I held her close.

Gravel crunched, and I stepped away to watch as Robbie pulled up beside us. "You tourists put yourself in a ditch? Don't worry, it happens every winter."

I gave him the finger, but he was out of the truck, scooping up Juniper into his arms. "Loonie Junie! It's good to see you, my friend. You never visit anymore."

She hugged him tight, laughing. "I've been busy, Robbie!"

He slipped her back onto her feet and looked between us, waggling his eyebrows. "So I see, girl. So I see." He whistled. "At least one of you finds it in himself to come and visit. Johnny's been down here, staring at his beer like a hound dog that's been kicked, ever since he took a ride on the Dynamite Express."

Juniper punched him in the shoulder. "Shut the fuck up. It wasn't like that."

He looked between us, his face losing its mirth. "You're gonna have to explain it to me soon, because I'm a little worried that everything's going to go to shit, if what I saw when I pulled up is a thing."

I tilted my head at him. "What did you see?"

He raised his eyebrows. "I saw you breaking the pact."

I laughed, because the pact was well and truly dead. Juniper put a hand on Robbie's chest. "We've got a lot to explain. Tow us out of this ditch, so we can do it over a few beers and not out here where my nipples are one gusty breeze away from cutting glass." We both imme-diately dropped our eyes to her boobs, and she punched Robbie in the arm, hard. I elbowed him in the ribs too.

"What? She started it!"

CHAPTER
Thirty-Five

JOHNNY

NEW GROUP CHAT REQUEST

LUDO CHANGED THE GROUP NAME TO
BUG'S BEAUS.

JUNIPER CHANGED THE GROUP NAME TO
BUG'S BITCHES.

LUDO CHANGED THE GROUP NAME TO
JUNIPER'S JOHNS.

ERIK CHANGED THE GROUP NAME TO
THE BOYFRIEND CHAT.

Ludo: Juniper and Jobbie are drnk af
and doing the 2 step on The Bars bar.

Ludo: The Bar's bar's bar. Ha trysayin
that ten times fast.

Ludo: I might also need a ride on Erik's
dick and probly back tto Bugs house.

YEAH, Robbie and Junebug weren't the only ones who
were shitfaced. Shaking my head, I cleared up my tools
from where I was working on Robbie's beat-up old

F100. I knew my way around a car from helping him and his dad when we were kids, but I wasn't quite as fanatical as Robbie had been.

I texted back.

Me: I'm on my way.

Erik: I'll put the coffee on.

I hopped in the truck and rolled down the driveway. I was glad they'd messaged me and not Marianne to get them from The Bar. That would have gone down pretty badly.

Even now, I could hear the kids yelling in the house. Sweet kids, but they were as wild as Robbie had been at their age. Twenty-three was pretty young to have a five-year-old and a three-year-old, though, so I didn't envy him. I fucking felt a hundred, and even I wasn't ready for kids.

Robbie and Marianne had gotten married straight out of high school; they seemed happy enough, so maybe I was the one doing it wrong. I had a sneaking suspicion that perhaps Marianne had been pregnant when they got married. I might be a dumb grunt, but I could count. But no one ever mentioned it, and we all pretended it was fine, even if it was a little archaic.

The Bar was in the center of town, and doubled as the general store too. You could buy a steak and get shitfaced at The Bar. Legit go out for smokes and a gallon of milk, and still end up at The Bar. There were a few cars in the lot already, more than there normally would be at this time of the afternoon. It wasn't often they got lunch and a show, by the sound of it.

The first person I saw as I walked in was Ruben, leaning against the backbar, grinning at Juniper and Robbie as they did their best *Coyote Ugly* impression, boot-scooting over the worn, wooden top of the bar while people hollered.

When Junebug spun on her sock-covered feet, I was convinced she was going to land on her face. But Robbie reached out and tugged her closer, holding her up while Ruben and Ludo stretched their hands out to grab her if she fell.

When she saw me, she squealed. "Johnny!" She launched herself off the bar and into my arms. I grunted as I went down in slow motion, my thigh protesting the blow of her against me. We ended up on the ground, her straddling my hips, her grin wide and sweet. "You caught me." She nuzzled my cheek, despite the two days worth of beard scruff. "You'll always catch me, right, Johnny?"

I ran my hands up and down her spine. "Always, Junebug," I said sincerely, and when she kissed my cheek, then my throat, I knew this was about to become something not fit for public consumption. I threw Ludo a *help me* look, but he just grinned goofily. Robbie was still on the bar. "Ruben!"

The man in question moved around the bar, tugging

Juniper to her feet. "Come on, Junie. You'll scare my patrons away with your free porn show."

She gasped. "I never would've taken my clothes off, and you know it."

I didn't know it, at all. Apparently, Ruben didn't know it either. "It was always your idea to go skinny-dipping when we were dumb teenagers, Junie. I don't think you've changed that much," he accused.

She laughed. "That's because my friends were all hot hockey players, and the eye candy was A plus. Hell, it was like A plus plus plus—you know what I mean?"

He sat her on the barstool. "Nah, because you were the only girl, and I'm pretty sure these three would have gouged out our eyes if we ever looked at you like that."

Damn straight, we would have kicked their asses. We weren't allowed to touch Juniper back then, and that sure as fuck meant no one else on the team was allowed to either. I guess that had fucked her up a little, but hindsight was twenty-twenty and all that. At the time, I was just a raging, jealous shithead who'd wanted that one shining piece of hopefulness to be mine forever, and not have to sit on the sidelines, watching someone else make her happy.

Juniper huffed. "Assholes."

I grinned at her, completely unrepentant. "Let's go, Junebug. Erik has the coffee on."

She sighed dreamily. "He's so handsome. And he

kisses like..." She bit her knuckles. "Not as good as when you do that thing with your tongue—"

I slapped a hand over her mouth, scooping her off the barstool and into my arms like she was a princess. "Nope. We're out. Let's go, you two." I tilted my head at Ludo and Robbie, who were both giggling like the knuckleheads they were.

Robbie pouted. "You aren't going to carry me out like a damsel too? I'm sad, Johnny." He lifted his arms in the air. "Carry me too."

Fuck, they were all wasted. "Only place I'm carrying you is to the dumpster, shithead. Let's go, unless you want me to get Marianne to fish you out of the trash can."

His face fell, but he followed behind me. Ludo was hugging Ruben, telling him how much he loved him, as the poor guy helped me corral them to the rental car. "But not like that, man. I promise, not like that."

Ruben threw me a panicked look, and I just laughed, shrugging. "I mean, I'm not exactly sad about that, Ludo."

Ludo sighed heavily. "I was worried you guys would all think I'd spent years looking at your dicks, when I didn't. I love boobs. And vaginas. Man, I *love* vaginas. But I never looked at your dicks. Maybe Johnny's. But that's because that fucker is a *monster* and we all looked at his dick to compare. Right? Robbie, back me up! You looked at Johnny's dick, right?"

Robbie snorted. "Fuck yeah, I did. I kept telling my

dick not to be sad. It's a grower, and there's nothin' wrong with that."

Ludo whipped his head back to Ruben. "See!"

Juniper was cackling in my arms, and I gave her a mock-stern look. "Not a single word out of you." She mimed zipping her lips, but there was still laughter in those pretty eyes. Fuck, I loved her. She was joy personified, and I wanted to spend every day of my life making her laugh like this.

I put her gently into the back of the car, buckling her in and shutting the door. I might have been a little less gentle with the other two. Robbie banged his head twice, trying to navigate the door of the sedan. "Fuckin' normal-people cars. Don't they know tall people have to fold in half to get in?"

Ludo was trying uselessly to put his seatbelt on. "Can't find the hole!"

"That's what she said," Junebug quipped back, and I snorted despite myself.

Robbie chuckled. "Never been the problem for Ludo. Too many holes—that's his problem."

"Not anymore. I'm a two-hole kinda guy." He frowned. "Four holes. Does a mouth count as a hole? Maybe six holes." He continued to frown as he counted on his fingers. He and Juniper got into a rousing debate about whether nostrils counted, and Robbie was snoring loudly by the time I pulled up at his house.

Dragging him from the car and maneuvering him to the door, I knocked softly. Marianne opened it, her mouth pulling into a tight line as she took in the drunken Robbie propped up by my shoulder. "I thought he was just going to have lunch and see if Ludo had been trying to fuck him all those years ago."

I ground my back molars. "Apparently, it was a liquid lunch." I pushed Robbie toward her, and he wrapped his arms around his wife.

"You're so pretty," he muttered drunkenly. Marianne rolled her eyes as the other two began to honk the horn, waving wildly at her. She shook her head with a scowl, closing the door in my face, ignoring the other drunkards in the car.

Such a fucking bitch.

I walked back to the car, climbing into the driver's seat. "In the back, you two."

Junebug grinned. "Will you spank me if I don't?"

Ludo groaned. "He spanks you? Fuck, I want to spank you too." He grabbed her up into his arms and kissed her, and I nearly crashed the fucking car. My eyes kept flicking to the rearview mirror as I watched their lips mold together, tongues tangling in a kiss that was more drunken mess than precision.

When did that happen?

They were both breathing heavily when they pulled apart. Junebug smirked at me in the reflection. "Nope, Johnny's the only one who gets to do that." She turned to Ludo, patting his face. "But you and Erik can watch."

I groaned, my dick now hard. Why did the idea of the guys watching me turn Junebug's pretty, heart-shaped ass pink with my palm make me feel so hot? Shaking my head, I turned and looked over my shoulder. "You both need to keep your shit together until we get home. Hands and mouths to yourselves."

Thank god Louviers was so damn small. Erik was waiting at the front door when we arrived, a soft smile on his face. I hadn't spent enough time with Erik to even consider what he was suggesting, but... wasn't that how all relationships worked? Friendships, too. I had to slowly get to know the man, but I liked him. He was nice, and knew when to push and when silence was golden.

I climbed out, and he came over, that smile spreading as he heard the other two bickering in the backseat. "They sound like they're having fun."

"They're definitely having a good time," I told him, opening Junebug's door. When I looked in, they were making out again. I looked over at Erik, expecting jealousy or something, but instead, there was just heat in his eyes.

They looked fucking beautiful together; that much was obvious. Perfect opposites, with all of Ludo's hard angles softened by Juniper's sweet curves. Like light and shadow.

I reached down and gripped her hand. "I hate to break this up, but unless you want Misha to ask some really hard questions, you're gonna need to stop." I pulled her gently from the car, and she came happily. It was a heady experience, having her fall into my arms after being right there with Ludo. I'd spent so many years in Ludo's shadow that it was nice for Juniper to *see* me. To *want* me. It was a mindset I had to shake, though, especially if I was seriously considering Erik's proposal.

Junebug wrapped herself around my body. "Mom is Team Johniper."

I blinked at her. "Johniper?"

She nodded solemnly. "And Henry is Team Judo." She leaned forward, dragging me down until her lips were beside my ear. "I'm Team Johnludik."

What the hell was she saying? "Baby girl, I have no idea what that means."

But she was already distracted, stomping toward the house. "Man, I'm hungry. Are you hungry? We should've gotten tacos." She frowned. "They don't have tacos in Louviers. That's sad. We should start up a taco truck."

I looked back over my shoulder to see that Ludo was kissing the crap out of Erik. Man, I wasn't breaking that one up. Erik was a big boy. He could fend off one professional NHL player, I was sure. I wrapped an arm around Junebug's swerving body. "Sorry, baby girl. No tacos. But I think your mom has leftover cake."

"Oooh, cake!" She raced into the house, and I could hear her pinballing off the hallway walls.

I peeked into the garage and saw it was empty, so thankfully Misha was out. When I made it to the kitchen, Juniper was in the fridge, leaning right in, her ass in those jeans absolutely perfect. I wanted to strip her naked and bend her over any surface she'd let me.

She grinned when she emerged, precariously holding a cake. Quickly rescuing it from her, I grabbed a knife from the drawer while she got plates. Then I put a huge slab on one of the little china dishes, hoping it would soak up some of the alcohol, because she was gonna have a hell of a hangover in about six hours.

She ended up with cream cheese frosting on her nose, and I couldn't resist the urge to lean forward and flick my tongue over it, sucking the frosting into my mouth. She looked up at me, her eyes burning with lust. For me. She was looking at me like she wanted me more than she wanted her next breath, and that was fucking heady.

In the next moment, she shook her head, shaking away the expression. "I'm sorry, Johnny. About yesterday. About throwing a tantrum because you didn't want me. Want more with me, I mean. How big does my head need to be to think you'd have this"—she pointed to her body with a scoff—"and then want to come back for more. I'll try not to make it weird, though maybe it's too late, and I've always made it weird. I just don't want you to think you have to—"

I leaned in and kissed her, swallowing her self-conscious words. I pushed all my feelings into that kiss, everything I wanted to tell her with words but was too scared.

"I want you so fucking much, but drunk as fuck

probably isn't the right headspace for this conversation." I cleared my throat. "I've talked with Erik and Ludo, about what they're proposing for your little group relationship. It's…" Fuck, this was so awkward. "Whatever you want, Junebug, can be yours. Or not. It's all up to you, okay?"

The guys finally came in the front door, and I stepped back as Juniper looked up at me, her eyes wide and shiny. "I want you to come home with us."

I let out a shaky breath. It wasn't a resounding *I'm yours*, but I'd take it. "Okay."

Ludo bounded into the room, his cheeks flushed either from the cold or the fact Erik had been kissing the hell out of him. "Cake!"

CHAPTER
Thirty-Six

JUNIPER

I WOKE up the following morning with a headache, vague memories of dancing on the bartop, and the inside of my mouth feeling like I'd been face-fucked by ALF. Luckily, I must have slept through the worst of my hangover, so I crawled out of bed, drank the large bottle of water beside my bed in one frat-worthy chug, and downed a couple of painkillers.

A knock on the door had me glaring at it blearily. "Yeah?"

Erik ducked his head around the door, his smile one of those smug Mona Lisa ones where they knew all the fucked-up shit you did last night but couldn't remember. *Ugh.*

"Hey, *Einiber.* Just letting you know I've been called back to Detroit early. Apparently, the Infernos want to 'discuss' my departure."

I snorted. Yeah, I just bet they did. They'd gotten

their ass handed to them and realized that a team was only as good as their goalie.

He sat down on the bed, and I pulled back the blanket so he could climb in. Being upright was making my head hurt more. He smiled softly down at me and climbed in. I snuggled into his warmth, the intimacy between us feeling so natural after we'd been through so much together. He pulled my head into the crook of his shoulder, wrapping his other arm around me.

"Have you booked a flight yet?"

He shook his head. "Wanted to talk to you first. They can wait." He kissed the top of my head. "You could come home with me and Ludo, or you can stay longer here and spend some time with your mom. I know you expected a whole week."

I chewed my lip. I knew Mom would be fine with me going home, as long as I promised to come back in the offseason. Ludo had a game in another two days anyway, so I could understand why Erik was happy going home early. I thought about Johnny, and I had brief flashes of him from last night, but not much. I really needed to clear things up with him before I could leave Louviers.

Erik stroked the frown lines on my forehead. "If you're worried about your soldier boy, I think he's already packed and ready to return home with you." His chuckle vibrated against my cheek. "He loves you so much, it's almost painful to watch." Erik tilted my chin up so I was looking at him. I could only imagine the state of my death breath. "I know this is confusing, *Einiber*, but know that none of us will deny you anything. I like Johnny. Ludo loves the man like he's kin. The one thing we have in common is that we all want you, though. If Johnny is willing to share, I'm happy to bring him into the fold. And something tells me he really needs the family now."

I shook my head, not caring how much it hurt. "You can't possibly be okay with sharing, Erik."

He raised his eyebrows at me. "Are you not okay sharing Ludo with me?"

Was I? I'd seen them kiss dozens of times now, maybe more. Behind closed doors, they'd never been particularly subtle with the PDAs. Sure, I'd felt jealous —not because I wanted Ludo all to myself, but because I'd wanted what they had. As soon as the option of being a part of what they had came up, that jealousy was gone. I loved that Erik appreciated Ludo with the same burning passion I did. I loved that Ludo let himself be vulnerable with the goalie the way he did with me.

Plus, I'd spent many a night pulling the idea of being between them in the bedroom out of the RubTub. I was more than happy for them to share me, and to share them in return.

"That's different. You have no other vested interest in Johnny." And there could be no way Johnny was okay with sharing me with Ludo, let alone Erik—who was basically an unknown entity—no matter how well they got along. Sighing heavily, I sat up. "I have to talk to him."

Erik laughed, sitting up with me. He towered over me, even in bed. "That's good, because he's downstairs with his army duffle of worldly possessions, looking delicious." I blinked at him in shock. "Drunk Juniper and Johnny had some serious conversations. Maybe your conscious mind needs to catch up with your subconscious desires." He winked. "I'll book us tickets?"

I chewed my lip, but nodded. "Yes. Please."

Leaning forward, he sucked the lip I was teasing between his own. I gripped the front of his shirt as he deepened the kiss, mastering my mouth until I was gasping. He pulled back, until all I could see were those beautiful ocean eyes, alight with desire, and maybe a little mirth.

One more quick kiss, and he pulled back. "I'll leave you to freshen up before I debauch you in your child-hood bed."

I grinned back at him. "You'd be the first."

He groaned as he pulled himself from the bed, then looked down at me, his eyes hooded. Tilting his head to the side, he stepped back toward my door and closed it softly. "You're too tempting, *Einiber*. I just need a taste."

He stalked back toward me, and my breath caught in my throat. I couldn't comprehend the desire on his face right now. I could only imagine how I looked, like a panda caught in the headlights. Or a Bigfoot sighting.

He reached down and wrapped a hand around my bare foot, his thumb pressing tightly into the arch in a way that felt way too good for a simple touch. "With your permission, sweet one, I'd like to lick your pretty little pussy until you come all over my face."

Breathing wasn't really an option when a Norse god was kneeling at your feet, begging to eat you out. I didn't want to say anything, in case I scared him away before he'd given me an orgasm with that tongue that uttered such filthy things.

So I nodded. Vigorously. *Hangover be damned.*

He grabbed my ankles and spread them wider on the bed, wide enough that he could fit those huge shoulders between them. I was in an oversized t-shirt and boyleg briefs—not exactly lingerie—but the way he was looking at me, it felt like I was wrapped in the most erotic lace and silk.

He kissed the inside of my knee, his lips traveling up my thigh to the edge of my underwear, and I could feel the hot puff of his breath against my damp center. I held my breath as his lips brushed against the gusset of my panties, but then he was back down to my left knee, starting the process of moving up my inner thigh again.

I groaned, and he looked up, grinning like a demon. He knew what he was doing, that was for sure. "You'll have to be quiet, sweet one, because we don't want your mother to hear, do we?" He nipped the fleshy part of my inner thigh as he tugged my underwear down. "Wouldn't want the others to come in and investigate why you're making such pretty noises."

The very idea of Ludo and Johnny watching me come on Erik's face had me trying to drag my thighs together, so I could create a little friction and hopefully some relief. But Erik's big hands spread me wide, his breath puffing across my overheated sex.

"Mmm, maybe you *want* them to watch you... I know they'd be stroking themselves as they watched you ride my tongue like a good girl."

Whoosh. Someone call the tourist bureau—there was a new Niagara Falls, and it was between my thighs, crashing onto the gorgeous planes of Erik's face.

He didn't speak anymore, instead burying his face in my folds, using that tongue to do some seriously wild things that my brain couldn't quite comprehend. It was like he had a forked tongue and fingers that vibrated.

"Unnghhhhgod," was the only thing I could pant out as my thighs slammed around his head. The man might like dick, but that didn't mean he didn't know his way around my vagina, like he could give a guided tour of all the happy spots. I grabbed my pillow and held it over my face so the whole house didn't hear me moaning like a poltergeist.

It felt like two minutes before I was coming in huge, shuddering waves, my hands gripping his hair so tightly that I worried I'd given him a bald spot. You wouldn't know it, though, the way he smirked up at me with that face that looked like an angel but was apparently designed for sin.

I relaxed my thighs, which was harder than it seemed, and disentangled his hair from my fingers. Erik moved up the bed a little until he could rest his cheek on my lower stomach. He stared at me, looking more than a little cum-drunk. "Do you think we can do that every day? I just know it's going to be my favorite way to start the day."

Uh, fuck yeah. I wanted to shout it from the rooftops, maybe get a demonic contract that he could sign in blood, agreeing to tongue-fuck me every morning. Instead, I cleared my throat, giving him what I hoped was a chilled-out smile. "I think that could be arranged."

When I came down from getting cleaned up and dressed, I tried not to flush when I looked at anyone in the room. Hell, I tried not to look at anyone in the room, period. Because if I did, I'd remember the dirty things Erik had whispered to me as he tongue-fucked me into outerspace.

Mom appeared with a coffee, and I gave thanks to whoever arranged for her to be my mom. "I heard you and Robbie did the final scene from *Dirty Dancing* over at The Bar yesterday afternoon," she said, her face somewhere between amused and disapproving.

I groaned. "No, we didn't..." I looked over at Ludo. "Did we?"

He shrugged, looking way too amused and not nearly hungover enough. "I don't remember. You did launch yourself at Johnny, though, so maybe that's where the rumor started."

My eyes flicked to the man in question, who was indeed sitting in the living room, a duffle bag at his feet. I flushed. "I'm sorry. Did I hurt you?"

"Nah. Though you did dry hump me on the floor, so maybe that's where the dirty part came in?"

I groaned again, burying my face in my coffee. God, I was never going to live this down. I stared imploringly at Erik. "You booked tickets out of here, right? Because I don't think I'll ever be able to show my face in town again." I looked at Johnny and tilted my head at the door. "Hey, can I talk to you for a minute?"

His face quickly shut down into that perfect mask of blankness. I *hated* it. I wanted him back to laughing, even if it was at my expense. He followed me out onto the back porch, and I'd obviously underestimated the chill of the wind, because I shuddered as goosebumps so big they were almost painful spread across my skin. Shucking his jacket, Johnny wrapped it around my shoulders, and I was immediately enveloped in his warmth and that scent that was one hundred percent Johnny.

"I'm not sure what I said yesterday, but I hope I didn't make things... weirder."

"I kissed you."

I choked on my own spit. *Dammit, why don't I remember that?* "Did I make you?"

He laughed, stepping closer. "Junebug, I'm a grown man who was in the Marines. I could incapacitate a man twice your size in seconds. I don't think you could *make* me do anything I didn't want to do, and I really, really wanted to kiss you."

"Oh," I breathed. "That's good, because I'm pretty sure I wanted to kiss you too. What else happened?"

His lips were so close to mine now that I could see the tiny scar he got from being hit with a hockey stick when we were in the U16s. "You told me you wanted me to come back to Michigan with you." It was like he was staring straight into my soul. "Do you still want that?"

"Yes." I didn't have to think about my answer. Didn't weigh up the pros and cons, didn't leave room for doubt. My gut said yes, and more than that, my heart said yes too.

The smile returned to his face, making me breathe a relieved sigh. "Okay. Lucky, because I already cleared out of my room at Robbie's house, and I'm pretty sure Marianne is turning it into a yoga studio as we speak, so I can never stay there again." I snorted, because that sounded like a Marianne thing to do. Johnny wrapped his hands around my waist and tugged me closer. "You can have it all, Junebug. Take what you want."

Those words in his dark, melodious voice echoed inside my head, like déjà vu.

So I leaned forward and kissed him. I knew what I wanted. I wanted him. I wanted *them*. And I was going to take it with open arms and an open heart, and hope for the best.

CHAPTER
Thirty-Seven

ERIK

MY AGENT, Nick, was pissed. Burn-it-to-the-ground level pissed. Firstly, because it had been a ridiculously backward notion to bench me, not for my performance, but for my sexuality. He'd seriously tried to convince me to sue the Infernos. If I didn't want this whole thing to be over and be well and truly out of the spotlight, I might have taken his advice.

The second reason was that they'd tried to negotiate my suspension without him present. He should have at least gotten a courtesy call that the meeting was going to happen, but the first he'd heard of it was when I'd called him, telling him I was quitting and running away to Colorado. That had put him seriously offside.

The final nail in their coffin was that they thought I was desperate enough to come back when they called, like I was a kicked dog. Nick had been very adamant that I make them sweat for a little while before coming back from Colorado for negotiations. Apparently, they'd been calling Nick, and me, since I'd walked out of that first meeting.

Fuck them, I didn't need them—a fact Nick made sure I knew.

"I've gotten three offers from other teams about picking up your contract, even though you haven't officially been offered for trade by the Infernos. If you want out, we can make it very clear to them that it's in their best interests to trade you."

The problem was, I didn't *want* to be traded. Not really. I liked being this close to Ludo and Juniper, and what if I was traded south, to Florida or somewhere?

Still, I needed the GM to believe that I wasn't bluffing. He needed to think that I really would fuck off back to Iceland until my contract expired. *Good luck staying below the salary cap, you bigoted asshole.* I'd play in the CHL in Europe if I had to, but I wasn't going to sit around and be the punching bag for anyone.

We were shown into the conference room, where the GM was sitting, looking extremely solemn. Coach King was there also, along with people from different departments who I didn't know. Stacey was conspicuously absent, and I clenched my jaw. Apparently, I was going into this meeting with no voice of reason.

There was a man a few decades younger than the GM sitting at the head of the table. I frowned at him, and Nick must have felt my tension, because he leaned in close. "Mac Wentworth. His family trust owns the team. The family doesn't usually bother with the front-of-house stuff like this, but I guess this was big enough to drag him home from Barbados."

I gave the man a respectful nod, and he gave me a crooked smirk back. Okay, so maybe he was only forty or so. Handsome, in a super rich way. Not my type, though.

The GM cleared his throat. "Thanks for attending, Erik." His tone suggested I'd been the problem, or maybe I was just being sensitive. He looked down at the papers in front of him. "We apologize for this whole mess. We have enacted team-wide sensitivity training, as well as refreshers on discrimination and harassment."

What, did he want an award for doing the bare minimum?

Nick was apparently unimpressed with their half-hearted attempts too. "That's great, Frank. Thank you for showing some common decency. But as you can imagine, my client has lost some serious faith in his team after this debacle. We'd all assumed that basic human rights were an unwritten clause in the player contract, but maybe we need to be more explicit?"

Frank, the GM, frowned at Nick, and I could see him trying to resist having Nick thrown out. "As you can imagine, it caught us off guard. We have Pride and

Inclusivity nights during preseason, so the Infernos clearly support the LGBT agenda."

I raised an eyebrow. "Agenda?"

He huffed. "Lifestyle."

"Lifestyle?" I echoed. Was this guy for real?

Luckily, someone from HR was there to reel the conversation back in. "We believe that the last two weeks have been a real learning experience for the team."

"This is bullshit. You want to talk about player contracts?" The contract manager gave Nick a shark-like smile. "We can sue your ass for breach of contract too."

Nick started yelling, as did the lawyers, each trying to out-balls the other one. I sat back, wondering how my dream of playing in the NHL had gone so fucking sideways. Well, I knew how it had gone sideways, but I'd never thought that me liking another player was going to be such an issue. That was probably pretty naive of me.

I didn't fool myself into believing I'd be sent back to free agency. I was too valuable a player, so they'd try to trade me—and trade me soon, before the deadline. The Infernos might be heading for the playoffs, though the last three games without me had been losses. I didn't think I was a one-man team, but there was clearly tension among the players, which translated on game nights.

I guess, in a way, that was my fault, but that tension had been building long before I got busted getting my dick sucked by the IceCaps star player.

Mac Wentworth leaned forward, resting his elbows on the table, his black shirt unbuttoned at the collar and his fingers steepled beneath his chin. "Do you want to be traded, Mr. Luthersson?"

It was a simple question, with a complicated answer. "I want to be in a club that respects me."

He shook his head. "That's not what I asked. Do you like the Infernos? Do you like Detroit?"

Fuck, he probably knew that I wouldn't leave unless I had to, just to stay close to Ludo and Juniper. "I like the area just fine. Most of the team are okay guys. Coach King is a decent coach."

"Don't give me a big head there, Luthersson," Coach muttered with mock irritation.

I gave him a tight smile, then looked back at Mac Wentworth. "If I could stay without compromising my self-worth, I would. But I won't stay just because it would be easier."

He nodded. "Daisy Monderra has informed me that the very concept of my team benching you for being gay is abhorrent. She appears to be on a one-woman crusade to drag the NHL into the twenty-first century."

"Who?"

Nick leaned close to me. "The daughter of the owner of the IceCaps. My friend Tony—he's the agent for a couple of IceCaps players—said she was pretty instrumental in the way their polyamory scandal was handled last year. Said she put her foot down and insisted that the team stay the hell out of players' relationships, unless they're unlawful." He grinned at Mac. "She seems like a firecracker."

Mac smiled, and there was more than a little desire on his face. "She's definitely something. She keeps staring me down and telling me that she's the future of the NHL, and I better get with it or get out of the way." He shook his head again, looking amused. "I think she may be right."

I didn't want to tell them what Melville had said to me—I wasn't about to out other players—but I nodded. "I think so too."

He chuckled. "She usually is." His face transformed, once again all business. "I'm asking you to stick out the season with us, Luthersson. I'm asking you to play like this is the team you want to stay with forever, and we'll work on making it worthy of long-term players. Because you're a damn fine goalie, and they aren't quite as common as members of this team seem to believe. While we could get a good trade with you, I don't think the league has a goalie that's of an equal value on the ice, so we'll do what we can to keep you." He looked me dead in the eye, though his tone remained light. "It's much easier to find defensive forwards or wingers than it is to find a goaltender of your caliber, especially at this stage of your career."

Was he telling me that he was going to replace the

players who had a problem with me? Because that seemed damn unlikely, especially when Rusket had several cronies who also made my life miserable. No one was going to change their whole roster to keep one player, no matter how valuable Mac Wentworth thought I was.

I looked at Nick, who tilted his head at me, a non-verbal way of telling me that this one was up to me. Sucking in a fortifying breath, I nodded. "I'll stay until the end of the season. Hopefully, this shit all blows over, but if it doesn't, I want to be traded." I'd deal with the fallout of that later. I doubted my time in the Infernos would get any better, though, considering Rusket was still on the team, and he'd been an asshole well before all of this media bullshit.

Mac thrust out his hand. "I hope it won't come to that, but if it does, we'll trade you. Somewhere favorable to us both, hopefully."

I shook his hand, hoping that a gentleman's agreement would hold up against the Board, should he go back on his word.

Nick worked out the finer details with everyone, so I sat back and just listened as the suits around this table decided my future for me. Autonomy was something you gave up when you got drafted into the NHL. A fundamental part of the dream, even if it was a shitty part.

An hour later, I stood, shaking hands with Mac Wentworth, as well as Frank the GM. Coach walked us out, silent until we made it to the elevators. "Stay with me and Mr. Wentworth for just a little longer, Erik. There are changes coming that are long overdue and well above my paygrade."

I nodded. I'd already agreed to that, but my brain turned over his words in my head, trying to make sense of them. I hated this league politics bullshit. I just wanted to play the game I loved, go home at night to whoever I wanted to, and be happy.

With that thought firmly in my brain, I said goodbye to Nick and Coach, and headed out to the parking garage. I would stop and get some flowers for Juniper and Ludo. I knew there was some rule that you weren't supposed to buy flowers for men, but I'd never understood why. They were a beautiful way to say that I was thinking about him.

Seeing a romance bookstore on the way, I had a better idea for *Einiber*. I'd seen those books that she liked to read on her e-reader, even though she made the font really small on the plane so I could only catch the titles over her shoulder. But the titles gave me more than enough clues, and I'd gone home to research.

To say I'd been pleasantly entertained was an understatement.

I walked into the romance bookstore, which had a surprising number of people in it for this time of the day. Someone gasped, and almost as one, they all turned to stare at me. Giving them a big smile, I tried not to feel like a deer in the headlights. I guess they didn't get many hockey players in here?

I looked at the closest woman who was wearing a name badge. "I would like a book about orcs who have sex with women. Actually, multiple orcs who have sex with one woman. Is there a word for that?"

"A gangbang?" a customer with crazy, curled hair suggested. Was she wearing a pin that said *Smack my ass and call me a good girl*?

A teenager shook her head from where she stood behind the register. Her hair was purple on one side and Cookie Monster blue on the other. "No, he means reverse harem. Sometimes we call it Why Choose as well. Because, you know, the leading female doesn't have to choose who to, uh, love? You want them all to be in love, right? Not just straight-up smut?"

Now it was my turn to look blank. "There's different genres depending on the level of smut?"

The teenager laughed at me. "There's different genres depending on the number of appendages, so yeah. Definitely different genres depending on the spice."

She disappeared into the shelves and returned with an armful of books, each of them with a buff-looking green guy on the front, wearing a furry loincloth and bearing tusks. Some had a bosomy woman on the front, who was one stiff wind from being completely naked. One even had a green guy in a business suit. Another was titled *Bride for the Twelve Orc Brothers*. That seemed like a lot of orc dick.

How the hell did I even choose? "I think I'm out of my depth…"

The women all laughed. And that was how I became a member of the Cinnamon Rolls and Alphaholes Book Club.

CHAPTER
Thirty-Eight

LUDO

THE TEAM RALLIED around me in a way that kind of made me want to cry, but quite frankly, I didn't want to appear weaker than I already did. Apparently, you suck one dick and you're no longer the macho ladies' man you've been since puberty.

Muss, Rigby and River in particular had all shut down anything even remotely negative coming from the team. River took it a little further during game day, nailing an opposing player who'd called me a faggot into the boards so hard, the guy hit the ground like a lead weight and struggled to regain his feet. After that, the slurs weren't so quick, and River mean-mugged every single person who looked in my direction.

I had something to prove—hell, maybe we all did—and I played hard, scoring another two goals that game. We trounced the Columbus Explorers 7-2 on their own ice. I smirked at those fuckers as we shook hands at the end of the game. I might like dick, but I liked hockey just as much, and I was fucking good at it.

Coach Toons didn't even chew River out for spending so much time on the bench throughout the game. It was like he knew we had something to prove and was happy to let us have our moment, especially since the game was such a solid win.

Erik was back playing tonight, and after I showered, I flicked on my phone, pulling up the livestream of their game in Chicago. They were losing, and it didn't take me long to work out why. I didn't know what the fuck the Infernos defense were doing, but they kept leaving Erik wide open. He could only block so many shots before one snuck past, especially with Rusket not doing his fucking job. By the looks of it, only one of the rookies was defending the goal with any kind of effort, but they were being swamped by Chicago's strong offense line.

"For fuck's sake, do something," I growled at my phone, and Muss came over with a frown.

"Something wrong?"

I turned my phone to show him the fact they'd once again left the goal wide open, and it was purely Erik's insane reflexes stopping it being the worst loss in recent memory. Muss frowned, watching Laurens yelling at Rusket, his hand wrapped in Rusket's jersey.

"Where the fuck is their captain?" Muss demanded, his tone thick with disgust. "Woodward always was a lazy fuck. How he's still their captain is a mystery. No wonder they're a mess on the ice—starts with shitty leadership."

The buzzer sounded to signal the end of the second period, and Erik ripped off his headgear. I didn't need to be on the ice with him to know that he was pissed. His jaw was tense, and his gaze was burning.

Muss huffed. "I don't know what they're trying to prove, but they're just making themselves look incompetent. The only person looking any good out there is your boy. I think Soukal would wet herself if he was ever traded to the IceCaps. A talent like that would ensure they both entered the history books."

Sighing, I flicked my phone off and put it in my pocket. "Yeah. I don't think he'll be traded, though, plus Virtanen's way too good to warrant a trade. We've put way too much into him now. If I was an Inferno, this game alone would tell me I had greater problems within the team, and they don't stem from Erik."

Muss made a noise of agreement and slapped me on the back. "Julieta wants to have a cookout before it gets too cold. Next weekend. Bring Erik if he's around, so he can get to know the family. Nova and the guys are coming too. And bring Junie and Friar Puck—the kids love that damn cat. Every time, they're like, 'Papa, we want a cat-dog.' God knows, those kids are enough work without a giant-ass cat as well."

I nodded. "Can I bring my friend from home? He's staying with me and Juniper."

Muss waved a hand as we walked to the bus. "Bring

whoever you like. Julieta always caters for a small army anyway."

We turned the corner to see one of the Explorers wingers—the one who River had knocked the fuck out —standing there. He scowled at me. "You're fucking disgusting. Your kind doesn't have any place in the NHL."

Muss stepped forward, fury on his face, but I grabbed his arm. The last thing I—or the team—needed was for him to be dragged over the coals for starting a fight in my defense.

"What kind is that? People who can hold a hockey stick and actually get the puck in the net? Or people who don't fuck their sister with their eyes closed, because it doesn't count if you can't see her, right?" I laughed right in his red, outraged face. "Fuck you, Cockington. You're a shit player, and an even shittier human. You're already a loser—don't add sore to the title."

I sneered at him, looking him up and down, like he wasn't worth my time or even the oxygen he was stealing from the rest of us. *Bigoted piece of shit.*

Turning, I strode away, but I should've known better. You didn't turn your back on an idiot, because they were usually too stupid to know when they were beaten.

Muss yelled something, but I was too slow. A blow connected with my temple, the fist of Cockington the only thing I saw as my head snapped to the side, throwing me off-balance. I went down like a sack of shit, the back of my head connecting with the concrete, making me see stars.

Then there was nothing but darkness.

I woke up to the team doctor standing over me, with arena security surrounding us. Coach Toons was yelling, but I couldn't make out the words.

Doc put a gentle hand on my shoulder. "Andrei, you've had a blow to the head. Can you tell me what year it is?"

"Did we win?"

Someone laughed, but it was a strangled sound. Doc just gave me a patient look. "The year?"

My head throbbed, making me wince. "2023. Did we win?"

Muss appeared in my periphery, looking rough. His eye was swollen, and he had a busted lip. "He won't chill out until he knows," he informed Doc. "We won, Ludo, but you got punched on the way out of the arena." He spat the words, with a slight lisp to his voice, like he'd damaged his jaw. I hoped the other guy looked worse. Rigby was behind him, his eyes worried.

I nodded, then winced. "The Matadors are good. I didn't think we would," I mumbled. "Definitely going to the playoffs."

Fuck, my head hurt, especially when Doc shone his little light in my eyes.

Panic flashed across Muss's face, and he looked back at the guys behind him. "Get Junie out here. Erik, too." Rigby's expression went from worried to straight-up panicked as he dragged his phone from his pocket. Muss looked over me at Doc, who was still trying to blind me with his little torch. "He's lost two weeks of his life. We played the Matadors twelve days ago."

Oh fuck. I knew enough about concussions to know that was a bad sign.

The EMTs rushed me off to their truck, Doc with us. My head throbbed, and I was so fucking tired, but I knew the pain would go away if I could just sleep.

"Open your fucking eyes, Ludo." Doc's gruff voice seemed irritated, more so than usual. He usually swore a lot, which was why he got on so well with Coach Toons. They both swore like sailors on shore leave.

I wanted Bug. And my cat. And Erik, though I couldn't say that out loud, because then everyone would know I was in love with a man. And probably my best friend.

The EMT next to me was trying to look professional, but whatever was on his face made Doc snap. "Patient confidentiality still applies to EMTs, boy, so keep what you hear to yourself or the IceCaps will sue the shit out of you."

Was I going to die?

"No, Ludo, you aren't going to die. You're just saying shit out loud. We all know about Erik—hell, the whole world knows. Junie is a bit of a surprise, but then again, not really. You've mooned after that girl for as long as I've known you. Muss is getting her down here. Erik, too. The cat will probably have to stay home, though."

I frowned, his words difficult to think about with the almighty pounding in my head. I closed my eyes again, but Doc woke me up once more.

"You've lost two weeks, Ludo, and that's concerning. I'm going to talk to the doctor in the ER, to make sure everything is okay. They'll do a few scans, then we'll see if you can rest, son. The police will probably want to interview you regarding the altercation before you got hit, though I'm not sure you're going to be a lot of help. Muss was there, luckily, and he'll be able to fill in the gaps."

I nodded, though the pain was fucking unbearable. "Will I be able to play tomorrow?" I didn't even know who we were playing tomorrow. Or if we even had a game.

Doc shook his head. "You just worry about getting better, kid. You might be good, but not even your big head could survive a kiss with concrete."

Fuck. "Is Muss okay?" He'd looked pretty fucked up when I saw him.

Doc nodded. "Yeah, he's all good. I checked him out, and he's in much better shape than the other guy. I imagine he'll meet us at the hospital."

"I just want Juniper," I mumbled. *And Erik.*

He grabbed my hand. "They're coming, Ludo. Don't worry. They'll be here soon."

I hoped so, because I wouldn't believe it would be okay until Bug was there, holding my hand, telling me so.

I couldn't hold my eyes open anymore, no matter how much Doc asked me to. I fell back into the blackness, away from the pain in my head.

CHAPTER

Thirty-Nine

JUNIPER

*Ludo's been injured. Someone sucker-punched him, and he's
got a brain injury. You gotta get down here.*

RIGBY ENGMAN'S words snapped at my heels like
a hound from Hell. Luckily, Johnny was here, and
he took control as soon as I got the words out past
my lips. He grabbed my keys, set up Friar Puck's
timed feeder, packed a bag of Ludo's stuff he might
need, and pushed me to grab some things of
my own.

We were out of the house and in Ludo's car within
fifteen minutes of the call. I still hadn't replaced my car
yet, after the… incident. Columbus, where the guys had
been playing, was three hours away from Ann Arbor,
and Rigby said the guys were at the hospital now,
waiting for updates.

I called Erik, but he was still on the ice. I left him

both a voice message and a text, telling him to call me, that Ludo had been injured.

I stared out the window as Johnny drove us down the freeway. Ludo had been hurt before, of course. It was the nature of the sport. You didn't survive in the league if you couldn't take a hit on the ice and just get back up. He'd never had a concussion, though. The helmets were there to protect the guys, and even when they fought on the ice, they rarely did it without their helmets. Concussions meant you couldn't play, and no matter how pissed you were, a hockey player wanted to be on the ice more than anything.

But this was different. Rigby had said it was a guy who'd been hounding Ludo on the ice, who'd approached him and Muss as they left the arena. Ludo had cut the guy down, and the guy punched him in the side of the head as he walked away.

Muss had broken the fucker's jaw before security turned up, but a look at the security tapes had absolved Muss of any assault charges, since the guy had been stepping toward Ludo to kick him while he was down. It was a clear defense of another person.

The guy himself was in hospital, getting his jaw wired shut.

The rage I felt was all-consuming. Not Johnny, though; his face was clear and determined. If I didn't know him so well, and didn't see the slight tic in his cheek, I'd think he didn't care. No, the Marines had taught my rage-filled, hot-headed friend to compartmentalize that fury. I wasn't sure if that was a bad thing or not, but right now? I appreciated the fuck out of it, because I was a mess.

> Rigby: He's got a bit of swelling, but no bleeding. They're giving him medication and putting him into an induced coma to keep the swelling under control.

> Rigby: They won't let us in to see him, but Doc's keeping us updated.

My phone rang, and it was Erik. His voice came through the car speakers. "What happened?" He was quiet as I filled him in on everything. "I'm getting a taxi to the airport now. I'll be there as soon as I can." His voice was soothing and calm, though he let out a shuddering breath. "Drive carefully, Johnny. I don't need all three of you in hospital beds."

The longest three hours of my life later, I flew out of the car toward the doors of the hospital. I paused, looking back at Johnny, but he waved me on. "I'll park. Go and check on Ludo," he said firmly, and I nodded, hustling to the front desk.

The receptionist was typing fast, but looked up with a harried smile. "How can I help you?"

"I'm looking for Andrei Ludokov's room."

The woman frowned. "Are you family?"

I nodded impatiently. "I'm his next of kin. His girlfriend," I informed her, trying not to stumble over the word.

She looked me up and down skeptically. Fury traveled through my veins, but she was saved by River. "Junie?" he called, and I scowled at the woman as I moved toward the big defenseman.

"Is he awake? Can I see him?" I asked in a rush, and River propelled me forward with a large hand between my shoulderblades.

He shook his head. "No, they're keeping him under for forty-eight hours at least, to make sure the swelling goes away and his brain's given time to rest. Doc will explain it all to you."

I nodded, my heart thumping hard in my chest. I walked into a quiet ward and noticed all of the IceCaps players there, overfilling the cheap plastic chairs, or leaning against the walls. Rigby was sitting on the floor, with Muss beside him, his head resting back against the wall. His face was a mess.

I looked between every single one of the men on the team, then back down at Muss, and I burst into tears. They were all here for Ludo.

River looked down at me, horrified, like my tears were made from acid, but Muss stood, making his way to me. He held out his arms, and I stepped into them, sobbing against his chest. He rubbed my back, making soft noises that I was pretty sure he used with his kids. "Shhh, it's okay. He's going to be just fine. He's got the hardest head around. It'd take more than a punch to keep him down."

He was in a fucking coma, and even though it was medically induced, I couldn't help the fear that maybe they wouldn't be able to wake him up from it. That could happen, right?

Muss continued to stroke my back, until Doc appeared. "Juniper?" I pulled back and looked at the grizzled old team doctor. "Come on back. Ludo's neuro specialist wants to talk to you, as his next of kin."

I stepped away from Muss, and he squeezed my shoulder. River patted my back gently, then Rigby was on his feet too, giving me a quick side squeeze. "Tell him we're thinking of him, okay?"

I swallowed hard, the tears brimming again. "Erik will be here…"

Rigby pushed me gently toward Doc. "We'll let you know when Erik gets here, and fill him in. Go."

I followed Doc through the doors to the ICU, past the curtained-off beds and loudly beeping machines. When we got to the end of the row, I saw Ludo and sucked in a painful breath. He looked so pale and was hooked up to a breathing apparatus.

"Miss Verne, you're Andrei's next of kin?"

I noticed the other doctor at the end of the bed. "Yes. Please, call me Juniper."

The doctor nodded. "Juniper, I know this all looks very scary, but it is more precautionary than anything. We are giving his brain a timeout, to prevent it swelling further, and to prevent further complications from occurring. The CT and MRI showed no hematomas, which is good news. He was unconscious for less than three minutes, with a small amount of amnesia, headaches, slurred speech, and confusion. All signs of a level-three concussion. We'll assess any lasting effects of the blow once we wake him in a couple of days."

He gave me a reassuring smile. "All in all, the signs are very promising that he'll make a full recovery, but we'll take it as it comes, okay?" I nodded. "Now, I got a fairly good medical history from the team doctor here, but I need to know if he's had any other concussions—maybe in his college days, or before that?"

I shook my head. "No, my mom wouldn't let us play without helmets, even in the backyard, so he's never had any kind of head injury." It was probably a miracle, really.

The doctor noted something down. "That's good. Any other health problems, or family history of strokes, high blood pressure, seizures?"

"No. His mom died of cancer a few years ago, but his dad's healthy, and his sister is a marine biologist in Australia." His dad was as healthy as an alcoholic could be, I guess.

The doctor smiled. "High-achieving family." He scribbled a few more notes. "Okay, let me know if you have any concerns." With that, he left, and I walked over to Ludo, grabbing his hand.

"Goddammit, Ludo," I whispered.

Doc gave my shoulder a pat. "I'll go and send the

players home, now that you're here. They didn't want him to be alone, even though no one was allowed back here with him but me."

I bit my lip, not able to drag my eyes from Ludo's sleeping face. "Thank you, Doc. And tell the team I said thank you too."

"He asked for you repeatedly. You and Erik."

Tears welled again in my eyes, but I managed to hold them in until Doc left. I leaned forward, resting my head on Ludo's chest, the steady beep on the monitor in time with his heartbeat against my forehead. I breathed in his scent, the hint of his cologne that was still on his skin after his post-game shower.

"I love you, you giant asshole, so you better wake up or else."

Keeping hold of his hand, I sat down on the hard plastic chair beside his bed, my head resting on the bars that kept him contained and safe. Breathing in and out in time with the ventilation machine, I let myself relax slightly. The doctor had seemed confident, and I had to trust that.

But this was my Ludo, and I loved him. I loved him so fucking much, but I hadn't even told him. He could have been stolen from me by a fucking punch from some hockey jock, and he would never have known that I'd loved him since I was fourteen, ever since he beat the snot out of Tony Meyer for pushing me into the goal.

I'd never been more scared in my life.

Pulling my phone from my back pocket, I slowly texted the group chat one-handed, informing them what the doctor had said.

> Johnny: In the waiting room. Not going anywhere. Tell the mouthy prick that I love him too, and I'm going to teach him to be more aware of his surroundings from now on.

> Erik: I've landed. I'm almost there. Keep our guy safe for me, Einiber.

Our guy. I tried to think how this would've gone if Johnny hadn't been there, making sure everything was done with cool efficiency, getting me into the car and focusing on the road. It would have taken me twice as long, and I probably would have crashed into other cars, distracted by what was happening.

I would have had to sit here, alone and worried, afraid to leave because I wouldn't want him to wake up alone. I'd have had no one to lean on, because for so long, Ludo was the only person I turned to when things went bad.

For the first time, I could see the ideal that Erik was herding us toward, the family he was weaving us into. The way I could rely on them all, love them all, and know they had my back.

I was all in, and to hell with what anyone said.

I HATED HOSPITALS. They all smelled the same, like disinfectant and death. I'd spent so long in the VA hospital, recovering from my thigh wound, that I'd hoped to never set foot in one again. I saw men there come and go; some left with family, some left in a body bag.

I'd messaged Robbie and told him what had happened, and he made me promise to keep him updated. Only Marianne being down south at her sister's place stopped him from getting on a plane here to sit with us, since he was stuck at home caring for the kids until she returned.

Pushing the fear from my body, I stared at the water-stained ceiling of the ICU's waiting room. They'd done the room up in soft furnishings and pale-colored walls, but they'd missed the growing stain on the ceiling. You could tell the type, a slow drip that came from nowhere and pooled in a low spot in the gap between the floors. You'd have to dig and rip to find the source of that leak, and everyone would probably deem it too hard. So they'd paint over it and hope for the best.

"Johnny?"

My head turned at the sound of Erik's voice. Ludo's teammates had just left at the insistence of the coach, but they'd all slapped me on the back and told me to look after Juniper and Ludo. Most of them I'd only met once, when I'd gone with Ludo to run drills after he'd booked some time on the ice.

Erik's face was brimming with concern. "How is he?"

I sucked in a breath until my lungs expanded painfully, then let it all out. "No more news since Junebug sent that message. I don't think we'll know if there's any lasting damage until they wake him up."

Erik nodded, sitting down beside me. "And Juniper? How is she?"

I'd never seen her so panicked. It was like she could see all her dreams slipping away, and the cool, confident woman I knew had dissolved into a jumpy, scared creature. "She was a mess, but she's better now she's spoken to the doctor, I think." I looked at Erik's knitted brows, the way his jaw was flexing with tension. "She'll be okay too. She hates it when we get injured. Hates to see us in pain."

The look of helplessness on her face after my flashback still haunted me.

Erik nodded. "And how are you?"

This time, I raised my eyebrows at him. "I went to war. Survived firefights. I'm fine."

He tilted his head, leaning in close until our arms were just touching. "There is a difference between a job where everyone knows the risks, and watching the people you love in distress. Besides, I can only imagine how you feel about hospitals."

My face snapped toward his, and the knowing look in those clear blue eyes made my chest constrict. "I'm *fine*."

He squeezed my shoulder. "I know you are. I'll let Juniper know I'm here. Maybe give her a bit of a break from sitting beside him." His fingers flew across the screen of his phone.

Moments later, Juniper reappeared.

"Make her rest, Johnny. She won't like it, but she'll need it. I'll stay with him." He stood and walked over to Juniper, dragging her into his arms and kissing her softly. They spoke in low tones, and I marveled at how easily Erik held her, like she belonged with him. I envied the ease they clearly felt together, unburdened by years of history between them. A fresh start as adults.

Finally, he kissed her again, before nudging her in my direction. He gave me a wink but as he turned to go into the ICU, I saw the worry lining his face. He was holding it together for Junebug.

We all were.

Standing, I took a page from Erik's book and pulled her close to me. "Okay, Junebug?"

She nodded, but it was half-hearted. "I'll be better when he's awake and giving me hell, you know?"

I grunted my agreement. We'd all be better then. I led her to the elevator, pressing the button for the ground floor. It was late now, two a.m., and Junebug's eyes were so heavy, I was worried she'd fall asleep before we got to the car.

I'd grabbed us all a room at the closest hotel, which was less than five minutes away. Fortunately, because I was exhausted too. The drive was short, but every mile made my body feel heavier. I was out of practice being awake for such long hours, and I hadn't been sleeping well anyway.

Juniper was barely awake when I pulled into the hotel parking lot. Grabbing her bag, I helped her from the car and led us up to the room. "Come on, Junebug. Let's get you into bed," I whispered, and she looked up at me with those big eyes that broke my heart.

"Kiss me, Johnny?" Her voice sounded so lost.

Shutting the door behind us, I led her over to the bed. She slumped down onto it, and I kneeled at her feet. "I'll kiss you anytime you ask, Junebug. But you don't have to worry. None of us are going anywhere; I swear it to you." I didn't care what deals with the devil I had to make, I was keeping my promise.

She grabbed my cheeks and pulled me closer, until her lips were brushing across mine. My hands bracketed her hips, and even on my knees, she was only slightly taller than me. "Don't make me beg," she breathed, and I gave in. Closing the distance between our lips, I kissed her softly. But my girl, she didn't want to be soft. She wanted to chase away her demons, and she pulled me in tighter, chasing my tongue with hers.

Groaning, I got off my knees, pushing her back onto the bed until I was above her, controlling the kiss. Controlling Junebug.

"Yes. More..." She breathed the plea, or maybe it was an incantation, because my dick was growing harder behind my jeans like it was being summoned to her hand. It had always been hers; every part of me had always been hers. Not that I hadn't tried to chase her memory away with a lot of meaningless sex. But I could never quite shake Juniper.

She wrapped her legs around the backs of my thighs, dragging me closer to her. Her sweet little body cradled mine, as if it was made to fit against me. I kissed my way down her body, over her collarbone, nipping her sweet little rosebud nipples until she rolled her body against me.

I would worship her body until she forgot her worries, forgot the fear that coated her like an oil slick.

She grabbed my hair, which had grown out a little since I'd been home. Pulling my head back gently, she stared up at me. I wanted to kiss those lips. She was an addiction now, one that I'd never be able to shake, even if I wanted to.

"Johnny?" she murmured.

"Mmm?" I answered, stroking her sex-wild hair.

"You know this isn't just because of what happened to Ludo, right? That I want you for you?" She rubbed her thumbs over the hard angles of my cheekbones. "I love you. I've loved you forever, but this is different. This is right. I didn't... I don't want to regret never telling you that."

My heart stuttered in my chest, growing three sizes, like I was the Grinch. The desperate boy who still lived inside me crowed with triumph and delight.

I kissed her upturned face. "I love you so much, Junebug. I've loved you forever. Just like this, until my heart stops beating in my chest."

She pulled me closer to her face, and I followed willingly, dying to taste those lips once more. "Then show me."

And I did. I showed her how much I needed her until exhaustion stole consciousness from us both, and we fell asleep, wrapped tightly in each other.

CHAPTER
Forty-One

ERIK

THE SWEET NURSE handed me another coffee and a small packet of cookies, giving me a kind smile. Well, maybe it was a little bit flirty too, but all the nursing staff seemed enamored by the sleeping Ludo. I had to admit, it just made him look like a tragic Disney prince, if a bit of a role reversal. I'd tried kissing him, but he hadn't woken. Not that kind of fairytale, I guess.

He'd been asleep for two days now, and every single minute had felt like torture. No matter how much I told myself that it was just medicine keeping him in this state, I felt his absence like a burning pit in my chest. They'd turned off the ventilator thing earlier this morning, and waiting for him to breathe on his own had been the worst fifteen seconds of my life.

Guilt swamped me. This was my fault. He was here, in a medically induced coma, because I'd opened him up to this hate.

It was almost time for Juniper to take her shift sitting beside him. Johnny had been ferrying us around, making sure we ate and slept, but he didn't sit beside Ludo. The wariness in his eyes, the way his gaze darted around whenever he was in the ICU, told me that he wasn't mentally okay with sitting in here. I wouldn't push him. He was helping in his own way, especially when Juniper always returned less stressed, more optimistic after she'd been to the hotel.

It was too late to have regrets about how this had all gone down. Logically, I knew that no matter how our relationship came out, players like Cockington were always going to be there, hiding in the shadows, ready to attack like cowards. But that didn't help the guilt.

A doctor appeared and frowned in my direction. "Oh, hello. You are?"

"Erik. I'm Ludo's boyfriend."

Both of the doctor's eyebrows rose in surprise. "Oh, I thought Juniper…"

I nodded, giving him my polite smile. I shouldn't have to explain this bullshit every day, but here we were. "She's his girlfriend. We're polyamorous," I said quietly.

He cleared his throat, his eyes darting over to the nurse, who just shrugged. Well, at least they didn't gossip about our relationship with the entire hospital. "Oh, I see. Well, Andrei seems to be breathing fine on his own now, so we're going to wake him. It may take a few minutes, or even hours, for him to be fully cognizant." He nodded at the nurse, and they began to prep him, attaching another small bag to his IV machine. As they did so, the doctor continued to explain how the whole thing worked, though it was hard to hear him over the thundering of my rapid heartbeat.

Before I had a chance to message her and tell her they were waking Ludo up, Juniper appeared at the curtain of the cubicle. I smiled softly at her. "They're going to wake him up," I whispered, as the doctor and nurses spoke back and forth. She walked toward me, trying to stay out of the way of the medical professionals. The doctor's eyes flicked to where my hand rested on her waist, but he didn't say anything.

"Will he wake straight up?" she asked softly, and I answered for the doctor.

"He said they were short-acting sedatives, so it could take minutes, or it could take hours." She nodded, her eyes on Ludo's face, like she would miss the moment he woke if she so much as blinked.

Finally, the doctor leaned down close to Ludo. "Andrei, can you hear me?"

Nothing. He didn't stir. Didn't blink.

I felt Juniper tense beneath my hand, and I rubbed the curve of her hip reassuringly. *It could take hours,* I reminded myself, even though I was feeling that same panic. He'd be fine. I just had to convince myself that was true.

"Ludo," Juniper said softly, leaning over his bed.

"Wake up now. I need you to wake up." I had a feeling if the doctor wasn't here, she'd goad him into consciousness. It was the kind of relationship they had. To prove my point, she leaned closer. "The doctor's really handsome, and if you don't wake up, he might sweep me off my feet." I snorted, and hoped the doctor in question couldn't hear her. "Wake up, Ludo. Come on, baby."

I watched his eyelashes flutter on his cheeks, my heart in my throat. "Come on, *Laglegur*. You've lain around for long enough. Wake up," I said firmly, and those lashes fluttered again. The nurse nodded encouragingly at us.

Juniper ran her thumb across Ludo's bottom lip. "I love you, Andrei Ludokov, so wake your lazy bones up before I get mad and kick your ass again. I love you so fucking much."

This time, his eyelids flicked open. He looked around, clearly confused, until his eyes landed on Juniper, and then me.

The doctor drew his attention. "Can you tell me your name?" he asked, and Ludo's eyes slid to him.

"Andrei Ludokov," he croaked. "Call... me... Ludo."

The doctor nodded. "Good work, Ludo. Do you know the month and the year?"

"November, 2023," he rasped out, and my shoulders relaxed a little more. Right month and year. "What happened?"

The doctor murmured a few things to the nurse beside him, then looked down at Ludo. "You sustained a brain injury from an assault. You've been in an induced coma for a couple of days. Do you know what state you're in?"

Ludo frowned, and I held my breath. "Michigan? No. Ohio? We were... playing Ohio."

The doctor made a hum of satisfaction. "Well done. And these two lovely people beside you. Do you know them?"

Ludo's eyes flicked to mine. "My boyfriend, Erik." He looked at Juniper, her eyes big and wet, and his face softened. "Juniper, my best friend and... girlfriend?"

She let out a sob and leaned forward, kissing him sloppily on the lips as her tears fell onto his cheeks. "Fucking hell, Ludo. You scared the shit out of me," she sobbed.

"Sorry... Bug," he rasped, and I pulled Juniper back a little so the nurse and doctor could work.

Soon enough, they finished the rest of their tests, and the doctor was happy with Ludo's progress. He'd go for a few more scans, but if all the tests from today were good, he could go home in a day or two.

Home. It wasn't in my tiny apartment in Detroit anymore. It wasn't even in Iceland. It was these two people in front of me, and even the stony-faced man sitting alone in the waiting room. Soon, we'd all find our home in each other, wherever we were, as long as we were together.

. . .

An awake, but still hospitalized Ludo was a bad-tempered Ludo. I'd heard one of the nurses muttering that they preferred him when he was unconscious, and when she caught me listening, she'd almost had a coronary. But I'd just grinned, because honestly, I didn't blame her. He was irritable and grumpy with anyone who wasn't me or Juniper.

The doctor had said it was part of the concussion, and eventually, he'd be back to his charming, loveable self. Being back home in familiar surroundings would also help.

I think the whole nursing staff breathed a sigh of relief as we left two days later. Johnny was bringing the car around, and when the nurse stopped with the wheelchair at the front door, Ludo popped out of it like a jack-in-the-box.

Johnny walked around the hood, his expression shuttered. "You scared Juniper," was all he said, and Ludo nodded. Something passed between them, something borne of decades of friendship, of loving a person for as long as you'd known what love was.

"I'll do better next time."

"Give me a name, and there won't be a next time," Johnny growled, grabbing Ludo and pulling him into a tight hug. "Sorry I didn't sit beside you. I..." He trailed off, but Ludo just slapped his back.

"I understand, man. Don't worry about it. If I had a

choice about whose face I had to stare at for hours, it probably would've been Bug's anyway." He slid me a mischievous look, his eyes alight. That look made my dick hard every time.

The nurse sighed, and I shook my head. Yeah, this was the Ludo who was so easy to fall in love with. I turned to her. "Thank you again for all your care," I said quietly.

"No thanks necessary," she murmured back as she turned, wheeling the empty chair back inside the hospital.

Juniper helped Ludo into the back of the car, and I knew if she'd been anyone else, he would have snapped at her that he could do it himself. But it was Juniper, and he was enjoying her attention. Plus she'd already threatened to punch him in the tit if he kept being a whiny crybaby.

Finally, everyone was buckled in, and I climbed in the front beside Johnny. "Let's get the hell out of here."

He nodded and pulled out onto the main road, toward the freeway that headed back to Ann Arbor. Within fifteen minutes, both Juniper and Ludo were asleep.

"Did they say how long before he can play again? Because he sprained his ankle mountain biking once when we were seventeen, and he was an asshole until they let him back on the ice. The guy needs skates on his feet like people need air in their lungs."

I knew that feeling. The freedom that came from

being on the ice, flying so fast that you felt almost weightless, was unlike anything. I would hate to lose it, even for just a little while.

"For two more weeks, at least. One more week to recover, and then they'll enact their concussion protocol, easing him back in. The IceCaps doctor will monitor him. There shouldn't be any risk, and they'll ensure he wears all the protective gear so he doesn't reinjure himself."

Johnny nodded. "This was bad, but it was also kinda good, you know?" he said gruffly, not taking his eyes from the road.

I had no fucking idea what that meant. "Oh?"

"Nice that no one had to do it alone. I didn't feel… helpless. Useless just because I couldn't overcome my own fucking head to be in there. I could still do *something*, even if it was just to look after you and Junebug."

This guy. "Juniper couldn't have done it without you. *We* couldn't have done it without you, Johnny. You belong with us."

He grunted his agreement. "I think you're right."

I knew I was. And Johnny was right that there was a silver lining to all this—it was that I was more sure than ever that this was the right decision for me. For us.

CHAPTER

Forty-Two

LUDO

BEING LAID up was the fucking worst. I hated it. But it did mean that either Bug or Erik slept in my bed each night, though neither of them would do more than spoon me. Soon, I wouldn't have to worry about having a stroke, because my blue balls would explode and I'd bleed out all over my silk sheets.

Johnny wouldn't even give me a beer. Doc wouldn't let me back on the ice yet; instead, I had to do gentle exercise and neurocognitive testing. Which was basically standing on a treadmill, walking average Joe slow, while doing a test on the damn tablet. Though tomorrow, they were going to let me go to the gym and lift weights with the guys, maybe do some stretching and balance drills while Doc stared at me as if I were about to keel over.

"Stop being such a fucking whiner," Johnny told me,

not taking his eyes off the TV. Erik was playing again tonight. Some of his team had finally pulled their head out of their asses, because they were doing a better job of keeping the puck away from the net. That could've been due to the fact that Rusket appeared to be benched, not having been out on the ice at all for the last forty minutes.

"I didn't even *say* anything," I grumbled back, glaring at his beer while I sipped my Dr Pepper.

"You're huffing over there like old Mrs. Porie when she saw us… well, anywhere."

Mrs. Porie had hated us. Hated we existed. Hated that we rode our bikes through the street. Hated that we were kids, and worse, boys. Hated that Juniper would hang around with us all, as it was "improper" for a girl to be alone with that many boys.

She'd taken that one to Juniper's parents, who'd put her right in her place. I could still remember the shade of purple her face had turned when Juniper's mom said it was concerning that a mature lady thought of children in that way, and perhaps she should be on a watchlist.

Hadn't stopped her huffing every time we came within twenty feet of her.

I pointed my soda can in the direction of the television. "That should be me."

He raised an eyebrow. "You want to be getting your ass kicked by the third worst team in the conference?"

I gave him a droll look. Juniper was in the kitchen making popcorn, her last free night now that she'd been recalled to her job. Apparently, she could resume her duties now that the narrative about my relationship with Erik had changed from "secret gay player" to "victim of a hate crime."

Unluckily for Cockington, his ejection from the Explorers meant no team would trade for him and his bad press. He was being thrown back into free agency. Not to mention that he'd already been picked up and charged with assault, and the prosecution was going to push for it to be upgraded to charges associated with hate crimes. I felt no remorse, because that asshole had targeted me purely because of my relationship with Erik. If him being charged in a high-profile case could bring that shit to light, then I would stand up there in my best suit and tell the whole world what an asshole he was.

I was tired of this shit. It felt like this whole season had been a shitshow, just one thing after another. I was ready to just settle down with Erik and Juniper into some seriously hot threeways.

I sighed heavily again, and for a second, I thought Johnny might actually punch me, concussion protocol be damned. "I've signed up to teach self-defense classes down at the Y," he said instead, as we watched Erik block another shot, the commentator somewhere between amused and disgusted by the game play.

. . .

"Luthersson once again blocking a sloppy shot from number seventy-seven, Goldsborough. Honestly, JP, Luthersson is really living up to his moniker of the Norse God over the last few weeks. I don't know what is happening with the Infernos defense but my peewee team played better D, and I have it on good authority that at least two of us were still in diapers."

"That's right, Ezra. There's only so much that good stick work and quick hands can do for Luthersson when San Antonio just keeps coming and coming from behind."

Ezra Phillips smothered a laugh. The best part of listening to Ezra Phillips and John Paul Renau commentate was the fact JP was oblivious to sexual innuendo, but Ezra definitely wasn't. Listening to him try to hold back the laughter and subtly rib him was hilarious.

"Indeed, San Antonio must have some big balls to keep coming and coming like that," Ezra teased. *"Number twelve for the San Antonio Vipers shoots it back down the other end, where it's intercepted by Melville, who is having a hell of a rookie year despite what's going on in the Infernos. Fired back down to Laurens, who takes a shot at goal... and SCORES!"*

. . .

I dragged my eyes from the TV back to Johnny. "Self-defense? For, like, women and kids?"

He shrugged. "For whoever wants it. I don't have any other skills, and that shit with Junebug a couple of months ago rattled me. How many other women are going on dates with psychos completely unprepared, you know? I have a little money saved, so I'm not worried about getting paid, but this seems important. At least it gives me something to do, while I wait for that thing I'm supposed to be doing to make itself known."

I squeezed his shoulder. "Take as long as you need. Be a stay-at-home husband if you want. I know I like having you here," I teased, and he gave me a flinty-eyed look. We both knew he'd go stir-crazy stuck at home, doing nothing. "Bug loves having you here, and so do I. Find what you want to do, and we'll support you. One hundred percent."

He nodded, and we went back to the game, while I sighed, wishing it was me out there on the ice.

Juniper came out to sit between us on the couch. She gave me a hard look, then turned to Johnny. "Is he still sighing like an old maid?"

He smirked. "I told him he sounded like Mrs. Porie."

That set them both off. Watching hockey together, just the three of us, was so like old times that it felt right.

Eventually, Erik's team won, and Johnny kissed

Juniper. "I'm going to bed," he said in a low voice that made her shiver. He met my eyes and nodded. "See you in the morning."

He was giving us alone time, and nerves ran along my skin like livewires. I'd played in the second round of the Cup Playoffs and hadn't been this nervous.

"Well, that was subtle," Bug laughed, leaning against my arm. "You're still on concussion protocol. I don't know what he thought would happen."

I frowned. I had blue balls, and she felt so good beside me that I was aching. Once I'd given myself permission to think of Bug *that* way, it had opened up a whole can of sexual fantasy worms that I hadn't been able to shake. Apparently, years of pushing that shit down didn't get rid of the desire, it just made it smolder hotter and hotter until it was threatening to burn me alive.

"I'm allowed to have sex, Bug. I'm not that much of an invalid." I didn't tell her that Doc had only passed me for it today. If she knew that, she'd definitely make us wait another week until she was sure he was sure.

She looked uncertain. "I don't want you to feel like you have to—"

I interrupted her right there. "Nope. Don't even start." I grabbed her hand and moved it to my lap, right over the bulge that was forming beneath my sweats. "I've been walking around with a semi for weeks, knowing I could have you but forced to wait."

"Ludo—"

"Nope, not done. You don't understand, Bug. This thing between us, this attraction that we've always had for each other—but chosen to ignore to protect our friendship—it didn't stop me *wanting* you. I wanted you every fucking time I saw you in a pretty dress, ready to go on a date. Or whenever you bent over to pick up Friar Puck. I almost returned him when I got him as a kitten, because you kept bending over to play with him, and your ass was so fucking perfect that it was giving me some seriously conflicted feelings."

She gasped in mock horror, but her eyes were wide and shiny and filled with this aching sort of hope and desire that had me bundling her into my arms, just so I could kiss her. I would never get tired of that. Just holding her close and kissing her how I wanted. She straddled my lap, kissing me back as I traced the curves that I'd always ached to memorize.

This was happening. Really, really happening.

But not here on the couch, that was for damn sure. "Come on, Bug. I want to make love to you somewhere more comfortable." Shifting her off my lap, I stood and pulled her toward her bedroom, all but running. I threw my shirt back at her, laughing when it got her in the face, then pushed her against the wall in the short hallway, kissing her until I felt dizzy. Not from the concussion, but from pure lust.

I undressed her too, tugging Erik's jersey over her head and throwing it on the floor, dropping to my knees to tug off her yoga pants, ignoring the glowstick cracks of my knees. Once she was gloriously fucking naked in front of me, I looked up at her. Her lips were parted, and she was heaving in breaths while she stared down at me. I was face to pussy, and I leaned forward, burying my face in the soft, trimmed hair between her thighs. Lifting one leg, I put it over my shoulder.

"Oh my god," she breathed, and I looked up at her and winked.

"You can call me Ludo."

She rolled her eyes as she gripped my hair and ground herself against my face, my nose bumping her clit, making her legs shake. "I'll call you whatever you like, if you don't stop," she gasped, and I grinned against her. Erik had said she tasted divine, and now that I'd gotten a taste, I believed him.

"I could take up residency between these thighs, Bug." As if to make my point, I skimmed my hand up her thigh and slid a finger inside her. As I curved it gently, she clamped down hard.

"Ludo!"

"Careful, Bug. I need these fingers to play. Don't want you to accidentally sprain one gripping me with that tight little pussy," I purred, slipping another one inside and moving my tongue to her clit. I sucked and flicked, and she squeezed my fingers so tightly, I wondered if I might actually sprain something.

Despite my teasing, I wouldn't give a single fuck if I

did. I'd wear the splint like a badge of honor. My face was wet with her juices, and I growled against her clit at the thought.

"Oh fuck, *Ludo*," she screamed, and I felt sorry for her downstairs neighbor as she came hard. She wobbled shakily, and I slipped her foot back to the ground for balance.

Slumping back with my ass on my heels, I grinned up at her. "I like the way you scream my name," I growled, and something hot and feral took possession of my sweet best friend. Dragging me to my feet, she pulled me down the hall, and I laughed as I shucked out of my pants. I wanted to be exactly where she wanted me to be.

"Sit against the headboard. I don't want to jostle your head."

I rolled my eyes at her overprotectiveness, despite the fact that I'd just made her come so hard, she almost broke my fingers. But I wasn't going to point that out. I wanted to be inside my best friend right now, with her pussy choking the life out of my cock. Climbing onto the bed, I sat exactly where she pointed. She straddled my hips again, kissing and licking her release off my lips and cheeks.

Holy shit. I was going to blow right there and then.

"Juniper," I groaned, my hands running all over that smooth, soft skin. Physically, she was the opposite of Erik in every single way, and every part of me was happy about it. I felt like I'd won the lottery being able to call these two mine.

Her sweet little pussy slid over me, and I gritted my teeth with the strain of not grabbing her and impaling her on my cock so I could rut into her like an animal. As if she was answering all my prayers, she grabbed my dick and lined herself up. Once I was notched against her entrance, the head almost pressed in, I grabbed her hips and held her still. I wanted to remember this moment—the exact second that I finally got the girl I'd always wanted but had been too stupid to know it.

"You're it for me, Bug. This might be the first time we'll make love, but I intend to know you inside and out. I want your insides to mold to the shape of my cock; that's how often I'm going to make love to you."

She kissed me hard. "You can tell you flunked biology, Andrei Ludokov, but I love you anyway."

All rational thought left me as she impaled herself on my cock. My head slumped back as I felt her wet heat. "You feel so fucking *good*," I groaned. I thrust up slightly, making her squeak out a surprised moan of pleasure. "You feel like home."

I wanted to roll her over and pound into her so I was indelibly marked on her body, but instead, she leaned down and kissed me. I met her rolling body with my own, and we moved together like a perfection I didn't know could exist.

"Ludo, fuck. *Yes*." Her voice was a chant against my face. I lost minutes, or hours, just absorbed in watching her face as she rode me, my hands gripping her ass so tight, I was probably leaving bruises. Every time I got close, I pushed it down again, riding out her orgasms. I didn't want this to end. I wanted to stay buried inside her until someone forced me to move.

Finally, she arched backwards, propping herself between my thighs, her body rolling up until I was hitting places that made us both wild.

"Jesus, fuck!" I shouted as my balls pulled up, my orgasm sneaking up on me like it was trying to jump me in the darkness. "Come for me once more, baby. One more time." She let out a whimpering cry, but a second later, she was clamping down on my cock. I was helpless to stop myself from coming inside her, filling her up.

The idea of me painting her insides gave me a primal sense of satisfaction. I wanted her big and round with my babies, though probably not yet. "Bug, you on birth control?"

She made a disapproving humming noise. "Lucky for you, Andrei Ludokov."

I pulled her close to me, not ready to be two separate people. "I don't know. I like the idea of you growing the next generation of Ludokovs here." I held her hips, rubbing my thumbs across her stomach. "I think it might even be a kink I didn't know I had."

"You have a breeding kink?" she said incredulously, not lifting her head from my shoulder.

I shook my head. "I have a breeding Juniper kink."

She laughed, and it was the most tired, perfect sound. "Love you, Ludo."

"Love you too, Juniper May Verne," I told her, with all the feelings I possessed. "You're mine forever."

By a quirk of fate, the first team we played once I was finally allowed back to full player duties were the Detroit Infernos. Unfortunately, whatever the coaching staff and front of house had said to the Infernos over the last two weeks had pulled their heads out of their asses. They were now back up to full skill, and a full team roster.

Which meant Rusket was back on the ice, which I fucking hated. I'd heard a little about the guy from Erik, and honestly, I wanted to punch him right in the face.

In my opinion, that whole team could burn in hell. Laurens was all right, and Erik had told me about the rookie kid who'd approached him, but the rest were irredeemable. Including the coaching staff. Who let that shit go on for so long?

Standing in the locker room, I was basically vibrating with excitement. Muss was all healed up from the brawl with Cockington, and officially cleared of any sanctions or legal charges, which was a relief. All geared up, he came over and slapped me on the back. "Ready to be back on the ice?"

I almost moaned in anticipation, but that would've probably been inappropriate. "Hell yeah, I am. Doc said he'll be watching me for the slightest issue, and he'll pull my ass if he has to. But I feel good, man. Strong. Hard-headed." I banged on my head, ignoring Doc's warning huff.

Muss laughed, wrapping an arm around my shoulders. "I've missed you, kid. Glad to have you back." He dropped his voice. "And what about playing against Erik? You gonna be okay with that?"

I frowned. Did they all think I was going to throw the game just because my boyfriend was the goalie? "Nah man, it's fine. I wouldn't insult Erik, or myself and this team, by giving anything less than a hundred percent. He's fucking good, and so am I." I grinned, remembering Erik's promise to give me a blowjob for every puck I got into the net, and I had to give him one for every one that he blocked. Win-win, but I wasn't about to tell the guys that. "No one will be able to find fault in how I play against him." I met Muss's kind eyes. He was a fucking good captain and an even better friend. "I promise, Muss."

"I know, Ludo." He grabbed my helmet and slapped it on my head. "Let's go and do what we do best, hey?"

Rigby looked over at us, his finger on his chin like he was pondering what I was good at. "Get busted fucking in public?"

I gave him the finger, making him laugh. "That was like… twice. No, three times. I'm a changed man, Rigby. You should know that this is it for me." I hadn't outright said that Juniper was mine now too, but I had a suspicion that Rigby and River knew. Because if anyone's minds were going straight to polyamorous relationships, it was those guys.

He chuckled. "Welcome to the club."

We stood around as Coach gave us last-minute instructions, and then we were walking out to the rink. Everyone slid onto the ice, while I paused at the edge. This was my first game back since my assault, and by now, everyone would know the whole sordid tale.

Would the crowd even like me anymore? Had they decided I was just too much drama?

Stepping onto the rink when my name flashed across the jumbotron, I held my breath, but the yells of the crowd ratcheted up another notch. The cheers and applause were almost deafening, and something in my chest cracked wide open.

As I skated around, I saw people on their feet, stomping and cheering. Signs about my hat trick, which had been lost beneath the rabid news cycle about my sexuality, were held up beside rainbow-painted cardboard with my number on it.

I shook my head in amazement. River skated up to me. "They're hailing this match as the most inclusive in the NHL's history, considering both you and Luthersson are opposing each other. But those signs have been at every match we've had since you got caught blowing Erik."

I looked down the ice at the man who held my heart. He was on his knees, stretching. As his eyes traveled around the crowd, his amazement was easy to see without his mask on. Feeling my gaze, his eyes found mine, and he grinned.

Winking, I continued to warm up with my team, and knew this was how it was meant to be.

CHAPTER
Forty-Three

ERIK

PLAYING the IceCaps was always a test of my skill. Rigby was an insanely good center, and Ludo backed him up beautifully on the right wing. The whole team played cohesively, and I knew that was why even with Ludo out, they'd held their own.

My team couldn't say the same, but they seemed to have gotten their act together lately, and we'd been winning games again. Laurens fired a great shot down the end, getting a puck in behind Virtanen, and the buzzer was deafening.

I lifted my mask and sucked at my water bottle. They were putting me through my paces, especially Ludo. Every time he took a shot that got through, he gave me a smug smirk that I couldn't wait to fuck off his face later on. He went hard, and none of the pundits would be able to say we were going easy on each other just because we were fucking. I'd saved more than a few of his sniper shots, my reflexes lifting to match the caliber of talent on the IceCaps. Our teams were still archenemies, and that translated onto the ice.

It was 2-2 in the third period, and I was sweating hard. The referee did the drop, and then my eyes were on that puck like it was my prey. It wouldn't get past me. Nothing would get past me now. I tracked the puck, but also the players, as they skated down the ice with a speed that was truly astounding. Rigby had to be the fastest guy in the NHL.

Rusket came charging toward Rigby, but veered sharply to Ludo, slamming him into the boards with an audible thump. I saw Ludo's head snap toward the glass, but he was back on his feet quickly. I dragged my eyes back toward the puck as Rigby shot it out to the left wing, Melville getting it and losing it rapidly. Rigby was there, right in front of the goal, hammering it at the left top corner, and I wasn't fast enough to block it.

The buzzer sounded. The home crowd was now on its feet, stomping until it felt like the whole arena was shaking. Rigby skated off, his grin infectious enough that I couldn't help but smile back. It was a good fucking shot. Beautiful, even. He deserved the insane contract he and River had negotiated last season.

Rusket slid into the space, spraying ice up into my face. *Fucking asshole.*

"If you want the IceCaps to win so much, why don't you go suck dick on the other bench, Luthersson?" he shouted in my face, his cheeks red with rage.

Standing until I was my full height, I glared down at the enforcer who was a couple of inches shorter than me. I growled at him. "Get back to the bench."

Rusket pushed me back, hooking his stick beneath my skates, tripping me. I landed on my pads. "Why don't you get back on your knees where you belong, fag."

Oh, fuck no. I rocketed back to my feet and shoved him. "Get out of my space, Rusket."

He just skated closer, until he was breathing heavily over my face with his rank breath. "This ice is all mine, Luthersson. You're in my space, my domain. You're the fucking reason I was benched."

I sneered. "This isn't the time, asshole. You're making a fool of yourself, but that isn't new for you—is it, shithead?"

My mask was still up, so while I saw the swing coming, I couldn't move back fast enough to dodge it completely, and his fist grazed my chin.

I stared at him in disbelief. "What the fuck is your *problem?*"

"You're blowing this game on purpose," he shouted back.

I had no idea how he'd come to that conclusion. It didn't matter, though, because the body of Ludo came sliding into view, taking Rusket down and into the wall. He had hold of Rusket's jersey as he laid blow after blow into the guy. River appeared, dragging him off, and Laurens was in front of me just as quickly.

"What the fuck was that?" he yelled, as the rest of the guys on the ice entered the brawl. I doubted they knew who was fighting who and why, but when all else failed, you tended to just hit the guy from the opposite team.

I held the back of Laurens's jersey, because if he waded in there, he'd get ejected from the game and probably get a fine, and fuck, who knew what else.

Rigby skated up to me, and I tensed, but he just stared at the brawl in front of us. "The fuck just happened?"

Laurens tossed down his stick. "Rusket fucking happened. Piece of shit."

I adjusted my grip on his shirt to keep him with me, and Rigby shook his head, but his eyes were alight, like he wanted to dive into the fray too.

He looked at Laurens. "Wanna take a swing?"

I gave him the stink-eye, but Laurens just laughed. "Thought you wanted to keep all your teeth?"

Rigby nodded. "True that. You need to get that fucker under control. He's reckless and bad for your team's rep. And the sport."

Laurens shook his head as the linesmen and ref finally managed to break the fight up, sending everyone to the penalty box. Rigby slapped me on the back, sliding back toward his bench, where I could see their coach shouting and red in the face. Laurens skated back to ours, but Coach King just looked pissed. Silent pissed. Even though it wasn't my fault, I knew I was going to get my ass handed to me at the end of the game.

Play resumed, and while most of the team were in the penalty box, Rigby still put me through my paces. Laurens was also still on the ice, and we played a glorified game of three on three until the other players started trickling back into the game. Neither Ludo nor Rusket were back on before the end of the game, though, and my jaw was clenched so tight, my teeth were going to crack.

The crowd went nuts as the final siren sounded. We'd lost 3-2, and it was going to be a hard one for our fans to come to terms with. This was bullshit.

I shook hands with everyone, keeping my eyes down, until I made it to Clint Vanmussen. "Chin up, kid. You did nothing wrong."

I gave him a tight smile and nodded. "Thanks. You run a good team."

He slapped me on the back and skated to the guy behind me. I ran through the whole team, none of whom seemed to bring the bad feelings of the fight to the end of the game. The same couldn't be said for Rusket, who spat at the feet of Ludo.

I watched Ludo tense, but River was behind him, nudging him forward, until he was in front of me and it was our turn to shake. "Good game," I murmured. "You shouldn't have done that."

He just winked at me. "No one touches my goalie."

This right here? This was the moment I'd tell people

about. The moment I knew that I loved Andrei Ludokov. A forever kind of love that lasted a damn lifetime.

Grinning back at him, I shook his hand, like I hadn't had these fingers wrapped around his dick this morning. "Juniper is going to kick your ass," I said with a laugh, and he winced. Yeah, no one was looking forward to that.

I skated off the ice, the intensity of Coach King's glare following us all down to the locker room. I saw Laurens's shoulders tense as we were met at the doors by Mac Wentworth.

"Fuck," I breathed, and Laurens looked over at me, his eyes wide with worry. He knew what I knew. I mightn't have been the problem on the team, but I was the catalyst. Sometimes it was easier to just get rid of the catalyst, rather than treat the problem.

Coach went over and talked to him, their conversation low but animated. Normally, after a loss, the locker rooms were silent as we all thought about what we'd done wrong. But the silence right now was unearthly. We showered and changed with the solemnity of a funeral procession. Even Rusket was quiet, for once in his stupid life.

I saw a flash of blue and gold, and the wild hair of Juniper appeared in the doorway, her eyes taking in the eerie vibe of the room. I walked over to her quickly, not wanting anyone to get it into their heads to take out their frustrations on the social media manager of the IceCaps.

"What are you doing here, *Einiber?*" I whispered.

She gripped my hand. "I just wanted to make sure you were okay. Ludo sent me; we're both worried."

I kissed her forehead, squeezing her fingers. "I'm fine. My jaw is like granite, obviously." My wink felt exaggerated. "It'll be okay. Go back and tell Ludo I'll see you both at home, okay?"

She nodded and scuttled away, and there was a small hum of noise behind me about her. Fuck them. I had nothing to explain to anyone about my relationship with Juniper.

But any sound that might have picked up vanished as Coach King stepped back into the room, his eyes fiery. "In all my years, I've never seen anything like what happened out there on the ice today." Mac Wentworth followed him in, and dread filled my veins.

Shit, fuck, shit.

Coach continued. "It was a *disgrace.* I didn't realize that this was who we'd become—an episode of Jerry Springer on ice." He shook his head, disgust etched on his face as he took in the team. "Laurens, you're on media duty. Keep it game-related, and deflect what you can." He turned, his eyes bouncing between me and the rest of the team. "As for the rest of you, Mr. Wentworth has had a serious conversation with me, and I agree with his decision. I'll see you all tomorrow morning at nine a.m. sharp to discuss the team and how I expect you all to conduct yourselves on the ice."

His eyes hardened as they looked in my direction. "Except you. You're fired."

It was like someone had reached into my chest and gripped my heart in their fist.

Fuck.

I PACED BACK and forth in front of Ludo's doorway. Johnny watched me closely, stroking Friar Puck's head where it rested in his lap. Ludo was sitting on the kitchen counter, the corners of his eyes tight with worry.

"Maybe I misunderstood Erik. Maybe he was going back to his house in Detroit?"

Ludo pulled out his phone, frowning to see there were still no messages from Erik. "Do you think we should call him?"

Johnny shook his head. "Give him ten more minutes. Maybe their coach gave them a proper forty-minute ass-chewing and they're only just leaving now."

I resumed my pacing. They hadn't seen that locker room. It had been as quiet as a tomb, like everyone was awaiting their turn on the executioner's block. There'd been real worry in Erik's eyes, no matter how much he'd tried to hide it from me.

Also, I was the social media manager. I knew Mac Wentworth when I saw him. He'd been up in the owner's box with Mr. Monderra and his daughter, Daisy. Ludo and the guys just called her Baby Monderra.

I'd seen Mac Wentworth's face when I'd walked toward the room. Seen the anger written in the lines of his body. He'd been *pissed*, and I was a little worried that his anger was going to be directed toward the wrong person. Erik seemed to like the guy, though he was wary. The owners and GMs moved players around like they were pawns on a chessboard. If he didn't like how Erik was impacting the team dynamic, he'd be able to do an amazing trade for him, even with the shitty press. Because Erik was a career goalie. A once-in-a-generation goalie. Easily a top-fifty player, almost unheard of for someone so damn young.

Selfishly, I didn't want Erik to be traded, because then he wouldn't be so close. I wanted him to stay here with us.

"Stop worrying. Whatever happens, we'll make it work," Johnny murmured, grabbing me on the way past and settling me into his lap. I relaxed against him, breathing in the spicy warmth of his scent.

Ludo was watching us with a soft expression. "You guys look good together, you know? Like every good memory I've ever had." His voice was wistful.

I nuzzled into the crook of Johnny's neck as he stroked my back. "It feels right," he said against my hair, his arms tightening a little. "We all feel right. And that's why it'll work."

Ludo laughed. "If you'd told teenage me that I'd be in a polyamorous relationship with you and Bug, I would have laughed in your face."

"After you Googled the definition of polyamorous," I teased, feeling the rumble of Johnny's laughter beneath my cheek. Happiness spread through me. He had the best laugh.

"Fact. Probably would have used a dictionary in the school library so my mom didn't think I was looking up weird porn," Ludo chuckled. The laughter was tinged with a bittersweet sound, the same way it always did when we talked about Ludo's mom.

Who knew what she'd have thought of our relationship, but I imagined she'd be happy. She loved Ludo more than life itself. It had been Ludo's mom, on her deathbed, who'd made me promise to look after her boy. She was the initial reason I'd followed him off to college, though not the only reason. I think Mrs. Ludokov had to have known that I had a giant crush on her son, or she'd never have suggested it.

Just then, there was a knock at the door. I shot off Johnny's lap, but Ludo was faster. He opened the door, and a freshly showered Erik stood there, his face solemn.

My heart sank at his expression. "*No fucking way.* I

swear, Erik, if they made this your fault, I'm going to march down there and give Mac Wentworth a piece of my damn mind. I don't care if he's a billionaire. I don't care if the IceCaps fire me. That shit isn't right!"

Erik grabbed my hands, which I belatedly realized were flailing around. He kissed each fist, his smile the kind that turned my insides to mush. "Thank you, *Einiber*. But that's not necessary. They fired Rusket. Scared the shit out of me, though. He was standing right behind me, and for a moment, I thought Mac was speaking to me." He let out a shaky breath. "Several other players are on probation, including me—" I opened my mouth to protest, but he shook his head. "It's unfair, but I can sit through some sensitivity training if it means I get to stay in Detroit and be close to you guys."

Tugging me to his body, he kissed me softly, then turned to Ludo, frowning. "What were you thinking, getting in a fight with fucking Rusket on your first game back? You're still on concussion protocol!" He shook his head, his jaw so tense, I could tell he was resisting the urge to shake him. "If he'd landed the wrong blow, you could have died, Ludo."

My stubborn-as-fuck best friend merely crossed his arms over his delicious chest, momentarily distracting me from the argument. Man, I wanted to bury my face between his pecs and blow raspberries. Was it still motorboating if I did it to a man?

"He was calling you slurs. He tripped you in your own goal." Ludo stepped closer, and I ducked out of the way, because I was fairly sure they were going to angry-kiss, and I wanted to be able to get a proper view. I loved it when they kiss-battled.

I sat back on Johnny's lap, and prepared for fireworks. He wrapped his arms around my waist, because we both knew that there was no way Ludo would admit he was wrong. Not even a little.

Erik grabbed his arms and held him closer. "I don't care if he had me on the ground and was beating me with his stick. I'm the most padded person on the ice. You do not throw yourself into a fucking brawl for me."

"You don't tell me what to do," Ludo growled. "You're fucking mine, and I'll defend you as much as I want. The same way as I'd defend Bug." He smirked over at Johnny. "And Johnny, but he brawls as good as I do. Though he knows I'd have his back anytime. We're in this together now, Erik. Me, Juniper and Johnny—we're all going to defend you, whether you think we should or not."

Erik grabbed the back of his head and kissed him hard. Watching their tongues battle, their bodies pressed together, made me moan softly. Johnny's hand slipped from my hip to my thigh, and he slowly moved it up the inside of my skirt. I turned to face him, but he nudged my gaze back toward the guys.

"Watch," he said softly, his fingers brushing across

my underwear, and I couldn't muffle the inhale in time. Erik pulled away from Ludo, his eyes snapping toward me.

Hooking both my ankles with his legs, Johnny spread my knees wide, my skirt dragged up by his hands. He leaned further back against the couch, holding me until I was pressed back tightly to his chest.

"Don't mind us. Our girl just likes watching you tongue-fuck each other, and I like burying my fingers inside her tight little pussy, so I figure it's a win-win."

"I didn't realize you were a voyeur?" Ludo choked out, though his eyes were devouring the path Johnny was creating with his fingers. "This isn't... weird for you?"

"Mmm, let's call it group bonding. I don't want to fuck either of you, but I'd really like to see Junebug riding your dick," he purred into my ear. "After she's come all over mine first."

Ludo's eyes flashed to my face, and I flushed pink at the fantasy Johnny was creating right now. As if he thought they needed a little encouragement, he stroked his fingers through my folds, opening me up to their gaze.

"Fuck..." Ludo breathed, tearing off his clothes so fast that he was almost a blur. Erik was close behind, and seeing the two of them naked together made me clench around the fingers Johnny was sliding inside me. Ludo took a step toward me, but Johnny closed my knees, his fingers still pulsing gently inside me, making my eyes roll back in my head.

Holy hell.

"Uh-uh. Our girl wants a show. Back to what you were doing," he ordered.

Bossy. Fuck, I loved it.

Ludo's hooded eyes took us in, and Erik was watching with a small smirk on his face. His hands reached out and wrapped around Ludo's thick body, fingers bumping over his eight-pack. Ludo flexed his abs, and the sight did something to me. Something wild.

Erik pulled Ludo back tight against his body, his hand traveling down further until it was wrapped around Ludo's dick. He stroked the length a couple of times, making me groan, my eyes transfixed. Johnny must have been half-watching him too, because he was moving his fingers in time with Erik's strokes. Or hell, maybe Erik was timing his strokes to Johnny's movements. Whatever it was, it was a perfect synchronization set to drive me mad.

Ludo widened his feet, rolling his own balls in his hand as Erik jerked him rougher than I would have even considered. Johnny pinched my clit, and I was suddenly a thousand percent focused on what was happening in my body. He flicked my clit until I was coming apart, a soft orgasm washing over me like a wave.

But Johnny wasn't done, and neither was Erik, by

the look of it. They had some kind of silent conversation, before Johnny moved us down the end of the couch, standing me on my feet so he could roll off his jeans. His dick popped out, hard as a steel bar.

What were the chances all my guys had great dicks? Both Johnny and Erik were hung, like they'd personally made a deal with the demon of dicks and tongue-skills, while Ludo's curved in this perfect direction that just hit something inside me every time he thrust. Like, every single time. It was basically a magic wand.

Pulling off my remaining clothes, Johnny stood behind me, his cock between my asscheeks and his hands wandering up and down my body, driving me crazy. He tweaked my nipples, scraped his teeth down my neck. Drove me wilder and wilder, until I closed my eyes, almost forgetting that Erik and Ludo were still in the room.

The wet sound of lube pouring out of a bottle broke me from my lust haze, and I looked over to see Ludo bending Erik over the arm of the couch, his cock achingly red.

Johnny grinned, and I knew for an unfortunate fact that this wasn't the first time they'd fucked in the same room. There had been the Bayliss twins in senior year. I was pretty sure they'd fucked most of Marianne's friend group too, just like this.

Pushing that shit from my mind—because this was different—I watched Ludo run his hands down the bunching muscles of Erik's back, his eyes hot and filled with more emotion than I'd ever seen. There was no doubt in my mind he loved Erik, and he loved me too.

He watched me as he traced his fingers between Erik's cheeks, sliding a finger inside him. At least, that's what I thought he did. I didn't have a great angle.

All thoughts of angles, or anything but Johnny's cock, disappeared as he spun me to face him, kissing me hard. "Mmm, do you want a better view, baby?"

"Yes," I breathed, and he grinned at me. Laying me down on the couch, he pulled me up until my ass rested on the low-profile armrest, my legs dangling over. I was laid along the couch, and when I looked up, Erik was right there, staring down at me in awe.

"So fucking beautiful," he moaned and moved forward until his mouth covered my nipples, sucking hard. If I looked straight back, I could see the hard length of his dick, too far away to reach with my mouth, but if I stretched…

I swiped up some of the lube that had run down from between his cheeks and used it to lube up his cock. As Ludo pushed inside him, he pressed forward into my slippery hand and groaned. "Fuck," he shouted around my nipple, biting down firmly and making me cry out with pleasure.

Just when I thought it was too much, Johnny grabbed my knee and spread me wide, before driving into my pussy with one definitive stroke.

I could hear Ludo curse, but it didn't matter. Between Ludo's thrusts, Erik's cock in my hand, his mouth around my nipple, and Johnny pounding my pussy like it personally owed him money, I was overrun with sensations.

I just held on for dear life as pleasure I'd only dreamed about coursed through my body. Johnny was playing with my clit as he snapped his hips into me, and I could hear the slapping of Ludo against Erik's perfect ass. My whole body felt like a rubber band that had been wound too tight, and I knew that when it snapped, I would shatter into a million pieces.

Erik's dick twitched in my hand, and he pulled back enough from my nipple to grunt, "Close your eyes. I'm going to…" That was all the warning I got as his dick painted my face with his cum. Hot ropes of it landed on my cheeks and lips, and there was something supremely filthy about it. I loved it.

"Fuck me," Johnny groaned, his thrusts becoming faster, more frantic, until I was tipping over the edge and he was following me down, splashing his release inside me in hot spurts.

Never one to be left behind, Ludo jerked himself out of Erik, moving around as he stroked himself harder and faster, unloading on my breasts and stomach.

I lay there on the couch, coated in cum, and laughed at how fucking happy I was.

Ludo knelt beside me and wiped Erik's release from around my eyes, tutting at the man who just watched with a satisfied smile on his face. Then Ludo lifted his finger and put it in his mouth, sucking Erik's jizz from the tip.

"You taste delicious. Let's get you showered and clean, because I'm not nearly done with you yet," he moaned, kissing me and sucking the cum from my lips.

Fuck. Me. I was so gone for these men.

CHAPTER
Forty-Five
JOHNNY

"I WANT TO BE A PONY."

I stared down at the kid who came up to my thigh, max. "You want to have a pony when you grow up?"

She frowned at me. "No, I said I wanted to *be* a pony." She looked at me like I was stupid.

"Uh, that's good. You can be whatever you want to be."

"Except a cult leader."

I choked on my beer. "Was that an option?"

"Daddy says it isn't." This kid legit pouted.

"That's, uh, a good piece of advice."

Muss, Ludo's team captain, came up and stared down at the little girl. "Cherub, are you harassing Johnny?"

"No," she said, looking at me with wide eyes, like I was supposed to back her up.

"We were just discussing our future employment

prospects. She wants to be a pony. Definitely not a cult leader."

Muss raised an eyebrow, but his eyes were laughing. "Go and play with Huey," he told the kid, and she ran off. I watched her crash-tackle her brother on the way, before dusting off her tutu and continuing toward the toddler, Huey.

What a firecracker.

Muss shook his head. "She gives me gray hair already. I'm not going to survive her to adulthood." He laughed. "Sorry about the cult thing. When people used to ask what she wanted to be when she grew up, she'd say she wanted to live on a big ranch with all her friends and classmates, and they'd worship her and give her all their money from when they went to work, and do everything she said. Couldn't work out if she meant a dictator or a cult leader, but neither seems like a positive career path."

I sucked back half my beer. "A pony is a much better option," I agreed. "Your place is nice." It wasn't nearly as big as I'd thought it would be, considering Muss had been a star in the hockey world for nearly ten years now.

He looked around, smiling. "Thanks, man. It's not as big as some of the other guys', but I know this career isn't forever, and neither Julieta nor I grew up rich. This is more than enough. More than either of us had when we were young. Better to save the money for them"—he nodded to the kids—"in case I blow out something important. It's a possibility every time I step out on the ice."

I let out a noise of agreement, because I understood that. Every time you suited up to go on a mission, there was a high possibility you'd never come back.

"Ludo says you guys used to play together when you were teens. Junie, too?"

I smiled. Those were still the best years of my life—though the other night had heralded the beginning of something that might just top it. "Yeah. The Dynamites. We were good, but that was because Juniper and Ludo were so damn competitive. Always trying to outdo each other. I don't think anyone else got Star of the Game for three years running. They just passed the title back and forth between them."

Muss snorted a laugh. "I can imagine. You never thought of going pro?"

The Johnny of my teen years only had one dream, and she'd been as unobtainable as the very concept of a sports scholarship. Not so unobtainable anymore, though.

"No, I was an angry kid. I needed the Marines, no matter how bad it fucked me up in the end. I, uh, had a shit start in life, and there were a few places I could have ended up, but the Marines was the best one."

Muss slapped me on the back. "I know what you mean."

Juniper let out a laugh so loud she snorted, and my eyes moved to where she sat with Julieta and Nova, drinking wine. Well, not Nova; she didn't have a wine glass.

The older guy followed my gaze. "Seems you ended up where you needed to be anyway. Only have to see the way Junie looks at you to know she loves you."

I shrugged. "She's special. She's got a lot of love to give."

"You got that right. Gotta say, though, I was surprised. We've been watching her and Ludo dance around each other for years, and honestly? I didn't think they'd ever get there. Then Erik came along, and we were all convinced Ludo would lose it. He loved her —it was clear as fucking day—but you young guys are oblivious to anything except your dicks sometimes." He laughed, and I shrugged again. I was probably just as guilty.

"Anyway, Rigby's been playing matchmaker with those two since Ludo's rookie year, but still nothing. Only time he ever showed any emotion but friendship toward her was when she got an actual boyfriend. A real one, I mean. Ludo was a fucking asshole for weeks, until Junie inevitably broke up with the guy. So when he took the fact she was with Erik so well, we knew something was up straightaway," he scoffed. "Didn't know quite what was up, though."

I smirked. "I've been his friend since we were four, and I didn't know either, so don't beat yourself up too much."

Julieta called Muss over, waving a hand at the grill.

Ludo and Erik were talking hockey with River and Rigby, but the third guy in their relationship wandered over to me. Devan Mayson had a darkness in his eyes that I recognized deep down. The kind of bruises we hid behind a hard shell, the kind that didn't heal well, because they'd happened when we were vulnerable and helpless, so they shaped who we became. River had that look too.

"Ludo tells me you were in the Marines," he said by way of greeting.

"Ludo tells me you're rich as fuck," I quipped back, making the guy laugh.

"He's not wrong. Making money had kind of become an obsession before Nova. Probably not a good one, but at least I can provide for my family now." We were both silent for a while, and I knew that where I could see the darkness in him, he could sense the same in me. "We cope how we can."

Juniper was looking over at me, her brows raised, like I was a child and she was a parent, watching me make friends for the first time. I waved a finger at her, grateful down to my very DNA that she was mine. Then she looked at Ludo and Erik, and it was like the sun had moved away. I wasn't jealous, not really. More like a little warmth had left me, though I knew it would be back.

"Any advice on being in a relationship like yours?"

He tilted his head at me, assessing to see if I was subtly insulting his family. Whatever he saw obviously reassured him I was being legit. "Good communication. And if you're anything like me, therapy." I snorted, because I was already getting so much therapy, I could probably write a textbook. "And don't leave all the emotional burden on Juniper. She's a sweet girl, and she'll take your problems on, but won't share her problems back. Do your share."

He looked at Huey, who was toddling at the speed of light, with Muss's kids chasing after him as he squealed, Friar Puck behind them. That cat really was like a dog.

"Also, wait a couple of years to have kids. Being able to have sex anytime, in any room, is a joy that disappears once you have kids. Though I wouldn't change it for all the money in the world, I would have liked time to fuck on the kitchen table…" He laughed, and the sound drew the eyes of Nova. She looked at him with so much love, I almost felt like a voyeur. She had a slight bump, her hands resting on it gently.

I lifted my chin in her direction. "Didn't seem to hold you back. Congrats, by the way."

Devan laughed again, winking at Nova. "Just gotta be creative. And have someone on lookout."

I chuckled along with him, and thought back again to the group sex we'd had the other night. It had been the hottest sex of my life, watching them move Juniper between them, kissing away her moans as she rode Ludo's dick. I'd thought I would be turned off, watching Erik and Ludo fuck, because damn, Ludo was my best friend and I definitely didn't think I'd be down to watch him fuck Erik like he owned him.

But the pleasure in the room, with Juniper wrapped around my dick, moaning as they fucked, it had been otherworldly. It was like being caught up in a mob or something, the lust a physical force in the room.

Clearing my throat, I turned back to Devan, but he was watching Huey, who'd climbed to the top of a playhouse and was standing precariously at the top of the slide. He stood there, still uncertain on his feet, and I thought he'd turn around and go back. Instead, he scrunched up his face and sat, babbling at the little Vanmussen to push him. She did, and he flew off the end, landing in the ballpit they had at the bottom with a cute baby laugh.

"Brave little guy," Devan said proudly, though maybe with a hint of exasperation. "You don't know stress until you have to let them explore the world on their own, not understanding they have your literal heart in their tiny little fists." He shook his head. "Wait to have kids. They change everything."

He cleared his throat, and the mogul was back in place of the doting father. "Juniper was saying you still haven't decided what you want to do, now you're out of the Marines. My security guy's about to retire, so there'll be a place opening up in the department, if you're interested. Mostly, it's just coming with me to meetings, sometimes ferrying Nova or Huey where they need to go, if none of us are available. I made one of those stupid Rich Lists, and there's always unscrupulous people out there who'll try and use Nova and the kids as a bargaining chip." His voice was hard, and the darkness was almost trickling out from wherever he kept it locked away.

"Have there been threats?"

He shook his head. "Not to Nova, but to an associate of mine in New York. It might be nothing, but I'd prefer if there was a guy with them who knew how to use a weapon, if I can't be there." His jaw flexed. "The rest is just building security—you know, basic shit that's going to bore the crap out of you. But the offer is there, if you want it."

I stared at the man in front of me. Was he serious? "I'll take it. Thank you."

He waved a casual hand just as Muss called lunch, and walked over to grab Huey before the little guy could climb the ladder to the slide again. Juniper came up to me, wrapping her arms around my waist, openly affectionate in a way that she normally wasn't in public. We were waiting for the furor around Ludo and Erik to die down a little before we launched the fact that we were following the IceCaps tradition of unconventional relationship structures. But here, we could be ourselves.

"They're nice people, right?" she murmured to me softly, as I wrapped an arm around her shoulders and walked her over to the large outdoor table, which was laden down with food.

The kids appeared like locusts, and Devan sat with

Huey in his arms, using his lap in lieu of a highchair. They looked like a family. River cut up his food, while Rigby doted on Nova like she was incapacitated, rather than just being pregnant.

"Yeah," I whispered back. Who knew that I wouldn't find the family I so desperately needed in the Marines, but here, in fucking Ann Arbor?

"Johnny?"

"Mm?"

"I love you," she murmured.

Every time she said those words, my heart beat faster, like it couldn't quite believe it.

"Love you too, Junebug. Let's go sit with your other boytoys while I tell you about the youngest Vanmussen kid, and what she has in common with Mussolini."

Later that night, Juniper lay beside me in her bed, scrolling through her phone. It was so damn domesticated, it made my heart happy just lying here.

"Holy *crap!*" she shouted suddenly.

I sat up, looking around for an intruder, or a giant spider, or something. "What?"

She thrust her phone at me. "This is the guy!"

I looked at the picture on her phone. "What guy?" I asked blandly, staring at the picture in the news article of an average-looking man, well-polished and smiling fakely.

"The guy from my date. *The* date. The one sent

straight from Hell. David Weinberg. Dean wasn't even his real fucking name. What a snake." She was silent as she read the article. "It says they found him floating in the Huron River, his kayak washed further down-stream. Police are assuming he fell out, hit his head and drowned." She narrowed her eyes at the picture. "Serves you right, you piece of shit."

She was silent for a moment as she read the rest. "It says that the police ran a routine DNA test to get a match on his identity, because he'd been floating for a while, apparently. His DNA matched twelve unsolved assault cases and one murder." Her face went gray, and I reached out, pulling her further beneath the blankets and wrapping her in my arms.

"Sounds like he got what he deserved then, don't you think? He went out as helpless as the women he preyed on. I'd call that karma."

She tilted her head at me, her eyes running across my face, like they were searching for secrets. She wouldn't find any here. All my secrets were hers already.

Finally, she rested her head on my chest. "Yeah, karma. I hope he rests in eternal misery, right in the bowels of Hell."

I kissed the top of her head. "Me too, baby. Me too."

Well, almost all my secrets.

About the Author

Grace McGinty is eclectic. She has worked as a chocolatier, a librarian, a forensic accountant and finally a writer. Like her professional career, the genres she writes are also eclectic. She writes romance, reverse harem romance, fantasy, contemporary young adult and new adult books.

She lives in rural Australia with her crazy family, an entire menagerie of pets, and will one day be crushed by the giant piles of books that litter every room.

Head over to www.gracemcginty.com and join my mailing list for sneak previews into what she is working on and to stay up-to-date with new releases and giveaways!

Turn the page for a sneak peek at *Pay-Per-Heart*, available now!

Pay~Per~Heart

CHAPTER ONE

BLAKE

I stood in front of the empty lot with two wieners in my hand, like this was amateur night on the Hub. You know which Hub. Don't make me spell it out.

There were large chunks of concrete littering the corner block, with pieces of rebar poking up at odd angles like a spider that suddenly died—the victim of a bigger, meaner spider, probably. I really felt for those eight-legged demons from Hell.

"You know, it's not going to suddenly reappear, no matter how long, or how often, you stare at it. You don't have to come back every day just to check."

I turned to the owner of Heinrich's Wiener, Schnitzel & Pretzel food truck. Heinrich had been here for my first visit to this empty lot, when I'd had nothing but two big suitcases and even bigger dreams.

He'd watched on with his sparkling blue eyes as I sank to the ground and cried like a baby, then he'd given me a soft pretzel. It had been hot and salty, just like my tears.

We'd bonded after that, Heinrich and I. At least, I thought we had.

"Are you trying to get rid of me, Hennie?" I asked with a huff, walking back over to the light blue outdoor setting he set out in the shade of his food truck. It was hot, but not like it was in Georgia. In Georgia, I'd always had so much boob sweat, the Georgia Forestry Commission could have declared my under-boob region it's own tributary. I took a bite of one of my wieners and sighed happily. Life had let me down, but these Vienna sausages were consistently the highlight of my day.

Hennie leaned forward on his elbows as I opened my laptop, and I tried not to stare at his bulging fore-arms. He was young, maybe in his late twenties, and he was so fit, it was like he'd never tasted his own pretzels. No one could have unlimited access to such bready goodness and look that hot. "Never, Blake, but stealing my wifi and staring at a building that was demolished over six months ago isn't going to help."

I glared at him, my fake outrage just making him smirk. "I'm not stealing your wifi. I eat two of your pretzels and at least one wiener a day. I'm a paying customer." Granted, that was all I ate every day, since most of my savings were being eaten up by the shitty-ass motel around the corner I'd had to check into while I mulled over my options.

There weren't many, so there wasn't much mulling going on, but I was in denial. This was what happened when I was impulsive. Well, not impulsive.

You see, it started a year ago. I'd dropped out of my Accounting course at college, because I hated it, and started a community college course on Graphic Design and Digital Art. I'd found my passion.

So when I got an invite to the exclusive Baldessari School of Art, for their piloted Digital Art and Design program, I'd jumped on board. I looked at the modern monstrosity of a building on Street View on Maps, had a video conference interview with the Dean of Admissions, paid the exorbitant amount of tuition fees upfront, and packed my bags.

The last month at home with my parents had been filled with fights; it'd been awful. Impulsive I wasn't, but stubborn? That's a whole different question. I was as stubborn as the day was long. So when my parents had said I was foolish to give up my Walmart job to play on my computer all day in LA, I dug in my heels and told them they were wrong.

When my friends had told me I was crazy to break up with Paul, the boyfriend I'd had since senior year, who refused to come to LA with me? I told them that if he couldn't support my dreams, he wasn't the right guy for me.

That decision I stood by. Paul had told me I was

being stupid, that I should stay in Dahlonega, Georgia, with him. He'd offered to move in together. Hell, he'd even said we could get engaged. He'd offered everything but support for my dreams.

I wasn't the type of person to settle. Besides, I was twenty-two years old; I wanted to live before I settled down and joined the Real Housewives of Dahlonega.

All completely justifiable, right? I'd done my due diligence.

Except when I arrived at the address on the admission forms, there was nothing. No pretty concrete and glass building. No students. Definitely no Digital Art department. Just rubble and Heinrich's wiener truck.

Cue the tears. And the soft pretzel.

Back to the options. Option one was I returned home and ate humble peach pie in front of everyone. I wasn't overly fond of this option.

Option two was that I tried to find another job in LA and maybe some kind of housing, all before my money ran out. Shouldn't be too hard during a housing crisis, an employment crisis and an absolute abundance of graphic designers, right?

Wrong.

I was determined to succeed despite this obvious first setback, which was why I kept coming back to this spot every day, to stare at the results of my impetuousness and, yeah okay, steal Hennie's wifi.

I glared at the man in question as the lunch rush began, but he just gave me that shiny white smile back.

He shouldn't be so handsome *and* sell the world's fluffiest carbs. It was almost unfair.

I flipped open my computer while he was busy, checking out the job guides. Graphic designers turned out hundreds of results, but mostly for people who wanted a decade of experience or wanted me to do it for free as "exposure." Well, guess what? Exposure didn't buy me wieners.

On a whim, I pulled up JeffsMarket, a kind of community noticeboard/platform for crazy people to share their alien abduction experiences. I typed in some general keywords and hoped for the best.

Pulling out my phone, I spent the next hour texting the numbers from job posts. In return, I got three dick pics, one photo of an impressive set of bolt-on boobs, one offer of a glory hole visit, and a legitimate marriage offer from a guy looking for a green card. More disheartening than one guy's shriveled little mole dick, however, was the amount of people replying that the position had already been filled.

I heavy-sighed when Hennie sat down beside me, sliding me a Coke. "The search continues?"

I nodded, chugging the cold soda. "No luck yet."

Hennie leaned back in his chair, making his black tee stretch taut across his chest. "There's always porn. I've seen the way you handle two Vienna sausages. There's gotta be a market for that."

I punched him in the chesticle. "Real funny, Heinrich. I'll be sure to sign you a copy of *Blake Bangs the Bratwurst*." I clicked on the next advert and perked up.

Wanted: Graphic designer and video editor for a collective of social media influencers. Position is on a commission basis, but does come with room and board for a shared house in Beverly Hills. Please text [login to reveal number].

"Hey, this sounds like something." I tried to keep the excitement out of my voice as I turned the screen to face Hennie.

He quickly read through the ad, his brows climbing higher and higher, before he laughed. "Blake, that one is definitely porn. Beware the Beverly Hills casting couch, *Liebling*." At my frown, he reached over and squeezed my shoulder. "It'll all work out. You'll see."

He stood, and I sucked in the groan that wanted to escape at the view of his super-toned ass. I was way off dating right now. I'd only just broken up with Paul. I had enough trouble and I certainly didn't need to add "rejected by the only pseudo-friend I had in this angel-forsaken city" to the list.

Still, I scrawled down the number on the ad onto a napkin, stuffing it in my notebook and continuing my search for a job, then shifted to a search for an apartment. I spent another thirty minutes using Hennie's wifi before I headed over to the public library to read smut and steal their wifi instead.

Stumbling into my hotel that night, I tried not to wince at the stale smell of old cigarettes and cheetos. Eu De Desperation. The concierge—a grand name for a guy with a greasy comb-over and a beer gut—caught me as I was climbing the battered old stairs to tell me next week's fees were due. I promised him that I'd get it for him tomorrow and tried not to cry.

I ate some ramen out of a mug and watched the only channel on the television, which happened to be Evangelical TV—twenty-four-seven hymns to heal your soul. I sang along, not because I was particularly religious, but damn, some of these songs were as catchy as Chlamydia in Vegas.

Putting my laptop on charge, I tried not to think about how desperate I was. I didn't want to spend another week in this shitty hotel. My mind flicked back to that ad that had seemed like it was the answer to all my problems. Maybe it was legit; maybe it was just a hype house of seventeen-year-olds dancing to twelve-second song snippets without their shirts on. I could do that, right?

It couldn't hurt to at least inquire. Pulling up my notes, I found the number and grabbed my phone, then quickly typed out my enquiry text. What had the world come to that you could text potential employers these days? Anyway, it was succinct and professional, introducing myself and listing my credentials, as well as attaching the link to a couple of examples of my work.

Throwing my phone down, I flopped back onto the bed, the only piece of furniture in this shithole.

I was humming along to Jesus being a boat on a river or something like that, while reading a book I'd picked up from the library, when my phone buzzed.

> Probably Porn: Blake, we love your work and would like to meet you tomorrow at ten. Please bring your portfolio and references.

There was an address listed below it, and I used some of my precious phone data to look it up. *Wow.* It was incredible, all glass and modern architecture, and was that a damn pool?

Every disaster-filled scenario of what could happen raced through my mind, my inner voice sounding—unsurprisingly—like my mother. The best worst-case scenario was some kind of sleazy porn producer. I'd pack my pepper spray. The catastrophic worst-case scenario was that they were human traffickers and I'd end up being sold for body parts.

I could always go home, I guess.

I shuddered at the thought of my parents saying "I told you so." Who needed two kidneys anyway?

> Me: See you at ten.

Impulsive Blake was back at the wheel, and I was just along for the ride.